**W9-AMX-717**

# On Joanna Russ

# On Joanna Russ

≈ ≈ ≈

EDITED BY FARAH MENDLESOHN

WESLEYAN UNIVERSITY PRESS
Middletown, Connecticut

Published by Wesleyan University Press,
Middletown, CT 06459
www.wesleyan.edu/wespress
Printed in the United States of America

With editorial assistance from Michelle Reid and Shana Worthen.

Samuel R. Delany's "Joanna Russ and D. W. Griffith" was first published
in PMLA 119, no. 3 (2004): 500–508.

Cover image © James Gurney, 1981.

Library of Congress Cataloging in Publication Data
On Joanna Russ / edited by Farah Mendlesohn.
　　p. cm.
　Includes bibliographical references and index.
　ISBN 978-0-8195-6901-1 (cloth : alk. paper) — ISBN 978-0-8195-6902-8
(pbk. : alk. paper)
　　1. Russ, Joanna, 1937 — Criticism and interpretation.　I. Mendlesohn,
Farah.　II. Title.
　PS3568.U763Z83 2009
　813'.54 — dc22　　　　　　　　　　　　　　　　　　　　2008044109

10 9 8 7 6 5 4 3 2 1

 Wesleyan University Press is a member of the Green Press Initiative. The paper
used in this book meets their minimum requirement for recycled paper.

# Contents

# Introduction

FARAH MENDLESOHN

In a frequently quoted letter to Susan Koppelman, Joanna Russ wrote that she does not trust people who can write without anger. I do not intend to begin with an apology, to explain "this is not what she meant" or to attempt to ameliorate the impact of rage (Russ 1998c, 63). Instead, I introduce a writer whose angry creativity burns the complacent veldt of narrative.

In the elegiac tale, "Mr. Wilde's Second Chance" (Russ 1987a), Oscar Wilde reaches a garden in limbo where he is invited to rearrange the pieces of his life. A lady, "Ada R—, the victim of the most celebrated scandal of the last decade" works next to him. " 'Of course, it is not easy,' said the lady. 'I try very hard. But I cannot seem to finish anything. I am not sure if it is the necessary organizing ability that I lack or perhaps the aesthetic sense; something ugly always seems to intrude' " (72). Mr. Wilde, the grand arbiter of taste, has no such difficulty. He reassembles his life as a successful Victorian novelist and dramatist, with three times the body of work, and two happy, healthy sons. Russ proceeds:

" 'Lovely, sir! Such agreeable color. Such delicacy.' . . . Oscar Wilde, poet, dead at forty-four, took his second chance from the table before him and broke the board across his knee" (73).

Beauty can be a lie: it can be the rich green stillness of the stagnant pond under which poison ferments; it can be a delicate silver chain, strung with pearls that ties the wearer to a life that chafes. Beauty can be the unchanging landscape of a wildlife reserve that masks the poverty of the evicted indigenes. What we call ugly may be the vibrant growth of industrial development or social upheaval. Who decides what is beautiful? Is the elegy of Mr. Wilde beautiful, or is it that last rupture? In her writing, fiction and nonfiction, Russ makes clear that she would choose the rupture, the apparent ugliness of anger and rebellion over the poisonous beauty.

Rupture, or the refusal to go along with the storying of the world, is the core of Russ's work: we can see it in *And Chaos Died*, in which the gay man does not die ignominiously, or become the sidekick in someone else's story, but instead goes on into a new future. It is there in *Picnic on Paradise* and in *We Who Are About To . . .* where the stories individuals tell themselves about who they are, and what their lives mean, collapse as the scenery and bit players are removed. It is most famously there in *The Two of Them* when Irene and Ernst fight: "Sick of the contest of strength and skill, she shoots him" (1978b 203). Burning through each tale are the questions, Whose narratives are these? Who benefits from this storying of the world?

Russ's work is metatextual: in itself it stands as a body of criticism of the science fiction field. The gray-eyed Alyx destroys many of the tropes of the heroic adventurer as she blithely wanders through the world demonstrating the value of intelligence. *We Who Are About To . . .* takes on the Robinsonade and leaves it gasping for a suicide pill, worn out on its own ludicrousness. Russ's work criticizes itself: as Lisa Yaszek and Graham Sleight both point out in their very different essays, many of the points one wants to make about Russ, she has already made about herself in her fiction and in her nonfiction. A novel like *The Female Man* dissects the world, the construction of fiction, the assumptions of science fiction, the responses of reviewers, and finally the responses of far future readers. It is steeped in genre consciousness.

Russ's work is intertextual; a reader must be able to follow fleeting references to Fritz Leiber, Charlotte Perkins Gilman, George Sand, and Emily Dickinson to follow the archaeology of the text down and down. The reader must be able to follow the stolen and subverted narrative forms, tracing not just the story but the poetics.

Russ's work questions the cosy consensus of author-reader relations. The reader must follow an author whose every book is written in a different form: the straightforward narrative of *And Chaos Died* is replaced with the casual but direct storytelling of *Picnic on Paradise* and then with the detached, almost academic tone of *The Two of Them*, and later the fractured, slightly distraught narrative voice of *The Female Man*. In *The Female Man*, as the visible narrator in Russ's fiction becomes more prominent, the proscenium arch of conventional narrative is replaced with all-round vision, angry and mocking, while the narrator becomes a participant in the action. Shifting between narrative and commentary, the narrative itself frequently encodes commentary. In "The Little Dirty Girl," the narrator's understanding of her own focal position slips and slides.

Voices: the narrator (named or unnamed) speaks directly to the audience (which is only sometimes us). At times, as in *The Two of Them*, the text feels as if it is written to be read aloud; the story is framed within the telling of it. This form of narrative is a critical tool in Russ's argumentative structure: stories are no longer neutral; they are the product of character—sometimes named, sometimes not—and in that they are products of a cultural positioning. Russ is always and ever the outsider but she is never a *neutral* outsider.

The observer narrator in Russ's work is one of her most powerful weapons: the observer identifies false allegiances; comments on the words not said; examines the cultural narratives of pink and blue books, of loving relationships; and exposes the muscle and nerve fibers of oppression. It is meet that the body becomes a canvas on which Russ paints resistance; oppression is written on the body. The Js of *The Female Man* share a genotype (perhaps), but they do not share a posture; their bodies do not confront the world in the same fashion. Janet slouches into the world, comfortable, spreading herself to accept space she takes for granted; Jeannine huddles, her body turned inward away from the world to its own core, while Jael's body faces outward in an stance of defiance/invasion. The world may be hers, but she does not fully accept that this is so. And Joanna exists as ghost, the observer narrator in-text who sees the layers of the world.

Russ's writing gets under the skin. It is a burr under the saddle blanket; sharp, uncomfortable, provocative. She is the science fiction writer who most encapsulates Wittgenstein's exhortation that aesthetics is ethics. Reading Russ can be exhausting, emotionally harrowing. Russ challenges your most radical analysis. There can be no excuses, no exceptions; niceness is not a mitigating factor in the structures of oppression. Difference isn't enough. Niceness merely pads the cell. Only rage is enough. Russ wielded her rage like a scalpel, in reviews, critical essays and in her fiction. Her purpose was to challenge the agendas of others.

Joanna Russ's career as a writer of fiction spanned thirty years. From her first published story, "Nor Custom Stale" (1959), through seven novels, several short story collections and three nonfiction collections, Russ produced a fierce, intense body of work whose influence has been complex. She is a writer whose work provokes reaction rather than emulation, and serves as an electric shock to the imagination. This collection of essays explores Russ's place within science fiction as a feminist, a science fiction writer, and a feminist science fiction writer, and sets out to assess what that means.

This collection seeks to do two things: to examine Russ's work as it appears on the page, and to place that work in the context of Russ's multifarious and overlapping professional worlds: worlds in which her position in a nexus of science fiction, feminist, and academic debates altered and shifted both with everything from the cover of a magazine to the personal partisanship of an audience. Russ's voice needs to be understood from these different perspectives; she is a thoroughly three-dimensional author and cannot be viewed through only one lens.

The first part of the book I have titled "Criticism and Community." We begin with Gary K. Wolfe's "Alyx Among the Genres," which considers Joanna Russ as a reader of science fiction and the way this consideration should affect the way her work is read. This chapter is followed by Edward James's consideration of Russ as a professional reader of SF, as a book reviewer for *Fantasy and Science Fiction* (F&SF) in the late 1960s and the 1970s. From here we move to Lisa Yaszek's essay on Joanna Russ's role in the creation of a feminist science fiction tradition and then to Helen Merrick's consideration of Russ's wider role in the feminist community as it developed within science fiction fandom. The last essay in this section is Dianne Newell and Jenéa Tallentire's discussion of the Merril-Russ intersection and the creative nexus between two very different women at a time when women in science fiction were still a reason for comment.

Part II offers a range of ways to consider Russ's fiction. Although her impact has been immense, Russ did not actually produce a huge body of work. Thus, rather than each essay's representing a single text, each takes a different approach to Russ's work: the texts considered reappear from different perspectives and are subjected to different critical approaches. Sherryl Vint discusses *The Two of Them* in the context of third-wave feminism, while Pat Wheeler considers anger and escape strategies in the same text. In the chapters by Keridwen N. Luis and Sandra Lindow, issues of alienation are highlighted as ways to understand *On Strike Against God* and *Kitanniny* respectively. Both authors home in on Russ's subversion of the bildungsroman, an inquiry that Andrew M. Butler extends in his psychoanalytic study of *The Female Man*. In all three of these chapters there is a strong sense that growth and change is central to Russ's conceptualization of feminism but that this is a growing beyond, rather than a growing into.

Violence and the uses of violence is a central argument of many of Russ's reviewers; Andrew M. Butler, Jason P. Vest, and Pat Wheeler all tackle this theme head-on in discussions of *The Two of Them* and *The Female Man* and *Alyx*.

Comparative work is always problematic and the more so with Joanna Russ, whose ferocity frequently raced ahead of her contemporaries. Paul March-Russell and Samuel R. Delany tackle the issue by using as foils Mina Loy and D. W. Griffith respectively, whose structural and aesthetic resonances provide new questions in the analysis of Russ's texts. Graham Sleight extends the emerging emphasis on literary aesthetics by returning us to a close reading of Russ's work with his focus on the poetics of her short fiction.

To conclude this collection on Russ, a collection that has been shaped by the fierce intensity of its subject, we have two essays on the narratives of joyous resistance: Tess Williams discussing carnival and satire in *We Who Are About To . . .* and Brian Charles Clark on *And Chaos Died* and *On Strike Against God*. In these final essays Williams and Clark encapsulate the tight spiral of argument and counterargument and the intense relationship between science and feminism in Russ's work to which Wolfe, James, Newell, and Talentire pointed at the beginning of the book.

# Part I   CRITICISM AND COMMUNITY

~

# 1 Alyx among the Genres

GARY K. WOLFE

I have also, by the way, seen first-rate adventure stories ruined by people who insisted on reading them as if they contained profound moral problems, though the story itself clearly had no such intentions. There is no reason on earth why a story *has* to be didactic, *has* to teach an explicit moral. But if you are going to moralize, you had better make sure it's above the kindergarten level.

—Joanna Russ, in a speech delivered before the Philadelphia Science Fiction Convention, November 9, 1968 [1]

The *Orbit* series of original anthologies edited by Damon Knight from 1966 to 1976 has often been regarded as one of the chief expressions of the American version of science fiction's New Wave, as well as one of the most highly visible: with some eighteen volumes appearing in less than eleven years, it very nearly achieved the periodicity of a magazine. Edited with an eye to innovative, literary fiction, the series featured early stories by such authors as Gene Wolfe, Thomas Disch, Sonya Dorman, R. A. Lafferty, Kate Wilhelm, Kit Reed, Carol Emshwiller, and others, as well as newer, more experimental tales by established authors such as Brian W. Aldiss and Philip Jose Farmer. With its second issue, *Orbit* 2 (September 1967), Knight took the unusual step of including two fairly long stories by the same author: "I Gave Her Sack and Sherry" and "The Adventuress," both by Joanna Russ and both featuring a character named Alyx, who begins her career as a mercenary adventurer, thief, and murderer in a sword-and-sorcery environment set in the Mediterranean world around 1500 B.C. A third Alyx story, "The Barbarian," appeared in *Orbit* 3 in 1968, the same year in which Russ published her first and only Alyx novel, *Picnic on Paradise*, with Ace Books; a fourth, "The Second Inquisition," appeared in *Orbit* 6 in 1970. (A fifth Alyx story, "A Game of Vlet," appeared in 1974, but was not collected in book form until Russ's 1983 collection *The Zanzibar Cat*.) Only thirty years old when the first of the Alyx tales appeared (the same age as Alyx herself in that first tale), Russ had previously published a handful of short stories in the genre, beginning with "Nor Custom Stale" in 1959 in the

*Magazine of Fantasy and Science Fiction*, a magazine for which she also became a frequent reviewer beginning in 1966.

The four Alyx stories (two of them retitled) and one novel were collected in 1976 in *Alyx*, an omnibus volume from Gregg Press, a division of the publisher G. K. Hall devoted principally to producing fine library editions of science fiction classics, under the editorship of David Hartwell. *Alyx* was one of the few new titles offered by this series, and the edition came with a thoughtful and insightful introduction by Samuel R. Delany, omitted in the first paperback reprint, which appeared in 1983 from Pocket Books's Timescape imprint (also edited by Hartwell) under the title *The Adventures of Alyx* (stories will be cited from the 1983 edition, unless otherwise indicated). This latter title was also that of the first British edition of the book, published by the Women's Press in 1985. Meanwhile, individual Alyx stories were reprinted in various anthologies during the 1970s: "The Second Inquisition" in *Nebula Award Stories 6, ed. Clifford D. Simak* (1971; the story was a Nebula finalist that year); critic Leslie Fiedler's odd but ambitious SF anthology *In Dreams Awake* (1975); and Pamela Sargent's second anthology of women's SF, *More Women of Wonder* (1976); "The Barbarian" in Gardner Dozois's *Another World* (1977); and "I Gave Her Sack and Sherry" in Knight's own *The Best from Orbit* in 1975. *Picnic on Paradise*, after being nominated for a Nebula Award in 1969, was reprinted as a stand-alone novel by Berkley in 1979. In short, even though the final original Alyx story appeared in 1970, Alyx herself remained a very familiar figure in the SF field for much of the 1970s and early 1980s.

My apologies for beginning with such a litany of bibliographical detail, but it's crucial to the intent of this essay, which is in part to reclaim and recognize Russ's identity and achievement *as a science fiction writer*—not simply a writer who used science fiction toward other ends—and to establish the extent to which Russ's work was deeply connected to the mainstream dialogue of genre SF prior to and concurrent with her most famous "breakout" works, the Nebula-winning "When It Changed" in 1972 and the now-classic *The Female Man* in 1975. While the Alyx tales have often been viewed as the early work of a feminist author in a formative phase,[2] the fact is that only a couple of years separate the final Alyx tale from those "later" classics, and the Alyx stories remained highly visible in the science fiction field throughout the decade in which Russ is now remembered for her more "revolutionary" works. Furthermore, they were measurably influential in their own way. Nancy Kress, in an address given at a 1993 fan convention, credits the tales with having given rise to an entire trend of women writers creating "female Amazon figures, warriors or wizards or assassins." "This trend," Kress continues, "started with Joanna Russ's stories about Alyx, an independent woman in a patriarchal preindustrial society who breaks free of its constraints. Russ's imitators, however, turned out characters who were less like Alyx than like female versions of Robert E. Howard's Conan." And Mary Gentle, in an online interview in 2000 with Nick Gevers discussing influences on her stories and the book *Rats and Gargoyles*, said "although Moorcock was undoubtedly an influence, the closer one—or the one I thought of at the time of writing—was Joanna Russ, and her "Alyx" stories: three of which are Leiberesque fantasy (with some science fantasy included), and then there's the novel, which is plain SF. And she doesn't apologize, and she doesn't explain. And if she could do it, I thought: why not me?" Gentle is not discussing the feminist content of the tales, but rather their sophisticated manipulation of genre materials, and it is this aspect of the tales that I intend to focus on here.

Kress and Gentle's mention of such writers as Robert E. Howard and Fritz Leiber might at first seem almost perverse, in the context of discussing an author whose principal reputation has been that of SF's most powerful, angry, and witty feminist voice, but their observations are not uninformed, and—like the publication history of the Alyx stories—they underline the degree to which Russ knew, understood, and manipulated the history and conventions of the field in her early fiction, and the degree to which she was *embedded* in the ongoing dialogue concerning the field's potential, both in her fiction and in her critical essays and reviews, which eventually won her a Pilgrim Award from the Science Fiction Research Association in 1988. Russ's reputation as one of the two leading "in-house" academic theorists of SF during the 1970s (the other was Samuel R. Delany) is well documented elsewhere in this collection; here, though, the focus will be on the Alyx stories as critical fictions, paying particular attention to the short stories, and on how such traditional SF forms as the sword-and-sorcery tale, the science fiction puzzle tale, the planetary adventure, and the time-travel story serve as a template for her more sophisticated and acutely gender-conscious narratives, while at the same time linking her to these earlier traditions, which she both celebrates and subverts. In a sense, the Alyx tales may be viewed as an account not only of the development of a feminist consciousness, but—particularly in the final tale—as an account of the birth of a science fiction writer.

That Russ was familiar with a wide spectrum of science fiction and fantasy traditions is evident in various ways throughout the Alyx tales. In the very first story, "The Adventuress" (retitled "Bluestocking" in the collection), Alyx describes a former lover to the young woman Edarra whom she has been hired to protect: "Ah! what a man. A big Northman with hair like yours and a gold-red beard—God, what a beard!—Fafnir—no, Fafh—well, something ridiculous. But he was far from ridiculous. He was amazing" (1967a, 26). The allusion might at first seem to be to the shape-changing dwarf Fafnir from Norse mythology (which would make little sense in the story's Mediterranean setting), but in fact, as Samuel R. Delany notes in his introduction to the Gregg Press *Alyx*, it is more likely an allusion to the hero of Fritz Leiber's long-running series of sword-and-sorcery tales featuring two rather disreputable heroes named Fafhrd and the Gray Mouser (Delany 1977, 194). Leiber—who supposedly coined the term "sword and sorcery" in 1960 (Clute and Nicholls 1993, 1194)—began publishing these tales at the very beginning of his career in 1939, and continued until 1988. In a 1979 review, revealing at least some familiarity with even the early tales in this series, Russ speculated, "I wonder if the very early "Adept's Gambit" was not the last of the Fafhrd-Mouser stories in which something really happened humanly, that is, in which somebody actually changed" (1979b, 64).

As Delany notes (1977, 194), Leiber returned the favor by including Alyx as a minor character in his story "The Two Best Thieves in Lankhmar," published in *Fantastic* in 1968, where she was described as Alyx the Picklock, a small, gray-eyed woman (she also appeared briefly in Leiber's later story "Under the Thumbs of Gods" in *Fantastic* in 1975). That same year Leiber provided a generous blurb for the paperback of *Picnic on Paradise*, describing it as "the only science fiction novel I've read in a single sitting in the past ten years." Meanwhile, as Edward James points out (see chapter 2), in her review column in the *Magazine of Fantasy and Science Fiction*, Russ had on more than one occasion expressed admiration for Leiber's work, particularly for his humor. In a review of Michael Moorcock's *Stormbringer* published in 1967—the same year "The Adventuress" was published—she mentions this humor while making some astute observations about the failings of sword-and-sorcery as a form: "Vividly colored, sensuously evocative but always a little vague, impressively single-minded and written with the utter conviction that is probably the indispensable element in this genre, Mr. Moorcock's sword-and-sorcery romances are near the top of the mark. I must add, though, for the benefit of those who came to sword-and-sorcery through writers like Fritz Leiber or Jack Vance, that Mr. Moorcock's romances are also entirely innocent of either the slightest trace of humor or what might tactfully be called the common operations of intelligence" (1967c, 20). In 1979, she noted that heroic fantasies "often begin with a delicious sense of freedom and possibility, only to turn dismayingly familiar and stale unless well salted with comedy (Leiber's technique)" (1979b, 68).

This generally sympathetic relationship between these two very disparate authors is less surprising when one recognizes Leiber's own relationship to the sword-and-sorcery subgenre, which, though it may have borrowed significant elements from the swashbuckling romances of Dumas and Sabatini, is most often associated with the work of Robert E. Howard. Howard, whose most famous creation remains the figure of Conan the Barbarian, was a pulp author associated for most of his short career (he committed suicide in 1936 at the age of thirty) with the magazine *Weird Tales*. Despite their narrative energy, the Conan tales can hardly be said to be characterized by any degree of wit or sophistication, or, for that matter, "the common operations of intelligence." Not surprisingly, the near-superhuman Howard heroes are all but invisible in Russ's variation on the sword-and-sorcery mythos (in fact, Delany reports that Russ told him she'd never read the Conan stories when beginning her own, but had only heard of them, just as she'd only heard of C. L. Moore's pulp adventuress Jirel of Joiry [Russ 1976a, 202]). But these superhuman figures are also increasingly invisible, or at least treated with growing irony, in Leiber's long series of tales. It may be significant that Leiber didn't begin publishing his Fafhrd stories until three years after Howard's death, and that the first story appeared in the John W. Campbell fantasy pulp *Unknown*, which was avowedly launched to provide a venue for more sophisticated fantasy tales than was common in the pulps at that time. Over the following decades, Leiber developed his own version of sword and sorcery into an increasingly complex and fertile arena for tales that ranged from horror to broad comedy, and that touched openly upon topics from fetishistic sexuality (which was hardly ever more than a disturbing subtext in early iterations of the subgenre) to urbanization; his corrupt and teeming city of Lankhmar likely provided the template not only for Russ's City of Ourdh ("that noble, despicable, profound, simple-minded and altogether exasperating capitol of the world" [1983a, 45]) but, directly or indirectly, for an entire tradition of such fantasy cities since, including Terry Pratchett's Ankh-Morpork or China Miéville's New Crobuzon. Equally important, his heroic but sometimes inept barbarian hero Fafhrd is balanced and to some extent undercut by the wily and wiry trickster figure of the Gray Mouser, who in many ways has more in common with Alyx than does Fafhrd.

In fact, when we first meet Alyx, she is described not as a statuesque heroic figure, but as a six-fingered "small gray-eyed woman" and a "neat, level-browed, governessy person" "of an intellectual bent" (9). Having arrived in Ourdh as part of a religious mission, Alyx quickly decides that the religion she's supposed to be promoting is "a disastrous piece of nonsense" (9) and takes up a living as a pick-lock. Soon she is hired as a traveling companion by the petulant teenage Lady Edarra, who is seeking to escape an arranged marriage. The two of them set sail in a decrepit stolen fishing boat and soon encounter a sea-monster—an unusual sea-monster, in that "it held its baby to its breast" (17)—which Alyx vanquishes with a spear. Shortly afterward, she defeats a small band of pirates through swordplay, and faces yet another crisis when the boat catches fire from a faulty firebox. The tale ends as the two of them encounter another fishing boat carrying two men, and the promise of a different life. In bare outline, this tale recapitulates several conventions of sword-and-sorcery tales, but with differences that must have seemed radical in 1967. Not only is the theme of domesticity foregrounded in ways hitherto unseen in this fantasy tradition—the sea-monster clutching her baby, Alyx and Edarra concerning themselves with matters as mundane as who does the laundry and who does the cooking—but the central action of the story concerns the evolving relationship of the hard-boiled, sardonic Alyx and the spoiled teenage girl Edarra, who is the first of a number of younger women that Alyx mentors in the remaining stories. Recovering from her burns after battling the fire, Alyx rather sadly mentions to Edarra "I had a daughter" (23), from whom she is apparently alienated. "But you . . ." she adds,' " "are here" (24).

In the second story, "I Gave Her Sack and Sherry" (retitled "I Thought She was Afeard Till She Stroked My Beard" in the collection), Alyx is a "wild hill girl" (31) married to an inept and abusive husband, whom she apparently kills during a fight after he's been humiliated and cheated by a band of smugglers. She takes up with a ship's captain called Blackbeard, again demonstrating her fierce independence and prowess in swordfights—in good sword-and-sorcery backstory fashion, she receives from him a sword which she will later have engraved with the motto "GOOD MANNERS ARE NOT ENOUGH" (44)—and eventually leaves him as well, arriving some six weeks later, alone, in the city of Ourdh. Samuel R. Delany, in his introduction to the Gregg Press *Alyx*, makes much of the fact that editor Damon Knight placed this story before "The Adventuress" when both appeared in *Orbit* 2, thus reversing the order of the first two Alyx stories to see print:

> My own suspicion (which I have never consulted the author about) is that, as a male, he saw Alyx born in the unhappy relationship with that husband, only to pass on through a fleeting encounter with religion. This probably seemed to him to preserve the "logical" (i.e. traditional) relation of men to women, and women to religion. That Alyx was born of an unhappy relationship with religion, only to pass through some fleeting encounters with husbands, puts husbands in such an untraditionally minor role in the scheme of things that it never occurred to Knight that it might be the right one. (Russ 1976a, 202–203)

Of course, one might respond in defense of Knight that there is indeed some internal evidence that the chronology of this tale places it earlier than the first tale, such as the fact that Alyx is described with "short, black hair" (10) in the first story and in this one is seen hacking off her long black hair that "fell below her waist" (32), or that the first story begins with her arrival in Ourdh and this one ends with it. Contrarily, the first story has her arriving "as part of a religious delegation" (9), while this one pointedly has her arriving there alone (45).

The most likely explanation, and one that Delany himself offers in apparent contradiction of his own hypothetical chronology, is that the Alyx stories were never intended to depict a particular chronology at all, or to imply the sort of narrative "mythology" that seems to so captivate fans of earlier sword-and-sorcery epics. As Delany puts it, only a few paragraphs after taking Knight to task for getting the chronology wrong:

> The critical temptation with a series is to try to read successive installments as if they were chapters in some particularly loosely-constructed novel. Almost inevitably, though, they present us with signs that insist, despite other signs of a serial chronology, that, rather than successive chapters, they are really successive approximations of some ideal-but-never-to-be-achieved-or-else-overshot structuring of themes, settings, characters. (Russ 1976a, 203)

Whether or not the Alyx stories represent "successive approximations" of a particular structuring of themes is open to question, although Russ's formula for ending all but the final story in the sequence with the line "But that's another story" suggests that something similar may be going on. And part of what's going on, I would suggest, is an exploration of genre materials, an ongoing experiment in what happens when a strong, intelligent, levelheaded, and competent woman is introduced into various traditional venues of SF and fantasy.

And these venues are not confined to sword-and-sorcery settings. The third Alyx story, "The Barbarian," set some ten years after the first, serves as a kind of transition between the historical fantasy milieu of the first two tales and the more purely science-fictional tales that follow, *Picnic on Paradise* and "The Second Inquisition." Alyx, now approaching middle age, is again hired as a guide and assistant, this time by a fat man who claims extraordinary powers and promises to show her wonders. These wonders are clearly science-fictional in nature: a small black box, featureless and indestructible, which glows with videolike images in response to thoughts, a knifelike object that disintegrates a wall of the tavern where they meet, an invisible force field that surrounds his "wizard's castle." And the always-skeptical Alyx greets these wonders with what can only be described as a kind of protoscientific attitude; of the featureless box, she muses that it must be some sort of machine: "*But magic? Bah! Never believed in it before, why now? Besides, this thing too sensible; magic is elaborate, undependable, useless*" (51). Later, trying to sneak into the "wizard's castle," Alyx even employs experiments and inferential reasoning when she encounters the invisible force field, described as "something at once elastic and unyielding" (60). She takes off one of her sandals and learns that it passes through unimpeded, then kills a crab and tosses it through as well. "The distinction, then, she thought, is between life and death" (61). But then she notices the crab, not quite dead after all, stirring on the other side of the barrier, and revises her hypothesis—"she now guessed at the principle of the fat man's demon, which kept out any conscious mind" (62). Pressing an artery on the back of her neck to cause herself to briefly lose consciousness, she falls through the barrier.

Jeanne Cortiel suggests that this barrier "has similar symbolic significance to the infamous 'glass ceiling' in women's careers" (1999, 50), but as almost any veteran reader of science fiction would have recognized in 1968, this incident marks the moment in which "The Barbarian" (and by extension the entire Alyx sequence) moves definitively from its sword-and-sorcery origins into the realm of science fiction. Alyx's conquest of the barrier is a direct echo of Fredric Brown's classic story "Arena," originally published in John W. Campbell, Jr.'s *Astounding Science Fiction* in 1944 and widely anthologized, and which (in the same year "The Barbarian" was published) placed fifteenth in a vote conducted by the Science Fiction Writers of America of the all-time best science fiction tales published prior to 1964 (this same vote provided the basis for the selection of stories included in Robert Silverberg's 1970 anthology *The Science Fiction Hall of Fame*). "Arena" had even been adapted as an episode of the TV series *Star Trek* in January 1967. Brown's tale is a classic puzzle-tale of the sort beloved by *Astounding*'s readers: in the midst of a long war against an alien race, a spaceman named Carson finds himself alone and naked on a strange planet, separated from a single alien only by an invisible and apparently impenetrable barrier. He learns that a vastly superior intelligence has placed the two of them there to act as champions of their own civilizations, and that the entire battle-fleet of the losing contestant will be annihilated so that the other civilization may survive and prosper. The puzzle, of course, is how to cross the barrier to engage in combat. When he's struck by a rock thrown by the alien, Carson first surmises that the barrier may screen organic from inorganic, but then realizes that a dead lizard can also pass through. He tries unsuccessfully to toss a living lizard through, then concludes—like Alyx—that "the screen was a barrier to living things" (Silverberg 1970, 236) Later, however, he realizes that the lizard he'd thought was dead was only unconscious, and that "the barrier was not a barrier, then, to living flesh, but to conscious flesh. It was a mental projection, a mental hazard" (246). By hitting himself on the head with a rock (somewhat less elegant than Alyx's solution), he is able to cross the barrier and vanquish the enemy.

Once Alyx attains the castle and confronts the "Wizard"—whom the reader, by now having shifted into SF reading protocols, recognizes as a renegade time traveler abusing his advanced technology and setting himself up as a kind of god in this primitive environment—she encounters another kind of force field borrowed from earlier SF tradition. He taunts her with his invulnerability:

> I wear an armor plate, little beast, that any beast might envy, and you could throw me from a ten-thousand-foot mountain, or fry me in a furnace, or do a hundred and one other deadly things to me without the least effect. My armor plate has *in-er-tial dis-crim-in-a-tion*, little savage, which means that it lets nothing too fast and nothing too heavy get through. So you cannot hurt me at all. To murder me, you would have to strike me, but that is too fast and too heavy and so is the ground that hits me when I fall and so is fire. (64)

Again, however, Alyx outwits the high-tech defenses in not one but three ways: she gouges his eyes with her fingers, bends him over a table to break his back, and finally smothers him with a pillow. The notion of a protective force field such as this is of course one of the oldest clichés in science fiction, and the term "force field" itself is often credited to early space opera author E. E. Smith, in his 1931 novel *Spacehounds of IPC*. But the notion of a force field sensitive to inertia—one that protects against violent attacks but is less effective against slow-moving threats—was of considerably more recent vintage, and has specifically been credited as the invention of Charles Harness in his 1953 novel *The Paradox Men*. As Peter Nicholls observes, this notion "gives Harness a good excuse to introduce swordplay (where the momentums are relatively small) into a technologically advanced society—an example that other writers were not slow to follow. (Clute and Nicholls 1993, 438) Though Nicholls does not mention these writers specifically, they include Frank Herbert and Larry Niven, both of whom gained wide prominence in the science fiction field during the mid-1960s.

"The Barbarian" serves as a kind of transition from the fantasy milieu of the earlier tales to the full-fledged science fiction of *Picnic on Paradise*, More important, it represents a quite conscious shift in genre from the sword-and-sorcery adventure to the science fiction puzzle-tale, with Alyx's competent swordplay replaced—or at least supplemented—by the newer model of heroism characteristic of such tales: her ingenuity and deductive ability. She rejects magical explanations for the advanced technology, reasons her way through two different force fields, and even realizes, after murdering the wizard, that he himself could not have been the maker of his mysterious devices. "*You hadn't the imagination,*" she thinks. "*You didn't even make these machines; that shiny finish is for customers, not craftsmen, and controls that work by little pictures are for children*" (67). And when she returns to her husband (presumably not the same one as in

"I Thought She Was Afeard Till She Stroked My Beard") at the end of the tale and explains how she killed the wizard, she gives only two reasons: "because he was a fool. And because we are not" (67). However blunt the message here may be that intelligence and ready wit are not bound to particular cultures (and however unlikely it may seem that an ancient "barbarian" could have reasoned through the function and even commerce of technologies thousands of years in advance of her own), the main point is that Alyx has now demonstrated her competence in yet another subgenre of the fantastic: she's become a science fiction heroine.

With *Picnic on Paradise*, Alyx moves into yet another subgenre of the fantastic, the planetary romance, sometimes viewed as a variant of the space opera. And once again, Russ alludes enthusiastically to earlier traditions. The first example of this is the "Trans-Temporal Authority," which has recruited Alyx to serve as a special agent assigned to assist a group of tourists stranded on the planet Paradise during a trade war. The notion of a kind of "time police" had been a popular one in the science fiction of the 1950s, whether conceived of as social engineers as in Isaac Asimov's *The End of Eternity* (which recruits its members from different eras) or as enforcers of historical order such as in Poul Anderson's "Time Patrol" stories (collected in book form in 1960 as *Guardians of Time*). But in *Picnic on Paradise*, it becomes clear that the main function of the Trans-Temporal Authority is as a means to get Alyx from the past into the future, where she again functions as a guide and, eventually, a kind of mentor. The Authority itself seems to function as nothing much more than "a study complex for archeologists" (160), regulating travel into the past for research purposes and taking exceptional precautions not to interfere with earlier eras. The nearly drowned Alyx was rescued by the time travelers purely by accident: she had been thrown into the sea off Tyre, tied to a heavy boulder, as a punishment for having stolen a chess set, and happened to be swept up in twenty cubic meters of water being transported back into the future for study. (We learn a great deal more about the Authority in Russ's later novel, *The Two of Them* ([1978]).

The only credible reason given for Alyx's assignment to rescue the group of tourists stranded on Paradise, apart from her hardiness and ingenuity, is her very ignorance of technology. Like "The Barbarian," and like a fair number of planetary adventures, *Picnic on Paradise* also features a significant aspect of the puzzle-tale. Alyx's assignment, simply enough, is to lead the tourists on foot several hundred kilometers across the snowy mountains of Paradise to a neutral base from which they will be able to leave the planet. But there is, of course, a catch: because of the ongoing trade war and the fact that the entire planet is monitored by satellite-based electronic surveillance, no advanced technology can be used to assist them in traveling or protecting themselves, lest they reveal themselves: " 'No fires . . . no weapons, no transportation, no automatic heating, no food processing, nothing airborne" (76), not even anything metal, although Alyx is given a nonmetal crossbow and synthetic knives to replace her own. This has the effect of leveling the playing field, of course: Alyx may be at a disadvantage because of her near-complete ignorance of the technologically advanced society in which she finds herself (she claims that the Trans-Temporal Authority taught her "not much" [74]), but the no-tech rule effectively strips the tourists of any advantages they may have because of their technological knowledge, and sets up the puzzle of how to survive a journey on an alien planet without benefit of any of the technology that got the tourists there in the first place. It also sets up the conditions for a classic wilderness survival adventure, a genre whose roots go far deeper than the origins of modern science fiction itself.

In keeping with the conventions of the survival journey, the cast of characters Alyx is hired to protect represent a familiar cross-section of social types; although all are considerably taller than Alyx and share a mixed-race heritage "as if they had crossbred in a hundred ways to even out at last" (79), they also are representatives of their leisure society's decadence, discussing various body modifications and the pleasures of installing free-fall in their bathrooms. (One such household amenity, "simulated forests with walls that went tweet-tweet" [79], might be a subtle allusion to Ray Bradbury's famous 1950 story "The Veldt," in which a similar artificial environment is installed in a child's playroom.) In general, they are a familiar crew: a famous amateur explorer, an artist, a politician, a pair of nuns (of an indeterminate religion), a young woman (who behaves like an adolescent, but is actually thirty-six, and who comes under Alyx's tutelage), her mother (who is dependent on rejuvenation drugs which she now cannot have), an alienated but beautiful youth called Machine (who tunes out the world with his psionic entertainment headware called a Trivia, in a rather remarkable anticipation of today's iPod generation). Machine eventually become Alyx's lover, but for the most part she retains her distance from the group. As Barbara Garland (1981) points out, all of these characters

> meet their own fatal weaknesses projected onto the landscape. Iris's mother, Maudey, unable to obtain her usual dose of rejuvenating drugs, falls over a cliff, the victim of her advancing age and of her inability to face death. Raydos, the artist, loses his vision. The explorer Gunnar, loses his machismo when he is unable to face real-life crises and is finally executed by Alyx for his cowardice. Machine, Alyx's lover, loses the perfectly functioning body which is his expression of life's meaning. Even Alyx herself loses her mental control, the ability to lead, the

refusal to accept dependence that has formed the basis of her own heroic self-image. (89)

In other words, the journey turns out to be anything but the "picnic"
Alyx had anticipated; after finally arriving at their destination base they find
it has been destroyed, and they must travel another five hundred kilometers
to a control embassy (protected by another invisible energy field). Alyx loses
about half her charges, including her lover Machine, before finally leading the
survivors to safety, where she says her farewell to them. *Picnic on Paradise* is
not merely a simple demonstration that the Competent Man role so common
to planetary adventures might as easily be assumed by a Competent Woman;
instead, it offers a subversive critique of the central assumptions underlying
that familiar form of adventure tale. Given the bureaucratic blundering of the
military on Paradise, the technological failures, and the moral and physical
weaknesses of her charges, it's rather remarkable that Alyx manages to get
any of them to safety. Nonetheless, the Trans-Temporal Authority regards the
mission as a success, and enlists Alyx to become a trainer, teaching her survival and combat techniques to other agents. The irony of such a misadventure
being touted as a triumph is not lost on Alyx.

The final story in *The Adventures of Alyx*, "The Second Inquisition," published in 1968, differs radically from all the others: instead of being set in
a mythical past or a science fiction future, it takes place in the distinctly
domestic setting of a middle-class household in an American small town
in 1925; instead of the voice of an ironically detached narrator, it is told by
a precocious sixteen-year-old girl; most important, Alyx herself seems to
be entirely missing from the tale. The narrator's family hosts a mysterious
boarder, pretending to be a circus worker, but who in fact turns out to be
another Trans-Temporal agent, a time traveler from 450 years in the future.
The story has confused some readers who regard this visitor as Alyx herself,
as the Trans-Temporal Authority figures significantly in the story.[3] But as the
very opening passage makes clear, this woman looks nothing like Alyx. In
place of the short woman with black hair and a milky complexion, we meet
a six-foot-four woman with "brownish, coppery features" (165) and reddish-
black hair, very much like the futuristic tourists from *Picnic on Paradise*. In
a letter to Jeanne Cortiel, Russ explained that the story is indeed an Alyx
tale because "the character in it is Alyx's great-granddaughter," and that she
meant to imply that the young narrator of the tale "went on to write the
other stories." But, as she also acknowledges, "That's impossible, of course"
(Cortiel 1999, 135), and trying to tease the chronology of the story to make
sense of this claim can be frustrating. The unnamed visitor from the future implies more than once that the sixteen-year-old narrator may be her

great-grandmother; at one point (in a scene that could easily be read as a figment of the narrator's imagination) she offers her a pair of silver sandals while explaining, "These are yours. They were my great-grandmother's, who founded the Order" (172). Yet elsewhere she explains that she has come back 450 years, which would place her many generations away from the narrator. And none of these chronological hints clearly connect either character to the Alyx of the earlier tales.

Nevertheless, there are useful hints in both the form and the technique of the tale, and Russ's claim that the narrator of "The Second Inquisition" may go on to write the other Alyx tales is tantalizing, and may have something to do with the fact that "The Second Inquisition" is the first of the Alyx tales to be narrated in the first person. Each of the earlier tales had ended with exactly the same formulaic closing line, "But that's another story." This one echoes that line with the variation "No more stories" (192, implying, at least, that the narrator's voice here may be the same voice that has told us the earlier tales. While this story may not be directly about Alyx, it may well be about the *origin* of Alyx. And again, this is closely related to the tale's roots in Russ's sophisticated understanding of science fiction and of what science fiction can offer to its readers. Like the earlier tales, this one is cast in the form of a familiar type, in this case the variation on the time-travel tale that features mysterious visitors to an almost idyllic domestic setting. The classic example of this trope—again, one that would have been familiar to almost any science fiction reader in 1968—is Henry Kuttner and C. L. Moore's 1946 novella "Vintage Season," which features a group of strange tourists who take up residence in a middle-class household overlooking a large city, and who are gradually revealed to be time-tourists seeking a safe vantage point from which to view a coming disaster.

Once again, then, Russ alludes to a familiar subgenre of science fiction tales—the time-travel tale—but here she brings the allusion directly into the text, and in so doing makes an elegant and critical point about the potentially liberating effects of science fiction as a form. Two novels figure prominently in "The Second Inquisition." The first, which the visitor describes as "a very stupid book," is titled *The Green Hat: A Romance*, and almost certainly refers to Michael Arlen's 1924 best seller *The Green Hat: A Romance for a Few People* (although Arlen is not mentioned by name), which later provided the basis for a London play featuring Tallulah Bankhead and a film starring Greta Garbo. In detailing the wildly romantic and decadent life of a pleasure-seeking young woman named Iris Storm, the novel was regarded as an anthem to a doomed generation comparable to F. Scott Fitzgerald's *This Side of Paradise*, and was exactly the sort of novel, like those of Elinor Glyn for an earlier generation, that seemed designed to scandalize parents of young women. Despite the time traveler's comment, she ends the book to Russ's narrator, who stays up most of the night reading it:

> When I slept, I dreamed of Hispano-Suizas, of shingled hair and tragic eyes; of women with painted lips who had Affairs, who went night after night with Jews to low dives, who lived as they pleased, who had miscarriages in expensive Swiss clinics; of midnight swims, of desperation, of money, of illicit love, of a beautiful Englishman and getting into a taxi with him while wearing a cloth-of-silver cloak and a silver turban like the ones shown in the society pages of the New York City newspapers.
>
> Unfortunately, our guest's face kept recurring in my dream, and because I could not make out whether she was amused or bitter or very much of both, it really spoiled everything. (167)

While these references to fast cars and flapper styles are directly borrowed from the Arlen novel, and seem meant to represent the kind of glamorous fantasy life available to young women in the 1920s through popular fiction, the key element in this beautifully written passage is the ironic presence of the time traveler's face, which "spoiled everything," presumably rendering the glamour false and trivial.

The next morning the narrator's mother discovers the book, and it leads to a moment of confrontation over the breakfast table with both parents. The time traveler effectively comes to her rescue, however, by claiming that she recommended the book to the girl after learning that the mother had special-ordered it from New York. She then takes the odd step of drawing for the girl a number of illustrations for the novel, which become illustrations concerning a family of white mice, one of whom is chasing the narrator's mother with a rolled-up umbrella. Later the narrator hears the visitor and her mother arguing in the kitchen, the visitor speaking "in a tone that would've made a rock weep" (170).

None of this has much directly to do with science fiction, of course, but it has a great deal to do with the kinds of fantasies available to young girls in the popular mainstream fiction of the day. In contrast to The Green Hat is a novel that the narrator reports finding on the visitor's bed: Wells's The Time Machine, which leads to a very different sort of discussion. The narrator tells us that after reading this novel, "I went around asking people were they Eloi or were they Morlocks; everyone liked it. The point is, which would you be if you could, like being an optimist or a pessimist or do you like bobbed hair?" (171). After complaining that "nobody in this town reads anything; they just think about social life" (171), the Morlock-Eloi question seems a direct comment on the shallow, bobbed-hair values depicted in The Green Hat. The narrator, as reader, seems to have reached a crucial point of discovery familiar to many science fiction readers: namely, that the genre as expressed by Wells invites intellectual speculation rather than fantasies of manners. As Russ herself wrote in a perceptive discussion of *The Time Machine*, Wells's novel "is not about a lost Eden; it is—passionately and tragically—about the Three Laws of Thermodynamics, especially the second."[4]

When the narrator asks the mysterious visitor if she herself is a Morlock, the visitor agrees wholeheartedly:

> I am a Morlock on vacation. I have come from the last Morlock meeting, which is held out between the stars in a big goldfish bowl, so all the Morlocks have to cling to the inside walls like a flock of black bats, some right side up, some upside down, for there is no up and down. . . . There are half a thousand Morlocks and we rule the worlds (171).

This odd exchange between narrator and visitor, which begins with the narrator telling us that she is in fact "talking to the black glass of the window" and ends with the comment, "It was almost a pity she was not really there" (171–172), seems to invite us to read it as a construct of the narrator's own imagination, an imagination that may be evolving into that of a science fiction writer.

Later, when the narrator becomes embroiled in the visitor's cross-time war involving a rebellion within the Trans-Temporal Military Authority—even helping the visitor kill an unwelcome cross-time intruder—they tacitly agree to adopt the term "Morlocks" to describe the other time travelers, of various shapes and sizes, who eventually come pouring through a mirrorlike portal into the narrator's home. In the climactic battle in the living room, during which the visitor loses an eye in a knife fight with a seal-like person, the rebels are finally forced back through the portal, but not before one of their leaders warns the narrator, " 'Do not try to impress anyone with stories . . . you are lucky to live" (189). But of course stories are exactly the legacy the visitor leaves her with. Confined to her bed with a nosebleed and anemia, the narrator learns that the visitor has departed, leaving no trace of her presence anywhere in the house. Toward the end of summer, however, she appears again in the mirror inside the narrator's closet door (again, as in the earlier passage, in a reflection). Unable to draw because of her damaged vision, she describes for the narrator three more sketches, each of which depicts a nightmarish overpopulated future with clear echoes of Wells's Morlocks and Eloi. She again disappears, and we learn that the narrator has patched together for herself a uniform of the Trans-Temporal Military Authority "as I thought it ought to look" (191)—in effect, a kind of science fiction fan costume. We also learn that her romantic dreams have shifted substantially from those she had derived earlier from her reading of *The Green Hat*. Instead of fast cars and romantic Englishmen, she now thinks, "Someday I would join a circus, travel to the moon, write a book; after all, I had helped kill a man. I had been somebody" (192). And the book she eventually writes, we can reasonably suspect, is this one. She is, perhaps, preparing to invent, or reinvent, Alyx.

Viewed in this context, "The Second Inquisition" (the title is drawn from a quotation from John Jay Chapman extolling independence of thought from one's townsfolk) is an appropriate and extraordinarily deft conclusion to a sequence of tales that form a subtle and celebratory critical survey of several forms of science fiction narratives. By the time we reach this tale, we have visited the sword-and-sorcery yarns of the pulp era, the science fiction puzzle-tale of the genre's "golden age," the planetary romance that has been so ubiquitous throughout the genre, and the equally ubiquitous time-travel story. It's of no small significance, then, that the final tale should be largely about reading, or that it should be narrated by a young girl who feels she is one of the few readers in a community otherwise obsessed by fads and fashions, or that this reader should herself be in the process of discovering the differences between fictions like *The Green Hat* and fictions like *The Time Machine*. In the very end, as she prepares to leave her room to return to the mundane world where her father is mowing the lawn and her mother weeding the flower bed, she thinks she sees something move in the mirror of her room, just on the edge of vision. "I wished for it violently," she tells us. "I wanted something to come out of the mirror and strike me dead. If I could not have a protector, I wanted a monster, a mutation, a murderous disease, anything! anything at all to accompany me downstairs so that I would not have to go down alone" (192).

Nothing comes out of the mirror, of course. Like generations of readers, she is left with her dreams and her stories, in a world of lawn mowers and gardens.

~

## 2  Russ on Writing Science Fiction and Reviewing It

EDWARD JAMES

Between 1966 and 1980, Joanna Russ contributed twenty-five reviews to the *Magazine of Fantasy and Science Fiction* (hereafter F&SF) covering some 110 books of all descriptions.[1] She was never more than an intermittent reviewer; when she started, Judith Merril was the usual reviewer for the magazine, and during her time at the magazine Merril, James Blish, and one or two others were far more prolific reviewers. But her magazine reviews constitute the bulk of her reviewing in the field,[2] and give us an insight into her approach to the writing of fiction, and the writing of reviews, which casts a sidelight onto her own fiction. I was inspired into writing this essay by an interaction many years ago, when a feminist critic of science fiction told me, in all seriousness, that she did not read science fiction written by men. My immediate thought was, "How can you hope to understand Joanna Russ, then?" It had become clear to me from reading Russ's science fiction that she was well versed in the science fiction of the 1950s and 1960s, the great bulk of which was written by men; understanding her work demanded a knowledge of what she was reacting against. It seemed to me that one way to investigate Russ's engagement with science fiction was not so much to look at her critical work, much of which has dealt with women's writing, but to look at her reviews. The ideal sample to take was that published in the *Magazine of Fantasy and Science Fiction*, where she was writing within and for the science fiction community; reviews in *College English*, the *Village Voice* or the *Washington Post* would inevitably have quite a different slant. F&SF during this period, all within the long editorial reign of Edward L. Ferman (editor from 1966 to 1991), had a circulation of more than 50,000,[3] and was widely recognized as the American magazine most committed to literary quality within the science fiction and fantasy field.

In taking on this prominent position, Russ was doing what numerous science fiction writers had done before her. Up until the 1970s, authors, as reviewers, were the predominant critics in the field: Damon Knight and James Blish (the latter publishing as William Atheling, Jr.) had set the standards in the 1950s. Other authors who were active critics in the period include Algis Budrys, Samuel R. Delany, M. John Harrison, and Judith Merril.[4] At least early in her reviewing career, Russ does not seem to have had any control over what she was sent for review. "Knowing my radical feminist tendencies, the Kindly Editor sent me only good books (by men) this month" (November 1971, 21).

As an author herself, Russ is well aware of the pressures of writing for a living, and is prepared to see the economic pressures as mitigating factors. She diagnoses Barry Malzberg as suffering from "that curse of all free-lance writers: lack of time. (Not time to write, but most importantly, time to think or just do nothing.)" (December 1972, 42). She feels guilty about dire criticism, and apologizes for her harsh words on Lloyd Biggle's *The Light That Never Was* (1972) by saying, "It's narsty to beat up on authors who are probably starving to death on turnip soup (*ghoti* soup) but critics ought to be honest" (February 1973, 27).[5] Likewise, of Anderson's *Satan's World* (1969), "it is rude to make nasty noises about half-loaves to someone who, must, after all, make a living from the stuff" (July 1970, 43). On the other hand, the lack of economic pressure can make a difference too: in relation to James Blish's *The Day After Judgment* (1971) she wrote: "It's my uninstructed impression that relative financial independence has allowed Blish to write more idiosyncratically than he ever did before, about themes he knows may not interest large numbers of readers" (November 1971, 23). She has no illusions about the difficulty of achieving "relative financial independence," noting that Ralph Blum's *The Simultaneous Man* (1970) is very poorly written in a technical sense (the science is "as bad as A.E. Van Vogt but without the charm"), but thinking the fine poems in it, if by Blum himself, show that he is wasting his time trying to be a mimetic novelist. She counsels him to "starve or teach like the rest of us" (February 1971, 63, 65).

Over the course of her reviews, Joanna Russ offers a minicourse in how to write science fiction, and—partly in response to letters, critical of her reviewing, which were sent in to the editor—in how to write science fiction reviews as well. This essay will show how she did this, and what lessons she had to offer. But it is worth pointing out first of all that, despite her academic status—she got her first university job in 1970—as a reviewer within the science fiction community, Russ had all the hallmarks of a fan. She clearly read very widely (unlike too many academic critics of SF then and since); she was a devotee of *Star Trek*; she was prepared to allow that science fiction offered different pleasures from those of other forms of literature; she was also—and this is important—prepared to tolerate and even enjoy schlock. Of Colin Wilson's *The Mind Parasites* (1967), intended as an imitation of H. P. Lovecraft (but actually more "in the Boy's Life Gee Whiz tradition, and ought to be called *Tom Swift and the Tsathogguans*"), she wrote, "It is one of the worst books I have ever read and very enjoyable, but then I did not have to pay for it." (January 1968, 38). (She recommended setting it alight with kerosene and subsequently reading Lovecraft's "The Shadow over Innsmouth" for relaxation.) *Omar* by Wilfrid Blunt, which is about talking badgers, is pleasant, charming and slight, she reports: "If your sugar tolerance is low, stay away. I liked it" (April 1969, 48). She seems to share the average fan's adoration of cats (the nearest thing to an alien in one's own house), saying of Fritz Leiber's "Spacetime for Springers" that "the less I say about this story the less I will slobber over the page and make a nut of myself" (July 1968, 55). Lloyd Biggle's *The Still Small Voice of Trumpets* (1968) is "innocuous and mildly analgesic, which is (I suppose) what this sort of book is for" (December 1968, 20). And when she comes across something she regards as really poor, she is inclined to blame the publisher as much as the writer. Of John Boyd's *The Last Starship from Earth* (1968), published by Berkley, she writes, "I forgive Mr Boyd the anguish his novel caused me and hope he will eventually forgive me the anguish this review may cause him, but for Berkley there is no forgiveness. Only reform. *Don't do it again*" (September 1969, 24). In the case of Ralph Blum, mentioned above, she is inclined again to blame the publishers: "A publishing house which goes into s.f. without some experienced person on its staff is heading for trouble: either incoherent drek or slick blandness" (February 1971, 65). Irresponsible publishers can indeed harm the whole field of SF: she described an Elwood-edited anthology as "one of that damned flood of anthologies that do nothing but cheapen the market, exasperate reviewers and disappoint all but the most unsophisticated readers" (October 1966, 37).

Russ certainly feels that science fiction can, and ought to, give something to its readers that can not easily be acquired anywhere else. This "something" she finds just as difficult to define as most science fiction readers do. It could almost best be determined by its absence, as in books written by outsiders to the field. *This Perfect Day* (1970) by Ira Levin caused her to reflect that it "makes science fiction written by science fiction writers look amazingly eccentric; I never realized what a freaky bunch we are, or what a strong impression of real, individual minds at work one gets from even the worst science fiction. I might add that a bad book written by a human being is infinitely preferable to a "perfect" book apparently written by a sales chart" (February 1971, 60). Like many fans, what really riles her is a book written by a sales chart, written, almost by definition (as few genuine science fiction books ever become best sellers), by someone from outside the field who thinks that cashing in on the science fiction market is going to be easy. *The Day of the Dolphin* (1969) is another example. The author, Robert Merle, writes for readers "whose delicate mental balance can be upset by the least sign of intelligence or originality" (January 1970, 37). His characters—"well-rounded, 'realistic,' ponderous, wooden dummies"—cause her to repent of her complaints in the past that there is not enough characterization in science fiction. "If characters have to be introduced to do utilitarian things in books—like turning on electric lights—I far and away prefer the lightweight, portable, flexible cardboard cutouts that science fiction writers are so fond of." She concludes, addressing herself to possible readers who are fearful that it might be science fiction: "Do not be alarmed, nervous readers. Even though the story is about dolphins, it will not hurt you, it is not really science fiction, it is full of recognizable things straight from novel-land, and nothing is real. M. Merle writes like this, by the way, it is very modish and experimental, it is called "run-in sentences," she flung herself down on the bed, I will kill all publishers, she thought" (January 1970, 38).

Russ remarks more than once on the vexed question of characterization. She complained about those SF writers who pay too much attention to critics outside the field, and try to learn about such things as characterization. "When will science fiction learn that we love it for itself alone?" she comments on James Gunn's The Listeners (1972). On the one hand, Gunn's book is a wonderful science fiction novel; on the other, it is a tale of "carefully variegated impossible people" who "go drearily through 'human interest' situations." The science is fascinating: "This is the subject. This is the soul of the book. The rest is flubdub. If Scribners insisted on it, Scribners must learn, and if part of Mr. Gunn insisted on it, he must learn." She concludes: "The book is good enough to be worth reading. But it hurts" (July 1970, 69–70). Although critics more recently have derided the idea that science fiction is a "literature of ideas," Russ still believes that the inspiration of "real, individual minds at work" is a major part of science fiction's appeal. Characterization, particularly if drawn from how-to-write-popular-fiction manuals, is unnecessary. Purple prose is unnecessary. Didacticism is not to be eschewed, and airy imagination should not be valued over hard fact.

Russ makes that direct comparison in an early review, in which she compared James Blish's The Warriors of Day (1951) and Michael Moorcock's two fantasy novels The Stealer of Souls (1963) and Stormbringer (1965). She castigates the Blish book, which "provides a beautiful display of Blish's defects." (There is a note to say that only after writing the review did she discover that it was a reprint of a book originally published in 1951.) Blish has "intelligence, logic, complexity, precision, wide knowledge, intellectual rigor (and vigor), and a natural preference for exact and telling detail." But "swashbuckling demands a certain suspension of the critical sense," which Blish in this book could not cope with. "He is a speculative realist trying to write a romantic novel; he cannot write it, and he will not give it up. And so he goes on, clashing gears and grinding (my) teeth." The writing is poor; there are wholly inappropriate comparisons. Moorcock's writing, on the other hand, is "vividly colored, sensuously evocative but always a little vague, impressively single-minded and written with the utter conviction that is probably the indispensable element in this genre." However, there is no humor, little common sense (both of which were abundant in Vance and Leiber, whose fantasy she clearly admired), no real geography, no real morality, no real characters, and hardly even any real weather, while some of the spellings (like Quaolnargn) made her "speculate whether Mr Moocock was Welsh, whether he was *very* Welsh, whether he had ever written for the Goon Show, and so on, quite against the purposes of Elric, the last Prince of Melnibone." "Myself, I find James Blish's sense of fact a hundred times more exciting—even in a bad book—than all Mr Moorcock's cloud-capp'd palaces. These are splendid but ultimately boring while fact is never either; fact is suggestive, various, complex and free—in short, it's fact—and this is the stuff with which writers like Mr Blish are trying, however erratically or imperfectly, to deal" (October 1967, 28–30). The didactic qualities of science fiction, which have seemed so incongruous to many critics, are for Russ part of what makes science fiction distinctive and enjoyable.

Russ can get enthusiastic about Blish (she reviewed four of Blish's books altogether), and she can get enthusiastic too about classic "hard SF" of the old school, such as Hal Clement's story collection, Small Changes (1969). " 'Old-fashioned' is a derogatory term nowadays, but it is the best single word for Small Changes, with the emphasis on 'fashioned.' Mr Clement's world is that of *homo faber* and within its confines the stories are nearly flawless" (August 1969, 27). She stresses the confines and the limitations of Clement's writing. Most of the tales are "almost completely devoid of social or psychological interest, and sometimes devoid of plot, except for this will-the-factory-run sort." But there are compensations. Clement's characters are sane and calm, and "Mr Clement is in love with the laws of basic physics, and they are in love with him right back; in no other set of stories that I remember do the words 'angular momentum' carry quite so much of a thrill." She concludes with the thought, "When people talk about 'pure' science fiction of the 'good old days,' this is what they mean. Unluckily the good old days had as little of this as we do; luckily Hal Clement is around now" (words that sadly, since 2004, are no longer true).

Like the most traditional reviews of science fiction, in the columns of *Analog*, Russ insists that the science be accurate. Seriousness is also a virtue. Poul Anderson's Seven Conquests (1969), for instance, she compares with Zelazny's story "For a Breath I Tarry." Anderson, by the late 1960s, was generally regarded as old hat; Zelazny was one of the hot new writers, a leading figure of the U.S. New Wave with two Hugo-winning novels and two Nebula-winning stories to his credit. Anderson's collection of stories "is a grim, low-keyed, joyless sometimes dreary book (not first-rate Anderson) which stuck with me and made me think—surprisingly, when you consider some of those cardboard personages. Zelazny's 'For a Breath I Tarry' is an emotional orgy that made me cry, but I didn't respect the story for making me cry, or like myself the better for it" (August 1969, 30). Anderson's stories were jerry-built, full of cliché and flat characters; but even if they start off as schlock, which most of them do in Russ's opinion, "they are all thoughtful and most pack a genuine emotional punch" (August 1969, 29). Zelazny's story, on the other hand, can be seen "working by sheer surface razzle-dazzle, as I suspect all Mr. Zelazny's writing does." She goes on to say that "If the story hasn't done so already, it will undoubtedly win the Hugo, the Nebula, the Comet, the Nova, the Pebble, everything else anybody chooses to toss at it" (August 1969, 29). Comets, Novas, and Pebbles did not exist, of course, and her over-the-top comment is just as likely to be a criticism as a compliment; this is the sort of story tailor-made for winning awards, she is implying, and not to her own taste. (It is certainly very different from her own Nebula-winning story, "When It Changed," published three years later.)

Stylistic experiments, in fact, meet with some suspicion (bizarrely, some might think, in view of her own The Female Man, which had been written by the early 1970s although not published until 1975). Brian Aldiss's Report on Probability A (1968, although written in 1962),[6] perhaps the most audaciously experimental novel to come out of the New Wave, was something to be admired, but it was too long, and sheer indulgence. "I had to work very hard to get through it at all and would on no account read it again" (July 1970, 45).

What she admires comes through in her comments on a number of people, and I shall take just five: Jack Vance, Kate Wilhelm, Keith Roberts, Robert Silverberg, and Ray Bradbury.

Jack Vance is a writer who inspires passionate devotion among some, and leaves others cold; and Russ does better than most to explain his appeal. She notes that Vance's Emphyrio (1969) is a fine book, and she talks about it in terms of Verfremdungseffekt and bildungsroman (both of which are explained in a footnote) (January 1970, 40–42). "Science fiction, like all literature, usually tries to make the strange familiar, but Mr. Vance makes the familiar strange." "Mr Vance knows about childhood, grief, love, social structure, idealism, and loss, but none of these breaks the perfect surface of the book; everything is cool, funny, and recognizable while at the same time everything is melancholy, real, and indescribably strange." She singles out in particular his gift for evocative naming: "What is one to say of a puppet play the title of which is 'Virtuous Fidelity to an Ideal is the Certain Highroad to Financial Independence'? Or of an author whose ear is so sure that among names like Ambroy, Undle, and Foelgher, he can serenely place a district called Riverside Park? Others grunt and heave to produce sophomoric diatribes against organized religion; Mr. Vance merely produces a Temple Leaper who asks the hero's father severely whether he has lately leapt to the glory of Finuka." (In the course of her reviews Russ more than once castigates sophomoric diatribes against religion.)

There are several women who are reviewed enthusiastically by Russ, including Carol Emshwiller (whose collection *Joy in Our Cause* (1974) is "a terrifying, inexplicable, totally authentic world in which even the commas are eloquent") (March 1975, 44). and Ursula Le Guin (who is an artist, not a hack or a craftswoman, and "potentially a writer of masterpieces") (March 1975, 42, 43). But it is probably Kate Wilhelm with whom Russ has most sympathy, despite her flaws. Of *Let the Fire Fall* (1969), she wrote that it was "brimful of the details of ordinary life—too full almost, for the people and places take on a liveliness beyond that necessary to the plot. At times this is confusing, but more often it's delightful—real people, recognizable people whose lives twist and shift, whose motives change, whose most commonplace decisions have unexpected effects" (September 1969, 22). Her review of Wilhelm's *Abyss: Two Novellas* (1971) immediately followed her puff for Shulamith Firestone's feminist classic *The Dialectic of Sex* (1971), which had some of the most exciting social extrapolation around, she said, although she warned potential male readers that "you will have a hard time with this book if you believe that Capitalism is God's Way or that Manly Competition is the Law of the Universe—but then you can go back to reading the Skylark of Valeron or whatever and forget about the real universe" (November 1971, 18). She ties Wilhelm's writing in with Firestone's insights. Firestone had noted that men and women live in different cultural worlds. This reminded Russ of what Orwell had said: that we did not learn authentically about many worlds, as to be a member of those worlds demanded that one not be an artist. Orwell instanced Kipling as an exception: someone who was inside Anglo-Indian society, and yet was able to escape it enough to write about it, yet not enough to cease belonging to it. Wilhelm, Russ suggested, was an escapee from the feminine mystique. Most women writers have "brought themselves up as men, since 'man'—in the general view—was the equivalent of 'human'"; here Russ inserted a footnote, "*e.g. myself and Anne McCaffrey*" (November 1971, 20). But "like Kipling, Kate Wilhelm manages to be both an artist and the voice of an experience *that is defined by its not having a voice*" (November 1971, 20; Russ's italics). In short, she can write about "real women," because she has found a voice by moving out of the culture of women, while still staying in it. Or rather, Russ qualifies, "Wilhelm almost does this." Russ does not like elements of these two stories, and she notes some clunky writing, but comments that "Wilhelm—luckily for her—has art but no conventional craft" (November 1971, 21). "Art" and "artist" are two of Russ's highest compliments.

Keith Roberts too is an artist. Russ reviews his most famous book, *Pavane* (1968; revised U.S. edition, 1969) with enthusiasm. (April 1969, 44–45). It has "a suggestive power science fiction so often lacks; the most important points in the book are not the most important parts of the plot, and at its best, the novel has that lyrical meaning that is so easy to feel and so hard to explain," above all in its description of "the extraordinary, half-expressed melancholy of a society that became static *after* the Renaissance." But Russ adds a new phrase to her critical vocabulary, and one that she does not use again in her *F&SF* reviews: he is "a real writer." She goes on to define this:

> By this I mean that he dwells on things for their own sakes, that he doesn't conceive of the details of his book as merely a means to get from point A to point B with as little sweat as possible (and with some superficially attractive tinsel thrown in). One feels that he would discard the plot instantly if the characters and the world decided to develop in some other direction; it is this risk that makes a book live. This is worth mentioning in a field that seems to conceive "good writing" (or "style") as either an irritating distraction or a mysterious gift before which we ought to be simultaneously awed and a little contemptuous. Style is respect for real life.

Robert Silverberg is a writer about whom many people changed their mind in the late 1960s, although Russ clearly found it difficult to describe her feelings about the change—or, more particularly, to explain that change in a way that made her feelings clear to her readers. Of a collection of Silverberg stories, *The Cube Root of Uncertainty* (1970), she noted that there were six stories by the Old Silverberg, and six by the New. "Old Silverberg is an idiot ('But it takes all sorts to make a continuum,' he philosophically decided), but New Silverberg is something else: a highly colored, gloomy, melodramatic, morally allegorical writer who luxuriates in lush description and has a real love for calamity" (April 1971, 66). Old Silverberg was an "extremely self-conscious and clever hack"; the New Silverberg still needed to flush some of that out of his system: "I don't like his feverishness, or his intense, mad romanticism." But the recent *Galaxy* serial, *Downward to the Earth* (published as a book in 1970) was a "genuine novel," and "the first use I have seen Mr Silverberg make in print of his really extraordinary wit" (April 1971, 67). Two years later she wrote of *Dying Inside* (1972) that it was "as close to mainstream realism as science fiction can get without moving out of s.f. altogether," and that "it's the first time that Mr Silverberg has used his extraordinary wit in print" (an unfortunate lapse of memory on Russ's part). "I wasn't in on its wavelength, but other readers will respond to it," she added (July 1973, 70).

The lapse of memory was nothing to the comment she made two years later in a review of Silverberg's *Born with the Dead* (1974). "Robert Silverberg is a sossidge-factory trying to become an artist. To my mind he's only done so only twice, in "Notes from the Pre-Dynastic Epoch" . . . and "Schwartz between the Galaxies" (July 1973, 70). She repeated the same idea just two months later, saying of the same short story "Schwartz between the Galaxies" that here "Silverberg becomes an artist for the second time in his life; the story is worth the rest of the book put together" (March 1975, 45). The following month, she felt obliged to add a REPENTENT SILVERBERG NOTE to her review section, referring back to the review of *Born With the Dead*, and saying that "I committed the kind of blooper about *Born with the Dead* that made me wish I was dead." She had said that Silverberg was a "sossidge-factory trying to become an artist," assuming that everybody knew that Silverberg's sossidge-factory days had ended fifteen years earlier, and that "by 'artist' I meant work so faultless and fully realized that one would not wish a word of it changed." Silverberg was a "*very ex-sossidge-factory still in the process of developing as an artist.*" These two stories were "true quantum-jumps" in this process. They were "absolutely satisfying works, without reservations, the kind of fully-fused writing that's rare in any writer's career. And *that* is what I meant" (April 1975: 67).

Part of this problem, of course, revolves around the question of what is art. Bradbury is art: which seems to go against what she has said before about the importance of scientific accuracy. But she almost believes Bradbury to be art against her own will. "Ray Bradbury does everything wrong," she begins (July 1970, 46). Anne McCaffrey can sing better, Poul Anderson can think better, "and compared with Brian Aldiss, [Bradbury] is as a little child." What Bradbury has is great economy of style and a very fine understanding of "a certain kind of childish or childlike emotion." The very fact that "there is little in his stories" provides "the effect of something spun gleaming out of nothing." Bradbury possesses few of the attributes of the most admired writers, yet his work is art: "Art can exist without encyclopedic knowledge, sophisticated morality, philosophy, political thought, scientific opinion, reflection, breadth, variety and a lot of other good things. What else can I say? Mr Bradbury strikes me as a writer on the same level as Poe, the kind of writer people will still be reading, still downgrading, still praising a century from now."

As Russ's career as a reviewer moved toward its second decade, she began to worry openly about the standards she was using to judge books: "The reviewer's hardest task is to define standard" (January 1975, 10). She commented that the word "good" could mean almost anything: "what the British call a 'good read,' 'for those who like it, this is what they'll like,' 'it won't poison you,' 'good enough for minor entertainment,' 'mildly pleasant,' 'intelligent, thoughtful, and interesting,' 'charming,' and just plain 'good'—excluding the range of better, from fine to splendid to superb to great." To make it more confusing, reviewers often adopted "a paradoxical sliding scale." A book that is very ambitious may not succeed in what it is trying to do, while books merely written to provide an entertaining read may actually succeed very well. Yet the former may actually be much more valuable and interesting than the latter. She instanced one of her own reviews in an apologetic tone, where she had not made the distinction sufficiently clear (July 1973, 69–70). She had reviewed James Gunn's *The Listeners* (an ambitious failure) and had managed to make it sound worse than Norman Spinrad's *The Iron Dream*, a much less ambitious work. Gunn's book was "bad" because parts of it were so good; Spinrad's was "good" "partly because it demanded so little of the reader—some of this by the author's deliberate choice, which only adds to the complexity of the whole business" (January 1975, 10).

Russ turned again to the topic of reviewing in her penultimate review, in November 1979, which responded to letters attacking her short but pungent demolition of heroic fantasy in the February 1979 issue, letters that had been inspired by the publication of Stephen Donaldson's *Lord Foul's Bane* (1977) and Joy Chant's *The Grey Mane of Morning* (1977), some of the first fantasy trilogies inspired by Tolkien. Some of the dozens of letters attacking Russ were published in the July 1979 issue, and she responded a few months later. Russ organized the attacks into seven categories; the italicized headings from which I quote from are hers, although what follows are my summaries.

1. *Don't shove your politics into your reviews. Just review the books.* "I will," Russ responded, "when authors keep politics out of their books." This, she noted, was an impossibility. Any attempt to describe relationships between human beings involved a description of power relationships, in other words, politics.

2. *You don't prove what you say; you just assert it.* As there is no way to "prove" anything in aesthetic or moral matters, such was an inevitable part of the reviewing process.

3. *Then your opinion is purely subjective.* It may be subjective by being the result of a critic's personal decisions, but that is not the same as arbitrary. It is based on a critic's whole education.

4. *Everyone's entitled to his own opinion.* She suggested that kids (American kids, obviously) discover "it's a free country" at seven, and graduate to "everyone's entitled to his own opinion" at fourteen, and she regards this as a problem rather than a solution. "The process of intimidation by which young people are made to feel humanly worthless if they don't appreciate 'great literature' (literature that the teacher often doesn't understand or can't explain) is one of the ghastly facts of American education" (November 1979, 104). Russ comments that sometimes the defensive mechanism asserts that great art doesn't exist, or that whatever is found moving is great art. Writing seems to be judged differently from other arts,

in that it is easy to accept that a dancer or a musician may be lacking in skill or technique, but we all deal with words and think that our opinion is as good as anyone else's. But writing is a craft too, and it can be judged. "And some opinions are worth a good deal more than others."

5. *I knew it. You're a snob.* The trouble is, Russ commented, that science fiction is a small world that often does not look outside its own bounds; reputations get inflated, particularly by those who are defensive about "high culture." But if Charles Dickens or Virginia Woolf are great writers, then the consensus in the outside world would be that C. S. Lewis and J. R. R. Tolkien are, at best, "good, interesting, minor authors."

6. *You're vitriolic, too.* Russ agreed: "critics tend to be an irritable lot," and she gives some examples of biting wit from George Bernard Shaw and Damon Knight. The only way, she suggests, to relieve oneself of the pain that has to be endured by reading every line, "with our sensitivities at full operation," is to express one's views vividly, precisely, and compactly.

7. *Never mind all that stuff. Just tell me what I'd enjoy reading.* "Bless you, what makes you think I know?" is how Russ starts her response (November 1979, 107). It is impossible for the critic to know, any more than it is possible for an editor. And it is particularly difficult in the field of escape reading; "i.e. something as idiosyncratic as guided daydreams." Some writers and publishers, she adds, do their best to give readers what they enjoy by reproducing more of the same, in series novels. But this "tends to eliminate from fiction these idiosyncratic qualities other readers find valuable, art being of an order of complexity nearer to that of human beings (high) than that of facial tissue (low)" (November 1979, 107).

This lengthy response to her angry readers was concluded by a clarification of her views on heroic fantasy. She apologized for upsetting people by saying that "something in which one has invested intense emotion is not only bad art but bad for you, not only bad for you but ridiculous." She did not do it to annoy, nor because she does not find "the promise held out by heroic fantasy— the promise of escape into a wonderful Other world" to be unappealing. Indeed, because she had spent her twenties reading Eddison and Tolkien, and adapting *The Hobbit* for the stage, she knew from personal experience how intense the demand for escape was, although it was ultimately impossible. "The current popularity of heroic fantasy scares me," she said; it is a symptom of political and cultural reaction, itself a response to economic depression. There is artistic worth in some fantasy. The strong point of Tolkien and Lewis is their moralizing; of Vance, his cynicism; of Dunsany, his irony; of Beagle, his nostalgic wistfulness. But if they are no more than daydreams, she implies, then the fantasy is not only worthless, but harmful. "Daydreams about being tall, handsome (or beautiful), noble, admired, and involved in thrilling deeds are not the same as the as-if speculation which produces medical and technological advances" (November 1979, 108).

Russ has thus neatly segued from an attack on heroic fantasy into a defense of science fiction and reality. Romancers may find reality horrible, and resort to painkillers (which can be bad for the health); but reality is all we have. "Once readers realize that escape *does not work*, the glamor fades, the sublime aristocrats turn silly, the profundities become simplifications, and one enters (if one is lucky) into the dreadful discipline of reality and art."

Ironically, perhaps, Russ might have been more at home in *Analog* than in *Fantasy and Science Fiction*. Her stated sympathies are with hard extrapolation, and not with the airy fantasies of "cloud capp'd palaces," such as are not infrequently found in the fiction published by F&SF. It is perhaps not coincidence that two months after her attack on fantasy she published her last review in this magazine.

What can the reader of Russ's science fiction learn from a study of her reviews of science fiction novels? First, that she is in many ways a very old-fashioned reader of science fiction. That she should write in praise, in her very last review, in 1979, of "as-if speculation which produces medical and technological advances," shows that she is a true daughter of Gernsback and Campbell, and apparently far removed from the reaction against the Old Guard by the New Wave. She enjoys schlock; she admits the importance of entertainment; she extols the value of scientific accuracy. If the Golden Age of SF is when one is twelve, then Russ entered her Golden Age in 1949, at the peak of Campbellian influence, and at a point that historians might well recognize as the beginning of science fiction's *real* Golden Age. Indeed, many of her values reflect her love and indeed nostalgia for that period. Obviously her feminism would lead her to criticize some of the assumptions made by male (and female) writers of the Golden Age, but in F&SF, at least, her main reforming tendencies are in other directions. She disapproves of the increasing popularity of fantasy, and wants a resurgence of truly scientific SF; she desires to see "art" in her writers (although rarely finds it), but is more interested in good science than in half-hearted attempts at characterization or other presumed "literary" qualities; she wants better writing, but (unlike several representatives of the New Wave) does not want an abandonment of the science fiction project. One might detect in her more than thirteen years of reviewing a gradual change in tone, from fannish reviewer to university professor attempting, delicately, to educate and enlighten her readers. Yet her own critical position remains much the same throughout this period: a radical feminist, and a booster for the true spirit of SF.

~

## 3   A History of One's Own

Joanna Russ and the Creation of a Feminist SF Tradition

LISA YASZEK

In her essay, "Recent Feminist Utopias" Joanna Russ proposed that contemporary women authors are compelled to tell stories about all-female futures for one simple reason: because men "hog the good things of *this* world" (emphasis mine; 1981, 140). Among these good things, of course, are literary tastemaking and canon formation. Although these processes are most often associated with critical assessments of realist or mainstream literature, they affect scholarly discussions of popular genre fiction as well. Such was certainly true when scholars turned their critical gazes on science fiction (SF) in the 1960s and 1970s. Given that feminists of this period were still fighting for basic recognition of their ideas, it is perhaps not surprising that most of the SF histories published in this era were indeed written *by* men *about* men—and, by extension, primarily *for* men.

The boom in feminist SF in the 1970s and the advent of feminist SF studies in subsequent decades signaled a significant shift in the ownership of taste- and tradition-making practices, and by now it has become commonplace to talk about the existence of a feminist SF tradition. Although feminist SF scholars vigorously debate the exact nature of this tradition, they almost universally recognize Joanna Russ as central within it.[1] This chapter builds upon such recognition to demonstrate the equally central role that Russ played in the development of feminist SF scholarship as well. I will begin by briefly reviewing the early decades of SF scholarship and the implicit construction of SF authorship as a masculine activity and then examine how the critical essays Russ published on feminism, SF, and women's writing between 1971 and 1981 constitute a counterhistory that positions feminist SF at the center of SF writing practices. I will conclude by considering the feminist SF tradition Russ constructs in relation to both prevailing assumptions about what constitutes "good art" and Russ's own early experiences as an SF author in her own right.

## Battle of the Sexes for Science Fiction
*Round One: History*

Although the SF community understood itself as a distinct, self-regulating entity throughout most of the twentieth century, there were relatively few formal histories of the genre published until the 1960s and 1970s. Such histories emerged at the very moment SF became a viable object of inquiry in academia: the first SF panel appeared at the Modern Languages Association's annual convention in 1959, and Mark Hillegas taught the first accredited SF class at Colgate University in 1962 (Parrinder 1980, 131). By 1976 there were three major SF studies journals (*Extrapolation*, *Foundation*, and *Science Fiction Studies*) and more than two thousand SF courses offered across a variety of disciplines (Gerlach and Hamilton 2003, 162).

More often than not, what early SF scholars had to say about the relationship of SF to Western history and culture took one of two forms. Throughout the early 1960s authors—including Kingsley Amis, Sam Moskowitz, and Robert M. Philmus—all discussed SF as part of a six-thousand-year-old Great Western Tradition of Speculative Literature that included Plato and Lucian, Kepler and Shakespeare, Vernes and Wells, and, in the present day, Frederik Pohl and John Brunner. Although their subject matter might have been novel to many literary scholars, these authors presented it in comfortingly familiar ways. For example, Kingsley Amis begins *New Maps of Hell* (1960) with the proclamation that "although what attracts people to science fiction is not in the first place literary quality . . . they may well come to find such quality there" (7). In a similar vein, Sam Moskowitz assures readers in his introduction to *Explorers of the Infinite* (1963) that "the men and women who shaped the direction of modern science fiction were by no standards ordinary people or hack writers. By any measure they were among the most colorful and nonconformist literary figures of their times, and a few of them were among the greatest" (14). By emphasizing the literariness of SF, Amis and Moskowitz take what otherwise might seem to be a crudely upstart form of mass culture and render it palatable to those institutional authorities who thought of themselves, in proper cold war style, as the gatekeepers of Western civilization.

By the late 1960s a second, more culturally specific mode of SF history began to appear with increasing frequency. Like Amis just a few years earlier, authors including H. Bruce Franklin, Sam J. Lundwall, Donald Wollheim, Brian Aldiss, Robert Scholes, and Eric C. Rabkin were quick to assure readers of SF's aesthetic and historical merit. Rather than placing it within the millennia-long sweep of Western tradition, however, these writers specifically approach SF, as Franklin puts it in *Future Perfect* (1978), as "a form of literature that developed as part of industrial society, and [that] is intimately connected with the rise of modern science and technology" (vii). Scholes and Rabkin (1977) take this premise a step further, describing SF authors as creating "a modern consciousness for the human race" (vii). Taken together, such claims echoed and extended arguments being forwarded elsewhere in academia by technology and literature scholars such as Leslie Fiedler and Leo Marx.[2] However, while Fiedler and Marx were concerned primarily with determining the unique qualities of mainstream literature, Franklin, Scholes, and Rabkin insisted that popular genre fiction was a significant part of the modern literary tradition as well.[3]

Whatever their chronological and disciplinary affiliations, early SF scholars had relatively little to say about the subject of women's contributions to the genre. At most, they acknowledged the impact of Mary Shelley's *Frankenstein* on the development of modern SF but then quickly concluded that few other women had followed in Shelley's footsteps. Amis (1960) claimed that fewer than one out of every fifty SF authors were female (51); meanwhile, Moskowitz (1963) described the field as a whole as "only meagerly graced by the writings of the so-called gentler sex" (33). Simply put, SF scholars didn't need to write about women's SF because women themselves seemingly were not becoming SF authors at any significant rate.

After the feminist revival of the mid-1960s and the rise of a self-identified feminist SF in the early 1970s, male scholars did indeed begin to address feminist concerns and include women authors in their SF criticism. Even then, however, they rarely made explicit connections between the politics of the women's movement and the aesthetics of women's speculative fiction. For example, Sam J. Lundwall (1971) noted that "in a world where women are at last being recognized as human beings, science fiction still clings to the view of the last century" (145). This inflexibility results in the bizarre situation where SF authors—most of whom pride themselves on their ability to logically extrapolate worlds based on current scientific and social trends—rarely even try "to base stories on the assumption that the woman's position might be different in another society" (149). Lundwall then goes on to briefly review the work of a few brave authors whom he applauds for bucking this trend. Somewhat surprisingly, his list includes only *male* authors: Frederik Pohl and Cyril Kornbluth (*Search the Sky*), Robert Sheckley (*A Ticket to Tranai*), and John Wyndham (*Consider Her Ways*). The only woman Lundwall mentions, Anne McCaffrey, is depicted as a brilliant but misguided writer whose stories reinforce rather than interrogate patriarchal social relations (144).[4] For Lundwall then, feminism certainly has a place in SF, but to date only a few visionary men have acted upon its potential.

Conversely, Scholes and Rabkin (1977) identify a number of contemporary women writers whose radical politics have clearly informed their SF, including Joanna Russ, Ursula K. Le Guin, and Anne McCaffrey. They never, however, actually discuss these women writers in relation to one another. Instead, they praise Russ—along with Samuel Delany and Thomas Disch—for producing SF that explores "radically different lifestyles" (97). They applaud Le Guin—along with Philip K. Dick—for illustrating "how fully adult and literate American science fiction has become" (80). And finally, they commend Anne McCaffrey—along with Philip Jose Farmer and Harlan Ellison—for creating more sophisticated representations of sex in SF (186). Thus Scholes and Rabkin do not connect feminist politics to the development of an aesthetically coherent feminist speculative fiction. Instead, they treat feminist authors as a series of unrelated individuals who use their politics to contribute to the more general (and determinedly ungendered) maturation of SF as an entire field.[5]

Of course, this is not to say that early SF critics were consciously or systematically excluding women as a united force from SF history. Rather, I believe the works produced by these men demonstrate the very real difficulty of naming emergent literary phenomena as such. This difficulty is perhaps best illustrated by Brian Aldiss's *Billion Year Spree* (1973). In a refreshing departure from other SF historians, Aldiss readily identifies the women SF authors of his time as loosely but provocatively united by their politics and poetics. Indeed, according to Aldiss, "much of the best writing in science fiction today is being done by women," a fact he attributes to "the disappearance of the Philistine-male-chauvinist-pig attitude [which has been] pretty well dissipated by the revolutions of the mid-sixties" (306). Aldiss provides contemporary women SF authors with a history of their own, noting that the SF magazine boom of the 1950s attracted a "wealth of talent," including Zenna Henderson, Marion Zimmerman Bradley, Miriam Allen de Ford, and Andre Norton, all of whom paved the way for other women interested in entering the field (264). Yet despite all this, Aldiss never quite manages to take the final step and name these women writers in the revolutionary language of his time with which he was obviously familiar—in other words, to name them as feminists. Once again then, the f-word, with all its radical critical potential, was somehow lost from SF history.

## Round Two: Herstory

While men wrote SF history in the 1960s and 1970s, women were actively engaged with making it. Pamela Sargent (1975) estimated that women accounted for anywhere between 10 percent and 15 percent of all SF authors—a solid increase over the 2 percent estimated by Kingsley Amis fifteen years earlier (xiv). This same period marked the publication of two landmark anthologies designed to introduce readers to the vitality and diversity of women's SF: Sargent's *Women of Wonder* (1974) and Virginia Kidd's *Millennial Women* (1978), as well as the first two feminist fanzines, Amelia Bankier's *The Witch and the Chameleon* (1974–76) and Janice Bogstad and Jeanne Gomoll's Hugo-nominated *Janus* (1978–80). In 1977 Gomoll and Bogstad also organized the first Wiscon, the world's only feminist SF convention. Taken together, these diverse endeavors by women associated with the 1970s SF community were key to the development of feminist SF studies in the 1980s. In essence, authors and anthologists provided their scholarly counterparts with a history of their own to critically assess, while fans created some of the first forums in which they could freely articulate their ideas about feminism and SF.

The 1970s also marked the beginnings of feminist SF scholarship—a field of inquiry that was all but created single-handedly by feminist SF author Joanna Russ. Between 1971 and 1981 Russ's essays on feminism and science fiction appeared in a range of scholarly forums including journals such as *College English* and *Science Fiction Studies* and critical anthologies such as Susan Koppleman Cornillon's *Images of Women in Fiction* (1972) and Marleen Barr's *Future Females* (1981). Although they did not appear together until the publication of *To Write Like a Woman: Essays in Feminism and Science Fiction* (Russ 1995i), these essays constitute a history of women's SF that both complements and corrects the SF histories produced by male scholars in the 1960s and 1970s.

As Sarah Lefanu notes in the opening pages of *To Write Like a Woman*, Russ has long argued "eloquently and persuasively for the importance and the originality of science fiction" (xi). She does so, I contend, by weaving together the concerns of the mainstream literary, feminist, and science fiction communities. For example, in "Towards an Aesthetic of Science Fiction" (1975g) Russ begins from the premise that "written science fiction is, of course, literature" (3). She then considers SF as an exemplary form of literary production, noting strong similarities between "George Bernard Shaw's insistence on art as didactic, Brecht's definition of art as a kind of experiment, and descriptions of science fiction as 'thought experiments'" (11). Like other early SF critics, Russ invites readers to think of SF not as something entirely new in the history of Western art, but as a mode of storytelling with much the same mission as avant-garde art the world over.

Elsewhere Russ—again, like other early SF scholars—insists on the unique qualities of her chosen genre. In "The Wearing Out of Genre Materials" (1971d) she argues that most genre fiction relies on culturally and historically specific conventions that become stale with the passage of time. By way of contrast, SF "is theoretically open-ended: that is, new science fiction is possible as long as there is new science." Thus it "need not limit itself to certain kinds of characters, certain locales, certain emotions, or certain plot devices" (54). For Russ, SF is unique both because it shares certain qualities with great art and because it is more flexible than other forms of popular storytelling.

As a feminist scholar Russ is interested in demonstrating the unique potential of SF for women writers as well. "What Can a Heroine Do? Or Why Women Can't Write" (1995h) begins with a proposition much like that advanced by pioneering feminist literary critic Kate Millet: that throughout the history of Western art there have been "very few stories in which women figure as protagonists" (80). For the most part books—and, more recently, films—have been populated by painfully stereotypical "images of women: modest maidens, wicked temptresses, pretty schoolmarms, beautiful bitches, faithful wives, and so on" (81). But Russ then identifies three types of genre fiction that, in the right hands, can be used by women writers to create female protagonists and explore women's concerns: detective stories, supernatural fiction, and of course, science fiction. SF is particularly useful in this respect because "the myths of science fiction run along the lines of exploring a new world conceptually (not necessarily physically), creating needed physical or social machinery, assessing the consequences of technological or other changes, and so on. These are not stories about men *qua* Man or women *qua* Woman; they are myths of human intelligence and human adaptability. They not only ignore gender roles but—at least theoretically—are not culture-bound" (91).

As a future-oriented mode of storytelling SF emphasizes the new rather than the old, which is why it need not repeat worn-out images of or assumptions about sex and gender. Moreover, as such it is inherently compatible with feminist political praxes because those praxes themselves are predicated on the utopian dream of intelligent and adaptable humans working together to create a new and more equitable society for all.

Of course, as an SF author in her own right, Russ also engages the concerns of the SF community in her early critical writing. As she readily acknowledges in the opening passages of "Towards an Aesthetic of Science Fiction" (1975i), Russ's thinking about the typology of SF strongly correlates with claims made elsewhere by SF scholar Darko Suvin and SF writer-critics Stanisław Lem and Samuel R. Delany regarding two of the genre's central characteristics: scientific plausibility and didacticism (4–5). She also applauds writer-critic Damon Knight for his eloquent description of SF's almost-religious tone as key to inducing a "sense of wonder" in its readers (5). By putting her own ideas in dialogue with respected members of the SF community Russ makes strategic advances in her argument regarding the importance and originality of the genre. SF is not only one of the few popular modes of storytelling that can be discussed fruitfully in terms of both mainstream literature and feminism; it is a genre with enough richness and depth that it merits its own distinct forms of scholarship as well.

And although she is far less explicit about it, Russ's understanding of what constitutes "good SF" is deeply indebted to one other prominent member of the SF community: *Astounding* editor John W. Campbell, Jr. By the 1970s Campbell had become notorious for his sexist thinking about representations of women in SF, a fact that led Russ to publicly dismiss him as "a coelacanth" (1974a, 85). Nonetheless he was also regularly recognized as a visionary editor who raised the standards of the genre to new levels by (among other things) defining good SF as that which explores the impact of new sciences and technologies on social relations (James 1994, 157; Westfahl 1998, 184).[6] This is precisely the sentiment at the heart of Russ's own arguments concerning the power of SF: at its best it critically analyzes and interprets both the hard and the soft sciences. Thus "one would think it the perfect literary mode in which to explore (and explode) our assumptions about 'innate' values and 'natural' social arrangements" (1974a, 80). Thus Russ adapts Campbell's dictate to her own feminist ends, suggesting that complex explorations of science and society are more than aesthetically pleasing pieces of political propaganda. Instead, such stories are, by definition, those that most fully meet the requirements of SF as a self-regulating and logically organized genre.

In the late 1970s and early 1980s Russ turned her attention to the project of mapping out a feminist speculative writing tradition that met (and sometimes exceeded) the political and aesthetic criteria for SF that she so clearly defined elsewhere. She begins this process in her 1980 essay "*Amor Vincit Foeminam*: The Battle of the Sexes in Science Fiction" (reprinted in Russ 1995i) by distinguishing between good and bad SF based on the plausibility of the gendered relations imagined by various authors. Here Russ focuses primarily on what she calls "Flasher fiction": storytelling about dystopic worlds ruled by cruel women who immediately realize their rightful place as men's subordinates upon viewing either literal or metaphoric displays of phallic power (43).[7] Flasher fiction is bad SF because it relies on magical solutions and mystical notions of biology to suggest that the battle of the sexes "may be won without intelligence, character, humanity, humility, foresight, courage, planning, sense, technology, or even responsibility. So 'natural' is male victory that most of the stories *cannot offer a plausible explanation of how the women could have [gained power] in the first place*" (43; emphasis mine). As Russ rather reasonably points out, bad SF is bad not simply because it treats men and women in stereotypical ways but because it abandons all pretense to logic whatsoever in order to preserve those stereotypes.

In the conclusion to this same essay Russ more specifically opposes Flasher fiction to what she calls the most "extraordinary phenomenon of the last few years": the appearance of feminist utopian SF. These new kinds of stories are "in every way the opposite of the Flasher books . . . They are explicit

about economics and politics, demystifying about biology . . . and serious
about the emotional and physical consequences of violence" (58). Such stories clearly meet the political and aesthetic requirements that Russ elsewhere
attributes to good art. Like the best kinds of mainstream literature they are
experimental; like the best kinds of feminist writing they offer depictions of
women that resonate with real women's hopes and fears; and like the best
SF, they are logically organized in such a way that they "explore and explode"
conventional, mystified thinking about social and sexual relations.

Russ addresses the notion of an emergent feminist SF tradition most extensively in the aptly titled essay "Recent Feminist Utopias" (1981). For Russ,
books including Monique Wittig's Les Guérillères, Sally Gearhart's The Wanderground, and Russ's own The Female Man constitute a "remarkably coherent group
in their presentations of feminist concerns and the feminist analyses that are
central to these concerns" (134).[8] Taken together, these stories imagine that
the better societies of tomorrow will be communal, ecologically sensitive,
classless, sexually permissive, celebratory of female agency and female bonding, and insistent on the consequences of violence. Moreover, they are logically constructed reactions to "what their authors believe society . . . and/or
women lack in the here and now" (144). As such feminist utopian writing
clearly meets one of the key requirements for good SF: it is logically plausible
because it is based on scientific knowledge about and systematic observation
of life as it is lived in the present.

But Russ is not content simply to describe feminist SF as a present-day
phenomenon. In the same essay she notes that contemporary feminist SF
strongly resembles at least two other, much earlier utopian works by politically progressive women: Mary Bradley Lane's Mizora (1887) and Charlotte
Perkins Gilman's Herland (1915). For Russ the correspondences between these
two sets of utopian fiction indicate a "parallel evolution" in the history of feminist politics and aesthetics: "it seems reasonable to me to assume that, just
as Gilman and Lane were responding to the women's movement of their time,
so the works I discuss here are not only contemporaneous with the modern
feminist movement but made possible by it" (1981, 134–135). Much like her
male counterparts in early SF criticism, Russ makes sense of SF—here, specifically feminist SF—by demonstrating its place in a larger historical tradition of speculative writing. In doing so she ensures that feminist SF will not
be dismissed as an anomaly in the greater sweep of literary history.

Russ further cements the notion of a feminist SF tradition in her introduction to David Hartwell's edited anthology of Mary Shelley's Tales and Stories (1975). According to Russ, what other scholars see as a flaw in Shelley's
fiction—her tendency to veer wildly between the real and the ideal—is actually a deliberate movement that indicates "there is much to be said about

her from a feminist perspective" (1995c, 120). Quoting from Shelley's letters and journals, Russ suggests that Shelley, like modern feminist authors, was a keen observer of reality with "good reason" to be melancholy about the state of sex and gender relations in her world (125). This despair led her to reject realist fiction writing in favor of an extrapolative, future-oriented mode of storytelling that, as Shelley herself put it, afforded "a point of view . . . for the delineating of human passions more comprehensive and commanding than any which the ordinary relations of existing events can yield" (Russ 1995c, 127). Although Russ merely follows up this quotation by briefly noting that it is "a very good definition of science fiction," we might more accurately say that it is a good definition of *feminist science fiction* as Russ defines it elsewhere (127). Thus Russ reclaims one of the SF community's earliest heroes as one of feminist SF's first heroes as well.

### Round Three: Putting Herstory in History

Literary tradition making is always a process of both inclusion and exclusion, and Russ's feminist SF tradition making is no exception. Logically enough, Russ did most of her writing about feminist SF in the early 1980s, after a number of feminist authors had clearly established their interest in the genre. Even as early as 1971, however, Russ had a very clear sense of who would *not* count as part of this emergent literary tradition: any of the authors who had published SF to date:

> Most science fiction is set far in the future, some of it *very* far in the future, hundreds of thousands of years sometimes. One would think that by then human society, family life, personal relations, child-bearing, in fact anything one can name, would have been altered beyond recognition. This is not the case. The more intelligent, literate fiction [simply] carries today's values and standards into its future Galactic Empires. What may politely be called the less sophisticated fiction returns to the past—not even a real past, in most cases, but an idealized and exaggerated past. (1972a, 80–81)

Although this seemingly wholesale dismissal of the entire corpus of SF literature might seem surprising at first, it does make sense in light of Russ's claim that feminist SF is almost always written in response to feminist politics (1981, 134). Such politics were, of course, most prevalent in American society during the woman suffrage movement of the early twentieth century and again during the women's liberation movement of the 1960s. Because modern SF emerged in midcentury, decades between these two waves of feminism, it seems to have little or nothing to say about explicitly feminist concerns.

Moreover, it is important to note that Russ specifically excludes the first few generations of modern *women* SF authors from her feminist SF tradition as well. Like Brian Aldiss, Russ acknowledges that "there are more women writing [SF] than there used to be" (1981, 88). She also concedes that "in general, stories by women tend to contain more active and lively female characters than do stories by men, and more often than men writers, women writers will try to invent worlds in which men and women will be equals" (89). In terms of formal literary concerns such as character development and world building then, such authors have indeed made important contributions to the development of SF as a mature literary genre.

Ultimately, however, Russ insists that these authors cannot be understood as part of a feminist SF tradition because they tend to set their stories in a kind of "galactic suburbia" that looks suspiciously like a high-tech version of life on Earth in the here-and-now (1981, 88). As space-age versions of "ladies' magazine fiction" such stories typically revolve around the adventures of a "sweet, gentle, intuitive little heroine [who] solves an interstellar crisis by mending her slip or doing something equally domestic after her big, heroic husband has failed" (88). Women who write stories about galactic suburbia might well imagine truly fantastic new sciences and technologies then, but they rarely take the next logical step to imagine how these new sciences and technologies might enable new sex and gender relations as well.

Just as Russ's identification of a distinctly feminist utopian writing tradition profoundly shaped later discussions of feminist SF, so too did her exclusion of midcentury women writers from that tradition. In her introduction to the 1975 anthology *Women of Wonder*, Pamela Sargent describes mid-century women's speculative fiction as "housewife heroine" fiction that largely "reflected the [conservative] attitudes of the time" (xxiii). Like Russ, Sargent is particularly dismissive of those stories that depict women solely as domestic creatures who "solved problems inadvertently, through ineptitude, or in the course of fulfilling their assigned roles in society" (xxiii).[9] Similarly, Lisa Tuttle (1995) argues that prior to 1970 women who were not interested in writing men's SF adventure stories had little or no choice but to write something akin to "ladies' magazine fiction, in which the domestic virtues of the sweet, intuitive housewife-heroine somehow saved the day" (1343). Given the obvious power of Russ's critical writing, it seems hardly surprising that the first generation of feminist SF scholars all but eliminated postwar women's SF from their own literary histories.

Over the past decade or so, however, SF scholars have evinced a new interest in tales about galactic suburbia. As early as 1991 Farah Mendlesohn reclaimed one of Russ's primary targets, midcentury SF author Zenna Henderson, through a careful reading of her fiction as consciously mobilizing

(rather than simply reiterating) gender stereotypes to comment on the patriarchal biases informing cold war politics. A few years later Jane Donawerth
(1994) identified a number of women writers who incorporated first-wave feminist principles into their pulp-era SF storytelling. More recently, Justine Larbalestier, Helen Merrick, and I have all proposed that what Larbalestier calls
the "sweet little domestic stories" produced by postwar women SF authors
were often anything but that (Larbalestier 2002, 172). Instead, they marked
the beginning of a sharply critical and politically progressive sensibility that
both inspired and informed subsequent generations of more overtly feminist
SF authors.[10]

My own interest in postwar women's SF initially stemmed from what I
saw as a surprising disjunction in Joanna Russ's critical writing. In *How to
Suppress Women's Writing* (1983b) Russ outlines a number of discursive tactics
that male critics have long used to downplay and erase women's contributions
to literature: claiming that "she didn't write it"; that "she wrote it but that she
was an exception to the rule"; and even that "in writing it she made herself
unwomanly." Ironically, Russ invokes at least one of these tactics in her evalu-
ation of midcentury women's SF, what she calls *false categorizing.* Russ herself
describes this tactic as a literary "slight of hand" in which "works or authors
are belittled by assigning them to the 'wrong' category, denying them entry
into the 'right' category, or arranging the categories so the majority of 'wrong'
[stories and authors] fall into the 'wrong' category without anyone's having to
do anything further about the matter" (49). By categorizing midcentury wom-
en's SF as "ladies' magazine fiction"—a label that, as we have seen, persists
in SF scholarship even today—Russ not only discounts this SF as feminist SF,
but also eliminates it from the category of "good SF" altogether.

So how did Russ, an otherwise perceptive thinker and staunch defender
of women's writing in all its myriad forms, wind up dismissing nearly half a
century of women's science fiction as little more than a failed experiment? To
answer this question, we must consider Russ's own history as both a critic
and an artist. It is important to note here that Russ's critical essays are very
much in tune with the prevailing attitudes of their times. For example, feminist cultural historian Joanne Meyerowitz (1994) argues that scholarly treat-
ments of midcentury women's popular writing have been profoundly con-
ditioned by Betty Friedan's *The Feminine Mystique* (1963), wherein the author
claims that midcentury magazine fiction did nothing but impose "damaging
images on vulnerable American women" (Meyerowitz 1994, 231). Although
Russ never directly cites Friedan in her own writing, her condemnation of
postwar SF stories that celebrate the "sweet, gentle, intuitive little heroine"
for doing "something . . . domestic" sound remarkably like Friedan's condemnation of postwar women's magazine fiction that celebrate the "fluffy

and feminine" heroine for being "gaily content in a world of bedroom and kitchen" (Friedan 1963, 36). Russ, far from being unusual in her assessment of her literary predecessors, built consent for her version of women's SF history by extending dominant feminist thinking about popular culture into her own area of expertise.

For Russ, the problem with stories about galactic suburbia is not just that they seem to celebrate stereotypical images of women, but that these images point to a failure of social extrapolation on the part of the authors who create them. In this respect, Russ is remarkably similar to early SF scholars such as Donald Wollheim and Sam J. Lundwall. A self-proclaimed communist since the late 1930s, Wollheim strenuously objected to SF authors who relied on satiric representations of present-day culture in their writing, arguing that such stories were devoid of "faith in humanity and in the future" (67). Similarly, Lundwall (a Swedish scholar whom Wollheim introduced to the English-speaking SF community) claimed that satiric SF "shows only one side of the matter. It is anti but never pro; it gives criticism but never even attempts a solution" (772). Russ does not explicitly discuss midcentury women's SF as satiric fiction, but the conclusions she draws about its limits are much the same: such stories may estrange readers from the present, but they do not logically extrapolate from it to imagine how people might create truly alternative futures as well.[11]

## Russ's Early Writings

I propose that we can most productively understand Russ's concerns about earlier modes of women's SF by closely examining them in relation to her own early authorial experiences. Although most critical discussions of Russ's fiction focus on the clearly politicized stories she produced after the revival of feminism in the mid-1960s, it is important to note that Russ actually began publishing SF in the late 1950s.

I suspect that critics (including Russ herself) have not addressed Russ's early career because she published seven of her first eight SF stories in the *Magazine of Fantasy and Science Fiction* (F&SF), a periodical that she would later condemn as one of the primary purveyors of "bad" women's SF (1972a 88). And of course it is true that under editor Anthony Boucher's guidance in the 1950s, F&SF became closely associated with stories that were told from a woman's point of view—which often meant stories told from a traditionally feminine point of view. Because Russ's name is synonymous with feminist SF, the early stories she published in F&SF might seem to be anomalies undeserving of critical attention. But it is equally true that Boucher did not insist that authors write from conventionally gendered viewpoints. Rather, Boucher's support of women's SF was part and parcel of his larger project to support *all* narrative experiments that expanded the boundaries and increased the literary quality of SF.[12] As such, it makes sense to consider Russ's own early writing in light of this project.

Perhaps not surprisingly, the stories that Russ published with F&SF between 1959 and 1966 are themselves highly diverse and highly literary. Three are explicitly fantastic and three are explicitly science fictional, while one combines elements of both: the fantastic stories explore the supernatural worlds of vampires, ghosts, and Christian souls in equal depth while the SF ones examine the technocultural worlds of bronze-age cave dwellers, Soviet politicians, and intergalactic suburbanites alike.[13] Moreover, Russ experiments extensively with narrative voice in all her early stories regardless of genre, writing one fantasy and one SF story each from masculine, feminine, and gender-neutral perspectives (the seventh, blended story is also told in a gender-neutral voice). As such, Russ's early oeuvre clearly reflects the interests of an author who is testing the limits of her chosen genre to see how it might facilitate or limit certain insights about the relations of science, society, and gender.

This project is particularly apparent in Russ's first two published stories, which are also her first two stories told from women's perspectives. The first of these, "Nor Custom Stale" (1959), is perhaps the most surprising because it is squarely set in that imaginative space that Russ elsewhere so roundly condemns: galactic suburbia. Of course, while Russ is entirely correct to note that tales about galactic suburbia tend to focus exclusively on traditional women's concerns, this does not mean that they cannot serve skillful authors as powerful critical tools. Indeed, as I have argued elsewhere, such stories were often used by midcentury women writers as lenses through which to critically assess new technocultural developments ranging from atom bombs and automatic coffeemakers to popular ideas about science, sex, and gender.[14]

As an author whose name later became synonymous with feminist SF, it should come as no surprise, then, that Russ uses her own experiment with galactic suburbia storytelling to interrogate midcentury America's most dearly held beliefs about love and marriage. "Nor Custom Stale" follows the adventures of Freda and Harry Allen, proud owners of a fully automated House that promises to prolong its inhabitants' lives "for a good many years" by supplying their every need: air, food, water, entertainment, and even animated window covers that blot out all the dismal aspects of seasonal change (75). After Harry's retirement the couple decide to test out this promise by enwombing themselves in their House for an extended vacation from the rest of society. The couple quickly settle into a domestic routine that surely would have been familiar to any midcentury suburbanite on vacation: Freda wakes early to make breakfast for Harry, and then the couple spend the rest of the day together doing crossword puzzles, reading novels, and watching television. And in some respects this experiment seems to succeed beyond the couple's wildest expectations: freed from the necessity of dealing with change, the Allens stop aging and live on for millennia past the rest of humanity, only perishing with the heat death of the universe itself. And thus "Nor Custom Stale" seems to celebrate precisely the kind of modern, technologically enabled "togetherness" that Betty Friedan argued was central to the ongoing success of mainstream midcentury women's magazines such as *Good Housekeeping* and *Ladies Home Journal*—and that Russ herself so roundly dismisses in her own later critical writing.

But of course this is only the story in its broadest outline. Ultimately, Russ anticipates her own ideas about the potentially radical nature of SF by using the technocultural setting of her story to "explore and explode" sentimental ideas about togetherness. As the story unfolds, a number of basic House functions fail and the Allens find themselves cut off from the world, with no access to phones, mail, or new books and films. Convinced that the House knows best and that someone will rescue them if the situation truly becomes dire, the Allens institute daily rituals of "forgetting," the better to endure the repetition of their days: erasing crossword puzzles after completing them and leaving the window screens set on perpetual summer to blot out the potentially frightening passage of time (80). The insanity inherent in this situation becomes clear when a rescue party finally shows up and the Allens dismiss it as a frightening hallucination that threatens to disrupt the perfection of their daily routine. As such, it is something of a relief when the end of the universe finally comes, releasing the Allens (and, by extension, Russ's readers) from the terrible vacation upon which they embarked millennia earlier. Thus Russ suggests that artificially enhanced togetherness might indeed bolster individual marriages, but that in doing so it severs married couples from the larger sweep of human society as a whole.

More specifically, Russ uses the microcosm of the Allens' marriage to demonstrate, in good protofeminist fashion, how togetherness is predicated on patriarchal privilege rather than mutual desire. When Harry first proposes the experimental vacation, he does so not because he wants to spend quality time with Freda but because he wants to prove to his former coworkers that the House can indeed prevent aging. Despite her misgivings, Freda accedes to Harry's plan because "they had all been talking about something scientific that [she] did not understand" and she fears that any protest she makes will simply reveal her ignorance (76). This pattern of masculine assertion and feminine deference turns out to be the defining characteristic of the Allens' relationship: each time the House malfunctions and Freda suggests that it might be time to call in the authorities, Harry dismisses Freda's concern as ungrounded hysteria that will only threaten the couple's great experiment. And each time her husband responds this way, Freda gives in quickly, telling herself that Harry must be right because "he had been working only a few days before, so naturally he enjoyed the vacation more than she did" (84). Here then Russ further challenges conventional thinking about the supposedly egalitarian nature of married togetherness, showing how male authority (especially when cloaked in the language of science) trumps female intuition and experience, even in that supposedly most feminine of all places: the home itself.

While Russ's first story relies on a science fictional premise to demonstrate the horror inherent in conventional gender ideals, her next one, "My Dear Emily" (1962), uses elements of gothic horror drawn from the vampire story to explore other, potentially more liberating sex and gender relations. As Peter Nicholls argues, SF authors have long used elements of the gothic to explore the limits of Enlightenment reason and the social order that derives from it. More specifically, "gothic SF emphasizes danger, and attacks the complacency of those of us who imagine the world to be well lit and comfortable while ignoring that outside all is darkness" (Clute and Nicholls 1993, 511). In vampire stories such as Bram Stoker's 1897 classic Dracula, this attack is figured in a specifically gendered manner, as masculine representatives of the rational and irrational worlds (such as the scientist Van Helsing and the vampire Dracula) battle to control the souls of individual women (such as Mina Harker and Lucy Westenra) who come to represent society as a whole. When humans prevail over their supernatural counterparts, as they do in Stoker's novel, the destruction of the vampire explicitly reaffirms the superiority of Enlightenment values while the redemption of the half-turned woman implicitly confirms the inevitability of normative heterosexual relations.

Much like her first SF story, Russ's first gothic tale begins by invoking both standard generic conventions and standard gender relations that generally accompany them. "My Dear Emily" follows the adventures of Emily, a seemingly prim young nineteenth-century woman who has reluctantly acceded to her minister father's request that she leave boarding school to marry his successor, the honorable but bland Sweet William. The Reverend's plans are drastically interrupted by the appearance of Martin Guevara, a dark, handsome vampire who claims Emily as his soul mate because she is "someone with intelligence, even with morals" who also embodies "desire made purely . . . walking the Earth" (100). When the Reverend and William learn that Martin is in the process of transforming Emily into a vampire they lock Emily away in her bedroom and prepare to battle Martin for her life and soul.

Once again, however, this is only the story in its broadest dimensions.

After establishing the scene for "My Dear Emily" Russ radically subverts both its generic and gendered logic by telling her tale from her heroine's point of view. As she does so, readers quickly realize that Emily is no mere victim, but an active protagonist in her own right, complete with her own opinions and (as Martin recognizes) her own desires. Although Emily initially claims that she does not want to become a vampire she soon realizes that "I shall like living forever. . . . I'll do anything I please" (103–104). And accordingly, once she is freed from her own mortality she quickly frees herself from conventional gender expectations as well, breaking off her engagement to Sweet William and abandoning her father's house for the excitement of the nighttime San Francisco streets. Ultimately, then, Russ's vampire story turns out to be not so much about the rational versus irrational worlds as it is about patriarchal order versus female desire.

This revised vampire story even allows Russ to explore, however tentatively, the relation of alternate worlds to alternate modes of sex and gender. Sweet William is, of course, immensely fond of Emily and perfectly willing to engage in deadly battle with Martin for her; in a similar vein Martin is desperately attracted to Emily and in the end even dies for her. The romance that is truly central to Russ's story, however, is the one that takes place between Emily and her friend Charlotte, an inseparable couple who "had loved each other in school" and who continue to share a bed when they return to San Francisco to prepare Emily for her marriage (91). Significantly, this love persists beyond both graduation and the grave: Emily's first act as a vampire is to make sure that Martin turns Charlotte as well, and later Charlotte risks a second death by sunlight to warn Emily that her father and former fiancé have captured Martin. Eventually Russ's protagonist realizes that she cannot save Martin—and that in fact she has no obligation to sacrifice herself for him pointlessly. Accordingly, she abandons all her men in the old graveyard that comes to represent her old life, running instead toward her true love and a new life in the new graveyard where "Charlotte in her new home will make room for her" (116). Although Russ's story thus ends on an extremely gothic note, it does so in a manner entirely congruent with what Russ would later describe as the mission of all good feminist SF: to challenge heterosexist myths about men qua Man and women qua Woman.

As even this brief review of Russ's early fiction indicates, it may well have been her own experiments with dominant modes of women's speculative fiction that later led Russ to valorize SF as an ideal political and aesthetic vehicle for feminist authors. At the same time, however, it also implicitly demonstrates just why Russ ultimately relegated the majority of early and midcentury women's fantasy and SF—including her own—to the sidelines of literary history. As Russ persuasively argues throughout her critical writing, feminist SF generally has two goals: to provide a systematic critique of patriarchy and to imagine more egalitarian social alternatives. However, even stories that are as surprising and dynamic as "Nor Custom Stale" and "My Dear Emily" only fulfill these dictates in part. Both clearly critique patriarchal relations, especially as they are linked to and justified by (quasi)technoscientific reason. However, because they remain largely focused on private relations in the home, such stories almost necessarily prevent authors like Russ from exploring how women (and sympathetic men like the vampire Martin) might come together in the public sphere to enact wide-scale cultural and political change. Given that death seems to be the only alternative to limitations of gothic and galactic suburban storytelling then, it is hardly surprisingly that Russ would look back to the past of feminist utopian writing and forward to the future of feminist SF for more thoroughly progressive modes of storytelling. In doing so, she has given feminist SF scholars both a literary canon of their own and a critical vocabulary by which to continue assessing and expanding it.

~

# 4   The Female "Atlas" of Science Fiction?

Russ, Feminism and the SF Community

HELEN MERRICK

Acclaimed as one of SF's most revolutionary, stylistically accomplished writers, recognized as an insightful and stringent critic, and marked as an angry polemicist: Joanna Russ is an inescapable part of SF history from the late 1960s. Moreover it is her presence as *feminist* writer and critic that is acknowledged—if not necessarily admired—by even the most trenchantly androcentric (dare I say sexist) accounts of the field. While her contributions to the development of a feminist sensibility in both science fiction and its criticism are widely recognized, there has been little overt attention to the less tangible fact of her presence and influence in the web of SF authors, fans, and critics. Yet there is ample evidence that Russ's views on SF, feminism, and politics in general were offered, debated, and attacked in numerous 'informal' forums within the SF community. Indeed, I would argue that an understanding of Russ's place in SF history is incomplete without acknowledgment of these more "informal" conversations in the SF community.

In this chapter, I suggest that the debates and dialogues (and outright fights) between Russ and other authors and fans are evidence of the active role Russ played in encouraging and often demanding serious political discussion of feminist issues. Just as important, these interactions, both positive and negative, suggest why despite its "masculinist" image, SF has provided such a unique space for feminist voices and debate. That Russ saw these SF conversations as further opportunity for, and manifestation of, political activity suggests both the limitations on and potential for the negotiation of feminist politics in the discursive space of SF.

From at least the time of her first consciously feminist fiction, the Alyx stories, Russ was participating in debates about women's place in SF and society in her critical writings, letters, and contributions to publications both inside and outside the SF field.[1] A particularly vital period in this "conversation" was the mid-1970s, which saw not only the publication of The Female Man, but also a flurry of debate (often provoked by Russ or her writings) around "feminist issues" in numerous fanzines and magazines. Due to her multiple identities as SF and feminist critic, as well as fiction writer and academic, there existed a number of possible catalysts for Russ's involvement in community debate: reviews of her fiction; responses to her critical articles; and more general issues-based discussion that did not directly cite her work, but for various reasons, incited (or provoked) her interest. I examine in turn specific instances of such exchanges, the first provoked by her story "When it Changed," the next a series of responses to her article "The Image of Women in Science Fiction." (Russ 1972a). Finally I shall consider her involvement in debates circulating within the emergent feminist fan and writerly communities.

## When it Changed: Battle of the Sex Organs

The habit of fanzine editors to send authors (and readers) copies of issues that referred to them in some way meant that Russ presumably was sent a large number of fanzines. What becomes evident in the cases examined here was that by the mid-1970s, Russ was already weary of explaining and defending feminist analyses—of fiction, criticism, or society in general, as can be seen in debates sparked by reception of "When it Changed" (Russ 1972c). Over a number of issues from 1973 to 1974, an oft-heated round of letters graced the pages of the fanzine the *Alien Critic*, edited by fan and writer Richard E. Geis.[2] SF author Michael G. Coney led the attack, in a letter describing "When It Changed" as a "horrible, sickening story." According to Coney, women's liberation was a topical "bandwagon," whose oppositional stance could be distilled to the view that "the-majority-is-a-bastard," a critique he suggests could be better represented through "blacks" versus "whites," or Catholics versus Protestants (Coney 1973). The source of Coney's displeasure was made clear when he situated himself as part of that majority ("quite the opposite of a crank") attacked by Russ: "I'm a white non-religious male of heterosexual leanings, a member of a vast and passive majority which seems to be the target of every crank group under the sun" (53). Coney here set himself up perfectly as part of the dominant group controlling the production of science and fictional meanings that was, indeed, the target of feminist (and later postcolonial and queer) interventions. It is worth quoting Coney at length to indicate the depth of passion that feminist positions—via Russ—could inspire in some sections of the SF community.

> The hatred, the destructiveness that comes out in the story makes me sick for humanity and I have to remember, I have to tell myself that it isn't humanity speaking—it's just one bigot. Now I've just come from the West Indies, where I spent three years being hated merely because my skin was white—and for *no other reason*. Now I pick up A, DV [*Again,*

*Dangerous Visions*] and find that I am hated for another reason—because Joanna Russ hasn't got a prick (53).[3]

In narratives like Coney's, the sociopolitical basis of feminist and Black critiques are refigured as biologically determined, direct attacks on his white, male person—who, because of his body marked by its color and penis, is vulnerable to (but not responsible for) such "bigoted," "unhuman" challenges.

Not surprisingly, a number of women responded to Coney's letter, including Russ and Vonda McIntyre. McIntyre states she would not subscribe to the fanzine due to her discomfort with its sexist tone, and takes issue with Coney's dismissal of women's anger "as penis envy (penis envy! In 1973 he talks about penis envy)" (McIntyre 1973). Another letter also ridicules the notion of penis envy and asks if Coney was suffering instead, from "vagina envy" (Aab 1973).[4] In contrast, one female reader describes herself as "one of the demon Women Libbers," but directs the brunt of her disproval at McIntyre: "I was goddamned mad to hear Ms. McIntyre refer to 'the anger and hostility of women' because women includes *me*—and I love my husband. All I want is equality Mr. Geis. I don't want to hate anyone. Why does Ms. McIntyre?" (Plinlimmon 1974).

In the following issue is a letter from Russ (who ironically, only looked at the zine because there was a letter from McIntyre) that opens: "Please don't send me any more copies of *The Alien Critic*. . . . You are certainly free to turn your fanzine into a men's house miniature world, but why you think I would like it or be interested in it—a mystery" (Russ 1974b, 36). Her letter focuses not on Coney's critique, but the editorial comments appended to McIntyre's letter. In a "one-man" fanzine like this, much overt sexism could reside in the "conversation" set up by the editor with other contributions. As in many of the letter columns of the pulps and other fanzines, Geis added his view to virtually every piece and letter he published. Following McIntyre's letter, Geis had argued that women's status as "sex objects" and "cultural victims" was due to men's capacity to commit physical violence upon women on a one-to-one basis. Russ in turn, feels compelled to once more adumbrate the argument that sexism is, rather, "enforced by ideology and economics" (37). Evidence of Russ's frustration at having to explain "feminism 101" again appears in her letter's postscript:

> P.S. Apologies will be cheerfully read, but nothing else. No explanations of how wrong I am, or oversensitive, etc. etc. (the usual stuff). After all, you don't have to print this. And I'm damned if I will get into another long-drawn-out argument. (the first was with—via Harlan Ellison and *Last Dangerous Visions*—guess who? Michael G. Coney.) (37)

Not surprisingly, Geis ignored Russ's plea, and filled a whole page (twice the length of Russ's letter) with his rebuttals.

## Images of Russ in SF: "Lady Militant" to "Rabid Feminist"

Another fascinating example of the complex responses to feminist critiques is provided by the SF community's reactions to Russ's classic article, "The Image of Women in Science Fiction." (1972a). The first critique of SF's representation of women consciously informed by the women's movement, "Image of Women" was first published in a small literary magazine, *The Red Clay Reader* in 1969. While it was reprinted (along with "What Can a Heroine Do? Or Why Women Can't Write") in the groundbreaking 1972 collection of feminist literary criticism *Images of Women in Fiction* (Russ 1972a), the article did not appear to attract much attention in SF commentary until its second republication in the magazine *Vertex* in 1974.

Subsequent issues of *Vertex* contained replies to Russ's article from two prominent male authors. The first was a rebuttal from Poul Anderson, whose tone of patronizing correction from a kindly, better-informed patriarch is signaled by his title "Reply to a Lady" (Anderson 1974). Beginning by situating Russ as a knowledgeable figure, "one of the perhaps half a dozen science fiction critics worth anybody's attention," he proceeds to recast her as a biased female (or worse, "lady") who had "let her political convictions influence her literary judgment to the detriment of the latter" (8). Like a number of his contemporaries, Anderson believed that women simply were not relevant to much SF: "the frequent absence of women characters has no great significance, perhaps none whatsoever" (99). Anderson's defiance of SF recalled earlier arguments conflating women and sex, arguing that in many works there was no need to introduce women or to "bring in a love interest":[5]

> Certain writers, Isaac Asimov and Arthur Clarke doubtless the most distinguished, seldom pick themes which inherently call for women to take a lead role. This merely shows they prefer cerebral plots, not that they are antifeminist
> . . . Ms. Russ' charge of sexism, like her charge of ethnocentrism, will not stand up unless one deliberately sifts the evidence. . . . I think she simply let her fervor in a cause run away with her. (99)

After establishing women's irrelevance to the genre, Anderson claimed that SF had never in fact been antifeminist, but indeed was "more favorable to women than any other pulp writing." Among the writers he brought to his defense were C. L. Moore, Leigh Brackett, and Zenna Henderson, while additionally citing examples of "sympathetic portrayals" of female characters by male SF writers, including those of Heinlein, and Asimov's "brilliant protagonist" Susan Calvin. These examples were, of course, unlikely to appeal to (or appease) feminists.[6]

A couple of issues later, there followed a rather ambiguous response to both Russ and Anderson (ostensibly supporting Russ) from writer Philip K. Dick (1974). Dick's "An Open Letter to Joanna Russ" illustrates the very complex reaction to feminist critiques from SF authors and critics accustomed to viewing themselves as "liberals."

> Ms. Russ has in the most polemical manner, familiar now to most of us, hit where it hurts . . . to make her point, even at the cost of strewing the landscape with the wounded and puzzled corpses of otherwise reputable SF writers unaccustomed to such unfair attacks . . .
>
> And yet . . . I suddenly realized that beneath the anger and polemics and unfair tactics, which remind me of my old Left Wing girlfriends when they were mad at me for whatever reason—under all her manner of expressing her views, Joanna Russ is right. And Poul and I and the rest of us are wrong . . .
>
> So Joanna is right—in what she believes, not how she puts it forth. Lady militants are always like Joanna, hitting you with their umbrella, smashing your bottle of whiskey—they are angry because if they are not, WE WILL NOT LISTEN.

Dick's letter begins by positioning himself firmly in the camp of "male SF writers": he acknowledges Anderson as a personal friend, and praises his article profusely, saying it was "superb," and "could not be bettered"—but for the fact that it was "wrong." In contrast to Russ's polemical tactics Anderson's article, although "reasonable and moderate and respectable" was, Dick concluded, nevertheless "meaningless":

> It was like telling the blacks that they only "imagined" that somehow things in the world were different for them, that they only somehow "imagined" that their needs, its articulations in our writing, were being ignored. It is a conspiracy of silence, and Joanna, despite the fact that she seemed to feel the need of attacking us on a personal level, shattered that silence, for the good of us all.[7]

Despite his avowed support of Russ's "beliefs," Dick traverses a fine line between acknowledgment of the necessity of "Joanna's" anger, and resentment toward what is perceived as a "personal" attack. A typical response to feminism(s) then as now, is that it does inherently consist of attacks on individual men: on their sexism, their particular acts of power, discrimination, and so on. This problem was if anything highlighted in the SF community, where so many people did indeed know each other personally, so that when examples were brought forth to display sexism in SF, they had often been written by contemporaries—even friends—of the (feminist) critic. Certainly the letters in *Vertex* suggest that Dick and Anderson's perception of Russ's "anger," "militancy," and charges of "sexism" are derived from more than just this one article, perhaps personal interactions with Russ, or awareness of her fictional texts, such as "When it Changed" or *The Female Man*.[8]

What the responses to "The Image of Women" most clearly demonstrate is a change in the context in which critiques of science fiction's androcentrism or sexism was received. Previously signaled as part of ongoing internal "quality control," from the time of Russ's article, critiques of women in SF are seen in the context of a feminist intervention, a politically motivated challenge (or attack). At first reading, the substance of Russ's arguments do not differ radically from earlier critiques (such as those by Amis and Lundwall), with the focus on the stereotypical nature of female characters, and the fact that this stereotyping signals a failure of SF's extrapolative imagination. Russ's position was distinguished by her particular investments in making such a critique: she was not only a woman, but a feminist, and she demanded a better standard of SF texts and authors. The image of women, in Russ's hands, is not just a "failing" (mostly located in SF's past) to be rued and mentioned in passing, but is a central fault line in SF that, if addressed, would disrupt SF's "business as usual."

The influence of Russ's feminism was most evident in her analysis of the causal factors that produced and continued to reproduce this lack of "real" women in SF. The lack of "social speculation," argued Russ, was owed not to a "failure of the imagination outside the exact sciences," but rather to an acceptance of cultural conditioning and stereotypes that SF authors, in particular, should strive to oppose. While Russ located sexism (not actually mentioned in her article, Anderson notwithstanding) in sociocultural relations, she also attributed responsibility for reproducing these relations to the author as an individual. Suddenly it was not "history" that was responsible for women's image in SF, but the SF authors and readers themselves. Most damning of all, Russ dared to be patronizing: "the [male] authors want to be progressive, God bless them, but they don't know how" (Russ 1974a, 56). As Russ only listed three male exceptions, Mack Reynolds, Samuel Delany, and Heinlein, all other male authors—like Dick—could take this comment as a personal attack. A respected SF critic and author, Russ charged SF with a failure to fulfill its potential of responsible and educated speculation.

A number of other authors and fans appeared more ready than Anderson to accept this critique, as evidenced by a series of letters in the fanzine *Notes*

*from the Chemistry Department.* The conversation opened not with a direct reference to Russ, but a rebuttal of Anderson's article by Loren MacGregor entitled
"A Reply to a Chauvinist" (MacGregor 1974).[9] While MacGregor aligns himself
with the "cohort" of male SF writers (and in this case male fans), he accepts
Russ's "charges" without qualification. Initially expecting, and indeed wanting to agree with Anderson (as many of Russ's points "hit uncomfortably close
to home"), MacGregor points out that "Mr Anderson had managed to ignore,
or misinterpret virtually all of [Russ's] assessments" (2). Most important, he
notes that the charge from Russ "was not one of antifeminism, but of male
chauvinism." Further, in MacGregor's eyes, Anderson's attempt to defend SF
from the accusation of "antifeminism" by referring to "sympathetic" portraits
of women was ultimately stereotypical and chauvinist.[10]

There were a number of responses to MacGregor's article in the following issues of *Notes*. As with other similar debates, many fans and authors who
did not accept feminist representations of sexism and chauvinism in SF still
claimed that they supported "equal rights" generally. These exchanges clearly
display representational contests over the meaning of equality, and whether
feminists should control the delineation of what "equal rights" might encom-
pass. The responses from fans and authors in the March 1975 issue of *Notes*
present an interesting range of political positions that all, to some extent,
agree with Russ's or MacGregor's conclusions about the limited portrayals
of women in SF, (even while some are explicitly opposed to "feminism" as a
movement or theory). In many of these examples, Russ's is positioned (often
almost metonymically) as representative of a stereotypical notion of feminism
that is antimale, "rabid," and blindly judgmental.

The article "Sexual Stereotypes" by Paul Walker (1975) begins by stating
that "in general" Russ and MacGregor are right, and Anderson is wrong, but
goes on to argue that women are just as guilty as men for promoting sexist
stereotypes, and indeed are *"far more* to blame for the inequalities that exist"
(emphasis in original; 9–10). Like many other commentators (including Dick)
Walker evokes the "danger"—and ease—of inciting Russ's anger: "I'm sorry,
but at the risk of bringing down the wrath of Ms. Russ, I do not beleive [sic]
men and women are identical" (11). In a similar vein, a letter from Victoria
Vayne (1975) expresses support for "a certain amount of equality in law, and
justice, and working remuneration," but sharply delineates these issues from
the arguments of feminists, whom she refers to as "rabid" and a "paranoid
bunch." Referring implicitly to Russ, Vayne observes: "Feminists seem to me
to be a touchy lot; they get so caught up in their cause they seem to have a
vendetta against men in general. They are generally too ready to boil over in
anger over some slight" (37).

The issue also includes letters supportive of MacGregor and Russ. In contrast to the antifeminist arguments of Walker and others who situated physical and biological difference as justification of sexual inequality, one letter emphasized the sociocultural context of gendered assumptions: "The fault . . . does not lie with the fiction or its creators, however. It lies in the culture that produced the creators and those who appreciate their works" (Franke 1975). In her own letter to this issue, Russ also reasserts the cultural, political, and economic elements of sexism: "sexism isn't a personal failing, it's institutionalized oppression" (1975c, 39).

The tone of Russ's letter is interesting to note: as I have already suggested, a certain weariness in having to explain sexism and defend her theoretical position has entered her writing. After opening with thanks to the editor for sending her a copy of the previous issue, she comments, "I'm glad the exchange in Vertex has sparked something, though I sometimes wish someone else had done it. Because, you see, I must answer . . . " (38). Russ answers, presumably, because she cannot resist the pull to try and explain—once more—that sexism is not always conscious, or personal, but can inhere in "small things" like the ratio of female contributors to male in the fanzine index, or the use of hearts and a (three-cup) brassiere in illustrating an essay on women in science fiction.

## Women in SF: The Symposium

Russ's interactions with fandom and participation in fanzine conversations were not all such combative, defensive affairs. Her presence and writings also had a vital impact on the nascent feminist criticism of SF and the developing feminist consciousness in fandom. Around this time, groups of feminist fans were coalescing, starting their own fanzines, the Women's APA,[11] and beginning to organize alternate "women's programming" at conventions. Susan Wood, convener of the first "women in SF" panel at the 1974 Worldcon and originator of the "room of our own" argued that the women's movement had begun to have an impact on SF in the early 1970s "chiefly through the fiction and criticism of Joanna Russ, seconded by Vonda McIntyre." Despite often open hostility to their public critiques of SF (including "trashings" for "being bitter, vicious feminist bitches") fans such as Wood were inspired to develop feminist spaces within fandom—both physical and discursive (Wood 1978a, 5) Indeed, the years 1974–75 were also a particularly fertile period for engaged informative debate in more supportive forums, such as the fanzines Khatru, The Witch and the Chameleon (WatCh), and Janus.

From September 1974 to August 1975 there ran a "round-robin" letter correspondence among SF authors, edited by Jeffrey Smith for his fanzine Khatru (Smith 1975). Reprinted in 1993 (with additional commentary from both original participants and contemporary authors) the symposium "Women in Science Fiction" is a wonderfully representative slice of SF discussions about women as subjects and authors of SF, as nine women, two men, and one woman masquerading as a man, debated, raged and agonized over sex roles, gender roles, literature, violence and rape—all those topics so much at the forefront of the feminist "consciousness-raising" atmosphere of the 1970s (Gomoll 1993).[12] One of the most intriguing and valuable aspects of this document of SF community history are the tensions and struggles over the meaning of feminism between women and men of different generations and backgrounds (from middle-class liberal to lesbian and socialist) and the contemporary reflections by Russ and others on their "previous selves" and earlier interactions.

Involving authors who were all at the very least sympathetic to "women's issues," *Khatru* featured none of the overt hostility to feminism displayed in some of the fanzine encounters discussed above. Nevertheless the issue of entrenched sexism, and Russ's apparent sense of exhaustion in being, once more, an "interpreter" for feminist theory and analysis comes through perhaps even more clearly in this symposium than elsewhere. At the same time, however, it also points to the fact that SF at least provided a space for the expression of this frustration. In particular, the sorts of "everyday" sexism Russ encountered could be revealed and denounced in a way that was impossible in her daily life in academe. At one point in the symposium she paints a very clear picture of the restrictions she operated within in her precarious position as an unmarried, career female academic:

> surrounded by colleagues whom I did not choose but who can fire me (and did) and upon whose extraordinarily sexist good will I am dependent for the money on which I live. I do not have a husband to fall back on. Nor do I have the social protection being married . . . affords. I have to face incidents like the bottom-pinching a dozen times a week. I cannot live a private life and choose my company the way a free-lance writer can. I cannot express my anger more than once a year. I avoid as much as I can but I have not the freedom every other woman in this Symposium has. (102–103)

This freedom, Russ suggests, came not just from the social and economic protection of marriage (not to mention heterosexuality) but also the professional location of all the *Khatru* symposium women (excluding, appropriately enough, Tiptree) predominantly within the SF field. For, despite its entrenched sexism, this community's vaunted commitment to liberal attitudes and (at times treasured) location on the periphery of the cultural mainstream allowed room for dissension and debate.

Thus it is hardly surprising that some of Russ's most vehement contributions to the symposium are pointed critiques of the men: particularly Jeffrey Smith, but also Delany and—most famously—"Tiptree" who provoked a number of "trashings" from Russ and others. First off the block was the editor of the symposium, Smith, of whom Russ comments:

> Every time you open your mouth, your foot goes in deeper.
>
> Stop it man! There is nothing more disgusting than a belligerent/ apologetic husband telling all us (women) how he was the one who *made* his marriage egalitarian because of course *she* would never have thought of it on her own.
>
> As I said . . . you do not have to apologize or defend yourself or explain. Just listen . . .
>
> Shut mouths do not engulf feet. (57)

Russ takes Delany to task through comparison of the differing constraints on their time and energy:

> Chip can reply at length partly because he does not have to live the problem all the time and can therefore gather his energies for one great analytic attack. I must defend my self-esteem so constantly and in such petty situations that at times I feel as if I were talking not to people but to phonograph records (41).

There is also the sense that in this fairly "safe" environment, Russ can vent steam at the continual demands on her to explain feminism to (mostly male) SF fans and authors. Ironically enough, it is in a response to "Tiptree" that Russ allows the full extent of her impatience to show: "I can't spend my time as a public library on feminism. It's like teaching frosh camp over and over. And *these* men [Delany, Tip, and Smith] are sensitive, intelligent, conscious, decent, and working very hard at their sexism. One ends up feeling like Atlas" (91).

It is not only the men whom Russ critiques, however; she takes the opportunity in this forum to expand upon all sorts of theories central to her feminist concerns: the nature of power and oppression, theories of social change, economics, and history. She also adumbrates many of the points about women and writing that are expanded in her later work, *How to Suppress Women's Writing* (1983b) When it is suggested that a women-only SF anthology is akin to creating a "ghetto situation" Russ counters it is, rather, "Us the Tribe getting together for the first time, after having been atomized, isolated, kept apart for centuries" (73). In another example, Russ confesses that she "couldn't help groaning a bit" at Kate Wilhelm's statement that her novel *The Clewiston Test* "is not a feminist book . . . not a polemic for anything except the right to be an individual human being" and comments: "It's funny, really; having disclaimed feminism, you go on to *define* it" (89).[13]

Russ's contributions to the dialogue also emphasized the movement of feminist theories beyond tangible goals of equal opportunity, forecasting, as does her fiction, the dissolution of modernist certainties about identity, and gendered binaries. She talks for example, of female and male feminists moving into "existentially frightening" territory: "a vision of the human race without the idea of sexual polarity": "There is no longer anyone to tell you who you are, what you 'ought' to do or be or feel, and it becomes frighteningly clear that we are not in nature but in culture, that sexual dichotomy or polarity are social constructs and not natural facts" (103).

Along with such ideas comes "the clear vision that Men and Women are impostors," that is, that gender is a social construction that is essentially performative (103)—a view that is of course suggestive of more recent developments, such as queer theory. Alongside these continuities or connections with contemporary feminist theories, there are also disjunctions and "outmoded" ideas—both in terms of Russ's own personal theoretical development, and within feminisms more generally. The commentary from the 1993 reprinting is particularly revealing of the schisms and competing threads of feminism that emerge in the original discussion as unsolved tensions—especially around the issue of motherhood, race, violence, and theories of power and oppression. Reflecting on the symposium in 1992, for example, Russ notes "how very radical Kate Wilhelm was then and how little I (or many of the other participants) perceived this." Echoing one of the core arguments in her survey of feminist theory, *What are We Fighting For* (1998c), she comments that Wilhelm's socialism "has begun to strike me as absolutely necessary to any decent future for almost anyone on this planet." (in Gomoll 1993 115).

## Finding Female Men: the Feminist Fanzines

In the same period as the *Khatru* symposium, we see the appearance of the first explicitly feminist fanzines, *WatCh* and *Janus* (later *Aurora*).[14] Together, these publications signaled the growing number of fans who wanted to bring together their commitment to women's liberation with their fan interests.[15] Readers and fans were thus developing feminist ideas in tandem with (and sometimes ahead of) the writers and texts they engaged with in the SF community; just as the writers were also "communicating with fan organizations and publications about their ideas in the process of developing them" (Bogstad 1977, 7). Indeed, Russ herself suggested in *Khatru* that fans were ahead of writers in terms of their engagement with feminist issues, theories, and consciousness-raising in SF. When bringing Wilhelm "to task" for resisting the label of "feminist," she adds "If you printed this in *WatCh*, for example, which is a small place to begin but I think important, you'd get howls of rage for that one!' (Gomoll 1993, 89).

Russ's approval of, and support for *WatCh* is reflected in the fact that the third issue contains a letter from her, as well as the hilarious series of stories 'Haven't we seen this before?' (which includes the 'Weird-ways-of-getting-pregnant Story').[16] Much more so than *Khatru* (at least judging by the edited version we are left with), *WatCh* and later *Janus* provided a fertile environment for feminist debate, particularly around issues of sexuality. Indeed, Russ's first letter to the fanzine is a discussion of lesbianism and the taboo against female homosociality (in response to an earlier letter on the subject from Andre Norton). Referring to Woolf's *Orlando* and *Room of One's Own*, Russ (1975d) notes that: "the taboo makes sure . . . that solidarity will never be shown. The message readers receive is that there is no solidarity or friendship between women, that all of women's affection, loyalty, interest, concern, compassion etc. is given to—who? To men, of course" (27).

*WatCh* was also the venue for a fascinating debate that clearly demonstrated the conflicts of analysis and response between feminists such as Russ and McIntyre and earlier successful female SF writers, including Marion Zimmer Bradley). A stringent feminist critique of Bradley's *Darkover Landfall* by Vonda McIntyre sparked an in-depth exchange between Russ and Bradley over a number of issues (Bradley 1974; McIntyre 1974). One of the most interesting facets of this conversation is Russ's changing response to Bradley as the latter reveals more of herself in subsequent letters. Russ gradually retreats from strident critique of Bradley's work toward a "gentler" negotiation of issues and acceptance of the political validity of differing personal experiences. Russ's first letter is an analytical critique of the assumptions about feminism displayed in Bradley's response to McIntyre's review, which notes that the question "of whether a woman's uterus belongs to her or to the community she happens to find herself in" was a "very hot political issue" that would necessarily provoke "vehement reactions" (Russ 1975e, 15). Emphasizing that books such as *Darkover Landfall* (and SF in general), could not be separated from the political and social assumptions that underlie them, Russ concludes that by relying on such assumptions, the book could be considered antifeminist. Summing up the anger felt by feminist readers such as McIntyre, Russ writes:

> to falsify biology (which Bradley does grossly in assuming that high gravity will have no effect on men, and no other effects on anyone) and to drag Anatomy-is-Destiny out of three-thousand-year-old mothballs in order to do so, is not an answer. Or an advance. It's the old you-can't-win slap in the face again. (18)

The debate takes on quite a different tone following Bradley's second letter (in issue 4), where she identifies with local women's groups and talks revealingly about her sexuality:

> I have not really intended to become the spokesperson for the gay community in science fiction, but I have always known . . . that I was just as strongly homosexual as I was heterosexual. . . . I have always felt free to write for lesbian publications, etc, under my own name, and have never made any secret of the fact that I consider myself at least bisexual, and probably, more honestly, an offbeat lesbian who simply manages to form occasional strong attachments to men. (Bradley 1975, 22)

In her second contribution, "A Letter to Marion Zimmer Bradley," Russ (1976b) apologizes for her previous letter, describing it as "too flip" and "heartless," and admits admiration for Bradley's "hard work, her grit, her honesty, and her bravery"—while still disagreeing with Bradley on many points (9). In this piece, Russ provides a wonderful review of the feminist movement, including the problems of "class snobbery and what . . . one might call . . . 'motherhood-snobbery'"(9). Once again, the notion of "sexism" is crucial: with Bradley claiming that SF is not sexist (Russ concurs to the extent that "in many ways fan groups are much less so than most of this country," 11), and Russ arguing that this must entail a lack of analytical understanding of what sexism means "beyond direct denigration," As so often in the past (but much more gently!) Russ emphasizes the difference between personal and social experiences, arguing it is crucial "to make distinctions between what people know and do personally and what is built into our social life, what is institutionalized" (11). This letter—the final contribution to the debate—is a wonderfully informed and persuasive delineation of many of the tenets of feminist arguments that would have been at home in any academic journal. It demonstrates the sophisticated and committed level of engagement that could occur in a small, amateur publication in the "ghetto" of the SF field.

The conflicts of generational difference evident in this "conversation" are neatly summed up by Russ, whose argument signals the importance and influence of personal histories and "travels" through or against feminism(s):[17]

> I wish I could castigate Bradley as a sexist—which would make everything so easy!—but clearly she's not. I do have a horrible feeling, though, that much of what she says in her letter is exactly what I would've said in or about the winter and spring of 1968, which is when I first met feminism. . . . I do feel that, having made sacrifices (including part of one's own personality) to get what one wanted, there's a strong human tendency to insist that the sacrifices were necessary (1976b, 12).

This was the last issue of *WatCh*, and thus the end of the "conversation"; nonetheless, there are interesting resonances in later writings by Bradley that suggest this exchange may have had some impact on her views. Her article "My Trip Through Science Fiction," for example, contains a reconsideration of the debate around *Darkover Landfall*. Here Bradley accepts, to some extent, the "outrage" felt by feminist readers and situates the book as part of a dialogue, initially between herself and Del Rey, and carried on by Russ (1977): "I am told . . . that Joanna Russ has written a novel where, in similar straights, the women of the colony refuse to bear children at all, on the grounds that a colony based on exploitation of women has no right to survive. Science Fiction writers are constantly amending, correcting, embellishing the ideas of their colleagues" (Bradley 1977–78, 16).

What becomes much clearer through these feminist fan conversations is the importance to Russ of emphasizing solidarity, communication, and "sisterhood" between women even while they may disagree on the theoretical nuances of feminisms. As she repeatedly argues in these fanzines, Russ felt it was vital that the irritation she and other feminists felt at teaching "frosh camp" over and over again, should not "spill over" into their conversations with one another (although she was not herself always entirely successful in this endeavor).

By the mid 1970s, what seemed most important for Russ was that women in SF not get distracted "from the real issues at hand"—in particular their writing—by constantly having "to answer those damned usual arguments about baboons and dishwashing" (Gomoll 1993, 87–88). Her feelings about such "time-hoggers" are, for me, perfectly encapsulated in her letter to the final issue of *WatCh*. Referring to a previous piece by Poul Anderson (which attempted to clarify his Vertex arguments, and reaffirm his belief that women and men should get "an equal break") Russ writes:

> He's a nice man in a personal way but it's hopeless; I feel like a rock climber at the 14,000–foot pass in the Rockies looking back through a telescope at an enthusiastic amateur in the Flatirons . . . who's proceeding Eastward, yelling "Hey! You're in the wrong place! The mountains are this way!" It's a sheer waste of time to argue with him; we'd better just let him go until he and his crampons and bolts (or whatever) hit Chicago. (1976b)

## What Did You Do during the Revolution, Grandma?
## The 1980s and Beyond

From the late 1970s onward, Russ appeared to be much less engaged in such fannish community conversations, probably due at least in part to her declining health (following an operation in 1978, she could only write by hand, while standing up). According to Wood, Russ had even by the early 1970s "retreated from the fray into teaching . . . and fiction writing" (Wood 1978a, 5). Nevertheless her presence and influence has remained vital to feminist fan and critical communities in SF, particularly in the "backlash" decade of the 1980s. Indeed, perhaps ironically, this decade saw the publication of some of her most influential works on feminist SF and feminist theory, "Amor Vincit Foeminam," "Recent Feminist Utopias," and *How to Suppress Women's Writing* (1995i, 1981, 1983b).

Russ's continued importance to the feminist SF community is evident in the fact that her name becomes synonymous with resistance to the very tactics she outlined in *How to Suppress*. In 1987, Jeanne Gomoll evoked Russ to explain her fear that the history and achievements of feminist fandom were being forgotten, suppressed, or rewritten (Gomoll 1991). By the 1980s, the feeling that feminism was in fandom to stay, that feminist, gay, and lesbian issues could no longer be excluded from fan debate, was dissipating. Many conventions had not embraced Wood's (1978b) ideal of "people's programming," but had remained at the level of the ubiquitous "women in SF panels" that slowly settled into a "generic" panel subject to mild ridicule: "Today I sit in the audience at all-male 'fandom of the 70s panels' . . . and don't hear *anything* of the politics, the changes, the roles that women played that decade (except sometimes, a little chortling aside about how it is easier now to get a date with a female fan)" (9).

This appeal to Russ is meaningful not only in the context of her critical work, which Gomoll explicitly references, but also in light of Russ's earlier support of and engagements with feminist fandom. Fittingly, the piece was published in the penultimate issue of *Aurora* (the continuation of *Janus*) alongside a response from Russ that praises the essay, situating it as part of a growing documentation of "the counter-reaction that's in full swing." Unable to "ever stop being a teacher," Russ also offers a reading list of feminist theory, which ranges from some of the founding texts of feminist science studies (Evelyn Fox Keller and Ruth Bleier) to central readings in lesbian and black feminist critique (Jill Johnston, Lillian Faderman, bell hooks, Audre Loudre, Gloria Anzaldúa, Barbara Smith).

A few years after Gomoll's essay, however, the future of feminism in SF looked much brighter, with what appeared to be a renaissance in feminist fandom under way. In 1993, SF [3], the fan group responsible for organizing the feminist convention Wiscon reissued the *Khatru* symposium (dedicated to Russ) and in 1996 celebrated Wiscon's twentieth anniversary. At the 1991 Wiscon, Pat Murphy announced the creation of the James Tiptree, Jr., award for "gender-bending" science fiction, which in 1995 gave "retrospective" awards to Russ, Le Guin, and Charnas. These developments can, I think be taken as renewed evidence of the SF field's potential for cultivating feminist activity and communities.

Despite the often challenging and conflicting relationship between her feminism and the genre, this potential is reflected in the history of Russ's ongoing engagements with the SF community. At one point in the *Khatru* symposium, Russ stresses the importance of taking political action "of whatever kind one finds congenial": "I tend to Write Letters [sic] myself, to magazines, Congress, NYS versions thereof, newspapers, even fanzines. There is nothing like public protest to lift the spirits. I consider it a civic act, like paying one's taxes, and personally satisfying" (Gomoll 1993, 73).

Thus letters to fanzines—even (or perhaps especially) combative ones— could be satisfying as well as frustrating because they constituted a political act of "public protest." Ultimately, what redeems SF for Russ is, I think, the very nature of the genre itself, as evidenced in her advice to a fanzine editor on challenging institutionalized sexism:

> But what am I to do? (I hear you cry piteously from beneath the sofa.)
>
> Keep printing articles, keep speculating, keep thinking. Which is what SF is about (speculating and thinking) anyway. (1975c, 39)

## 5  Learning the "Prophet Business"

### The Merril-Russ Intersection

DIANNE NEWELL AND JENÉA TALLENTIRE

The year 1968 appears to have been pivotal in the evolution of Joanna Russ as an author and an authority in SF circles. In 1968, Russ was a thirty-one-year-old beginner who was gaining recognition in the field of American science fiction through her intelligent 1960s stories in the *Magazine of Fantasy and Science Fiction* (F&SF) and her inclusion in an anthology of New Wave science fiction. We see this year as emblematic of a transitional phase, as Russ struggled to succeed to a place of leadership and authority in the SF world, originally on its terms, before forging her own. This struggle can be seen in the interaction between Russ and Judith Merril, the foremost editor and critic in American science fiction in the late 1960s.

Dubbed the "little mother of SF" by Damon Knight and widely regarded as the foremost editor of science fiction through the 1950s and 1960s, Judith Merril in 1968 was an accomplished author-anthologist at the peak of her power and influence in Anglo-American science fiction circles. A political radical since childhood, she had been active in the New York Futurians in the 1940s and cofounder of both the New York Hydra Club and the influential annual Milford Writers' Conference. As an author, her influential work ranged from groundbreaking woman- and family-centered science fiction ("That Only a Mother," *Shadow on the Hearth*, "Daughters of Earth") to classic space opera (*Gunner Cade*, coauthored with Cyril Kornbluth). She also turned her hand to supporting the best new SF authors with her editing projects, including her best-of-the-year anthologies in the late 1950s and the 1960s and her catalytic books column in F&SF (1965–69). Through the 1960s she increasingly called for a more political, speculative, and stylistically adventuresome approach to writing for broader themes and styles, which she specially promoted with the term "SF" and others called "New Wave." In 1968, at forty-five years of age, she had just published the first anthology of British New Wave experimental stories for an American readership, titled *England Swings SF*, and a retrospective anthology of what she judged to be stories ahead of their time: SF: *The Best of the Best*.

By the time Russ published her first novel, *Picnic on Paradise* (1968), which featured a smart, tough, autonomous female hero, Alyx, and hinted at her emerging feminist stance, she was a regular invitee to Milford and had become an occasional substitute in the F&SF books column for the increasingly experimental and tardy Merril—sure signs of a rising star. She was, like Merril, a woman who stood out. When David Laskin (2000) describes the young Mary McCarthy writing for New York magazines in the early 1960s as "weighing in as an intellectual contender" and gaining clout by way of her bold, intelligent reviews, "her style and for her precocious assumption of authority" (39), he could just as easily have been writing about Russ's contributions to Merril's books column. Merril, by contrast, was seriously reconsidering the worth of her own leadership within the American SF community.

At this pivotal moment—a point when a torch could be passed, from established authority to rising star—instead, a break emerged that would have resonances in Russ's own scholarship and conceptions of women's literary contributions to SF. Despite Russ's later reputation as *the* innovative and first truly feminist science fiction author and critic, in 1968 she was still grappling with the tenets of traditional, "hard" science fiction. In fact, she publicly set herself against Merril's already established position as the foremost editor of superlative new SF authors who distanced themselves from traditional science fiction in trying to access the radical potential for social change inherent in the genre.

Given Russ's reputation just a few short years later for her commitment to women's writing, the transformative nature of science fiction, and feminist practices of solidarity and inclusion, this break initially seems strange. Not only were the two women rare examples of respected female reviewers and critics, but they shared an interest in new, experimental forms of science fiction writing, and they also shared a circle of top professional male colleagues. But perhaps it should not be surprising. Russ did not spring, Athena-like, from the heavily male-oriented traditions of science fiction as a full-fledged feminist champion. Instead, her development can be traced over time: from her 1959 debut writing much in the mode of other female (and male) authors of the day; her experiments with form, genre, and voice in the later 1960s; and her 1970s emergence as a determined advocate of science fiction's revolutionary potential, shaping her work as a vehicle for overt feminist principles.

The failure in the meeting of minds between Russ and Merril tells us something of the generational and intellectual tensions within science fiction in the late 1960s, a turning point for radicalism in the West (Kurlansky 2004). It also speaks to the difficulties women faced in forging successful careers in male-dominated worlds such as literature; although second-wave feminists of the 1960s and early 1970s called for the harmony of sisterhood, the reality for most women who pushed at the boundaries was not solidarity but fierce competition for the seeming few positions of power open to them.

## Transitions

Through the 1960s Merril fought to open up the field to ideas and formats that did not depend on "hard" science and technology to drive their plots, but instead on questions of social, moral, and political change. She understood the politics of mythologizing and the unique role of science fiction, if reconfigured as "SF," as modern myth (1967a, 3). Merril championed her vision in her anthologies from 1959 forward, and in her reviews, her mentoring projects (such as Milford), and her important critical essay "What Do You Mean: Science? Fiction?" (1971) for the first journal of science fiction criticism, Extrapolation. The openings thus created by Merril and her supporters in the 1950 and 1960s would also generate the very experimental environment that Russ and her feminist SF contemporaries enjoyed by their advent in second-wave feminism.

In many respects, Merril was of the "last generation" before second-wave feminism took hold in literary circles. Merril was understood to be a "gender-bender in a man's world" and was certainly nonorthodox in her attitudes and practices of sexuality, authority, experimentation, and ideas about women's capacities, as revealed both in her life and her writing (Merril and Pohl-Weary 2002, 11). However, she disavowed the term *feminist* and did not connect her own individualist feminist principles of personal equality and competence to a wider movement of women's liberation. This position was not uncommon among intellectual radicals of Merril's generation. Feminism was a problematical "brand of radicalism" that eluded the famous group of left-of-center writers and critics known as the New York Intellectuals at this time, argues David Laskin (2000, 246). The women in the group and "most of the women they knew and listened to didn't notice, weren't interested, or actively opposed 'women's lib' until it was a fait accompli. In fact, the whole business irritated the hell out of them" (247). Indifference, rather than outright opposition, appears to have been Merril's reaction to feminist discourses. It was a subject she never discussed in her SF writing and reviewing. But in a 1993 letter to her old Futurian friend and her longtime literary agent, Virginia Kidd (reproduced in her memoir), she reflects on feminism and Joanna Russ: "All these years, when people went on about my supposed feminist role-modeling in SF I laughed and laughed, because I knew I wasn't doing anything like that. SF was ready for that change; it accepted me eagerly . . . nobody but nobody advised me to use a man's (or neutral) name; some stories were hard to sell because editors said they wanted 'the woman's angle' from me. Etc." (Merril and Pohl-Weary 2002, 258).

But certainly Merril was promoting the subversive nature of the genre, to stir up questions of all kinds of social issues, including but not excusive to gender: "I do not mean just in its special uses as a vehicle of political analysis and social criticism," she cautioned in 1967, "but in its essential character. A literature dealing in possible-futures and alternative-presents, concerned with how things *might be*, rather than how they are, is inevitably (in any state short of Utopia) going to stir up some degree of dissatisfaction with the world-as-it-is. And just as certainly it will attract writers with vigorous opinions about how things ought to be" (1968b, 4).

At the time, however, Merril was completely discouraged in her efforts to have the American science fiction field respond to the new political and social climate of the late 1960s. She felt there were social revolutions all around her but little to "chew on" in American—as opposed to English—science fiction, even by those Americans who laid claim to writing and editing in the new mode.[1]

One of those American SF authors operating in the new mode was surely Joanna Russ, whose writing was undergoing a crucial transitional period, reflecting the place of a "hard" SF advocate up-and-comer in the mid-1960s to feminist forerunner and lesbian activist a decade later. As Gary K. Wolfe notes in chapter 1, the Alyx stories in particular can be read "not only of the development of a feminist consciousness, but—particularly in the final tale—as an account of the birth of a science fiction writer." Jane Donawerth (Donawerth and Kolmerton 1994) observes that Russ's fiction changed in this period from "writing love stores to writing stories about women in which the woman won," and her criticism, which "began in the general aesthetics of science fiction," moved on to "passionate feminist critiques of science fiction and other literatures" (1–4). Thelma J. Shinn (1985) agrees that Russ's work shows a progression from "isolated superwoman" to characters engaged in community and questioning wider structures of inequality (212). Shinn also concurs with Samuel Delany that Russ's novels can be read as "mounting critiques of her own earlier works" (211).[2]

A hint of the personal side to this literary trajectory emerges in an autobiographical essay, originally published in 1980, that Russ included in her 1985 essay collection *Magic Mommas, Trembling Sisters, Puritans and Perverts*. In it Russ recounts her struggles with stifling normative gender roles and heterosexual identity, and her attempts at finding her own power. She notes, "I kept 'falling in love' with inaccessible men until it occurred to me I wanted to be them, not love them" (27–28) and sought to turn her energies to her own needs and development. Although she cites no dates, it seems clear that this life-changing transition began around the period of the late 1960s. She also marks this turning point in terms of her political thought: "by this point, feminism was bursting out all over us" (28)—which would seem to place this moment in or around 1968, the year that she notes in a fanzine debate in 1976 was "when I first met feminism" (Russ, 1976b, 12). Significantly, Russ sees starting to publish some SF stories and being invited to writers' conferences and SF conventions (and building meaningful connections with the SF community) as part of that process (1985a, 27).

By the time she began "weighing in as an intellectual contender" with occasional reviews in Merril's books column in the mid-1960s, Russ had already entered the inner circle of new SF writers at the illustrious annual Milford Writers' Conference cofounded by Merril with Damon Knight and James Blish in 1956. Among Russ's colleagues there in 1966 were promoters of new writing such as Thomas Disch, Harlan Ellison, Carol and Ed Emshwiller, Damon Knight, R. A. Lafferty, Kate Wilhelm, and Samuel R. Delany (Disch 1998: 137; Delany 1968, 20). (Merril was absent from the event that year, abroad in London exploring the new mode in science fiction with the *New Worlds* SF magazine writers.) The rousing support for Russ by the most successful male writers in science fiction was evident from her earliest novels—a point highlighted in Robert Silverberg's introduction to Russ's 1970 novel, *And Chaos Died*. Silverberg (1978) writes that decorating the dust jacket for Russ's first novel, *Picnic in Paradise*, was jacket-copy praise by Theodore Sturgeon, Fritz Leiber, Poul Anderson, Hal Clement, and Samuel Delany, which "succeeded against the odds in giving the appearance of merit in such high-powered hype" (vii). Yet all of those high-powered hypesters were also part of Merril's circle of close friends and supporters. The people who respected and admired Russ, as a rule, respected and admired Merril as well.

Perhaps the most important connection that should have allied Russ and Merril was the relationship of each to Delany. It was through and around Delany that the two women may be seen to have had great potential connections on a personal and an aesthetic level. The divide between Merril and Russ was in part generational and Delany could have bridged that gap. He was five years younger than Russ but by 1968 had published ten science fiction novels and was beginning to publish short stories; thus he was considered the youthful prodigy of the field. To him, Merril was of the generation (or even two) before him and Russ the one after (Delany 1985, 103–104). Merril had no difficulty connecting with Delany and championing his writing; she felt very maternally "connected" to him, she wrote to a friend in 1967: Delany "is the same age as my oldest daughter, and has about him the same new-youth feeling I get from my younger one."[3] Merril was captivated by his challenging latest novel, *The Einstein Intersection*. "I read the book at a gulp, delighted page by page, and disappointed at the end, without quite knowing why," Merril writes in her books column (1967d, 34–35). In Delany's case, Merril is willing to go an extra mile: "When I went back to skim through and refresh myself before writing about it, I found myself re-reading instead: and found out that it was the gulping that gave me that faint indigestion the first time" (35). Here, Merril seems able to provide her typical generous gesture to readers: sharing with them the practice of reading the new mode of science fiction. Her conclusion is that Delany's is "a charming book, a gay book, a story of true love and roving adventure, full of strange music, a song of changelings and dragons and a Dove and a devil; where Orpheus battles Billy the Kid, and is saved from the Minotaur by a compassionate computer; but is also and absolutely a story about where-it's-at, right here, right now" (35). Yet as we shall see, in the same column Merril dismisses Russ's stories in Damon Knight's *Orbit 2* anthology, and will later offer a negative review of Russ's *Picnic on Paradise*, in both cases for not being science fiction. The question remains, What makes Delany's experimental writing science fiction, even exemplary of "The New Thing" science fiction (Merril 1967d, 35), yet Russ's similar writing to be relegated beyond the pale?

Delany, one notes, had no trouble connecting with Russ or identifying her as a writer of science fiction. Just as Merril enthusiastically interpreted early Delany for serious readers, Delany interpreted early Russ as praiseworthy for the same audience. In a review for *Nozdrovia* Delany establishes *Picnic on Paradise* as definitely science fiction and even a "work of the highest art" (1968, 21). Reading and rereading the novel, he discovers on the third reading that the book is all about the present (a reason Merril gives for declaring Delany's *Einstein Intersection* definitely science fiction). "For me, however," writes Delany, "one of the book's magnificences was that for all its terribly skilful blending of the archaic and the alien, the world generated is consistently and absolutely of the present. Were it any other, the book would be pointless. As well, the glistening set on which this psychological saraband is choreographed gives us a myth turned inside out. . . . [sic] the only sort we can use today" (23). Delany also goes beyond the book itself to talk about the writer, about her powerful, effective presence at the Milford writers' gathering. Russ struck Delany as a writer's writer (20).

Yet despite the many connections, in 1968 Merril and Russ seemed on opposite sides—at least in print.[4] Russ, the future advocate of science fiction as a socially revolutionary literature, a natural for any kind of radical thought, used her review of Merril's work to knock Merril precisely for her adherence to the "new writing" in a self-conscious defense of "hard" science fiction and its adherents, while Merril would contest that Russ was a true SF writer at all.

The question remains, Why was it that the foremost advocate for social transformations inherent in science fiction in the 1960s, and its champion of the mid-1970s, should not have a meeting of minds in 1968, but instead a sharp conflict? It might simply be that the intellectual, personal, and professional currents of these two powerful personalities could not come together: too soon for Russ, too late for Merril. But we believe that there are other, contextual elements at play here. As we shall argue, and as Lisa Yaszek and Helen Merrick have also argued, the struggles of women of talent and ambition to survive and succeed in the male-dominated world of literature militated against an accord, or cooperation between science fiction's foremost female practitioners. Russ herself, as Sherryl Vint points out (chapter 6, this volume), was not unaware of this dilemma and wrote about it in much of her fiction. Yet only in her struggles to win at this game could Russ reach the place of relative success and safety to start to dismantle the system itself.

## The Women Science Fiction Did See

Russ was from the outset in 1966 an intelligent, tough-minded reviewer who routinely tempered her harsh criticism with just the sort of faint praise she handed out to Merril. James Tiptree, Jr., a decade later likened corresponding with Russ to facing a "conflagration." One minute she was an "absolute delight." The next, she "rushes out and bites my ankles with one sentence" (Phillips 2006, 306). To Ursula Le Guin, Tiptree complained that Russ "[p]ees all over your leg, interspersed with the converse of angels" (Phillips 2006, 306).

In a similar vein, Russ slams (albeit with a feather pillow) Merril's SF: The Best of the Best anthology (1967). In her review of it (as a guest contributor in Merril's books column), Russ criticizes the "Merrilian bent" of the collection for being "human," "poignant," caught up (through "retrospective interest") in "New Thing" writers such as Carol Emshwiller and J. G. Ballard, and a "reaction against too much hardware in the s-f field (both now and back then)" (1968c, 54).

The most damning critique is that in Best of the Best "the hard sciences are conspicuously absent" (Russ 1968c, 55). In Russ's view this made for a "surprisingly monotonous book," which she is careful to lay not at the feet of the authors, whose stories she individually lauds, but at the editing hand of Merril, who here is clearly not fulfilling her reputation as a science fiction "connoisseur."[5] The code is not all that subtle: "hard" science fiction being of course the continuing measure of true or pure science fiction in the eyes of much of the contemporary SF community. Justine Larbalestier observes of the history of American science fiction that science, so central to the genre (in theory, at least) "has always been lamented for its absence" by SF critics and fans (2002, 171). Yet, given the clear association in SF circles of "hard" science

with masculine writers and writing, it was by any measure a remarkable statement to be made by someone like Russ, who would only a few years later rise
to become the leading feminist SF writer. Russ's own early promise in science,
however, was part of her professional credentials as a science fiction writer.
Reference to her Westinghouse Science Scholar connection was standard in
introductions to her stories and novels and still meaningful to her persona
in the 1970s. When interviewed in 1975 by Paul Walker for *Moebius Trip*, at
the question "When did you begin to write?" Russ broke through her train
of thought at one point to confirm the, by now, very old connection: "Did you
know I was one of the ten top finalists in the Westinghouse Science Talent
Search in 1953?" (Walker and Russ 1975, 5).

*Best of the Best* is dismissed finally with the praise that it would be an excellent choice for someone who did not usually read science fiction, or who
did not follow Merril's anthology series—a primer for the uninitiated and a
catch-up for those who, despite Merril's reputation, missed (or rejected) her
earlier work. The target is not only Merril's reputation as a foremost editor-
critic, but her credentials as an intellectual leader and a connoisseur of science
fiction who was pushing science fiction in the new, experimental directions
to which Russ (later) seemed committed. Russ concludes the backhanded
compliment with praise for the book's size: "One of the best things about
THE BEST," she writes, "is that it is fat, the way anthologies used to be in the
fifties" (1968c, 55).

Given Tiptree's comments on Russ's critiquing style, it is tempting to
dismiss Russ's review of Merril as simply par for the course. And, as is well
known, spats and temporarily warring factions proliferated in SF circles in
this era of change. But we suggest that in this case there was more to it than
that. Russ would gain a reputation in her feminist fiction of the 1970s for daring to construct female characters that were unafraid of killing off powerful
women. Here, in her early years as a reviewer, Russ seems to have already
adopted the philosophy that if one were to succeed, one would need to challenge and defeat the master on her own turf. Taking apart a volume that could
be seen as the best distillation of the editing skill and avant-garde projections
of the top editor in American science fiction was certainly one way to step up
to the portals of the SF community and pound loudly.

Merril returned to her column with a salvo of her own. Reviewing
Russ's *Picnic on Paradise*, Merril found that Russ had all the potential but was
missing the key element, the "binding energy that holds a [science fiction]
novel together: that is, 'Prophetic Power'" (1968d, 35). As a first novel it was
"startlingly superior," Merril gushes "I cannot think when I last enjoyed so
much reading anything so unconvincing" (36). "The girl can *write*," she says
(37). "Joanna Russ *writes* so well, it doesn't really matter if she makes sense"

(36). Nonetheless, she simply "didn't believe *anything*" (36) of the characters, events, or world Russ created. Merril finally decides that it is only the novel's "false-science-fiction front" that she disagrees with; as fantasy or other genre it would be excellent. She speculates that in time a fine writer like Russ might even be able to "learn the Prophet Business too" (37).

This was not Merril's first opportunity to separate Joanna Russ's work from that of proper science fiction. As mentioned, the previous year she had an opportunity to review Russ's stories in an anthology of Damon Knight's purporting to be New Wave writing: *Orbit 2: The Best New Science Fiction Stories of the Year* (1967d). Merril reviewed *Orbit 2* in the context of an entire books column, which was devoted to answering critics' attacks on the new wave of "soft" science fiction and of Merril's advocacy of the new practice and its practitioners. Merril is not buying Knight's claims to avant-garde status. Only two of the stories in *Orbit 2* (Kate Wilhelm's "Baby, You Were Great" and Brian Aldiss's "Full Sun") would, just barely, she suggests, "satisfy any reasonable, traditional definition of science-fiction-proper," including even Knight's various definitions of the genre. And only one, Kit Reed's "The Food Farm," could "unarguably" be considered The New Thing (30–31). Excluded from both The New Thing and even the science fiction category are "two delightfully literate but otherwise routine sword-and-sorcery stories by Joanna Russ ("I Gave Her Sack and Sherry" and "The Adventuress"), which Merril neglects even to name (31).[6]

And not too long after her *Picnic on Paradise* review, Merril vanished from the scene, an antithetical transition of leadership. We know now that the production of *Best of the Best* was Merril's swan song, her penultimate anthology in the American science fiction context, In her final columns and in her final annual anthology, *SF12: New Dimensions in Science Fiction, Fantasy, and Imaginative Writing* (1969), Merril would move beyond professing to expand the definition of science fiction, to admitting to no longer being able to recognize the best of genre in its current "moribund" state.[7] To British author Brian Aldiss, Merril wrote that year, "I guess I'm getting farther and farther removed from attachment to the whole science fiction scene. I find more and more that the essence of science fiction, the stuff that hooked me way back, is coming at me from different places."[8] She had lost faith in contemporary American science fiction's coming to grips with contemporary social and political change; it had become, she lamented in her January 1969 column, the literature of great escape, rather than great hope. Her disgust at the American position on Vietnam—in particular the violence she witnessed towards the antiwar demonstrators at the Democratic National Convention in Chicago in the summer of 1968—and the uncomfortable position of power she had achieved in the SF field as foremost editor, reviewer, and controversial "prophetess" of New

Wave SF writing (1967d, 28), solidified her decision to leave the United States for Canada, leaving the American SF community behind as well (Newell and Tallentire 2007).

Thus this moment in the rise of one of the "next generation" of SF writers and the bowing out of one of the original leaders of the postwar SF field was not a passing of a torch or baton between the two women but a harsh, splintering break. In retrospect, it seems clear that Merril would not have shed her individualistic identity to make room for a newcomer like Russ. And Russ had not yet completed the profound paradigm shift from up-and-comer to authority, from critic of "soft" science fiction to advocate of science fiction's revolutionary potential, and from unconscious embedment in hetero/sexist structures to committed feminist and lesbian.

## How to Suppress (Other) Women's Writing

Given her later dismissal of women writers of the 1950s and 1960s (as examined by Lisa Yaszek in this volume as well as Connie Willis [1992]), it is somewhat ironic that Russ should, in 1983, compose a feminist volume titled *How To Suppress Women's Writing*. The book is divided into sections, each based on the strategy used by men to deny women the authenticity, genius, and sheer existence of their artistic endeavors. "Bad Faith" is the tile and theme of her section describing the root cause of denial of women's artistic accomplishments; bad faith lay behind whatever method is used to "bury the art, explain it away, ignore it, downgrade it, in short make it vanish" (1983b, 17). It seems that elements of bad faith may have been at work for both Russ and Merril in their attempts to discredit, or undermine or at best marginalize, each other in the late 1960s. In the section on "False categorizing," Russ is speaking of literary genres generally (the novel, poetry, letters) and the ghettoizing of women's work as belonging to substandard or outside genres. But the themes apply just as well to the subgenres of science fiction: "soft" versus "hard," fantasy versus science fiction. Both Merril and Russ use false categorizing to attack the other: Merril to dismiss Russ as nothing new, or not even a writer of science fiction; Russ to dethrone Merril as not "hard" enough and out of touch, a producer of fat anthologies, throwbacks to the 1950s.

A need to carve space and claim a reputation seems to have led Russ to adopt a posture of exceptionalism—"I was the first, the only"—rather than the mentorship model more commonly found in SF circles. Perhaps because she had been called in a pinch to take over for Merril as a guest contributor to the books column, Russ had seen herself as the logical replacement, one who could complete all her assignments and get her columns in on time to boot. Perhaps behind-the-scenes politics gave her the confidence to tackle the foremost editor and top female critic and reviewer in her field. By 1968, Russ was a regular guest reviewer while Merril was increasingly absent.

Russ continued in this vein in her attack on Ursula K. Le Guin's 1969 novel The Left Hand of Darkness, which won both the 1969 Nebula and 1970 Hugo awards for best SF novel (the first awards in the category to a female writer). Le Guin was arguably the foremost female rising star in science fiction at the time. In "The Image of Women in Science Fiction," a pioneering 1971 study reprinted in the first anthology of academic feminist literary criticism (Cornillon 1972), Russ argues that despite the closer attention that women authors pay to female characters and to inventing worlds marked by gender equity, the gender stereotypes that pervade science fiction by men show up "just as often" in the science fiction written by women. It is not sufficient to consider only gender relations in the workplace, argues Russ. One must regard the more intimate settings; it is "in the family scenes and the love scenes that one must look for the author's real freedom from our most destructive prejudices" (Russ 1972a, 89). To Russ, Le Guin's The Left Hand of Darkness was emblematic of these stereotypes, and she devotes the last third of her essay to listing its failings on technical and feminist grounds: for example, "family structure is not fully explained" and "child-rearing is left completely in the dark." Most important, "the great love scene in the book is between two men: the human observer (who is a real man) and the native hero (who is a female man)" (90). Russ adds a lengthy endnote to her analysis that tries to soften her attack, admitting she is "too hard" (94 n. 29) on the "beautifully written book" (89). Yet, Jane Gallop (1989) finds that this does not repair the damage done to Le Guin: "after three sentences of trying to be fair to Le Guin, the lengthy note closes with the most damning statement Russ makes about the other woman: '[Le Guin's] earlier novel, City of Illusions . . . is surprisingly close to space opera, he-man ethos—either anti-feminism or resentment at being feminine, depending on how you look at it' (94)" (619). Gallop feels that "the condemnation is, in a sense, more devastating because Russ is apparently going out of her way to be fair" (619).

Russ was far from alone in her objections to Le Guin's acclaimed novel. British feminist author Sarah Lefanu remembers that her own review of it on feminist grounds in the magazine Spare Rib (May 1975) was scornful (Lefanu 2004). Yet, regardless of who else would agree with Russ's objections to Le Guin's novel, Russ's discussion of Le Guin is remarkably aggressive. And this is Jane Gallop's point: Russ's extensive endnote demonstrates a "particularly effective intensity about criticizing a woman writer" (619). For Gallop, the heart of the matter is in fact competitive, not critical: "Russ is herself a science fiction writer judging a more successful sister. The psychological scenario is more apt to involve the aggressive aspects of identification, a complex we can call rivalry" (620). Most telling for this present study is Gallop's suggestion that this "troubled endnote to Le Guin—displaying a combination of admiration, guilt, and aggression"—might be a prime example of a type of rivalry phenomenon: "as bespeaking a certain kind of woman-to-woman relation: the view of a more established woman by a woman with ambitions in the same field. We might call this the little sister's discourse on the big sister" (620).

Russ was equally, pointedly harsh on another female, prizewinning up-and-comer in the field: Anne McCaffrey. McCaffrey was a double prizewinner in 1968, the first woman to be awarded either a Hugo for short fiction (for her novella, "Weyr Search") or a Nebula for a novella ("Dragonrider"). Still contributing the occasional review in the *Magazine of Fantasy and Science Fiction*, Russ attacks McCaffrey's *The Ship Who Sang* (1969), a novel featuring a heroine named Helva made cyborg when she is built into an interstellar spaceship. *The Ship Who Sang* extended McCaffrey's original short story of the same name and it quickly became (and remains to this day), like Le Guin's *The Left Hand of Darkness*, a classic work associated with the new presence of women in the genre. Russ challenges the sense, the science, and the writing. "Some very important things are never explained," she argues. "Is Helva sexually mature? We know she is sterile, but what about her ductless glands? I would also like to know what life without olfactory or tactile sensations does to the human psyche . . . . And why *does* Helva lack these? . . . All these confusions seem to me to be the result of a lack of rewriting" (1970d, 40–41). Russ damns McCaffrey's book with faint praise for signs of improvement toward the end, taking one more poke at the author: "one of the pleasures of reading SHIP is watching it progress from some rather awful gaucheries through the middling treatment of middling ideas to the two final sections in which the author at last begins to dramatize scenes with ease and some polish" (40). For all its "silliness," Russ writes, the book is not without its "contagious joyfulness" (42).

Feminists in particular can be disappointed and bewildered when open competition between women is found, not sisterly cooperation. But Jane Gallop (1989) argues, that we need to "consider those aspects of 'sisterhood' which mean not solidarity but hostile competition" (620), and Helen Longino and Valerie Minor (1987) note: "Feminists have long been fiercely critical of male power games and so often ignored or concealed our own conflicts over money, control, position, and recognition" (1). More recently, Lyn Mikel Brown (2003) has explored the roots of conflict between women—"girlfighting"—in the socialization of girls from infancy to accept subordinate status and turn their anger and anxieties born from their positions in patriarchal society on one another. Central to this conflict is what Brown calls the "nice girl" versus "bad girl" game: being "nice," pleasing those in power, being the

proper champion of men's interests or the competent "exception" to the infe-
rior feminine. "Internalizing a culture that centers male authority and trivial-
izes femininity," from an early age girls learn "how to strip away other girls'
support and depose other girls who threaten their positions of power" (180).
Women are taught from young girlhood the acceptable avenues to power: "be
nice, stay pure, look beautiful, act white, be chosen" (21). The "bad" girls (and
women) "ask the "wrong" questions, know or want too much, act too sexual, speak too loud, like themselves too much, dream too big" (180). The real
source, and rightful focus, of the anger and fear that girls and women feel in
a heterosexist society too often gets lost, trained as girls are to see other girls
as the target rather than wider society.

The lessons girls learn about how to be a "proper" girl are carried with
them to shape their adult relationships and careers. A barrier to connection
and mentorship between women is the traditional pattern of competition for
scarce resources and recognition in male-dominated enterprises. McGuire
and Reger (2003, 62) argue that the weight of gender inequality and the need
to be "exceptional" to achieve the success of mediocre men builds barriers
between women in predominately male enterprises: quoting Rosabeth Moss
Kanter, "For token women, the price of being 'one of the boys' was a willingness to occasionally turn against 'the girls' "(228).

Speaking more specifically about literature, Elaine Showalter (2000)
notes: "The dominant myth of this century has been that of the Dark Lady, the
token woman or exceptional intellectual in a community of men" (137). Showalter's dissection of "the idea of the Dark Lady as the only girl in the gang,
fighting off competition from her rivals" (137) seems appropriate to consider
here. Earning her stripes in science fiction in the 1950s and achieving the top
spot as a critic-reviewer and anthologist by the mid-1960s, Merril was to some
extent the first Dark Lady of science fiction, a heavily male-dominated field
that Russ would later, in the 1970s, rightly dissect in her critical writing. Yet in
1968, Russ seems to have been more immersed in this culture of exceptionalism than Merril. In a candid letter to James Tiptree, Jr., in the mid-1970s, when
Tiptree was still believed to be a man, Russ described growing up female but
not being able to identify with women: "Women never did anything remotely
interesting, so I identified with all the men in the books and films and in
life, too, almost." In the end, she wrote, "I decided I would be an exception"
(though, by this point in her life, she concludes that "one can't use that as a
model or guide to real living") (Phillips 2006, 303).

Poised between what seemed the two choices available to women—to
be uselessly female, or to be the exceptional competent "female man"—Russ
quite understandably chose the latter. In "Powerlessness and the Women's
Movement" (also in the Magic Mommas collection), Russ identifies two dis-

tinct adult female identities formed out of the "Feminine Imperative" to serve others, an extension of the "nice girl" paradigm outlined by Brown. The "magic momma" is capable and competent, and is expected to only serve others; she "pays for her effectiveness by renouncing her own needs," The "trembling sister" is by definition ineffective and expects the magic momma to take care of her needs (1985c, 45). Magic mommas, having gained some kind of visible achievement, must use it for the good of other women (sisterhood), or be decried as selfish for the ultimate (female) crime: using her power on her own behalf (49). (Trembling sisters, on the other hand, assume that powerful women lie about other women's abilities to get ahead.) Russ is firm that whatever the seeming benefits of fitting into the framework of the "good woman," the "magic momma," and "trembling sister" positions ultimately mean powerlessness for women. She strongly hints in this passage why she might have taken a different path, one that would leave her open to criticism:

> Both are engaged in ritualistically sacrificing the possibility of a woman's being effective on her own behalf, not needy and ineffective, not effective and altruistic, but *effective for herself*.
> It's selfish, vicious, and nasty, and will cause everyone within a thousand miles to faint flat.
> But it beats being dead. (1985a, 54)

## When It Changed

In the late 1960s and into the early 1970s, Russ had played the game, by the rules as she saw them. Russ's "aggressive" attacks on key female authors and pursuit of the Dark Lady paradigm was not a surprising stratagem in such a male-dominated field as science fiction. It appears that by the time she published her celebrated feminist novel, *The Female Man*, in 1975, Russ got what she aimed for: the top spot, a clear field, the mantle of leadership, and the space to promote her new ideas about science fiction. And Sarah Lefanu, in her critical study of feminism and science fiction, could declare that Joanna Russ was "the single most important woman writer of science fiction" (1988, 173). Russ was also successful among fandom in establishing herself firmly as the leader of a group that "broadened the scope of SF exploration from mere technology to include personal and social themes as well" (Gomoll 1986–87, 1).

Yet the introduction to feminism and the feminist movement around 1968 also gave Russ the conceptual tools (and, we would argue, the strength and community) to slowly abandon that game. Just a few years later she would begin to create a new space for women writers and feminist thought that challenged the limits placed upon women's identities and ambitions in a deeply sexist society. Although Russ retained her conviction that good science fiction required good science, as Edward James demonstrates in his essay in this volume (chapter 2), Russ would construct her vision of science fiction in nearly the exact terms that Merril had used in the 1960s. Cathy Silverstein's (1976) interview with Russ in *Cthulhu Calls* confirms Russ's transition from a strict adherence to hard science fiction to the New Wave writing: "Joanna Russ defines Science Fiction as a literature that 'portrays the state of affairs of things, not as they are, or were, or as we typically characterize them to be. It portrays things as they *might* be, may be, or might have been.' . . . Professor Russ believes that "SF can [also] play a role in all sorts of political or social revolutions)" (14). When interviewed with Delany several years later, Russ voices similar (and oft-quoted) thoughts: "Science fiction is a natural in a way for any kind of radical thought. Because it is about things that have not happened and do not happen. It's usually placed in the future, but not always. It is very fruitful if you want to present the concerns of a marginal group because you do it in a world where things are different" (Delany and Russ 1984, 29).

Perhaps just at the point of the Merril-Russ intersection, then, Russ was struggling with what it meant to be not a magic momma but a person of achievement without oppressive labels, a true leader who was effective as herself. That her own fictional themes transitioned from superwoman to community is a sign of this later maturity as a feminist theorist and spokesperson.

Interestingly enough, when offered the permanent books editor position vacated by Merril at the beginning of 1969, Russ turned it down, although she would continue to do reviews through the 1970s.[9] The proliferation of the female and feminist science-fiction authors through the 1970s made tokenism and the exceptional less possible and less necessary. By the mid-1970s, Russ could feel confident enough in her position to reach out to feminist science-fiction authors as a group, claiming a leadership of equals rather than maintaining the fiction of an exceptional, lone figure.

The transition we can trace, through Russ's fiction, her reviews, and her scholarship, might best be seen as a tale about *community*: from the old community of male authors and traditional "hard" science fiction to a new community of female authors and feminist ideas. As Helen Merrick notes in her essay in this volume (chapter 4), a series of feminist debates between 1974 and 1976 show Russ's feminist ideas maturing and her position as feminist leader solidifying. Russ was also coming out as a lesbian. "Her whole idea of herself," she said, in her April 1975 letter about the discovery of her lesbian sexuality to James Tiptree, Jr., "had been turned upside down" (Phillips 2006, 345). Lillian Faderman points out that those lesbians who came out in this period existed in a society that benefited from feminism and other radical movements. More crucially, a support community had emerged, both physically and in the lesbian-feminist literature that blossomed in the 1970s. In short, these "New Women did not need to come out in isolation" (Faderman 1981, 383–384).

Having found a community, published her iconic novel, and made the crucial paradigm shift to coming out as a lesbian, Russ could by 1975 shed many of the Dark Lady tactics that had seemed so viable and necessary back in 1968, and pursue instead a new paradigm of feminist critique and community—arriving at a more nuanced and complex vision of feminism and connection with other feminist writers, even in disagreement. Thus, in contrast to her 1971 nascent feminist critiques, Russ could go on to use Le Guin as an iconic SF success and reliable source for women's experiences in SF publishing (1983b, 22–24). As for Judith Merril, while it seems clear that she could not have followed Russ on her particular journey, her break with the American SF community and move to Canada in 1968 took her down a rather spectacular, radical path of her own.[10]

This dissection of the Merril-Russ intersection in 1968 is meant to be a reflection on how far Russ was to travel in a few short years, in her novels and in her politics. However far she might have gone to promote feminist writing, and even a canon of feminist science fiction, she did so from a position of strength forged from a model of isolated superwoman, the achievement of a Dark Lady status that brooked no equals. And she reaped the benefits, as well as the scars. In reviewing her own trajectory, Russ noted in 1976: "I do feel that, having made sacrifices (including part of one's own personality) to get what one wanted, there's a strong human tendency to insist that the sacrifices were necessary" (1976b, 12).

Perhaps this brief "rivalry" between Merril and Russ is best seen as emblematic of a process Merril describes in her 1952 novella, *Daughters of Earth*: that exploration and adventure would skip a generation, each daughter becoming the polar opposite of her mother and taking the path of her grandmother, a cycle of rooted women holding to home, and mobile women attracted to the stars. It would seem that (if we compress Delany's "generations" to see Russ as Merril's direct heir) at first Russ also took her place in that cycle of opposites, rejecting the "soft SF" focus of Merril and presenting her own credentials as the innovative hard-science "isolated superwoman."

Yet through the 1970s Russ began to shed that position, moving instead to embrace and, through an evolving feminist framework, expand upon many of the SF ideals that Merril had fostered before her—her own new vision of "the prophet business." Russ's extraordinary trajectory and substantial legacy and influence reminds us that authors and critics do not come to their careers fully formed and changeless, but develop over time, and with "the times"—and the 1960s and early 1970s were the most profound for women in science fiction.

# Part II    Fiction

~

# 6 Joanna Russ's *The Two of Them* in an Age of Third-wave Feminism

SHERRYL VINT

The master's tools will never dismantle the master's house.

—Audre Lorde, *Sister Outsider*

You are the liberal who might concede (if pushed into a corner and yelled at by twenty angry radicals) that morality does indeed begin at the mouth of a gun (though you'd add quickly, "It doesn't end there") but do you realise what does end at the mouth of a gun? Fear. Frustration. Self-hate. Everything romantic. (This depends, of course, on being at the proper end of the gun.)

—Joanna Russ, *On Strike Against God*

Ernst is one of the few men she's ever met who likes women. Most men don't. Most women don't, most boys don't, most little girls don't.

—Joanna Russ, *The Two of Them*

*The Two of Them* (Russ 1978b) is the most troubling and most pessimistic of Joanna Russ's works. The novel ends, as Sarah Lefanu (1988) notes, not with a vision of utopia or hope, but rather with the killing of Ernst and Irene left alone, "a thirty-year-old divorcee in a hotel room in Albuquerque, with a child to support" (195). Two things trouble critics and reviewers of the novel: the shooting of Ernst, a mainly sympathetic character, and the ambiguity at the conclusion which leaves it unclear as to whether Irene really has achieved enlightenment. The shooting of Ernst is the central focus of the denouement and our decision to interpret this act as murder, justified homicide, or as an expression of Irene's loss of sanity shapes our interpretation of the entire novel. My argument is that Ernst's death is necessary in order for Irene to escape the structures of patriarchy, structures that continue to shape her identity and leave her filled with fear, frustration, and self-hatred. Irene can move beyond such feelings and begin to truly like women only when she finds herself at the "proper" end of the gun. Thus, Ernst's death, although troubling, is necessary to the novel's desire to avoid a romantic conclusion and to its argument regarding the necessity of radical, rather than merely liberal, feminism for the emancipation of women.

Carl Freedman (2000) argues that *The Two of Them* is distinguished from Russ's more polemical and better-known works, such as *The Female Man* (1975), because it is "ultimately concerned with estranging liberal patriarchy and normative heterosexual relations *at their best*, or in any case at what initially appears to be their best. The target here is the subtlety as well as the grossness of sexist oppression" (135). Freedman goes on to read the novel in terms of Irene learning to distance herself from her Orientalist attitude toward Ka'abah culture. His reading points to one of the limitations of second-wave feminism, the insufficient attention it has paid to class, orientation, and racial difference among women, and its own tendency to erase the voices of some of the very women it claims to champion.[1] The voices of those feminists—of color, lesbian, working-class—who have critiqued second-wave feminism for this blindness have sometimes been referred to as the "third wave" of feminism. Their critiques are quite valid—and have been responded to by feminism—and such interchange is not the focus of my discussion today. Instead, I am focusing on a more recent and new "third-wave feminism" that has emerged, that defines itself in terms of generational differences from the second wave. Arguing that their experience of patriarchy is quite different from that which formed feminists of the second wave, these third-wave feminists contend that new strategies and goals are therefore required for feminist struggle.

Feminists who identify with this third wave believe that what they see as the exclusion of their priorities from many feminist agendas is no less significant than the problems of racial, class, and orientation bias. In "The Decentering of Second Wave Feminism and the Rise of the Third Wave" (2005), Susan Mann and Douglas Huffman argue that "the new generation, in its attempt to open up and broaden feminism, introduced a number of less restrictive ideas, strategies and ways of conceptualising feminism that sparked condescension, controversy, and rather hostile critiques from their second wave sisters. . . . It is precisely such feelings of condescension and exclusion, experienced by women of color and ethnicity here and abroad, and now felt by a new generation, that fostered the decentering of the second wave" (70). Many third-wave feminists focus on what they perceive to be the overnarrow vision of feminist identity articulated by the second wave. Their critique of second-wave feminism tends to focus on two issues: sex and capital. Many feel that second-wave feminism was over concerned about the sexual exploitation of women within patriarchy and thus left no place in its analysis for women's own sexual desire, which might even be expressed through embracing such things as lipstick, hooker chains, or strappy shoes. Others feel that second-wave feminism has been overfocused on seeing women as a class and working for structural change of systems that oppress women, leaving insufficient space for the celebration of female agency and strategies that would focus on victories women might achieve within the structures of democratic capitalism.

Some women's decision to turn away from feminism because they no longer see a need for solidarity with other women is part of what is explored by Russ's novel. The Two of Them is the most pertinent of Russ's novels for the present cultural moment because it suggests a way to help us think past the stalemate between second- and third-wave feminisms. The novel is the story of two Trans Temp agents, Irene and Ernst, who are sent on a mission to the planet (or perhaps parallel world) Ka'abah. Irene and Ernst are partners, former teacher and pupil, and lovers. They come from different worlds: parallel earths with some things in common and others that are not. The Trans Temp agency for which they work seems to be egalitarian as regards gender. The opening lines of the novel stress for us that Ernst and Irene are almost the same, using the non–gender-specific, plural pronoun: "they're entirely in black" and "both are tall" (9). When the novel does move to distinguish between them, it is age rather than gender that is the pertinent category. In Ka'abah, Ernst and Irene discover a society quite unlike their own, characterized by the most rigid of gender distinctions. The women of Ka'abah are kept in a state of purdah and are entirely at the mercy of the goodness of their husbands who, if they are "good" men, don't "divorce" or "send . . . back to [the wives'] parents" or "knock . . . down" (82) their wives. On this world, Irene and Ernst meet Zubeydeh, the young daughter of their contact, 'Alee. Zubeydeh is too young to have been fully repressed by the gender conventions of her society and dreams of being a poet, an honored profession reserved entirely for men.

Ernst and Irene are there on a minor diplomatic mission, unrelated to gender politics. Of her own initiative, and against Ernst's wishes to a degree, Irene decides to rescue Zubeydeh from the limited life she would have on Ka'abah and take her to be raised at Center. When Irene makes this decision, she sees herself as saving Zubeydeh from a life in which her opportunities would forever be limited by her gender and taking her to a place that is "for all its faults, a better world" (131). What interests me in Irene's analysis is the gap she constructs between her own experience of gender and gender oppression and that which she perceives in Zubeydeh's life. Irene's analysis is very similar to that offered by some third-wave feminists whose greater access to education, work, and other opportunities causes them to perceive a large gap between their experience of gender and that of earlier generations. Irene and such third-wave feminists are guilty of taking their own, exceptional, experi-

ence to be the norm and thus failing to see the degree to which gender discrimination remains a problem. Over the course of the novel, Irene comes to
realize the continuity between her experience and Zubeydeh's and, in the process, to realise the need for radical feminist consciousness, collective feminist
solidarity, and systemic change.[2]

Paula Kamen (1991) suggests that young women no longer identify as
feminist precisely because of the failure of second-wave feminism to respond
adequately to the context of young women who have experienced a measure
of gender equality within patriarchy. As Carolyn Sorisio (1997) points out,
they are compelled by a narrative: "We are postfeminist. Women don't want
to call themselves the 'f' word. . . . Worse yet, feminism is cast as a tragic
hero crafting its own demise. A monolithic 'we' considers women passive victims of male sexual and economic violence. 'We' have deployed a 'fem police'
that regulates the thoughts, sexuality, and choices of women in the name of
equality. Our dogma is stale, our ideology rigid, our fashion tastes hopelessly
passé (134).

Various voices have emerged within the third-wave to reclaim the mantle
of feminism from those second wavers who have thus "betrayed" the cause,
and the history of the feminist movement itself is being written in these
struggles over the rightful "heir" to the label. Naomi Wolf (1993) suggests we
should distance ourselves from a "victim feminism" that focuses on how patriarchy hurts women and instead embrace "power feminism" that focuses on
opportunities rather than impediments. Christina Hoff Sommers looks back
to the "good old days" of first-wave "equity feminism" when the movement
had its priorities straight. In *Who Stole Feminism?* (1994) she argues that feminism lost its way when it was taken over by second-wave "gender feminists"
who try to brainwash us into believing that "that women, even modern American women, are in thrall to 'a system of male dominance' variously referred
to as 'heteropatriarchy' or the sex/gender system" (22). That Hoff Sommers
seems shocked that "even modern American women" could thus be duped by
men is telling of the race, class, and other biases that persist in this version
of third-wave discourse. Perhaps most distressingly of all, Katie Roiphe suggests in *The Morning After* (1993) that the second-wave feminist concern with
the systematic discrimination of women under patriarchy does not merely
keep the focus on ways that women are victimized; in fact, it misleads women
into seeing themselves as victims when the reality is much less dire. The existence of "blue light" phones, for example, placed on remote and dark areas
of many campuses to allow instant access to the police, means that a woman
will "learn vulnerability and lurking dangers in the bushes. She'll learn to be
afraid walking around at night" (28).[3] These arguments all fail to understand
persistence of systemic discrimination in the power relations of everyday life

under patriarchy, a position that resonates with Irene's view at the beginning of *The Two of Them*.

I must stress that in talking about a number of different groups who have embraced the label of third-wave feminist I am not suggesting that all are the same. Although I have some reservations about the third wave taken as a whole, I also find much that is valuable in some third-wave thought, such as many of the essays collected in the anthologies *Third Wave Agenda* (Heywood and Drake 1997) and *Adiós, Barbie* (Edut 1998). These women's work points to the need for us to address the fact that feminism has had a significant effect on culture in the past thirty years; thus the ways in which patriarchy structures our lives are different from the ways of an earlier era. Many of these voices I do find to be authentically feminist. The third wave of feminism, of course, is no more homogeneous or unified than was the second wave, but what is disquieting is how easily some third-wave concerns can be translated into a distinctly antifeminist agenda such as that put forward by Roiphe or by Hoff Sommers, all the while retaining the feminist name. Despite the heterogeneity of third-wave feminism, two trends do appear in most of its discourse, and it is upon these commonalities that my argument focuses. The first is the contention that second-wave analyses are incapable of speaking to the situation of young women today, women whose experience of patriarchy is quite different from that of the previous generation given the victories of second-wave feminism. The second is the focus on the individual over systematic analysis that characterises most version of third-wave feminism. Both trouble me, for related reasons.

There is a tendency to take women in privileged positions (Roiphe, Hoff Sommers, and Wolf all might be slotted into this category) and generalize from such women to a conclusion about the "victory" of feminism and the lack of remaining barriers to women's emancipation. Not only are such arguments tremendously naive; they also do a grave disservice to many women still struggling with the pernicious affects of patriarchy, women who are made all the more invisible when comparison to their wealthy and successful "power" sisters is taken to render null any argument that systemic discrimination rather than personal failing is at the root of their suffering. As we shall see in my analysis of *The Two of Them*, this belief that one is "special" and that one's own achievements despite the sex/gender system deny the continued dominance of this system is something with which Irene struggles. She must learn to overcome this perception as she develops her radical feminism. To take the experience of women who have escaped some of the consequences of gender discrimination as the norm means that third-wave feminism itself is responsible for erasing the experience of many women. Thus, I would argue that while we should not deny that many women experience the sex/gender system in different and perhaps less oppressive ways than those experiences from which second-wave feminist analysis developed, it is nonetheless imperative that we look for continuities and the new strategies of patriarchal discrimination rather than view such gains as a complete break with the past.

Irene, too, needs to learn to see continuities rather than seeing herself as entirely different from Zubeydeh. Although Irene has a relatively more equal and autonomous existence, the key point is that both she and Zubeydeh live in patriarchal worlds, even though worlds that express their patriarchal structure differently. Early in the novel we are given hints that all is not so equal as it might seem to be on the surface, but the contrast between Irene's life and Ka'abah distracts us from the continued structural gender discrimination that persists in Irene's relationship with Ernst. Although their similarities are emphasised in the novel's opening lines, we are also quickly told, "Some things to know: that she was his pupil for seven years before she became one of The Gang. . . . That earlier he had got her out of a very bad place" (13).[4] This, along with the twenty-year difference in their ages, suggests that Ernst is in the dominant position in their relationship. Although Irene continually tries to assert her independence from him, she is always and inevitably in the role of supplicant not through any particular conspiracy or desire for power on Ernst's part—and this is key—but merely because she is *structurally* in the weaker position. Thus, when a teenage Irene, increasingly disaffected with the limited gender roles and opportunities she sees for herself in her own world, encounters a mysterious stranger (she doesn't yet know that he is *literally* from another world, but she does know that he seems sympathetic to her ambitions), she is forced to tell him, begrudgingly, "I guess I've got to say 'Take me with you' though I'd rather cut my tongue out. But what I really need is to get right out of this world" (73). That Ernst knows the "real" her is confirmed for Irene when her mother introduces her to him as "i-REEN" and he responds by pronouncing her name the British way, "i-REE-nee" (32), a pronunciation that corresponds with her own alter ego, a powerful inner identity that she has constructed for herself as compensation for all that her world does not offer.

Irene is at first blind to these structural power imbalances that persist throughout her relationship with Ernst. It is only her association with Zubeydeh—and the insight that Zubeydeh's much less subtle experience with patriarchy contributes to the situation—that makes such homologies clear to Irene. When they arrive on Ka'abah, Ernst tells 'Alee, "This trip Irenee is the doer and I am the conscience. Next trip it will be the other way around. . . . I mean that I am not in charge" (28). However, when Irene and Ernst get into a conflict over how to respond to Ka'abah's sexism, it gradually becomes clear that Ernst really is in charge. He is able to prevent Irene from rescuing

Zubeydeh's mother (against the woman's will, granted) simply by refusing to help her with the operation so that they run out of time and have to leave. Near the end of the novel, when Irene has decided that she will defy Trans Temp and try to find its "real" agenda (something that has been kept from them), Ernst makes some efforts to talk her out of this plan and, when they are not successful, he simply cancels her I.D.s without discussing the matter with her. When Irene discovers that her very identity can so easily be taken away from her, she truly begins to realize how precarious her privilege is, how much her seeming equality had been "a game" to Ernst and Trans Temp (just as Zubeydeh's brother had encouraged her poetry but immediately changed his position as soon as their father demanded stricter compliance with gender conventions). This is an epiphany for Irene: she recognizes that as long as the structures of gender discrimination remain in place, the success of some individuals despite them is not enough. She and Ernst were never truly equal, she recognizes, because she had "*no such power*. She has never had the numbers of Ernst's I.D., not even when she was his Conscience. Yet he must have a record of hers and must have gotten it from Trans Temp at Center, months ago at the very least" (184).

Irene had moments of doubt before, but it is only when she is confronted with the most naked expression of inequity that she realises that her goals should have been structural change of the system of gender discrimination, not individual transcendence of this system by aspiring to the status of one of the Gang, one of the guys. Her moments of anger in the novel suggest that on some level she has always known that there was a problem even if she was unable to articulate it. In her earlier incarnation, Irene moves from moments of angry outburst at Ernst to moments of apology, a pattern not sufficiently different from the experience of her mother, trapped in a more overtly oppressive gender system, who "alternated periods of loud heartiness . . . with fits of weeping" (29). Irene gropes her way toward making this connection, reflecting:

> *My expensive weapons, my expensive training, I'm exceptional, I should know better.* She thinks idly of her own mother. . . . She thinks, *My expensive position, my statistically rare training, my self-confidence, my unusual strength.*
>
> And I'm still afraid. .
>
> *Of what?* (145)

Irene needs to listen to her fear, to stop thinking of herself as exceptional, and to realize the continuities between her experience and that of her mother and Zubeydeh. Ernst cannot understand the source of her fear and rage, telling her "you dress as I do, you work as I do, you're paid as I am! If

you were in your mother's situation. . . ," and concluding, "If there's a difference . . . I'm glad of the difference" (180; ellipses in original). He might well
be glad, of course, as this difference privileges him. Zubeydeh, on the other
hand, sees the truth from the very beginning. Observing Ernst and Irene arguing, "Zubeydeh thinks that the lady will lose the argument, although the
man looks like a nice, pliable man, but if he gets really roused the lady will, of
course, have to give in" (138). The obviousness of male dominance is apparent
to Zubeydeh, given its much more overt form on her world; Irene's relatively
greater privilege serves in this instance to blind her to the fact that she and
Ernst, while lovers and partners and friends and potentially even allies, really do live in different worlds, not only the different parallel worlds of science fiction convention but also the different worlds of gendered experience.
Ernst is also blind to the ways this difference privileges him, as is suggested
by a place-name game they play near the beginning of the novel, a game
Ernst wins by using a word for a place that exists on his world but not on
Irene's. "It is really true in my world," he tells her when she objects, "so it's all
right" (16).

So long as Irene perceives things in terms of her personal relationship
and individual experience only, she is blind to the larger structures of patriarchy that continue to limit her options based solely on her membership
in the category of women. The focus on individualism in many versions of
third-wave feminism is precisely what prevents us from perceiving a need for
continued solidarity among women. Too often third-wave feminists rely on
a concept of self as "free individual" unaffected by the structures of cultural
meaning except to the extent that one chooses to submit oneself to these
structures. Such a position leads to a very limited sense of power and agency,
a power often expressed through sexual attractiveness or consumer power.
Naomi Wolf's *Fire with Fire* (1993) is the most influential example of a text
urging women to embrace both sorts of power as the new agenda for feminist action. Anna Quindlen (1996) has labeled this form of feminism "Babe
Feminism" and notes that it was called "do-me feminism" in a 1994 issue of
*Esquire* magazine. Quindlen suggests that anxiety about this sort of feminism
is "certainly just as stupid" as the "days when Gloria Steinem's politics were
overshadowed by her streaked hair" (4). Nonetheless, she does suggest that
the focus on this sort of feminism will be "cheering" to "men who have grown
tired of complaints about equal pay and violence against women" as it tends
to reduce feminism to "Good Feminism = Great Sex" (4). Quindlen believes
that "babe feminism" will soon pass away and that what is really important is
the structural changes won by feminist struggle over the last three decades,
structures that ensure that women do have access to education and jobs and
more equitable (if not equal) pay, noting that even in *Esquire*'s "do-me femi-

nism" issue, a survey of one thousand women asked whether "they'd rather be brilliant but plain or sexy but dumb" (4) showed a 74 percent vote in favor of brilliance. Like Quindlen, I am cheered by this result; nonetheless I worry that third-wave feminism's focus on individual rather than structural change, liberal rather than radical agendas, will limit the progress of feminism. It keeps women fighting among themselves instead of fighting patriarchy.

Irene achieves a true feminist consciousness when she learns to perceive the two of them in the title as referring to her and Zubeydeh rather than to her and Ernst. Zubeydeh not only teaches Irene the persistence of gender oppression in its more subtle form; she also draws her attention to the strategies that it employs in such contexts. It is the strategy of making those dependent realize their dependence that ensures the persistence of patriarchy. Zubeydeh tutors Irene on how the withdrawal of affection or the threat to withdraw affection is the most effective policing tool that patriarchy has: "He wouldn't even speak to me until I stopped. I mean stopped whatever it was. That's the way an older brother should discipline you. He didn't beat me, you know. . . . Husbands don't beat their wives, Irene. That's silly and barbaric. That's what outsiders think about Ka'abah. . . . We're really not so different from other places, you know" (167–168). This strategy has worked on Irene as well, evident in her persistent apologies to Ernst after outbursts, evident in the self-doubt that accompanies them. The effectiveness of this strategy is apparent also in the discourse of some third-wave feminists, who insist that feminism is not about "hating men" or trying to appease men, to a degree, by emphasising sex (the very difference of which Ernst is glad). The need to resist this sort of domination is why Ernst has to die. It is not Ernst as an individual whom Irene must kill, but Ernst as a symbol of the continued influence of patriarchy in Irene's thoughts. Irene finds Ernst "barring her way" (199) when she tries to leave with Zubeydeh, and it is only by killing him rather than letting him exercise his real (and greater) power over her that she can escape, both physically from Ernst and also emotionally from her desire to please him.

The murder of Ernst is the first blow that Irene strikes against the system of patriarchy that he represents. Thus it is vital to the novel's themes that he be killed (even though he may be a nice individual): the death emphasises the importance of structural analysis and structural change. It is important to understand this is a deliberate and rational—if painful—choice that Irene makes, not as a glamorization of violence or "male" models of power. The shooting is not narrated in any detail and the preceding fight emphasises only the degree to which the structural differences between them will always disadvantage Irene so long as she plays by patriarchy's rules. During the fight, Ernst contemplates whether or not he is willing to "hurt Irene" and decides he will "have to" (201). Although Ernst is still presented as a sympathetic character who does not *want* to hurt Irene, what is also evident in this quotation is that for Ernst winning is a matter of deciding to. Irene, on the other hand, is engaged in a serious struggle. In the past she has told Ernst, "*I fight well because I'm bad at it and I practice. You play at it*" (201). Russ emphasizes throughout the novel that gender relations can be a game only for the gender with power, a point made even more strongly in another of her novels, *On Strike Against God* (1980c). This later novel considers the desire for violence that years of systemic discrimination can inculcate in women, and ends with a direct address to the reader: "How can I tell you never to kill for pleasure, never to kill for sport, never to kill for cruelty, but above all, don't play fair, because when they invite you in, remember: we aren't playing" (105).

Recognizing that while gender struggle and violence may be a game for men, they are deadly serious for women, Irene decides to kill Ernst. She does not feel joy or even anger when she kills him, but rather does so with the realization that she will continue to lose so long as she plays fair. This analysis is suggestive for third-wave feminists, who believe that they can "play" with gender roles, choosing for themselves how much or how little they want to embody the various female stereotypes that circulate in our culture. I am not suggesting that all such ludic and ironic feminism is "wrong" or is simply internalized patriarchy. I *am* arguing that it is important to remember when engaging in such play that women enter the field on disadvantaged terms. We cannot "play fair" as the game, the culture, is not fair to us. It is to our own peril that we lose sight of the structural persistence of patriarchy, as Irene had lost sight of it. However, as she kills Ernst: "She's coming out of a thirty years' trance, a lifetime's hypnosis. She used to think it mattered who won and who lost, who was shamed and who was not. She forgot what she had up her sleeve. Sick of the contest of strength and skill, she shoots him" (203). Ernst had thought of her strength as a "nuisance" (201), but one that he could overcome if he so chose. The gun is Irene's only way to be more than mere annoyance.

It is essential to remember that killing Ernst is about removing the structural and systemic impediment that he represents, not about attacking Ernst as an individual.[5] The novel makes it clear that this situation is not Ernst's fault, but he nonetheless bears some responsibility for it simply because of his unwillingness to live in Irene's world as Irene sees it. Irene knows that Ernst is always gentle and kind to her, but just as consistently condescending and closed. He listens to her, but follows his own counsel and overrules her in times of disagreement. His very reasonableness is the source of some of her rage, although at first Irene tries to see things as Ernst does and thinks, "it can't have anything to do with him. She knows that she's perceiving him through some kind of distortion, that it's not fair to him" (166). From one point of view, this statement is accurate. Irene's rage has nothing to do with Ernst as an individual and she does perceive him in a "distorted" way. From another point of view, however, the distortion is merely what it feels like to live a life structured by systemic but often unacknowledged gender discrimination.

Although there are third-wave feminists who try to reduce the feminist movement to misandry (Hoff Sommers, for example, favors this argument) or attacks on individual men, this approach is not the point. Just as women need to recognize that we need to address the systems of discrimination structurally, at their root, we also need to recognize that a critique of patriarchy is not the same as nor reducible to a critique of individual men. Clearly, one can always find examples of men who are friends and allies. Nonetheless, the system of gender oppression continues to privilege these men (though not through their own culpability), and attacking this system may indeed appear to be attacks on such men. From this point of view, we need to see the murder of Ernst as a symbol rather than as an act between individuals. It is important to note that the novel shifts modes when this violence is introduced as well; what had been a largely realist adventure story becomes a self-reflexive narrative in which the author directly addresses the reader's disappointment that things had to come to this violent impasse. Irene herself notes that Ernst "was kind and gentle, he was a truly good man; nonetheless, he was going to return her to Center (for her own good), stick her in a desk job (if they had one), or maybe just send her home. . . . As the ladies of Ka'abah would say, there are the gentlemen who, weeping, send you back to your parents because you are not stable enough; there are the gentlemen who refrain; there are the gentlemen who push you down a flight of concrete stairs; there are the gentlemen who (for your own good) lock you up, either on Ka'abah or not on Ka'abah" (165). From this point of view, Ernst is killed not because of his individuality, but because he is functioning as an agent of a system that is going to take away Irene's identity. Eliminating him is the only way she can prevent that from happening.

Thinking about the withdrawal of affection as the primary disciplinary mode of nominally equitable patriarchy is particularly instructive here. The fear, frustration, and self-hatred that are the consequences of living under such a system, of continually but delicately being reminded of your precarious status within this system, are what produce the anger and desire for mastery that might be expressed through things such as murder. Other Russ protagonists also feel this urge, from Joanna in *The Female Man* who slams a man's finger in a car door (although she is then consumed by guilt by this minor act of insurrection) to Esther in *On Strike Against God* who responds to being asked by a condescending male companion "what's it like to be a woman" with "I took my rifle from behind my chair and shot him dead. 'It's like that,' I said.

No, of course I didn't" (6). The desire to be able to assert mastery if only for an instant is "what it's like to be a woman" under patriarchy. Zubeydeh also shows evidence of this tendency. One night Irene finds her bullying and sexually molesting a younger child, Michael. When confronted with her behavior, Zubeydeh knows that it is wrong and displays some of the self-hatred that is one of the sources of her desire in the first place, saying, "I'm bad, I'm bad, I'm bad" (126). She goes on to explain that her actions emerged from her feeling of helplessness and dependence, her realization that men "can do without us. . . . Uncle knows that. When he wants to show me he disapproves, he just gets very quiet; that's to show that he can withdraw his love. He doesn't have to fight about it." She adds "That's why I dragged Michael around, because he's so little and alone that he needed me more" (162).

Thus, our discomfort with the murder of Ernst in the novel cannot be used to condemn Irene or transform her action into one of despair or irrationality. It is a very rational—if horrible—response to an intolerable situation. To remove Irene's action from the category of protest and place it in the category of pathology does her and the novel a great disservice. When the system is biased against you, only revolutionary options are efficacious, as Esther and her friend Jean decide in On Strike Against God: "What do you do when the club won't let you in, when there's no other, and when you won't (or can't) change? Simple. You blow the club up" (85). We must also remember that the murder of Ernst is not the first act of violence in this struggle, although it is frequently described as such. Understanding The Two of Them within the context of the later novel is also useful here. In On Strike Against God, Esther and Jean take up shooting as a hobby and—although they shoot only bottles—they fantasize about shooting a man. Esther points out that this desire is only shocking when removed from its context of systemic patriarchy. If the desire is placed back in its context, however, it becomes rather more ordinary. Esther wonders, "Why is wanting to be able to kill a man so bizarre? Men kill men. Watch TV. Men kill women on TV." Jean's response is "Monopolistic practices" (96). We see violence against women as normal (expected if not condoned) while violence by women seems shocking. Irene notes with irony: "The ladies go mad with guilt if they leave the gentlemen or stop caring about the gentlemen or say nasty things about the gentlemen; the gentlemen run the ladies over with cars or shoot them or rape them or break their necks or strangle them or push them off high buildings (the taped stories in the library)" (164). That Irene has learned these norms from the taped stories shows the role that culture plays in producing such expectations and stresses all the more why it is important for us think about a novel, The Two of Them, that uses violence in another way.

The narrator recognizes that violence, particularly violence against a well-liked character such as Ernst, is a problem. The text notes that other ways of trying to conclude the novel and facilitate Irene's escape with Zubeydeh have been explored: "I've contemplated giving Ernst stomach 'flu and letting the other two run while he's retching, but I don't think so. Not really. I don't think it happens like that" (198). The text also briefly offers the consolation of Ernst being stunned rather than killed by the shot, "and that he'll come looking for her, penitent, contrite, having learned his lesson. Well, no, not really" (205). Although emotionally appealing on one level, neither of these conclusions is satisfactory because they leave Ernst in place as the "daddy" from whom both Zubeydeh and Irene continue to want approval, the figure of patriarchy who can still withdraw affection and approval and thus "discipline" the "ladies." As Irene notes, despite her personal pain and at times her desire, she is "*too old for a Daddy*" (163).

This desire to appease, to have "a daddy," also seems to be something that troubles third-wave feminism and its sometimes too-anxious desire to insist that it is not "against" men. In this, third-wave feminists mistake a critique of a gender system that structurally privileges men over women with an attack on the individual men who are thereby privileged. It is not surprising that third-wave feminism is unable to make this distinction between attacking men and attacking patriarchy: the structural level of analysis is precisely what this version of feminism too often lacks. It is equally interesting to read some third-wave feminist statements in light of *The Two of Them* and its struggle to escape the desire for "daddy's" approval. Hoff Sommers, for example, is quick to see a conspiracy on the part of any woman she sees promoting a "gender" feminist agenda in education and elsewhere. When she encounters such a program being championed by a *man*, however, she is quick to leap to his defense:

> When I heard Mr. Goldberg say this [that adjustments need to be made to the curriculum as "a vindication of the simple and honest concept that scholarship should reflect contributions of all"], it confirmed my belief that many well-meaning government officials do not understand the implications of the feminist demand for a more woman-centered curriculum. Goldberg is not a "gynocrat"; he is probably an old-fashioned equity feminist who wants a fair deal for women in education. (83)

Similarly, Roiphe feels that men who consume pornography need to be defended against "overzealous" crusaders such as Catherine MacKinnon. Against MacKinnon's reading of pornography as a literature of male domination of women, Roiphe argues: "How many of these men are compensating for how short they are or how little money they make? She overlooks the numbness, the mechanical way in which they reach into their pockets for money. The joy and elation, the naked will to power, and the male pleasure in subjugating women she describes doesn't seem to be the whole story" (157).

Reading these defenses, I cannot but think of Irene's struggle *not* to appease Ernst, to see him as an ally (even when he does not act as one). When Irene and Ernst fight about her plan to find out what Trans Temp is really up to (a plan he resists), she finds herself thinking, "*He's old, that's all it is*, but hears Zubeydeh saying: Daddy loves my poems" (172). Even after her father rips up her poems in front of her and insists that she should abandon this "male" goal, a part of Zubeydeh still wants to believe that "Daddy doesn't want me to be a poet, but that's only because he's afraid I'll fail. He doesn't understand, but I'll convince him. I know it's not good for women to be poets, but I'm different" (110). Such third-wave feminists need to learn to kill the patriarchal voice within—symbolized in the novel by Irene killing Ernst—and discover the painful truth with which Irene finally confronts Ernst: "you like me being aggressive as long as I don't cross you" (178). We must learn to "question the system" not just "insist that [we are] outside it" (111).

By recognizing the continued need for radical feminism, for feminism whose goal is to enact systemic and structural changes to patriarchy, third-wave feminism will truly be able to continue the feminist tradition and move on to address the needs of a new generation of women. So long as it remains focused on personal fulfillment or exceptional women, the third wave will be feminist in name only. Those who call themselves feminists but promote a backlash agenda (such as Roiphe and Hoff Sommers) are a warning of what third-wave feminism risks becoming unless it can learn, as Irene did, the importance of feminist collectivity, of seeing continuity among women, even between those more privileged within patriarchy and those still struggling with its more overtly oppressive forms. There are third-wave feminist voices that recognize this problem and one can only hope that they will be heard and will enable many younger women to experience an epiphany like Irene's. In *Third Wave Agenda* (1997) Leslie Heywood and Jennifer Drake acknowledge that this noncollective vision is a limit of third-wave ideology: "Despite our knowing better, despite our knowing its emptiness, the ideology of individualism is still a major motivating force in many third wave lives" (11). Like Irene, third-wave feminists need to recognize that gender oppression shapes not only the past and other places but also continues to shape their own lives. Not until they are able to recognize the persistence of patriarchal power will they be able to escape it by refusing, as Irene eventually does, to play its games.

It is painful but necessary that Irene's escape must come at the cost of Ernst's death. Were he to survive, the transformation would not be sufficiently radical. My third point is that we need new stories to tell, new gender roles, entirely new logics through which to structure our experience. The novel must thwart our conventional expectation that a sympathetic male character such as Ernst might be redeemed and allow Irene to learn to "make it on her own," just as Mary Richards on *The Mary Tyler Moore Show* (which Zubeydeh watches at the end of the novel) tries to do. Conventional endings allow conventional gender assumptions to creep back in; thus, however emotionally satisfying they might be, they are politically unproductive. As Russ (1980c) stresses in *On Strike Against God*:

> At this point some hapless liberal sees the end-papers approaching and has started looking frantically for the Reconciliation Scene. It (the liberal) is either cursing itself for having got entrapped in what started as a perfectly harmless story of love, poignancy, tragedy, self-hatred, and death or—rather smugly—is disapproving of me for not possessing Shakespeare's magnificent gift of reconciliation which (if you translate it) means that at this point I must (1) meet a wonderful ideal man and fall in love with him, or (2) kill myself. (101)

Instead of reproducing this tired old plot, feminism—third wave and beyond—must rediscover collectivity, must do without the consolation of Ernst's survival, and must remember that we are not alone. Irene has only entered on the first step of this journey by the end of *The Two of Them*, having moved from reliance on "a daddy," a couple formed with Ernst, to the new "two of them," Irene and Zubeydeh, struggling to make it without the support of Ernst or Center. Two is not a collectivity, of course, but we hope that Irene and Zubeydeh will find other women; the novel ends with a vision of something arising out of nothing: the last lines are "they rise" (226). Cortiel (1999) argues that in this conclusion: "The two female protagonists . . . come to discard their status as extraordinary individuals and cooperate in a rescue operation which ultimately aims at the 'rescue' of all women from patriarchy" (107). The ending of *On Strike Against God* is a much more overt call to a feminist collective, compensating the reader for the lack of the Reconciliation Scene with an offer of community instead: "Hello. Hello, out there. . . . Did you think you had no allies? What I want to say is, there are all of us; what I want to say is, we're all in it together" (106).

I would like to conclude with one more pair suggested by the title of *The Two of Them*, the "pair" of second-wave and third-wave feminism (both heterogeneous within themselves, one must remember). Despite their differences, so long as we remember "we're all in it together," that the root of gender oppression is structural and it must be fought on this level, then second- and third-wave feminism might be allies. This is possible so long as second- and third-wave perceive themselves to be a pair, which is possible only if third-

wave feminism learns Irene's lesson. It is important for second-wave feminism to listen to the voices of a younger generation and acknowledge the ways
in which their oppression is not like our own precisely because of the very victories that second-wave feminism has won. It is equally important for third-
wave feminists not to let a sentimentality about these victories blind us to the
ways that equality has not been achieved. Gender discrimination still shapes
experience. Both Irene and Zubeydeh need to learn to stop being exceptional
and realize that it is the gender system that needs to change, not their individual circumstances. Feminism as a movement and individual feminists
within it must do likewise.

~

## 7 "That Is Not Me. I Am Not That"

### Anger and the Will to Action in Joanna Russ's Fiction

PAT WHEELER

> But holy peanut butter, dear writer . . . do you imagine that anyone with half a
> functional neuron can read your work and not have his fingers smoked by the bitter,
> multi-layered anger in it? It smells and smolders like a volcano buried so long and
> deadly it is just beginning to wonder if it can explode.
>
> —James Tiptree, Jr., letter to Joanna Russ

In an article written over ten years ago, "Empathic Ways of Reading: Narcissism, Cultural Politics, and Russ's 'Female Man,'" Judith Gardiner (1994) says she was "struck not by how fresh it was but by how dated it seemed." She goes on to say: "This is a heavy-handed treatment of a situation that I now find embarrassing even to recall. It's hard for me to recapture the fresh moral indignation of that time, its conviction of rightness, the enthusiasm and group solidarity of its feminist anger yet also its despair at patriarchal odds, its effrontery in demanding to overturn all of human history, and its blithe effacement of potentially troubling differences among women" (87).

It seems obvious that women's writing reveals something about the world of women during particular periods and the rage and anger in Russ's seminal novel certainly keyed into the zeitgeist of radical feminist politics of the day. Russ's protagonists are frequently angry, even downright unpleasant; they are prepared to risk conflict and even to kill in order to make transgressive crossings to new spaces, to new areas of representation. As Jael says, "Murder is my one way out" (Russ 1975b, 195). The contemporaneous radical readings of Russ's fictions are, of course, products of their time, but equally, when third-wave feminists look for new strategies, women's continued oppression cannot be overlooked. Not *all* women have achieved agency and Russ's angry rhetoric still has plenty to say. Sarah Appleton Aguair (2001) contends that in certain feminist fictions the reclamation of "unsavory behavior, flaws, failings and downright nastiness" is essential in order that women are not simply objectified as any other "silenced heroine." (6) And Clare Watling (1993) argues that

contemporary women writers explore violence, anger, and their relation to sadism so that female readers "might experience certain satisfaction at the victorious conclusions of the exchange" (196, 199). Anger is a unifying force in Russ's fiction, an oppositional strategy that offers ways of reading and writing that subvert the notion that the female subject is acted upon, rather than active.

In her discussion of transgressions and borders, Gloria Anzaldúa (1987) argues that "whatever the ground on which one stands, whether the center or the margin, one faces in each movement an Other/ground which is threatening—the unknown. Only by violating the boundaries of the familiar and proper, risking conflict, can one reach toward connection" (45). Russ transgresses those "familiar and proper" boundaries in her storytelling, in both the subject matter and in the telling of her stories. She uses anger to communicate powerfully women's sense of alienation, as well as the dissatisfaction that arises out of estrangement and social fragmentation. Russ's stories are carefully constructed and utilize a full range of emotions and styles in which she explores the ways that women and girls are acculturated into social attitudes. Her writing exemplifies the ways in which anger can be amplified and used to instigate women's vocalization against oppression and silence. She creates imaginative visions of the strength and intensity of women's rage that are indispensable to the intellectual and political potency of women's writing. And she uses the anger of her protagonists and narrators to "move women from unconscious passivity into clarity and the will to act" (Kaye/Kantrowitz 1992, 24). In a letter to Susan Koppelman, Russ (1998c) writes about a young woman's paper on one of her stories: "I ache for her—because she's young—but *where is her anger?* I think from now on, I will not trust anyone who isn't angry" (63; emphasis in original). Russ's writing self-consciously keys into the anger that is one of the most powerful forces shaping contemporary women's writing. Anger will not go away and in Russ's writing it becomes part of an affirming self-knowledge.

Russ's work displays tangible renderings of anger that makes visible women's disaffection and feelings of alienation and estrangement. She deploys this aesthetic of anger to address issues of gender and sexuality and provides a reading experience that is transformative. Russ subverts the unifying affirmation and recognition of women's position in society and shows how escape can be actuated through contact with other women (the "rescue" theme apparent through much of her work). In *The Female Man*, with Joanna's narrative, Russ offers a multiplicity of experiences ordered through the appearance of verisimilitude, where differences may be reconciled under the mutual recognition of the oppression. Those experiences that are "knowable" and therefore shared are public, and those that are "unknowable" or impossible to reconcile, are private. Jael's fearlessness and ferocity challenge received notions of gender and her overt anger empowers the other Js. In "The Book of Joanna" she informs us: "I committed my first revolutionary act yesterday. I shut the door on a man's thumb. I did it for no reason at all and I didn't warn him; I just slammed the door shut in a rapture of hatred and imagined the bone breaking and the edges grinding into his skin. . . . Horrible. Horrible and wild" (203). Russ offsets the "realities" of Joanna's position with those experienced by her other protagonists to offer a balance of form in which subjectivity and judgment, based on individual personal perceptions of patriarchy and oppression, can coexist with wider externally observed facts regarding the position of women in other worlds and other societies.

In much of Russ's work the tropes of space/time continuums fulfill important roles: they provide both the sites of struggle over cultural meanings of gender (in the world as we know it) and they offer (in other worlds) the potential for future emancipation for women. *The Female Man* has four women who could travel to one another's worlds, to one another's past and futures. This time-traveling device, or time loop, is used to great effect in Russ's oeuvre, particularly in stories such as "The Second Inquisition" (in Russ 1983a), "The Autobiography of My Mother," and "The Little Dirty Girl" (both in Russ 1987a, to which this essay is referenced). This narrative convention allows disparate women, or versions of the same woman, to connect. Women of different generations and from parallel universes interact, often in the most personal and intimate ways and frequently giving voice to their anger at women's lack of autonomy or women's lack of will to effect change.

The narrator of "The Autobiography of My Mother" is on an endless quest as she visits her mother at various stages in her life; she is caught in a perpetual mother/daughter time loop. In a series of encounters with her mother the narrator seeks to explicate feminism's project of emancipation. She turns on a "bullying, leering, ironical boldness" to force her mother to consider her life (208). "Consider what you gain by not marrying," she says. "Be the first one on your block; astonish your friends" (209). Russ calls for women to seek agency, to go against the grain of society's expectations. The narrator seeks to "rescue" her mother from being a victim. The various scenarios enacted by the mother/daughter examine the ways in which women both validate and nullify each other. The narrator informs her mother: "When women first meet they dislike each other (because it's expected of them)" and that this soon "gives way to a feeling of mutual weakness and worthlessness." Inevitably the "feeling of being one species leads in turn to plotting, scheming and shared conspiracies" (210). Russ's anger at the ways in which society devalues women is tangible, although paradoxically it is not clear whether the women conspire against each other or with each other. The narrative never fully reconciles this

dichotomy and the narrator's desire to conspire both with and against her
mother's choices in life is only partly successful. Russ shows how anger can
be used constructively to compel women to examine the systems that dominate their lives and the role they play in their continuance.

In "The Second Inquisition," the final story in The Adventures of Alyx, Russ
examines the ways that young girls are inculcated into acquiescent modes of
behavior and how, through connection to a woman from 450 years in the future, the narrator begins to see a different life for herself. In this story the anger is symbolic, more an assertion of growing rebellion against the status quo
and the event of struggle against parental oppression. At one stage the father
asks: "Is my daughter being angry? . . . Is my daughter being rebellious? (168).
The story encapsulates the changing sensibility of the girl and is perhaps the
least "science fiction" of the Alyx stories, grounded as it is in a traditional
realist narrative that only occasionally deviates into other worlds and other
possibilities. And even this deviation is tentative; we are not sure whether the
interior narrative of Morlocks at war is part of the young narrator's imagination, as she reads H. G. Wells's The Time Machine, or if Wells's fictional race is
evoked as a metaphor for the girl's fear and uncertainty. The visitor from other
worlds is ostensibly the great-granddaughter of Alyx, but the narrator says at
one point, "it was almost a pity she was not really there." It is almost as if the
imaginative young narrator conjures up the woman in order to have an outlet
for her boredom and frustration.

The science fiction elements of the story are most clearly realized when
the two women combine to kill the man who threatens them both and in
the fight among the "Morlock" aggressors. The violence takes on a symbolic
meaning when the woman kills the visitor with a hot poker, crushing his wind-
pipe so he cannot speak and "finishing the job on his throat . . . with the thick
heel of her silver shoe" (181). It is clear that the woman has to keep the young
narrator alive, or at least keep her anger at her oppression alive. At one stage
she says to her, "without you all is lost" (172). The time-travel device offers a
call to women to connect, but connection alone is never enough. Women must
speak out about their estate. The visitor in "The Second Inquisition" tells the
young woman, "I am not you . . . but I have had the same thoughts and now
I have come back four hundred and fifty years. Only there is nothing to say.
There is never anything to say" (190). It is up to the young woman to speak her
story in her own time; the visitor can only free her imagination (indeed, she is
probably only in her mind). She says, "My dear, I wished to take you with me;
but that's impossible" (191). The narrator is left looking at herself, dressed in
the uniform of the Trans-Temporal Military Authority. There can be no resolution to the vexing questions of women's ordained existence—for Russ there
can never be—the fight goes on. The uniform from the future tells us that. In

"The Second Inquisition" there is more emphasis on recognition rather than resolution. Through her engagement with the older woman the young narrator comes to knowledge of herself, in the same way that the older narrator of "The Little Dirty Girl" comes to self-knowledge through the acceptance of her younger self, who visits her in the form of a ghostly girl.

Russ's preoccupation with mother/daughter and older/younger women relationships comes to the fore in many of her short stories. In "The Little Dirty Girl" the narrator, A.R., meets a "passionate and resentful" child, "a wandering Fury, with the voice of a Northwest-coast Raven" (8). The child, a manifestation born out of her relationship with her mother, is alienated and angered by her mother's apparent disinclination to love her. In this story Russ exemplifies notions of abjection as an examination of repression. The abject, angry child needs to be loved and accepted and the narrator learns to embrace all of her: "her shit, her piss, her sweat, her tears, her scabby knees, the snot on her face, her cough, her dirty panties, her bruises, her desperation, *her anger* [emphasis mine] her whims" (16).

The maternal body (in this instance the self as both daughter and mother) is a model for the relationship between the self and the actual mother/daughter relationship. In accepting the abject she achieves autonomy. Nonetheless, the anger the child expresses still resonates in the older woman's relationship with her own mother. Once she accepts the child she decides she will be "openly angry" with her mother, "only there was nothing to be angry about, this time" (18). The woman who had kept "her fury and betrayal and misery to herself" finds that once she had embraced the dirty little girl to herself she was able to move forward in her relationship with her mother (20). What is apparent here is that in Russ's writing, conceptions of identity are plural and flexible. According to Julia Kristeva (1982) women achieve agency when they can shape and participate in more than one discourse. There is little doubt that within "The Little Dirty Girl," there are many divergent voices—the child, the narrator, the mother—that fulfill the dialogic conventions required to reach agency. As Kristeva would argue, women are always negotiating the other within, and this is what Russ makes visible.

In these short stories Russ draws on other literary works, and uses intertextual references to other stories, other novels (both her own and other authors'), to further break the narrative frame. Each story is simultaneously independent and stands alone in its examination of women's lives, but taken as a whole, the body of work constitutes an important engagement with women's political fight for autonomy. In the above short stories Russ enacts what critics have called "the rescue of the female child theme"—a theme also apparent in *The Two of Them*. In *Demand My Writing* (1999), Jeanne Cortiel's authoritative study of Russ's work, she argues that rescue elements are present in Russ's work "in most, if not all intimate relationships between women." I tend to agree with Cortiel's assessment that the "rescue" element is ever-present but that it does not always end in freedom from oppression (133). According to Russ for the adolescent girl, entry into women's estate is often not a broadening out but a diminution of life. This can be seen in The Two of Them, where Zubeydeh, a twelve year-old girl, living in a quasi-Islamic, misogynist society finds her childish exuberances to misbehave tolerated when young, but her freedom beginning to diminish as she reaches puberty. For Zubeydeh, Simone de Beauvoir's notion (evoked by Russ in "Recent Feminist Utopias") of "the prison bars of femininity," that on puberty, "shut the girl up for good" are a self-fulfilling destiny (Russ 1981). She is "rescued" from her family and her planet by agents of the Trans Temp Agency. They do so at the request of the child because she wants to be a poet and this is an honor only allowed boys in her society. Ironically Irene, one of the agents, who is so angry at the way in which the women on the planet are treated, fails to see how she is the victim of a more covert form of misogyny from her partner and the agency for which she works.

The rescue of the female child, is, as discussed above, important to Russ's work. She argues that this act "speaks to an adolescence that is still the rule rather than the exception for women, one made painful by the closing in of sexist restrictions, sexual objectification, or even downright persecution" (145).

Russ does not offer "imaginary solutions" to the problems women face. In The Two of Them Russ again revisits what she sees as the main source of women's oppression: the family. In this novel she coalesces the lives of all four women protagonists in The Female Man into that of one woman, Irene, who is a skilled agent of the Trans Temp Agency, on a mission to the planet Ka'abah. The family, a site of patriarchal power and a microcosm of the wider influences that are brought to bear on women, figures in all its guises on Irene's Earth, on the planet she visits, and in her filial relationships with her mother, Rose, and her rescued "daughter" Zubeydeh. Her partner, mentor, and lover, Ernst, the company she works for and her relationships within The Gang function within the novel to show how, when women believe themselves to be free of constraint, they are still in chains. Irene's relationship with Ernst is not as it seems and in her emancipatory journey to understand this Russ very consciously moves the narrative through various emotions; from comedy to anger and through hope and potential emancipation to something much bleaker at the end of the novel. Russ uses the "paraliterary" conventions of genre fiction to "express what can't easily be contained in realism" (1995i, 162). This typical postmodern trope is a conscious destabilizing of realist narrative conventions that occurs throughout the novel.

In *The Two of Them* the interior thought processes and narrative complexity are resonant of her earlier work, *The Female Man*, but Russ takes her writing strategies a stage further here, drawing more heavily on the power of satire. Russ is fully aware of the power this has. James English (1994) argues: "The potential comedy of ideological narratives is not only that of a society whose defining law or principle of selection, whose quintessence, excludes its own actual members, but that of a field of action on which the would-be political subject can never be in the right place at the right time" (161).

If the "field of action," as English argues, is patriarchy, or women's oppression, or compulsory heterosexuality, then feminist practice must be the refusal to play by the rules. The politics of identity are at the forefront of the narrative in Russ's angry, satirical exposition of gender ideology on the planet. In her discussion of gender identity, Judith Butler (1990) makes the point that primary gender identity can be parodied within cultural practices of drag and cross-dressing. The performance of drag plays upon the distinction between the anatomy of the performer and the gender that is being performed. In making 'Alee believe that Irene is a man, Russ shows the dissonance not only between sex and gender but between what Butler calls the regulatory fiction of heterosexuality. On Ka'abah: "There is a saying that no man is truly fine-looking who could not play the role of female impersonator in the theatre" (22).

'Alee's comment reveals both a radical disunity of heterosexual coherence and a potential transfiguration of male sexuality. However, the same metamorphosis is not available to women on the planet. It is a given that while men can and do play the role of women in Ka'abah society, "a real female could not impersonate a female-impersonator. That would unbalance everything" (27). Russ shows that masculinity and femininity are transmutable—and that the attributes that have been socially adjudged as masculine can be found in women *and* men, and those adjudged as feminine can be found in men *and* women.

The potential that transgendered bodies (with their temporary shifts of gender identity) offer to a denaturalization of "natural" gender attributes is clear. For 'Alee, however, this only works in one way: masculinity can incorporate attributes of femininity, but femininity in women must stand alone. When his wife begins to fail in her role he reminds her of her "duty": "[He] talks to her seriously . . . driving home his points with unnecessary repetition (but it relieves his feelings) and representing to her that she is neglecting her duties, that she has abandoned every woman's lifelong project of forming a feminine personality—and has become unbalanced inside in consequence" (40).

The maternal function is used here to emphasize the dynamics of oppression. Irene is a threat to 'Alee as she stands outside the subjective group identity of women on the planet. The wish to exclude or negate through vilification anything that lies outside the knowable community is considerable. He accuses Irene of having discarded all those elements that would determine her femininity, saying "where are your children?" and wondering "why has this unnatural woman removed her veils and her beauty spot, her necklaces, the dye on her fingernails?" (30). Irene the woman, according to 'Alee masquerades as a man. Russ's ironic re-creation of gender bias on Ka'abah is played out in other aspects of Irene's life. Not until later does she realize that misogyny is rife in the Trans Temp Agency and in her own relations with Ernst (Freedman 2000, 135)

Ernst initially seems to approve of Irene's liberation from gender constraints. Nonetheless, we are constantly reminded that beneath the "new" man exterior lurks something darker. He calls her Sklodowska (ostensibly a pet name) but which means: "*I know your anger is only put on.*" He secretly thinks: "*You'd complain in Heaven, just to keep your credit up*" (13, 14; emphasis in original). He becomes distant, withdrawing his attention from early on in the mission until she is forced to ask: "All right, Conscience Neumann, what have I done wrong this time." She finds herself constantly apologizing: "Ernst, I'm sorry. Really I am. It's unprofessional. It's not objective. It's all that. Why you hired me I'll never know. . . . I still don't know what you see in me" (33). As Ernst constantly undermines Irene while appearing to validate her as autonomous (and thereby alienating her), so Zubeydeh comes to be more important to her. Irene, apparently "rescued" by Ernst from a stultifying existence on her world, determines to rescue Zubeydeh from hers.

It is through Irene's relationships with David and Ernst that Russ satirizes notions of essentialism and biological determinism. In a short encounter that the young Irene has with her lover, David, Russ's ironic humor predominates, but the anger that underpins their encounter is always palpable. Irene has already fully embraced her sexuality: "she wanted to laugh and say coarse things, bite him, throw him down and sit on him." She knows this goes against the grain: "It occurred to her that she wasn't normal . . . she always seemed to want more" (52). After they have sex, David proposes to her but she replies that she does not want to get married. He says, "don't you want children?" When she replies in the negative he calls her "neurotic." This produces in her "a nagging feeling that she wanted to fuck again, really hard this time; she wishes she could tape his mouth and throw him down" (54). The incongruity of (and identification with) the situation in which Irene finds herself evokes self-conscious laughter—a knowing awareness of Irene's sensations and thoughts.

Russ uses the anger of her protagonist, offset by humor, to accentuate a highly politicized debate about gender and sexuality. She uses the situation to both reveal the (supposedly) inappropriate and unsuitable behavior of Irene (in 1950s America, young women were not supposed to even *think* in this manner) and to offer a clear indication as to why Irene has a strong desire to change her situation. In *The Female Man*, Russ memorably wrote that to be a woman is to be a "honeypot . . . the vagina dentata and the stuffed teddy bear that is every man's prize" (134). David obviously believes Irene is his "prize," but she has other ideas. This section exemplifies many feminist concerns about women's "nature" and about the socially constructed determination of both gender and sexuality. Russ is savagely satirical about the roles women are expected to play as David puts forward the following arguments:

> "A mother who works is neglecting her children";
> "But you've got to stay at home when the children are young";
> "Of course I wouldn't mind my wife having a career, but the children come first. I couldn't allow anything else";
> "I feel very sorry for women who don't want children; they're just not normal";
> "Your mother had the normal fulfillment of a woman's life."
> Irene's response is swift: "She hit him." (54–56)

The humor of the situation and the violence perpetrated by Irene brings together what Umberto Eco (1984) calls a "disturbing ensemble of diverse and not completely homogeneous phenomena"; that is, irony, parody, satire, and wit (1). In the encounter between David and Irene, Russ exemplifies a range of primary theories of humor. These are, according to most theorists, superiority theories, repression/release theories, and incongruity theories. They can loosely be understood as laughter that is associated with the glorification of the self, usually at the expense of someone else; the release of repression (usually sexual and emotional) and the collision of two seemingly disparate worlds within a single context. Eco refers to "the broken frame" of reference (which must be presupposed, but never spelled out) for humor to occur and argues that one must understand "to what degree certain behaviors are forbidden" in order to appreciate their transgression. In the above quotations humor "breaks the frame" of patriarchal reference to "underscore the absurdities" inherent within that frame. In Russ's narrative anger and satire combine to empower Irene; she becomes what Aguair (2001) calls a "vital woman" armed with ruthless survival instincts.

Russ's protagonists frequently disregard the laws and rules socially imposed on them and indulge in quite exuberant transgressions. Russ's skill at satire is occasionally overlooked in the earnest criticism of her work and her reputation as a radical, materialist feminist. According to Simon Critchley

(2002), for humor to work there has to be "a sort of tacit consensus," implicit shared understanding as to what constitutes the joke. He argues that "in order for the incongruity of the joke to be seen as absurd," there has to be congruence between the structure of the joke and the social structure. In other words, if there is no social congruity, then there is no comic incongruity (4). Henri Bergson (1921) believes humor "must answer to certain requirements . . . it must have a *social* significance" (65). In the encounter between young Irene and David, the humor derives from our understanding of the social significance of Irene's behavior and her acknowledgment of it; she has behaved inappropriately and feels furious and vulnerable. She compares her behavior to that of Irene Adler (Iren*ee*), the only woman to have outwitted Sherlock Holmes. In Arthur Conan Doyle's, "A Scandal in Bohemia" (1892) Irene Adler ("*the* woman") "has a soul of steel . . . the face of the most beautiful of women, and the mind of the most resolute of men" (12). Holmes is "beaten by a woman's wit" (32), not by violence. Even so, the strength of Russ's writing lies in our identification with Irene and the vicissitudes of her life. We experience vicarious pleasure from the fact that she hits him.

The stultifying atmosphere inherent in Ka'abah society and the technical advancements for surveillance and control on the planet are the means by which Russ maps the painful issues of women's lives. Zubeydeh's brother is aware of the restrictions placed on girls and thinks: "[It's] a shame that you girls can't have part of the country to yourselves, to live together and have love affairs, as we do. And we could pay you a good lot of money to raise the children until they were five. And then we could take the boys, maybe, I don't know. And have big parties a few times a year in which we all got together and danced and recited" (136).[1]

In this nod toward women's separatist utopian/dystopian science fictions, Russ directs our attention to the actuality of oppression and simultaneously envisions an escape from it. This escape, however, is not achieved without cost. The humor so clearly observed in the first half of the novel is gradually replaced by a darker, more pessimistic narrative and shows "a shift in perspective from the self and its ability to create a moral ambience through an act . . . to an emphasis on all the moving forces of life which converge collectively upon the individual" (Schulz x). The discovery of Zubeydeh's aunt locked in a cell evokes Charlotte Perkins Gilman's ghost story *The Yellow Wallpaper* and precipitates the rescue of Zubeydeh and the flight from Ka'abah.[2]

The evocation of women's madness in the novel is essential to examining the oppression of women. Zumurrud is crazy, medicated, and nullified; Rose (Irene's mother) has moments of madness, and both David and Ernst say that Irene is "crazy." In fact Ernst has always believed Irene was "deformed" (20). Toward the end, the feelings he has kept hidden rise to the surface. Our new man does not hesitate to question whether women can step outside their designated roles—whether they are up to a "man's job." He realizes: "*This is not the woman to be my successor* but things flash in his mind. *Are women—and Women don't—*, thoughts he knows are treasonous to Irene" (156).

Irene, as much a victim of cultural conditioning in her own way as Zubeydeh and Zumurrud, just apologizes over and over again: "Ernst I'm sorry. . . . I'm sorry. I'm sorry. I know. I'm sorry." She also begins to question her own sanity. Zubeydeh asks Irene if she enjoys being crazy and says: "Women always go crazy. My mother was crazy. . . . I go crazy too; I become my Bad Self. . . . I don't mind going crazy now and then and becoming my Bad Self; I think it's good for me. Poets need something like that. Anyway the gentlemen are always calling the ladies crazy and that's wrong" (173).

Russ's focus on issues of madness exemplifies the misogyny that confronts women when they express ideas and emotions that fall outside socially constructed modes of behavior. Irene serves as a means of expressing the ways in which women are inevitably invalidated. In the same way that the child enters the social order by paternal threats, so women are shown to remain under the same subjective process. Irene believes she "shouldn't have asked to be listened to," she says. "It's absurd." Rage. Defeat. Fear. Something is getting to her. She wonders if it's a replay situation, something from her earlier life (166).

The way in which Russ gradually introduces the everyday slights against Irene shows just how pervasive this form of (covert) subjugation of women is. Because she argues and rails against him, Irene becomes firmly ensconced in Ernst's mind as simply another "crazy" woman: "In his mind's eye she's surrounded by madwomen: Zudeydeh's mother, Zubeydeh's aunt, Irene's friend, Irene's mother, maybe Zubeydeh herself. They're sealed-off, self-possessed unhappy women, sinking back in to that sinister matrix Irene herself has always abhorred, something unformed and primitive, a paranoia so complete that it closes over its victim like a swap" (200).

According to Carl Freedman (2000), what Russ helps us to see is that "the psychiatric category of madness is among the most important of those putatively liberal and thus gender neutral tools actually used to perpetuate the subordination of women." He believes that *The Two of Them*, like no other novel, "powerfully demonstrates the relations that link social power, everyday details of routine and intimacy, and the formation and deformation of subjectivity itself" (143–144).

One thing Russ makes absolutely clear in her work is that transgression of the rules of "femininity" requires great strength of character. In *The Two of Them*, Irene's anger empowers her actions, and her will to change. Her rage at Ernst's actions against her is so absolute that "she almost breaks her hand against the wall." Ernst was "going to return her to The Center (for her own good), stick her in a desk job (if they had one) or maybe just send her home." He turns out to be the same as the gentlemen of Ka'abah, "who weeping, send you back to your parents because you are not stable enough; there are the gentlemen that refrain; there are the gentlemen who push you down a flight of concrete stairs; there are the gentlemen who (for your own good) lock you up (206). As Russ disintegrates the narrative frame, the author and the narrator come together to discuss the manner in which the mood changes: "Confess it; this is all very much nicer as comedy. . . . You don't want to know how Irene hates looking at that good man and neither do I. . . . I've contemplated giving Ernst stomach 'flu and letting the other two run while he's retching, but I don't think so. Not really. I don't think it happens like that" (198).

But this is not a comedy and Irene realizes she must fight Ernst to escape. After a prolonged struggle Irene becomes "sick of the contest of strength and skill" and so shoots him. The act is shocking in itself but particularly so as it follows a section where Ernst reflects on his own failings. Once again Russ intervenes: "It occurs to me that she only stunned him, that soon he'll get up, facing nothing worse than a temporary embarrassment . . . that he'll come looking for her, penitent, contrite, having learned his lesson. Well no—not really (205).

Ernst *has* to be removed from the story in order that Irene achieve the freedom to take that step toward agency. Irene and Zubeydeh escape from the ship and end isolated and alone, unimportant and powerless on a planet that may be Earth. She has, in effect, become her mother: Irene Rose Waskiewic and Irene and Zubeydeh are now "the two of them." Again Russ uses the time loop of mother/daughter relations—Irene is now the mother—inevitable, as she took Zubeydeh on her lap and soothed her tears. For Irene it is "Back to Square One. . . . Always back to Square One" (176).

Lefanu (1988) argues that Russ "challenges our own desires for happy endings" and certainly Russ firmly eschews a happy compromise at the end (xiv). Nonetheless, the feelings of desolation and helplessness are undercut by Russ's narrative of inclusiveness at the end of the novel. There are other women, "other unimportant and powerless people," and together something will be achieved (178). There is hope at the end of the novel as Irene realizes that for the first time "something will be created out of nothing" (226). As with other stories the older woman will empower the daughter figure (releasing her, we hope, from her ambition to be Mary Richards). Russ shows that anger or aggression, overt curiosity or explicit sexuality led, in many cases, to the vilification of the woman concerned. As Sarah Lefanu argues in her introduction to the new edition of *The Two of Them* (Russ 1987b), "the questions raised . . . have not been resolved . . . since its first publication." As Irene says:

"To come so far. . . . And all for nothing. . . . To make such a big loop—even into the stars—and all for nothing. She thinks: *What a treadmill*" (140). Ernst's insidious misogyny, cloaked by versions of a "new man" still has much to say about gender relations.

In her later work, *On Strike Against God* (1980c), Russ's anger *appears* to be somewhat tempered. The narrator, Esther, who is a professor of English, says, "after a while you tame your interior monsters, it's only natural. I don't mean that it ever stops; but it stops mattering" (8). Esther's disingenuous musing, however, belies the narrative thrust of the novel, which sees Russ's anger still razor-sharp and constant. "Shredder," a male academic, says to Esther, "You're strange animals you women intellectuals. Tell me: what's it like to be a woman?" In response she says, "I took my rifle from behind my chair and shot him dead. 'It's like that.' " She did not really do this and, unlike Ernst, he remains alive. Esther goes on to say, "It's not worth it, hating, and I'm going to be mature and realistic and not care, not care" (6). Whereas Irene *needed* to kill Ernst in order to move to that transgressive place of freedom, Esther knows she can make that change by her own volition. We follow her journey from a woman who (at her analyst's suggestion) tries to overcome her "compulsion to always have the last word with men" (5) to a radical feminist who believes women should "*Demand the Impossible*" (107; emphasis in original). Esther rages against a society where women "badmouth . . . [other] women . . . with that venomous sweetness that shows you how very feminine the woman is—she can't get angry openly, not even at another woman. Pathetic and awful" (13). Esther is not prepared to make a deal to be a woman. She is "something else," not a woman, and "never, never will be." The word is meaningless to her and she is "defeated by the irrelevant idiocy" of the classification. She says, "they got to my mother and made her a woman, but they won't get me" (18).

Despite attempting to "not care," Esther cares very much. She argues with friends, colleagues, and strangers, unleashing what she calls a "burst of idiot demonhood" (30) wherever she goes. Esther's monster refuses to be tamed: "The demon got up. The demon said Fool. To think you can eat their food and not talk to them. To think you can take their money and not be afraid of them. To think you can depend on their company and not suffer from them."

For Esther, and for Russ, women's estate never stops mattering. Esther says, "if we're going to talk about [women's liberation], let us please talk . . . seriously." She knows the man she talks with will say that "they always take pretty girls seriously," she will get angry and then she will say, "Why don't you cut off your testicles and shove them down your throat?" (31). She has tried being nice, but being nice does not get her anywhere and her encounters throughout the rest of the novel are striven with angry exchanges and thoughts of violence. She says "something is changing within me. . . . My demon . . . is back now, and now I don't mind" (29).

At the end of the novel Russ reflects on the ways her book might be read. The liberal, she says, is either "cursing for having got entrapped in what started as a perfectly harmless story of love, poignancy, tragedy and self-hatred and death—or rather smugly—is disapproving of me for not possessing Shakespeare's magnificent gift for reconciliation." The same liberal might concede "if pushed in a corner and yelled at by twenty angry radicals" that "morality does indeed begin at the mouth of a gun" (101). Russ argues that women's fear, frustration, and self-hate *can* end, and the call to militant action is clear: "You will some day soon see us on TV asked at a demonstration, or someone like me until she turns round—

> *Interviewer:* Who are you?
> *We (smiling):* Oh, somebody. A woman.
> *Interviewer:* But what's your name?
> *And we'll say very lightly and quickly:* My name is Legion." (102)

Esther's tamed demon has been set free. In Mark 5:9, Jesus asked the demon entity what its name was, and it replied, "My name is Legion for we are many." Russ goes on to describe many women, and then asks of them and us, "Did you think you had no allies? What I want to say is, there are all of us we're all in it together. . . . I've hung my red petticoat out on a stick and I'm signaling like mad, I'm trying to be seen" (106). The discovery of women's unity is, for Russ, a beginning. She warns of complacency:

> When I smile flatteringly at you, we're a liar.
> When we hate and need you, I'm dangerous.
> When they become indifferent, run for your life. (101)

Do not be seduced into thinking Russ has renounced anger when she writes: "The amazing peacefulness, the astonishing lack of anger, the sweetness and balm of being at last on the right side of power" (100). Her protagonist's greatest wish is still "*I want to be able to kill a man*" (98; emphasis in original).

Neil Nehring (1997) argues that "one encounters anger everywhere in women's writing about their own condition," and that "anger became guilt by association with its advocates' heavy-handed treatment of novels as direct embodiments of their authors' intentions and emotions" (120). We cannot assume that all texts written by women are feminist texts and that they may always and without exception be held to embody somehow and somewhere the author's anger against patriarchal oppression (Moi 1991, 62–63). Russ's images of disruptive or angry women serve as symbols of the potentiality of women's transgressive behavior. In part, feminism's ongoing fight is to examine essentialist constructions of women and to engage in debate regarding the multiplicity of female experience. Russ's fiction renegotiates the constraints of gender roles and compulsory heterosexuality and validates women's anger as part of the debate against essentialism. Anger is expressed against cultural, physical, and ideological oppression and is used as a positive force of expression. It is translated and transformed into violence, extremes of expression, and sexually liberating behavior, and the alienated, estranged, and isolated women are transformed by their anger. Russ's writing of and with anger provides a perceptive and penetrating narrative device for women writers: its continued application is a signifier of women's resistance, then and now.

## 8 Les Human Beans?

### Alienation, Humanity, and Community in Joanna Russ's On Strike Against God

KERIDWEN N. LUIS

Joanna Russ's *On Strike Against God* (Russ 1980c) is remarkable for its deft intertwining of many themes: not only the overt one of "coming out," but many intricately (and inevitably) interlaced stories of alienation, a search for community, and rebellion against how our society defines women. These themes are interdependent: how our society defines women leads to alienation leads to a search for a community for the "something-elses of the world" (19). The question of whether lesbians *can* be women—and, indeed, the related questions of what women are, and whether it is worth being one—are explored throughout the book as Esther, our intellectual narrator, chronicles her experiences of not fitting in with the world. These moments have as much to do with being an intellectual woman as with being a lesbian. The parallel is clear: being a lesbian is no more alienating than being a female English professor. For a lesbian, however, there are moments of joy. In fact, it is *through* being a lesbian that Esther is able to overcome her alienation from her own gender, and to find a community that includes not only other lesbians, but all women.

In chronicling Esther's journey, Russ makes available a new model—or, as she calls it, a new myth for women who experience a similar desire to go "on strike against god." Esther provides a demonstration of feminist principles that Russ discusses in her nonfiction work, as well as a reflection of women who had previously been all too invisible. Esther's story validates and illuminates these experiences.

### Myths, Gender Roles, and Literary Inversions

What kind of story is *On Strike Against God*? What "literary myths"—to use Russ's own term—does it employ? Russ, in her 1972 essay "What Can a Heroine Do?" (1995h) argues that the conventional myths of modern literature *cannot* be successfully used by women to describe their own experiences. She adds that "there seem to me to be two alternatives open to the woman author who no longer cares about How She Fell in Love or How She Went Mad. These are (1) lyricism, and (2) life" (87). After her deconstruction showing how limiting the story of How She Fell in Love is to women writers (and, one presumes, readers), it is thus surprising that the subtitle of this work is "A Lesbian Love Story."

This work, while undoubtedly a love story, subverts the entire genre of heterosexual "love stories," both because the protagonist falls in love with a woman and because the love story does not end in the conventional way. Jean moves to New Zealand; Esther remains a lesbian. Gender roles cannot be reinforced through their relationship and Esther's rebellion against female gender roles is a constant throughout the text. Indeed, one could say that the book is more about loving *lesbianism* than it is about an intense love affair between two women, providing a very different gloss on the phrase "A Lesbian Love Story."

Interestingly, the other "female" literary modes are also present, if in somewhat unconventional forms. How She Went Mad is copiously referenced in the imagery of the text, for example, through the device of Esther's "demon," and her revealing and poetically funny conversations with her imaginary therapist, Count Dracula. But Esther does not, in fact, go "crazy"; Russ provides her with a different option. The mode of the story is lyrical, by Russ's definition—"*the organization of discrete elements* (images, events, scenes, passages, words, what have you) *around an unspoken thematic or emotional center*" (1995h, 87; emphasis in original)—and is also realistic, life-based. Russ notes that "the lyric structure, which can deal with the unspeakable and unembodiable as its thematic center, or the realistic piling of detail . . . may (if you are lucky) eventually *add up to* the unspeakable, undramatizable, unembodiable action-one-cannot-name" (1995h, 90). Both of these forms are abundantly used in the story. Yet the story also goes beyond them, *naming* those actions, themes, and struggles.

For example, the question of what a woman is comes up again and again as Esther tries to understand just what it is that women are and why anyone would do what "women" do. Through Esther's reflections, Russ articulates and names this struggle with limited, repressive gender norms.

> But the name is bad. The name is awful. I mean that everyone I've met, everyone I know well (unless they're lying, as I always am in a social situation—you don't think I want to get locked up, do you?)—anyway, every female friend of mine seems to have accepted in some sense that she is a woman, has decided All right, I am a woman. . . . Perhaps

they've lost something, perhaps they've hidden something. When they
were sixteen they could say, "I'm a girl, aren't I?" and not be stupefied,
stunned, confused and utterly defeated by the irrelevant idiocy of the
whole proceeding. (1995h, 17–18)

Esther's bewilderment is clear as broken glass. What is a woman? What
makes a "woman" and why? And why do they have to act that way? Instead of
"writing around" Esther's predicament, Russ chooses to let Esther speculate,
reflect. Esther herself is "stupefied, stunned": she does not intuitively grasp the
doxa of society, does not internalize the message that a gender role goes with
the genitals. Bourdieu (1995) calls doxa culture's "naturalization of its own
arbitrariness" (164). The doxa is a structure of concepts on a basic level that
tends to "naturalize" culture and that also tends to be unexamined—and is
all the stronger, indeed, because it is unexamined. Bourdieu "distinguish[es]
it from an orthodox or a heterodox belief implying awareness and recognition of the possibility of different or antagonistic beliefs" (164). It is Esther's
ability to question doxa, to turn doxa into orthodoxy and her own position
into heterodoxy, that makes her aware of her alienation. It also alienates her
further.

Russ likewise possesses the gift for speaking the unspeakable. The ability to articulate the unspoken assumptions (thus enabling one to explicitly
resist them) is one that Russ counts as particularly important. She notes:
"The problem of 'outsider' artists is the whole problem of what to do with
unlabeled, disallowed, disavowed, not-even-consciously perceived experience,
experience which cannot be spoken about because it has no embodiment in
existing art" (1995h, 90). The problem of trying to express something that has
no means of expression becomes the problems of invisibility and muteness,
both of which easily lead to a lack of existence in the well-known equation of
silence and death. As Russ states grimly, "make something unspeakable and
you make it unthinkable" (1995h, 90). In On Strike Against God, Russ is speaking
the unspeakable and thus allowing us to think what was previously unthinkable. The importance of clearly articulating experience that is not mirrored
in available, conventional myths cannot be exaggerated. As Russ says, "The
[gender] roles are deadly. The myths that serve them are fatal" (1995h, 93).

Esther's open rebellion against her classification as a "woman" includes
a lyrical, articulate discussion of experience and a declaration of revolt against
these fatal gender roles. Esther states simply and baldly, "I'm not a woman.
Never, never. Never was, never will be. I'm a something-else. . . . I have a
something-else's uterus, and a clitoris (which is not a woman's because nobody ever mentioned it while I was growing up) and something-else's straight,
short hair, and every twenty-five days blood comes out of my something-else's

vagina, which is a something-else doing its bodily housekeeping" (1980c, 18). Russ has Esther focus on the very foundations of what society thinks makes a woman—biology—while denying femininity in the social sense. While she possesses the body, she disavows the name, the social role, and all of culture's "naturalization of its own arbitrariness" about how she should look, act, and be in the world. Social gender, as we see below, is an *impersonation*:

> This something-else has wormed its way into a university teaching job by a series of impersonations which never ceases to amaze me; for example, it wears stockings. It smiles pleasantly when it's called an honorary male. It hums a tune when it's told it thinks like a man. If I ever deliver from between my smooth, slightly marbled something-else's thighs a daughter, that daughter will be a something-else until unspeakable people (like my parents—or yours) get hold of it. I might even do bad things to it myself, for which I hope I will weep blood and be reincarnated as a house plant. I do not want a better deal. I do not want to make a deal at all. *I want it all.* They got to my mother and made her a woman, but they won't get me.
> Something-elses of the world, unite! (1980c, 18)

By defining herself as something other than a woman (while still claiming her physical body) Esther declares herself on several levels. On the surface is an open rebellion against the gender roles of society: even her daughter will be a something-else "until unspeakable people (like my parents—or yours) get hold of it." Clearly, she knows that being a woman is *not* innate; it is something that is *learned.* She also knows that being a (womanly?) woman keeps people back; it is a form of restriction. She says, "I do not want a better deal. I do not want to make a deal at all. *I want it all.*"

A deal implies giving something up in exchange for something else. Esther does not want to give up anything she has; she wants to be fully acknowledged, a complete, equal, whole human being, who happens to be female. This desire connects to a parallel discussion in *The Female Man* (Russ 1975b). In *The Female Man*, Joanna "becomes a man"—a female man—claiming privilege and rights (20). In both scenes, narrators refuse to be "the *second* sex" (in de Beauvoir's famous appellation), instead claiming primacy as full human beings. In "wanting it all," and by turning into "a man," Russ asserts that her narrators want the unacknowledged, *automatic* rights that society tends to assign to men. In *The Female Man*, one of the narrators declares, "for years I have been saying *Let me in, Love me, Approve me, Define me, Regulate me, Validate me, Support me.* Now I say *Move over*" (140; emphasis in original).

Esther is not the only person to find the "name" bad. Kim Chernin (1982), in her examination of body image in Western society, presents what must be one real-life example among many: the case of Ellen West, a young woman who also refused female gender roles. Ellen West, who lived in the 1920s, refused these roles through many means, including refusing to eat. The incident in West's life that shows a strong parallel to Esther's case involves a bird's nest: "We learn that one day, when she is shown a bird's nest, she insists that it is not a bird's nest and nothing would make her change her mind" (Chernin 1982, 166). Chernin interprets this as a refusal to accept the feminine role: "'This bird's nest is not a bird's nest,' she says. And she means: I will not accept your vision of reality; I am a woman who will not accept this nest as destiny" (168). Esther similarly reshapes her role and place in society by calling herself something other than a "woman," which is something that society has a place for and can control.

Ellen West's story ended in suicide, but Esther transforms her refusal of the female role into a powerful and positive act. Her rebellion leads to alienation, but within that alienation she remains positive that she is a human being: she refuses to disappear. She reminds us that we are, indeed, all human, and that we need not be strangled by the limitations of "the name." Esther is alienated, but she remains convinced that there are other "something-elses" out there.

Russ, in explaining "why women can't write" (the subtitle of "What Can a Heroine Do?"), notes that there are particular types of fiction that expand the horizons constrained by male-oriented myths:

> Science fiction, political fiction, parable, allegory, exemplum—all carry a heavier intellectual freight (and self-consciously so) than we are used to. All are didactic. All imply that human problems are collective, as well as individual, and take these problems to be spiritual, social, perceptive, or cognitive—not the fictionally sex-linked problems of success, competition, "castration," education, love, or even personal identity, with which we are all so very familiar. I would go even farther and say that science fiction, political fiction (when successful), and the modes (if not the content) of much medieval fiction all provide myths for dealing with the kinds of experiences we are actually having now, instead of the literary myths we have inherited, which only tell us about the kinds of experiences we think we ought to be having. (1995h, 92)

Yet in *On Strike Against God* she does *exactly* this—and it is not science fiction, parable, allegory, or exemplum. It is, instead, a work that subverts, transforms, and transcends the boundaries of the literary tropes it references. Esther's situation is not blamed on a particular person; her troubles are societal, communal. Her story arc, despite the happy ending, is not wish-fulfillment ("the kinds of experiences we think we ought to be having") but is instead built on experiences that are all too familiar to many of us. Just as the work itself opens up these new possibilities, it also provides a model (a myth?) for us to use in interpreting and transforming our own lives. As Russ notes, "the lack of workable myths in literature, of acceptable dramatizations of what experience means, harms much more than art itself. We do not only choose or reject works of art on the basis of these myths; we interpret our own experience in terms of them. Worse still, we actually perceive what happens to us in the mythic terms our culture provides" (1995h, 89–90). By writing a new way to think about lesbian experience, Russ provides us all with a profoundly insightful myth that enables us to break out of traditional gender roles, articulate our experience, and find/establish a community in each other. As Esther reflects, "Lesbians. Lez-bee-yuns. Les beans. Les human beans?" (70), humanity is inherent in all of us.

## On Strike: Alienation

Joanna Russ's *On Strike Against God* (1980c) is named after a labor strike by women. Russ's analysis of labor and gender has always been particularly acute. In using the words of the judge condemning one of the strikers, Russ echoes the courage of women "holding out" for a better world, one with equitable pay, better working conditions, better hours, and so on. The use of the phrase "on strike against god" evokes a notion of being on strike against not only their employers, but the entire order of their existence; a revolt not just against the factories, but against the world in which those factories exist.

Why does Esther want to strike? Much of her desire springs from a persistent feeling of alienation, a feeling that the world itself has no place for her. "I remember being endlessly sick to death of this world which isn't mine and which won't be for at least a hundred years; you'd be surprised how I can go through almost a whole day thinking I live here and then some ad or something comes along and gives me a nudge—just reminding me that not only do I not have a right to be here; I don't even exist" (16). Esther doesn't exist because she is not mirrored in society as an intellectual woman, as an unmarried woman, as a woman who would greatly prefer not to be condescended to. The poignancy of going through "*almost* a whole day" before being reminded of one's invisibility emphasizes the ubiquity of gender messages in our society—messages about what women *should* be like. Russ, in her essay "She Wasn't, She Isn't, She Didn't, She Doesn't, and Why Do You Keep Bringing It Up?" (in Russ 1998c), describes some of the difficulties and consequences of invisibility. Although she is discussing lesbians in particular, her analysis also applies to Esther's status as an intellectual woman who exists without societal (or mythic narrative) support. In speaking of invisibility (of lesbians, intellec-

tual women, women writers, women artists . . . ) Russ says, "note please that
the little woman (or man) who isn't there is not merely invisible. She is also
punished" ("She Wasn't, She Isn't," in Russ 1998c, 114).

> It is not happy or comfortable to be forced to lie, forced to remain silent
> about most of your personal life, forced to invent stories about an "ac-
> ceptable" life so people won't wonder about you, forced (sometimes) to
> join in the baiting of others like yourself. "Silence is like starvation,"
> says Cherríe Moraga, and Adrienne Rich calls invisibility "a danger-
> ous and painful condition." She describes the sensation of seeing the
> world described by authority—and not seeing oneself in it—as "psy-
> chic disequilibrium, as if you looked in the mirror and found yourself
> missing."

That "psychic disequilibrium" is clearly rendered in Esther's situation, both
in her lesbianism and her unwillingness to adhere to expected gender roles.
Russ *depicts* Esther's invisibility, paradoxically making her (and women like
her) present and visible, showing them in a textual mirror.

Esther narrates her own experience with invisibility as well as commenting acutely on the societal pressures that produce it. "Since I crawled into
this particular ivory tower it has not been better, hearing about the typical
new man in the department and his work and his pay and his schedule and
his wife and his children (me? my department), well that's only comedy, but
what goes right to my heart is the endless smiling of the secretaries where
I work, the endless anxiety to please. The anxiety" (16). Esther emphasizes
economic as well as social invisibility, highlighting the fact that the department's status quo is male with a female support staff, thus making her invisible as a female professor. Her invisibility is reinforced by the disposable jobs
of the lower-status, lower-paid secretaries, who must kowtow with smiles.
Those disposable, ill-paid jobs are crucial to the structures of heterosexual
marriage, and crucial also to the class status of Esther and women like her;
a comment that Russ would later amplify in "Why We Women, Sloppy Creatures That We Are, Can Never Find Anything in Our Pocketbooks" (in Russ
1998c). This gendered economy is a societal message of which Esther is quite
aware. She is uninterested in the unpaid labor of a heterosexual marriage,
is working in a "man's job," and yet can comment on the conventions surrounding work and expected female behavior that constrain her as well as
the secretaries. Again, instead of "writing around" this issue, Russ names it
and brings it out into the open.

As a female professor, Esther is, like Aesop's bat, between the beasts and
birds. While she finds women easier to talk to, the threat she represents to
the gender hierarchy as an intellectual woman is as threatening to the faculty

wife as to the male professor. Although Esther says "I love women—I mean, I just decided that, talking to her; I mean women don't come up to you and go sneerk, sneerk, menstruation ha ha" (27), and even goes on to note that conversations with women are less fraught, unlike "taking your life in your hands, as I seem to do every time I talk to a man" (27–28), the threat she presents is still present. Her "simple lovely conversation" (28) cannot be sustained, for other (heterosexually married, "traditional") women see Esther as a threat, although Esther does not seem to return the sentiment. "She said *she* wasn't a woman's-libber, she wouldn't burn her bra, but with such a frightened look that I wanted to put my arms about her" (28). One wonders exactly what Esther's conversation partner is frightened of. Changes in society? A deep-seated desire to go braless? A sense of her own powerlessness and how she was trying to appease the powerful by saying what she thought they wanted to hear? Esther responds to that fear with compassion, even though this faculty wife is, in her own way, just as nasty to Esther as her male colleagues are and perhaps more competitive.

> "I think," said my neighbor, her chin *very* high in the air (and still spiffed, I am glad to say) "that women who've never married and never had children have missed out on the central experiences of life. They are emotionally crippled."
>
> Now what am I supposed to say to that? I ask you. That women who've never won the Nobel Peace Prize have also experienced a serious deprivation? It's like taking candy from a baby; the poor thing isn't allowed to get angry, only catty. I said, "That's rude and silly," and helped her to mashed potatoes. (29)

Esther seems to feel guilty, or as though she has failed the other woman somehow, yet that failure is inevitable in a culture that sets women up as intractable rivals. Ironically, in this case, that rivalry is only illusionary, as Esther wants nothing of what her conversation partner has.

The rivalry of women makes Esther sad. Being attacked by men, however, makes her angry, her anger arising from the power differential inherent in their social positions. "After all," Russ remarks in "For Women Only, or, What Is That Man Doing Under My Seat?" (1998a), "the real question, of course, is not whether women will practice separatism against men, but whether men will continue to practice it against women" (95). Esther echoes this almost exactly when she says, " 'My politics,' said I in a glorious burst of idiot demonhood, 'and that of every other woman in this room, is waiting to see what you men are going to inflict on us next. That's my politics' " (30).

Esther's alienation stems not only from her invisibility, but also from the ways in which her experience is rendered powerless through definition.

"Piggy" says, "You can't get along without us" (30) meaning, of course, that
women are dependent on men, a situation that Esther does not experience
personally or romantically. She in fact *does* get along without men as often as
society lets her (she lives alone and earns her own money), so this comment
again makes her invisible and alienated, as well as reminding her that she is
dependent on men for things like her position in the department. "He twin-
kled at me. 'Disappointed in love,' he said," to which Esther reacts, "*I think he
thought that I thought that he thought that I thought I was flirting*. This is unbear-
able. I'm absolutely paralyzed" (30; emphasis in original). The assumption
of disappointment in love and of flirtation (an assumption so monstrous, so
invasive that Esther finds it paralyzing) reduces her anger by transforming it
from something rational into something irrational. It makes her motivations
something more acceptably feminine, thus diminishing both her anger and
her just reasons for that anger. It also self-aggrandizes Piggy (allocating her
sexual interest to him) while leaving Esther to deal with the disgusting and
unanswerable assertion that she would have such an interest.

Esther cannot win such verbal battles. The odds are stacked against her
because her experience is invisible and those whose experience is not, vastly
prefer to keep it that way. Her opponent, Piggy, goes on to state (monstrously):
"We love you. What bothers us is that you're so oversensitive, so humorless, of
course that's the lunatic fringe of the movement—I bet you thought I didn't
know anything about the movement, didn't you!—but seriously, you've got
to admit that women have free choice. Most women do exactly what they
want" (31).

Piggy's remarks about women having "free choice" and being humorless
are a particularly nice piece of irony, in a book that is so humorous and aware
of itself as part of that same "lunatic fringe." These remarks are of course
unanswerable, and Esther does not attempt to answer them. They are not unanswerable because they are true, but unanswerable because there is no language, no conceivable way to make him listen to the truths that Esther knows
and which are by now present in the text. "The solution is to be defeated over
and over and over again, to always give in; if you always give in (gracefully),
then you're a wonderful girl" (32). Yet Esther does not particularly *want* to be
a wonderful girl; she simply does not know an alternative to allowing defeat:
"My mother used to tell me not to hurt people's feelings, but what do you do
if they hurt yours? But it's my own fault. But the worst thing is that you can't
kill that kind of man" (32). It's not a matter of trying to hurt other people;
it's a matter of not knowing what to do when she herself is hurt. Lashing out
(even verbally) at the perpetrator is not an option. "You can't kill them; they
grow up again in your nightmares like vines" (32). Esther understands that it
isn't really her colleagues who are the problem; it is the way she's internalized

those messages, made them into her nightmares, her bindings, her limits. "The demon got up. The demon said Fool. To think you can eat their food and not talk to them. To think you can take their money and not be afraid of them. To think you can depend on their company and not suffer from them" (31). It is this *dependency* that creates Esther's suffering.

Esther's later quarrel with her friend Ellen springs out of Ellen's unwillingness to acknowledge that women face oppression; she would rather believe that everyone has free agency and the ability to pull themselves up by their mythic bootstraps. The distance between them comes from Ellen's inability to acknowledge Esther's reality—an inability that springs from a fear of admitting the validity of Esther's arguments, a fear of being forced to examine her own life. Ellen would have to see herself—"Superwoman; if Ellen's responsible for anything, that's because it's her choice; Ellen still exists on five hours sleep a night" (82)—as constrained. That is, she would have to acknowledge an influence on her life other than her own free choice, and such and admission is clearly unacceptable to her.

This situation calls to mind the dynamics of the shared social oppression of lesbians and heterosexual women as articulated in Adrienne Rich's famous essay "Compulsory Heterosexuality and Lesbian Existence" (1994 [1980]). Rich reflects on the limitations imposed on both lesbians (violent prejudice, internalized homophobia) and heterosexual women (fear of being called lesbian, inability to choose *freely* to be heterosexual), and writes "within the [heterosexual] institution exist, of course, qualitative differences of experience; but the absence of choice remains the great unacknowledged reality, and in the absence of choice women will remain dependent on the chance or luck of particular relationships and will have no collective power to determine the meaning and place of sexuality in their lives" (1994, 87). Russ articulates the same problem in "I Thee Wed, So Watch It: The Woman Job" (1998b): "heterosexuality as a personal erotic or affectional preference is absolutely different and distinct from the heterosexual institution, which is public and compulsory. The latter must be challenged and eradicated, and this process includes the female achievement of economic independence . . . and an end to homophobic bigotry. The demystification of lesbian presence and lesbian visibility . . . is an important part of this process" (143). In the conflict between Ellen and Esther, Russ weaves this idea into the narrative, mythical work of her protagonist, presenting us with this demystification and its consequent challenge to that which is "public and compulsory."

Furthermore, by clearly illustrating the ways in which Ellen (as well as Esther) is both constrained by and collusive in this mystification, Russ demonstrates just how important it is for *all* women to participate in the process of demystification:

Ellen knows better than to believe in bra-burners; she thought for
a minute and then said carefully, "I suppose I've always been a feminist.
You know, where I grew up it was impossible for a woman to have a
career at all; she could only be a wife and mother, but here I am with
both."

I said, Yes, wasn't that wonderful.

She smiled.

"And Hugh does half the housework," I said, "and takes care of the
baby." (Anya was at the baby-sitter's because I was there.) "Ah! That's
unusual."

"He helps," said Ellen. Then she said, "I don't mind doing it." They
all start out assuming you mean somebody else: Third world women,
welfare mothers, Fundamentalist Baptists, Martians. (80–81)

*They all start out assuming you mean somebody else.* Esther's point that Ellen's
husband still does not do a fair share of the housework is glossed over with
"I don't mind doing it," and given a false sheen of voluntarism. When Esther
goes on to note that Ellen had to get up at five o'clock for four years to write
because she had no other time in her life, Ellen remarks, "If one wants something, one makes sacrifices" (81), and when Esther asks whether the same is
true of Hugh, she replies, "We are different people" (81). By reverting to an
individualistic argument, Ellen deflects Esther's point, which is that Ellen's
sacrifices are inevitably gender-based, and that Ellen is certainly not making
such sacrifices alone. She is part of a system, but as long as she focuses on her
individual choices (or those of others), she does not have to acknowledge the
system at all.

"You're bitter!" said she.

"Sure," I said. "Malcolm no-name saw his daddy killed before his
eyes at the age of four and that's political: but I see my mother making
a dish-rag of herself every day for thirty years and that's personal."

Ellen said that my mother was responsible for that, if it was true,
and we didn't have to repeat our mother's mistakes. (82)

The victim-blaming of Ellen's last line here is particularly acid: *if* it is
true, then it is *entirely* the fault of Esther's mother. Not of society, which taught
her that making a dishrag of herself was her job, and which made other jobs
difficult or even impossible to get, nor of all of the other people around her
who agreed with that message and told her it was her destiny. Ellen believes,
like Piggy, that women have free choice.

Ortner (1996) in an essay analyzing agency, writes, "studies of the ways in
which people resist, negotiate, or appropriate some feature of their world are

also inadequate and misleading without careful analysis of the cultural meanings and structural arrangements that construct and constrain their 'agency,' and that limit the transformative potential of all such intentionalized activity" (2). This conclusion applies equally to Esther's mother—who was doubtless constrained by many things from running away to join the circus or from otherwise choosing not to do housework—and to Esther, who must deal with many "structural arrangements" and expectations that limit her choices. It also applies to Ellen, who will not admit it.

Despairingly, Esther asks, "Why did Ellen forget the classic exchange? I mean the one where they say But aren't you for human liberation? and you say Women's liberation is for women, not men, and they say You're selfish. First you have to liberate the children (because they're the future) and then you have to liberate the men . . . and then if there's any liberation left you can take it into the kitchen and eat it" (84). This resonates with Russ's observation: "yet whenever any woman or group of women propose to use its own resources for its own ends, there is an enormous amount of shock and horror at such ghastly behavior" (1998a, 92). Why did Ellen forget that exchange, that bald statement that even in a movement for women's equality, women are expected to work for others first? Probably because in her own life, she is working for others first, and no one cares to be reminded that they haven't made their own choices freely. Ellen is accepted as a woman because of those choices; Esther, as the alienated outsider, sees the consequences more clearly: "There's this club, you see. But they won't let you in. So you cry in a corner for the rest of your life or you change your ways and feel rotten because it isn't you, or you go looking for another club. But this club is the world. There's only one" (84).

Esther's alienation is so complete that she sees herself as completely shut out from the world; her friend Ellen is willing to accept the status of being a woman (and all that entails, including the housework and only five hours' sleep a night) but Esther is not. She is not admitted to the club; she is utterly excluded. "If Jean had stayed with me I wouldn't have cared, but now I must put on my putrid ankle sox and my cheerleader button because there's no right of private judgment and you can't think of yourself; you have to be thought. By others" (84). "You can't think of yourself" is beautifully phrased to mean both putting other people first, as women are classically supposed to do in the culture Esther grew up in, and to mean that you are not allowed to conceive of yourself, to create yourself: "you have to be thought." That is, other people have to think you, have a concept of you. Otherwise, you are invisible and have no niche in society.

## Something-Elses of the World, Unite!

Esther's hope that Jean, her friend, might be a something-else (18) is also her hope that she is not entirely alone in being out of alignment with the conventional feminine gender framework. It is that hope and the very act of falling in love that leads her out of alienation and into connection with other women. Esther's romance with Jean and her discovery of a new way to connect with women creates both hope and happiness for Esther, and her intellectual connections help form this sense of community. All of these connections forge the discovery of a community/connection of women that Esther revels in as a joyful and subversive alternative to the world she has found so alienating. Russ (1981) notes that "the positive values stressed in these stories can reveal to us what, in the authors' eyes, is wrong with our own society. Thus, if the stories are family/communal in feeling, we may pretty safely guess that the authors see our society as isolating people from one another, especially (to judge from the number of all-female utopias in the group) women from women" (145). This reasoning applies also to *On Strike Against God*. Yet it is not a utopia, but instead a myth-model for finding or creating community. If Esther can find community, so can we.

Esther's intellectual connection with other women is profound in that it not only indicates community, it also represents an act of creation and foreshadows her other types of connections with women. For example, when she talks with her friends Jean, Sally, and Louise for six hours,

> I had a terrible shock, something so profound that I couldn't even tell what it was; for nothing had changed—the sun sank, the light breeze blew though my enormous open windows. . . . But nothing had exploded or changed color, or turned upside down, or was speaking in verse. Nor had the wall opened to reveal a world-wide, three-dimensional, true-view television set playing for the enlightenment of the human race and our especial enjoyment, a correct, truly scientific (this time) film about a runaway computer in Los Angeles in which all the important roles were played by grey-haired, middle-aged women. That would violate everything. (The other way, only we are violated.) (21–22)

Esther's vision is of a world turned truly upside down, a world in which women—middle-aged women, at that—are seen as having the intellectual capital to play major roles. It is community and revolution in one. Esther experiences this intimacy of the mind as an act of creation and connection. She has a vision of creation as "both voluntary and involuntary, in the mind and in the body, so as to bear the stars and planets—indeed, the whole universe—She had not only to grunt and sweat with the contractions of Her mind, but think profoundly, rationally, and heavily with Her womb" (22).

   This episode of speaking and thinking together is also when Esther first has stirrings of *something* for Jean. "I started thinking again and my first thought was very embarrassing: I realized I had been staring very rudely at Jean, who was sitting in front of the window and whose breasts were silhouetted through her blouse by the late afternoon sun" (22). The mind and the body are indeed intimately connected here: the intellectual intimacy cannot, perhaps, be divorced from Esther's admiration of Jean's breasts.

   Russ's depiction of the dizzy joy of being in love is intensely personal, as narrations of this sort tend to be, but also looks outward toward community from the very beginning. When Esther writes, "I decided I must babble of something so that she would think I was behaving normally, while the sun shot arrows through my bones—although I do not look like a truck driver with a duck-tail haircut, do I?—while my sex radiated lust to the palms of my hands, the soles of my feet, my lips (inside), my clumsy, eager breasts, while they radiated it back to between my legs and I very obligingly thought I was going to die" (41), she is already referencing, through the cliché of the truck driver with butched hair, a community of lesbians. She pokes fun at and deconstructs the stereotypical image of "the butch lesbian" and at the same time uses it to connect to a hypothetical community of other women.

   By writing about a connection between women that is both erotic and emotional, Russ provides a model that validates choice and the important place of female sexuality. Russ describes the "consequent lesbianism" of all-female utopic fiction as "expressing the joys of female bonding, which—like freedom and access to the public world—are in short supply for many women in the real world" (1981, 142). Although *On Strike Against God* is neither utopic nor all-female, Russ manages to express that joy all the same: "Sexually, this amounts to the insistence that women are erotic integers and not fractions waiting for completion. Female sexuality is seen as native and initiatory, not (in our traditionally sexist view) reactive, passive, or potential" (1981, 142). The revolutionary possibilities of female sexuality are, in this instance, linked to seeing women as whole unto ourselves, but also possessing the ability to bond with one another in community. In "Is 'Smashing' Erotic?" (in 1998c), Russ discourages those who would discount the erotic dimension of women's interactions: "There is no sense in colluding with the patriarchy in this area; our sexuality ought to be named for what it is, as it is our very great resource" (169).

   Beyond eroticism, there is also the issue of lesbian continuum. Adrienne Rich (1994) defines this as "a range—through each life and throughout history—of woman-identified experience, not simply the fact that a woman has had or consciously desired genital sexual experience with another woman" (51). It is more than narrowly defined romantic experience: it is participation in a network, a community of women. The experience is not of "woman" but of women, separately and together, as discrete human beings with their own identities: "You breed cats. You ride. You fix cars. You can't stand my mother. Sometimes you are my mother" (Russ 1980c, 104).

This is the thing Esther feels connections to. Her lesbianism is not an isolated sexual experience—it is not isolated at all, nor is it exclusively erotic. Her community is not just lesbians, nor even just intellectual women, or women who are rebelling against gender norms. She feels a connection with *all* women: "What I want to say is, there are all of us; what I want to say is, we're all in it together; what I want to say is, it's not just me, though I'm waving too; I've hung my red petticoat out on a stick and I'm signaling like mad, I'm trying to be seen too. But there are more of us" (106). Through Esther's boundless affection for and sense of connection with all women, Russ demonstrates—and makes a powerful, usable myth of—the power of "the lesbian continuum" described by Rich.

That community, that continuum is also powerful beyond the formation of connections. Even before Esther confesses her love to Jean, she worries, "What if Jean . . . won't?" (48). That worry is assuaged by "another marvelous discovery . . . a vision of the local Howard Johnson's (East of the campus, on the superhighway), full of healthy, comely young women. *There are others besides Jean!* For the first time in my life I felt free. In fact, I felt perfectly wonderful" (48). This epiphany of community grants freedom from the intolerable pressure of trying to belong, and additionally provides the joy of knowing that there are others in the world, that one is not alone. Esther takes strength from knowing that her mere existence is an act of rebellion. "What do you do when the club won't let you in, when there's no other, and when you won't (or can't) change? Simple. You blow the club up" (85).

Access to the lesbian continuum is what gives Esther the tools to "blow the club up." Between the first and second episodes of Esther's lovemaking with Jean, Esther reflects, "The world belongs to me. I have a right to be here" (58). In this simple statement we see that, paradoxically, being a lesbian gives Esther the courage to claim the whole world for herself. Not Esther's love-connection with Jean, nor even her intellectual and emotional connection with other women, but her access to the lesbian continuum in what gives her the entire world.

This connection, this willingness to love the entire community of women, represents not only Esther's connection to a new community, but also a new conception of gender. Her rebellion against being "a woman" does not prevent her from connecting with women who have embraced that gender role—the community still exists. She has transcended the limitations of that gender role, created her own role and agency and abilities, yet still reconnects with other women in a way that is deeper than the imposed rules of society. Linda Nicholson (1994), in her argument against "a feminism of difference," (99), suggests a Wittgensteinian category for "women": an "elaboration of a complex network of characteristics, with different elements of the network being present in different cases" (100). Russ does not explicitly articulate such a theory, yet Esther's all-embracing connection with and category of women agrees with such inclusivity.

This lesbian connection is the source of Esther's hope that others may be able to be fully themselves—whatever that may be—without artificial limitations. This echoes Gayle Rubin's (1975) comment: "I personally feel that the feminist movement must dream of even more than the elimination of the oppression of women. It must dream of the elimination of obligatory sexualities and sex roles" (204). Esther does this both through becoming a lesbian, and also through her feeling of being connected with all women, regardless of how they "perform" their gender, and her support for women both as we *are* ("A Christian American Anti-Hippie Mother" [105]) and how we *can be*:

> we should all trade poems, we should all talk like mad and whoop and dance like mad, traveling in caravans on camel-back (great, gorgeous, sneery eyes, haven't they?) and elephant-howdah and submarine and hot-air balloon and canoes and unicycles and just plain shank's mare toward that Great Goddess-Thanksgiving Dinner in the sky; Jean can rough-house with Stupid Philpotts and tie his hair back with a red ribbon and then roll up her sleeves and make her batter better.
>
> We must all get some better butter; that will make our batter better. (106)

The book ends as Esther quotes from some graffiti: "*Let's be reasonable. Let's demand the impossible*" (107). Haven't feminists have been demanding "impossible" things for the entire history of the movement? Whether it is Rubin's (1975) vision of "an androgynous and genderless (though not sexless) society, in which one's sexual anatomy is irrelevant to who one is, what one does, and with whom one makes love" (204) or Dworkin's (1993) radical demand for a single day where no woman is raped, feminism is known for its impossible and reasonable demands. *On Strike Against God* also looks outward to community, Esther's demand is not made to a specific other person, but to society as a whole, to every reader. Esther's rebellions against the norms of her society seemed impossible at first: simultaneously frightful, terrible, and in the case of Jean, too wonderful. Yet Esther could not reasonably exist in a world that refused to acknowledge her; the only reasonable thing to do was to demand the impossible, the right to exist as she was. In this mythic narrative about resistance and transformation, Russ both demands the impossible, and achieves it.

~

# 9  Kittens Who Run with Wolves

## Healthy Girl Development in Joanna Russ's Kittatinny

SANDRA LINDOW

$P$sychologists and educators have argued that the stories we tell children change how they see the world and their place in it. As a reading specialist with more than thirty years' experience working with disabled and emotionally disturbed children I believe in the importance of giving children stories that will help them live happy, productive lives. For those who have a difficult time finding anything optimistic to say about themselves, it is important to help them re-story their experiences by providing model stories with more optimistic plotlines than their own. Girls, in particular, can get bogged down in a learned-helplessness, dysfunctional personal story. Joanna Russ's allegorical hero's quest, *Kittatinny: A Tale of Magic* is a young adult novella, a Pilgrim's Progress for Girls that represented the forefront of feminist thought in 1978 when she first published it and still provides an excellent road map to healthy gender role-modeling today.

Since the 1960s, Joanna Russ is one writer/critic who has examined traditional folktales and mythology and found them poor representatives of women's real lives and experiences. In her thoughtful essay, "What Can a Heroine Do? Or Why Women Can't Write," Russ (1995h) explains that traditional hero tales handicap women writers because "there are so few stories in which women can figure as protagonists. . . . Both men *and women* conceive the culture from a single point of view—the male" (80–81). Furthermore, Russ (1983b) believes, the "social invisibility" of women's experience is not just "bad communication" but "a socially arranged bias" that has persisted long after accurate information has become available (48). When women realize that their experience is radically different from the stories told to them, they are forced to be cultural outsiders: "The problem of 'outsider' artists is the whole problem of what to do with unlabeled, disallowed, disavowed, not-even-consciously-perceived experience, experience which cannot be spoken about because it has no embodiment in existing art. . . . Make something unspeakable and you make it unthinkable" (1995h, 90). Thus, it is important to create new myths where women transcend the traditional stereotypes of "modest maidens, wicked temptresses, pretty schoolmarms, beautiful bitches, faithful wives"; in other words, women seen through a male lens: "Cloud-cuckooland fantasies about what men want, or hate, or fear" (1995h, 81).

Kittatinny (1978a) follows the structure of the traditional hero's tale: separation, initiation and return. Living in New York along the valley of the Delaware River in the foothills of the Kittatinny Ridge, Kittatinny Blue Eyes ("Kit" for short) is born into an early machine-age culture where rigid sex roles and family vocations define the lives of the inhabitants. Kit is a fairly normal, bright eleven-year-old girl until she becomes interested in the machinery involved in milling grain. She wants to become a miller not "marry a Miller" as someone jokes. Disgusted with hearing "girls can't do this and girls can't do that," Kit goes for a walk and ends up running away from home (4).

Beginning with the groundbreaking publication of Carol Gilligan's (1992) In a Different Voice, the problems of finding authentic women's voices and experiences have been carefully studied by psychologists as well as writers and critics. In Reviving Ophelia: Saving the Selves of Adolescent Girls, psychologist Mary Pipher (1994) describes girls' problems to be like those of the gifted children Alice Miller (1997) describes in The Drama of the Gifted Child. They "faced a difficult choice. They could be authentic and honest or they could be loved. If they chose wholeness, they were abandoned by their parents. If they chose love, they abandoned their true selves" (Pipher 1994, 36). Pipher believes that it is not the parents but the entire culture that tends to abandon girls for choosing wholeness (37). When Kit is told what she can and cannot do as a girl, she is receiving what Pipher calls "false self-training" (44). Pipher explains that authenticity means "owning of all experience, including emotions and thoughts that are not socially acceptable" (38). Adolescent girls, however, experience considerable social pressure to be nice rather than authentic and honest, thus becoming "female impersonators" who must fit their whole selves into small crowded spaces (22). Through her practice with girls, Pipher has learned that bright, sensitive girls are most at risk for developing emotional problems in response to gender roles.

They have the mental equipment to pick up our own cultural ambivalence about women, yet lack the cognitive, emotional, and social skills to handle this information. They are paralyzed by complicated and contradictory data they cannot interpret. They struggle to resolve the unresolvable and to make sense of the absurd (Pipher 1994, 43)

Making sense of the absurd is a common theme in stories Russ has written for adults, one where she gives no easy answers. Her characters are predominantly gawky outsiders, ill at ease in their environments. For instance, in "The Autobiography of My Mother" the thirty-five-year-old time-traveling narrator and her mother "live on different ends of a balance," making it possible to first meet when the mother is a two-year-old—and one the narrator doesn't particularly like (1987a, 206). In "The Little Dirty Girl," the main character meets herself as a neglected, even-younger child and doesn't recognize herself until the end (1987a, 3). On the whole Russ's fictional family relationships can best be described as dysfunctional with varying amounts of attachment disorder. In order to grow up with strong self-esteem, children need to be emotionally attached to their parents in deep, nonverbal ways. But when parents are abusive, solipsistic, emotionally distant, seriously ill, or even rigidly conventional, the normal process of attachment often breaks down and children can grow up as disconnected misfits. Growing up authentic is never easy within a Russ fictional family.

Thus, it is necessary for Kit to leave the stifling confines of the Valley culture in order to search for her true self. As in all good hero tales, Kit is provided with guides through trial and danger. She meets a male wolf with "an enormous mouthful of frighteningly efficient teeth and a long, doggy tongue" and follows him (9). For the first part of her trip a wolf is a suitable guide. As an eleven-year-old girl, Kit lacks wilderness smarts, the well-developed ability to recognize and protect herself from danger. In *Women Who Run With the Wolves*, Jungian analyst Clarissa Pinkola Estés (1992). writes that, "Healthy wolves and healthy women share certain psychic characteristics: keen sensing, playful spirit, and a heightened capacity for devotion" (4). Later Estés explains: "A wolf shadows anyone or anything that passes through her territory. It is her way of gathering information. It is the equivalent of manifesting and then becoming like smoke, and then manifesting again" (456).

Kit's wolf takes her as far as an opening in the forest where she finds a group of naked wood nymphs and satyrs cavorting around an open fire. When Kit comes near, she is pulled into the "hooting and bawling and piping" of the ring (13). Amid goat-legged men and shrieking, naked women, Kit is whirled dizzily around and then left hungry, tired, and alone when the couples suddenly go crashing off into the bushes. It is here, though, that she finds her next guide, an infant satyr or faun complete with tiny hooves and tiny bumps on his forehead that would eventually become horns (15). Although Kit has not much enjoyed child care prior to this moment, she reluctantly agrees to care for the infant satyr and names him B.B., short for Baby Brother. By seeing him as her brother, Kit claims kinship with Pan, one of the oldest gods in the Greek pantheon. Connected to Dionysian fertility rites, Pan becomes a symbol for sexuality (Warner 1983, 765). As the wild wood god of the nineteenth century romantic poets, Pan symbolized a move away from the restrictions of urban behavior. Thus, Kit's alliance with the faun is important because it symbolizes her willingness to live in harmony with nature rather than having dominion over it, as is the tradition in paternalistic versions of Christianity

(Johnson 1990, 130). B.B. convinces Kit to carry him because he will be light as "a piece of paper" and she will not have to worry about food for him "My food is a person's heartbeat. . . . And if you sing to me once in a while, that will feed me, too. And in return I'll feed you; I'm a magic baby and you won't need to eat while I'm with you" (18). By being light as paper and nourished by song, B.B. represents the essence of myth and story. Furthermore, physical closeness, heartbeat, and song are all part of the attachment process between good parents and healthy, emotionally secure babies. B.B. is helping Kit become her own healthy parent.

B.B. explains that the nymphs and satyrs mate by chasing each other in a wild *panic*—Greek for "magic yell" (Johnson 1990, 130). If they run fast enough and yell loud enough, babies are created and left in bushes and streams (16–17). B.B. wants to go with Kit because he finds the nymphs and satyrs "very sad and dull." By going with her he expects to become human. "I want to eat porridge! I want to wear clothes! I want to have feet!" (18). Although Kit is only eleven, she, as a child living in a farming community, does know the rudiments of sexual contact and baby-making. Being able to recognize the obvious lack of tenderness and warmth in the satyr/nymph sexual panic is an important part of her psychosexual initiation.

As Kit walks, seasons change and B.B. begins to take on human characteristics. In a thunderstorm, they enter a magical, dreamlike cave where they encounter the gold and jewels of a dragon's Hoard. (25). Kit is strongly attracted to the Hoard but believes that by touching it she could be turned into a dragon. When she tries to hurry away, her path begins to shake and the Hoard becomes the body of Taliesin, a huge female dragon. (27). Russ here refers to the ancient Welsh bard, Taliesin, and also recalls Le Guin's dragon Kalessin from *The Farthest Shore* (1972). Taliesin was a poet and musician who served early kings of Britain around the time of Arthur. The work most associated with him is *The Book of Taliesin*, which scholars consider to have been written in tenth-century Welsh. Once again Kit is confronted by myth and story. When the dragon transforms to become a giant woman made up of many women of all races, it is apparent that Taliesin also represents the ancient Goddess Tiamat, "the womb of creation," who is sometimes depicted as the dragon of creation (Walker 1983, 998–999). In *Womanguides: Readings Toward a Feminist Theology*, Rosemary Radford Reuther (1985) describes her as the Babylonian Mummu-Tiamat, the mother (39). Taliesin initiates Kit with secret knowledge:

> Know, thou: all greed is greed for love. Know: My body is more golden
> than the mines of Asia, My eyes more precious and jeweled than the
> sum of Peru. I am the Hoard which men hunt. My food is the heat which

bubbles and burns at the center of the planet. My natural home that white-hot, molten core. Once all mountains moved in fire; once all beasts were of My kind, even thou and that pale Idea on thy back. All was fire, joy, and transformation. All was the many-shaped Goddess.

So will it be again! (29–30)

Thus, Kit's kinship to dragons is established. Taliesin, as deity, is larger than the earth itself, able "to sip red-hot metal from the center of the earth like a dragonfly snacking from a flower" (30). Kit is dizzied, hypnotized by her closeness, and dreams of a stone woman who holds a sword in her lap, not knowing how to use or even pick up the sword. Then another woman, a real one this time, springs to her feet and, like a magician, draws a "shining ray of light" out of her head that becomes "a sword made out of thought" (31). Here Russ implies that a traditional woman, trapped in stone by cultural bias, can't use a sword, but a "real" woman can jump into action, reforming her thinking to become the sword-wielding protagonist of her own hero tale. The dragon/Goddess disappears and Kit wakes in a sea of grass with a "golden sword and buckler" beside her. The sword is named "Taliesin." By receiving the sword, Kit is given a traditionally male way of protecting herself but, by making it a gift from the Goddess, Russ feminizes the icon, providing a yin-yang balancing of imagery. Lisa Tuttle (1997) writes, "The sword is an equalizer, allowing individual women free passage in a male-dominated world" (394). But it is not just a sword. Through the power of naming, it represents the beauty, power, history, and mythology of English poetry and song.

In *Stealing the Language: The Emergence of Women's Poetry in America*, Alicia Suskin Ostriker (1986) writes: "A major theme in feminist theory . . . has been the demand that women writers be . . . thieves of language, female Prometheuses" (210–211). By this she means that women must make the fire of language authentically their own. Ostriker goes on: "Where women write strongly as women, it is clear that their intention is to subvert and transform the life and literature they inherit" (211). By giving Kit a traditionally phallic sword rather than a knitting needle or a buttonhook, Russ remythologizes girl as hero and takes back the language.

After accepting the sword, Kit's journey becomes much harder. The object of Kit's quest is intellectual, emotional, and moral maturity. Becoming a morally mature adult requires the ability to recognize emotions and use them appropriately. The sword, now plain steel, represents the double-edged problem of anger—specifically, whether Kit will channel her anger into effective action or strike out at others. When Kit gets hot and tired, she tries to control herself, but begins to quarrel with B.B. When he shrieks like a "police whistle," she grabs one of his feet and twists it. When he bites her, she unties

her shawl and throws him away from her "like a stone out of a sling . . . a soap
bubble" (33). They have entered an emotional Slough of Despond.

All adolescents have moments of anger and despair. Despair is anger
turned inward. Russ knows that girls are not always nice. They can do serious
harm to others if they are only taught to hold back or repress anger. Even as
the sword loses its gold color, Kit's bildungsroman, her coming-of-age story,
must be emotionally real and not gilded. Within her culture, being openly
angry is a privilege usually relegated to men. When Kit's increasing anger
makes it impossible to be nice, she becomes abusive. Pipher (1994) writes,
"Young girls are egocentric in their thinking. That is, they are unable to focus
on anyone's experience but their own" (60). Kit blames B.B. for her discomfort
and takes it out on him. As part of a revisionist mythology for girls, the event
becomes a worthwhile talking-point. Hearing the anger stories of others is
a good way to learn when and how to be angry. In "No Docile Daughters: A
Study of Two Novels by Joanna Russ," Marilyn J. Holt (1981) remarks, "Russ
makes a clear delineation between patriarchal power and feminist power. Patriarchal power seeks to control others: parents saving their daughter for a
husband, the husband owning the wife. Feminist power seeks self-control:
the control Bettelheim described as 'following their right way with deep inner
confidence'" (94).

To transcend learned-helplessness, Kit must gain this deep inner confidence. When B.B. runs away, she is able to act quickly and effectively, using
her sword to save him from huge, predatory, rocklike Slonches, cutting their
sticklike legs out from under them (36). Despite mastering this anger/action
lesson, Kit has entered an unexpected world where there is still much to learn.
She, like the girls Pipher describes, is still fairly aimless in her journey, "happy
when praised and devastated when ignored or criticized," a sailboat without a
centerboard (Pipher, 1994, 37).

At the edge of a ruined city, Kit finds a book written in Cyrillic. After
touching it with her sword, she is able to read the story of "Russalka" the little
mermaid (41). In this version, Russalka suffers deeply for forcing herself to
be someone she is not and dies miserably, no true healing available. Kit cries
at the end, but B.B. announces that he has enjoyed the story and happily suggests alternative endings: "I think it was a most true story and very exciting. I
think Russalka should've pushed the throne over on the old wizard, grabbed
the Prince's sword, and made everybody get out of the way while she escaped.
I think she should've kicked the old wizard and run down to the sea" (52).

Russ's ruined city is much like Bunyan's "City of Destruction." Those
who choose to remain there will "sink lower than the grave into a place that
burns with fire and brimstone" (Bunyan 1882, 11). Russ suggests that accepting female role models provided by folktales is a spiritual death "lower than

the grave." By restorying "Russalka," B.B. teaches Kit to go beyond the old, false myths. As they travel, Kit starts telling her own versions, "Sometimes she went to Tahiti to fight the sharks or was a famous professor at the University on the edge of the Pacific Trench." At this point the book transcends historical fantasy. The insulated Kit of the beginning chapters likely would not have known about the Pacific Trench.

Although Kit has gained the imagination to reframe her experience and be the hero of her own life, she still needs strong woman role models. As her dream-time Pilgrim's education continues, she meets a Woman Warrior who is practicing throwing her sword in a clearing. Woman Warrior represents another aspect of the Goddess and harkens back to Maxine Hong Kingston's (1989) *The Woman Warrior*, a book that effectively mixes fantasy and mythology with real-world events. Soon Woman Warrior is demonstrating prowess, battling a thunderstorm. "Ah! My old enemy," she greets him. "The storm threw another lightning-bolt and the Woman Warrior turned her back, caught the lightning-bolt on her heel, kicked it up, caught it with one hand and threw it back" (58). At this point the omniscient narrator suggests that thunderstorms make good training partners, but Warrior Woman's real enemies are "the great warlords and the evil kings," in other words, the good old boys of the patriarchy (59). Pipher (1994) writes, "Resistance means vigilance in protecting one's own spirit from the forces that would break it" (264).

Woman Warrior recognizes Kit as the initiate and invites her home (56). Despite the excellent lessons Kit has already learned about passivity and action, her education continues when Much Wanted, a child in Woman Warrior's house, decides to show Kit the "magic" of fire. Unfortunately, Kit's manners are "too good" and she doesn't stop Much Wanted until it is too late and the dry grass of the meadow has caught fire (60). Pipher (1994) writes:

> Girls learn to be nice rather than honest . . . Adolescent girls discover that it is impossible to be both feminine and adult. Psychologist I. K. Broverman's now classic study documents this impossibility. . . . Healthy women were described as passive, dependent and illogical, while healthy adults were active, independent and logical. In fact, it was impossible to score as both a healthy adult and a healthy woman. (39)

Fortunately Much Wanted's multiracial, multicultural relatives answer her call and fight the fire. All are historical role models of strong women. Sacajawea, for instance, actually talks the fire back into the earth (62). When Western Cousin (Calamity Jane) goes down on one knee and shoots "the fire between the eyes with a long rifle" the flames go out (61). Impressed by the strength, competence, and authenticity of the family, Kit asks to stay, but Woman Warrior sadly tells her that she can't, "Because we are legendary people . . . and you are real. If you lived with us, you would starve and die, like the sea-maiden trying to breath air. . . . You must become a Warrior in the real world" (63).

Kit is desperate to create a new family for herself, but Woman Warrior's family is made up of "Ideas," not flesh-and-blood human beings (61). Here Russ seems to be saying that adolescents feed themselves on human connection and will "starve and die" on ideas alone.

As Kit resumes her journey, she feels rejected and sad and takes it out on B.B. "She hated having B.B. on her back, and even if she had to carry him she certainly wasn't going to talk to him" (65). Pipher (1994) argues that adolescent girls can be paralyzed by the expectation of external disapproval, "easily offended by a glance, a clearing of the throat, a silence, a lack of sufficient enthusiasm or a sentence that doesn't meet their immediate needs. Their voices have gone underground—their speech is more tentative and less articulate. Their moods swing widely" (20).

When B.B. says that they're going the wrong way, Kit thinks, "You ninny, whatever way *you* go, I'll go the opposite!" and continues in the same direction because all ways look the same to her (65). They enter a deceptively beautiful countryside with "the stately spires of a castle rising from behind trees" (66). When B.B. refuses to go forward, she continues to the castle. After pricking her hand on a thorn, Kit passes through a magical opening in the hedge and enters Sleeping Beauty's castle. In her thought-provoking essay, "The Wilderness Within: The Sleeping Beauty and 'The Poacher,'" Ursula K. Le Guin (2004c) suggests that the sleeping castle stands for childhood: "It is the secret garden; it is Eden; it is the dream of utter, sunlit safety; it is the changeless kingdom / Childhood, yes. Celibacy, virginity, yes. A glimpse of adolescence: a place hidden in the heart and mind of a girl of twelve or fifteen. There she is alone, all by herself, content, and nobody knows her" (111).

No wonder Kit is attracted to the castle. It provides an easy way out, never really having to grow up, spending Ever After dreaming of an impossibly perfect prince and a ridiculously easy life that will be magically provided without the pain of having to make mature, trial-and-error life choices, what Le Guin calls "love marriage child bearing motherhood and all that" (2004c, 111). However, the reader already can guess that Russ will not give Kit this romantic "stereomyth." Even though everyone in the castle appears to be frozen in sleep, Kit discovers that the princess is not the expected innocent flower, but a successful child/vampire who has never been asleep even though centuries have passed. The Princess tells Kit that she was pampered, sheltered, and warned of worldly danger until there wasn't anything she *wasn't* afraid of (72). Finally, her father hired a witch to put her under a sleeping spell until she was old enough to be married to a suitable prince: "You see, they couldn't lock me up in a trunk or in the palace food locker, so they did the next best thing. Only something went wrong and now I'm the only one who doesn't sleep" (72).

When the spell went awry, the Princess's mirrored reflection slowly faded away and she became a vampire with needle-sharp fangs for draining blood from unsuspecting wannabe rescuers: "When I drink their blood they die, and when they die they turn white and cold and look like marble. First I tried to get them to talk to me but they wouldn't, they wouldn't—and now I don't even try, I just go down and kill them. I kill more than I need; I do it for fun" (75).

In other Russ stories (for example, "The Second Inquisition") mirrors are important props for revealing the true self. Russ suggests that when a girl is overprotected and forced to remain an emotional child, she can lose her sense of self. Whatever culturally induced *beauty* she has becomes so inauthentic that she becomes a vampire, living off the lives of others. Pipher (1994) writes that "all mixed-up behavior comes from unprocessed pain" (257). Because the princess has had no one with whom she can process the pain of her abandonment; she becomes criminally disturbed. Because Kit is also a little girl, Beauty doesn't want to kill her and pushes her away saying, "They made me scared of everything in the world and now I'm the scariest thing in it" (76). Princess Beauty has been reduced by "a girl poisoning culture" (Pipher 1994, 267) to a reflectionless vampire because she can't participate in experiences that will help her see herself clearly and grow.

Terrified by the evil and emptiness Princess Beauty represents, Kit runs out of the castle to find B.B. Together they lock "an enormous iron gate" by sliding a piece of iron bigger than they are through its hasps (76). Kit looks back and sees the castle rising and shining "like cake icing under the moon. It was horribly beautiful" (76). Pipher explains that the cult of feminine beauty or "lookism" is a trap that many adolescent girls fall into. Cosmetic and clothes ads first make young women feel inadequate then promise to make them into beautiful princesses (Pipher 1994, 243–244). Girls struggle with mixed messages. "Be beautiful, but beauty is only skin deep" (Pipher 1994, 35–36). She suggests: "The luckiest girls are neither too plain nor too beautiful. They will eventually date, and they'll be more likely to date boys who genuinely like them. They'll have an identity based on other factors, such as sense of humor, intelligence or strength of character" (56).

When Kit and B. B. lock the castle gate, they are making a decision to turn away from the moral reductionism of falling for the culture's false promises about beauty. They had argued before, but now they agree never to allow anyone to lock them up even (supposedly) for their own good (78). This unity of purpose is similar to that experienced by Bunyan's Pilgrims after leaving the Enchanted Land. "They could see each other better, and the way wherein they should walk" (Bunyan 1882, 368). Kit's clear-sightedness regarding gender roles once again causes the land to change. Suddenly there is no fence, no castle (78). In a "pleasantly musky" forest a "Parlement of Foules" attenuates to only a few birds (79). "What she'd thought was an ostrich . . . was a fallen tree trunk wedged upright between the live ones" (80). The magic is fading away. "This is the way stories end" (80), B.B. says.

Discomfort with the way stories usually end is common in Russ's other work. After winning important battles against evil, returning to a mundane world where nothing has changed can be deeply damaging to a young hero: "Nothing came. Nothing good, nothing bad. I heard the lawnmower going on. I would have to face by myself my father's red face, his heart disease, his temper, his nasty insistencies. I would have to face my mother's sick smile, looking up from the flowerbed she was weeding, always on her knees somehow" (Russ 1970e, 39).

Kit's decision to turn away from the deadly cult of feminine beauty has provided the portal for returning to the world of her home village. As they pass through the first of the trees that surround it, B.B., who is now Kit's own size, disappears like a candle going out and Kit comes home to the valley alone "with the taste of tears in her mouth" (80).

The initiate has returned. Kit has been tested and has learned from her experiences. However, whereas the goal of the traditionally male hero's quest is the validation of manhood and happy reintegration into his community, Kit's quest has not provided her with validation for her village's concept of womanhood. Having passed through the fire, Kit now no longer fits in. Knowledge has made her different. She is not ready for comfortable reintegration. Lisa Tuttle (1997) in her article on "Gender" for the *Encyclopedia of Fantasy* concludes: "Knowing too much or knowing something different, makes a woman an outsider; while a man, accustomed to defining himself in oppositional terms of power and freedom, will consider the achievement of a quest to be the end of a story—his own story—women, who customarily define themselves within a web of mutually reciprocal relationships and responsibilities, cannot rest until the impact of their actions has been accepted by others" (394).

As Kit enters her village she discovers everything to have shrunk in size. On entering her parents' house she finds Ondry Miller waiting for her. It is apparent that she, like others who enter magical realms, has been gone six or seven years (81). However, it is also apparent that a part of her has been in the village all along. Ondry is not surprised to see her. Pipher (1994) writes, "Most girls choose to be socially accepted and split into two selves, one that is authentic and one that is culturally scripted. In public they become who they are supposed to be" (38). Unlike real-world girls who have to go through every dreadful moment of their puberty and adolescence, Kit lucks out. Her consciousness goes on a quest while her social self stays home and goes through the motions. She has matured into a young woman. She sits down on a bench next to Ondry and, when they kiss, he asks her to marry him. Kit, however, suddenly finds herself on the other end of the bench (82).

Annis Pratt suggests that women's life choices are "disrupted by social norms dictating powerlessness for women. . . . Young girls grow down rather than up" (in Shinn 1986, 152). But Kit has indeed grown up. She demonstrates positive changes in both her maturity and her moral development.

When Kit does not respond to Ondry's proposal, he leaves and she stays to wash the dishes and douse the fire (a symbolic response to Ondry's proposal.). Kit's friend Rose Bottom, now a beautiful woman, stops in to tell of a dream where, in a room with increasingly modern printing presses, Kit and a little naked boy meet a printer who has just printed the Sleeping Beauty story. Kit knows it is "all lies" but is "too polite" to criticize it (83). B.B., however, begins to yell for her and the words come out of Kit's mouth (85). Pipher (1994) suggests that when parents don't tolerate anger, the unacceptable feelings may be projected onto others (36). B.B speaks for Kit because she is not yet able to be angry for herself. In a scene reminiscent of Christ turning the moneylenders out of the temple, Kit tries to break the printing frames and she is forcibly removed from the shop. As Pipher (1994) reminds us:

> Simone de Beauvoir would say that strength implies remaining the subject of one's life and resisting the cultural pressure to become the object of male experience. Betty Friedan would call it fighting against "the problem with no name. . . . Gloria Steinem calls it "healthy rebellion." Carol Gilligan refers to it as "speaking in one's own voice," and bell hooks calls it "talking back." Resistance means vigilance in protecting one's own spirit from the forces that would break it. (264)

Out on the street B.B. is delighted by Kit's temper tantrum but she feels "torn up inside," a common female post-anger response. Rose's dream demonstrates strong empathic understanding of Kit's life and emotional experience. Later when they, too, kiss, Kit responds more passionately to Rose than she did to Ondry even though she knows she is not supposed to feel that way. The two pull away from each other, frightened.

After Rose leaves, Kit sees B.B. standing in the doorway to the pantry but now transformed into a girl. "I told you about legendary creatures, didn't I? I told you I would turn into whatever you were. . . . Is it my fault you think only boys can lose their tempers?" (87). The separate lives Kit has lived for the last seven years begin blending in a very confusing way. Coming closer, Kit sees "the swaggery, grown-up, self-confident smart aleck" B.B. and then realizes it is her own reflection in a full-length mirror. With a yin-yang kind of symbolism, the integration of Kit's boy/girl self is now complete. She has become an androgynous mix of male and female characteristics. According to Pipher (1994), androgynous adults are the most well adjusted because they are free to act without worrying if their behavior is feminine or masculine (18). Kit prepares to leave the village without seeing her family. Wondering what she has learned from her adventures, she is thinking about change and beauty when she sees someone dressed for travel coming toward her. It is Rose.

John Clute (1999) writes: "For thirty years, Joanna Russ has been the least comfortable author writing SF, very nearly the most inventive experimenter in fictional forms, and the most electric of all to read. The gifts she has brought to the genre are two in number: truth-telling and danger" (1035). It is apparent that Kittatinny, despite its deceptive simplicity, is as dangerous a book as Russ has ever created. Written nearly twenty years before Pipher's (1994) groundbreaking Reviving Ophelia, Russ's intuitive grasp of girls' developmental issues effectively predicted the research that Pipher explicated. When, at the end of her quest, Kit is able to transcend the heteronormativity of her culture and choose Rose as her traveling companion, Russ's girl readers are given permission to be their true selves and to find their true loves, whatever their gender. This is dangerous business indeed.

~

# 10 Medusa Laughs

*Birds, Thieves, and Other Unruly Women*

Andrew M. Butler

There is a moment in a chapter of Joanna Russ's *What Are We Fighting For?* that threatens to sink this contribution before it even gets going: "A combination of Freud, Chodorow, and Cixous is not enough equipment for the study of anything" (Russ 1998c, 64) As it is my intention to offer a reading of some of Russ's fiction using the ideas of Sigmund Freud and Hélène Cixous without even progressing so far as Nancy Chodorow—although I would trade her for the possibly more ambivalent figure of Jacques Lacan—it might appear that I am on a fast track to nowhere from the outset. Russ is right to be suspicious about psychoanalysis, given its deeply problematic situating of women within Freud's sexual and psychic schemes, not to mention the damage a wrongheaded psychotherapist could inflict upon a patient. She is right, also, to be suspicious of the academic paper that grabs at theorist *X* as a too blunt tool to excavate the meaning of *Y* or *Z*; I am sure that I am as guilty of this kind of thing as any other academic. But the narratives of psychoanalysis are very seductive.

This is the path that I am navigating here, and I take comfort from the knowledge that Russ does not necessarily dismiss Cixous as much as the *use* made of her by some critics. Indeed, she acknowledges: "I find Hélène Cixous's 'The Laugh of the Medusa' . . . moving and at times even inspiring" (in Russ 1998c, 77). In this chapter I offer a sort of chiasmatic reading[1] of Russ's work, suggesting congruences between it and Cixous's, in particular "The Laugh of the Medusa." (Cixous 1981). I find the echoes between "Laugh" and, especially, *The Female Man* (Russ 1975b) to be interesting, although the coincidence of publication dates mean that no actual influence is possible in either direction, aside from the unlikely chance that Cixous read the novel in manuscript between its completion in 1969 and eventual publication in 1975. The most I can suggest is that both are coming out of the same cultural epoch, albeit on opposite sides of the Atlantic. I wish to trace the figure of the Medusa and the role of laughter through a number of works by Russ, taking in a close cousin to the Medusa woman, the unruly woman—identified by

Natalie Zemon Davis (1975)—along the way. I shall also draw upon three models for the purposes of laughter, and note how it has been suggested that they might be put to feminist use. The discussion of Russ's work will be somewhat skeletal and suggestive, as it is necessary to outline the theoretical frameworks first.

In order to situate Cixous's ideas, it is necessary to go back to Freud and Lacan, although it needs to be noted that Cixous does not take their ideas onboard uncritically.[2] Freud's notorious theories of gendered identity produced through differing responses to castration anxieties is specifically linked to the figure of the Medusa in a short piece called "The Medusa's Head": "The terror of Medusa is thus a terror of castration that is linked to the sight of something. Numerous analyses have made us familiar with the occasion for this: it occurs when a boy, who has hitherto been unwilling to believe the threat of castration, catches sight of the female genitals, probably those of an adult, surrounded by hair, and essentially those of his mother" (1995b, 273). The hair, particularly hair in the form of snakes, symbolizes phalluses, indeed, a multitude of phalluses and an excess of phallic power. The Medusan figure is thus paradoxical; she is both castrated and castrator, both evidence that someone can be castrated and a figure of power to be feared as castrator.[3] The male spectator has in turn a paradoxical response to the sight: "The sight of Medusa's head makes the spectator stiff with terror, turns him to stone. . . . [B]ecoming stiff means an erection. Thus in the original situation it offers consolation to the spectator: he is still in possession of a penis, and the stiffening reassures him of the fact" (275). At the moment of absolute terror this emotion is apparently disavowed by the reassuring reappearance of the threatened organ, as yet undamaged.

Lacan (1977) places importance on the power structures between the participants of the Oedipal drama, although the end result is still dependent on the sex of the child.[4] The female child, defined as a lack because always already castrated, cannot enter comfortably into the Symbolic Order as a male child could, and has to retreat into pre-Symbolic babble, into what Julia Kristeva (1982) calls the semiotic, or what might be referred to as an *écriture feminine*, feminine writing. While this approach is hardly less problematic than Freud's scheme, it has offered a female-centered space for feminist philosophers to explore—including Cixous.

Cixous (1981) says: "I shall speak about women's writing: about *what it will do*. Woman must write her self: must write about women and bring women to writing, from which they have been driven away as violently as from their own bodies. . . . When I say 'woman,' I'm speaking of woman in her inevitable struggle against conventional man; and of a universal woman subject who must bring women to their senses" (245). The situation is made more complex because writing cannot simply be split into masculine and feminine as products of males and females: two of the examples she gives of woman's writing are male writers, James Joyce and Jean Genet. But Cixous's own writing, her tone, her rhetoric, is rather different from most male writing.

In *The Female Man* Russ (1975b) does at one point satirize the idea of a female language: "You will notice that even my diction is becoming feminine, thus revealing my true nature. . . . I have no structure . . . my thoughts seep out shapelessly like menstrual fluid, it is all very female and deep and full of essences, it is very primitive and full of 'and's' " (137). While it would be unfair to say that Russ is entirely unsympathetic to Cixous's ideas, she is skeptical about her attitude to language: "[Her view] that women cannot express themselves in existing language but only by subverting existing language—or by inventing a totally new one—seems to me extreme . . . perpetuating long-held sexist stereotypes of women" (Russ 1998c, 77). This invocation of a new language risks maintaining a too-rigid essentialism of the distinction between men and women, and seems too much like withdrawing from a battle for rights into a sterile separatism or isolationism that could end up settling for second best.

It also potentially blames women for being inadequate rather than taking men to task for their excluding behavior. Russ notes that not being allowed to speak was much more of a problem than not being able to: "Cixous's viewpoint . . . seemed plausible to me . . . until I remembered the early days of the women's liberation movement and the forces that actually kept us from speaking up. These included the fear of losing our jobs (or losing the job of marriage), being publicly ridiculed, having friends desert us and being insulted, threatened, or beaten up" (Russ 1998c, 78). But if the means of expression is up for debate, the fact of woman's testimony, woman's writing, woman's experience being expressed is surely a positive thing, if only to offer potential role models for those who follow.

Nevertheless, this element suggests an intriguing parallel between Russ's and Cixous's work. Cixous 1981 asserts: "A female text cannot fail to be more than subversive. It is volcanic; as it is written it brings about an upheaval of the old property crust, carrier of masculine investments; there's no other way. There's no room for her if she's not a he. If she's a her-she, it's in order to smash everything, to shatter the framework of institutions, to blow up the law, to break up the 'truth' with laughter" (258). In masculine space, she has to follow the masculine rules if she is to be accepted—rather than being a "her-she" she has to turn into a "her-he" or what we might call a female man. Her-he has to masquerade, cross-dress, to fit into male rules. Or, as in *The Female Man*:

> I sat in a cocktail party in mid-Manhattan. I had just changed into
> a man, me, Joanna. I mean a female man, of course. (1975b, 5)[5]

and:

> For a long time I had been neuter, not a woman at all but One
> of The Boys, because if you walk into a gathering of men, profession-
> ally or otherwise, you might as well be wearing a sandwich board that
> says: LOOK! I HAVE TITS! . . . there is this giggling and this chuck-
> ling and this reddening and this Uriah Heep twisting and writhing . . .
> I back-slapped and laughed at blue jokes, especially the hostile kind.
> Underneath you keep saying pleasantly but firmly No no no no no no.
> (1975b, 133)

This version of the female man is "an honorary male," and is no better
than the feminine female: "Turning certain, select women—or all women—
into honorary males is not what women's liberation is about" (Russ 1980a,
179). The "honorary male" is a category recognized by the "good guy . . . [who]
believe[s] in equal pay for equal work . . . and [has] gone out of [his] way to
bring a woman into the organization/department/business . . . [He] treat[s]
her like just like a man, just like one of the boys . . . and even tells dirty jokes
when she's around" (1980a, 179). The awkwardness of such behavior may recall Sigmund Freud's identification of smut as humor designed to wound. He
notes: "Smut is like an exposure of the sexually different person to whom it is
directed . . . Among country people it is not until the entrance of the barmaid
or the innkeeper's wife that smuttiness starts up. Only at higher social levels
is the opposite found, and the presence of a woman brings the smut to an
end" (Freud 1976, 141, 143). The Manhattan cocktail party is clearly a higher
social class situation, and yet the smut continues. From the context it is obvious that this is not really treating woman as equal, even if she is one of the
boys; rather, it is a continuation of the old patriarchal hierarchy. Any claim to
equality is here undermined by the fact that the narrator feels uncomfortable
in such a homosocial environment. Indeed, she is actively being made to feel
uncomfortable.

To be a woman, to be a real woman, rather than a woman who is there
purely to serve the needs of men—"women's business is to keep men comfortable" (Russ 1980a, 182)[6]—is an almost revolutionary act. A simple reversal
of "masculine" rationality and logic into "feminine" irrationality and illogic
is not enough, of course. The categories have to be muddied and rejected. A
"feminine" text often admits to more than one meaning at once, rather than
being tied down to a single linear sense.[7]

Cixous (1981) also seems to attempt to subvert the notion of writing from within, or perhaps from the position to which masculinist thinking has marginalized her. By rewriting the story of the Medusa, and creating a Medusan woman, she ridicules the underlying assumptions of men about women: "[Men] need femininity to be associated with death; it's the jitters that give them a hard-on! for themselves! They need to be afraid of us. Look at the trembling Perseuses moving backward toward us, clad in apotropes! What lovely backs! Not another minute to lose. Let's get out of here" (255). Here you cannot but feel that Cixous has smuggled female desire—an emotion barely acknowledged by patriarchal society—into her account of the Medusa story. There is that Greek hunk, Perseus, edging backwards toward her, sneaking glances at her in his polished shield, and her first thought seems to be, "H'mm. Nice ass. Get yer coat, you've pulled."[8] But in order to prop up the oh-so-fragile male ego, he has to be defined by his presence, in opposition to her absence, her lack, her emptiness, even though Cixous seems to suggest that it is a male problem rather than a female one: "If they believe, in order to muster up some self-importance, if they really need to believe that we're dying of desire, that we are this hole fringed with desire for their penis—that's their immemorial business" (1981, 260). This misguided belief is part of a masculinist ideology, and she wants to have no responsibility for the consequences: "Too bad for them if they fall apart on discovering that women aren't men, or that the mother doesn't have one" (255).

This male ideology has situated women as two sides of the same coin, as castrator/castrated: "They riveted us between two horrifying myths: between the Medusa and the abyss. That would be enough to set half the world laughing, except that it's still going on" (255). This positioning is either laughable or tragic. But, of course—and this really needs to be emphasized—woman is *not* lack, *not* absence, *not* withdrawal. She has rarely been castrated in the sense that Freud suggests. It is just a story to prop up patriarchy, and another story could (should [must]) be recounted against it. Cixous asks: "But isn't this fear convenient for them? Wouldn't the worst be, isn't the worst, in truth, that women aren't castrated, that they only have to stop listening to the Sirens (for the Sirens were men) for history to change its meaning? You only have to look at the Medusa head on to see her. And she's not deadly. She's beautiful and she's laughing" (255). In a coming together of the power of female sexual desire and the power of laughter, Cixous suggests: "Undeniably (we verify it at our own expense—but also to our amusement), it's their business to let us know they're getting a hard-on, so we'll assure them (we the maternal mistresses of their little pocket signifier) that they still can, that it's still there" (260–261). Ridicule becomes a political weapon for the physically weak as Regina Barreca (1992) notes: "In contrast [with men], women's comedy takes as its material the powerful rather than the pitiful" (13).

In a comic yet serious touch, Cixous yokes together the concepts of theft and of being a bird, drawing on the double meaning of the French verb *voler*, meaning to steal/to fly: "Flying is woman's gesture—flying in language and making it fly . . . for centuries we've been able to possess anything only by flying; we've lived in flight, stealing away, finding, when desired, narrow passageways, hidden crossovers. It's no accident that *voler* has a double meaning, that it plays on each of them and thus throws off the agents of sense. It's no accident: women take after birds and robbers just as robbers take after women and birds. . . . What woman hasn't flown/stolen?" (Cixous 1981, 258) Just as Cixous's appropriation of the Medusa as a feminist role model risks reinscribing misogyny, so the alignment of women with thieves and birds is a dangerous rhetorical ploy. In British ideolect, "bird" is of course slang for a woman;[9] but the caged bird is a recurring image of the fragility, repression, or flightiness (read: hysteria) of intelligent women trapped in supposed domestic bliss.[10]

Birds occur at a crucial point in *We Who Are About To . . .* (Russ 1977) the fragmentary account of the survivors of a spaceship crash, narrated by Elaine. Elaine refuses to take part in the clichéd activity of trying to rebuild a civilization of one's own when marooned, and does not want to reproduce to "save" the species. She alone sees how futile that would be, and she is not averse to hastening the extinction of the passengers and crew by killing in self-defense. This mind-set marks a distinct contrast with how she behaved at home in New York, when she was woken up in bed by a noise:

> Like a siren right under your pillow. The damnedest sound. The bed quaked. I thumped him in the ribs, said, "Bang on the wall." He said, I think sitting up, "What? What?"
> I said, "Sparrows. Bang on the wall."
> There was a nest in the air-conditioner . . .
> He said, "Kill them."
> I sat up. "Why? They're just babies."
> "Babies? They're banshees." (Russ 1977, 156)[11]

These birds are enclosed, if not exactly caged. The rest of the mission's survivors are seen as baby birds, unable to help themselves, and unfit to survive; Elaine has no compunction in killing them when they conflict with her needs. On the other hand, Sarah Lefanu (1988) compares Elaine to a bird: "The narrator herself is a greedy baby bird: she has got rid of the audience that won't listen to her, the six who imagine they can survive on an alien planet, and now demands another audience, us, her readers. . . . [In] reading Russ . . . a reaction is forced from us, as the baby bird forces a reaction from its parent" (177). Russ's text, too (if not Russ herself) becomes viewable as a bird, demanding our attention—although given Elaine's statement that there is nothing "uglier or stupider than a baby bird" (157) this revelation is not exactly desirable.

Sparrows also figure significantly in *The Female Man* when one of the narrators, Janet, recalls the experience of falling in love: "In our family hall, like the Viking meadhall where the bird flies in from darkness and out again into darkness . . . I felt my own soul fly straight up into the roof" (Russ, 1975b, 76). This image borrows from a passage in the Venerable Bede's (1969) *Ecclesiastical History*: "When we compare the present life of man with that time of which we have no knowledge, it seems to me like the swift flight of a lone sparrow through the banqueting-hall where you sit in the winter months. . . . This sparrow flies swiftly in through one door of the hall and out through another. . . . Similarly we know nothing of what went on before this life, and what follows" (127).

What in Bede is a spiritual metaphor—for the time before and after existence—is here an image of a woman in love with another woman; it also is changed into an image of transcendence, reversing the original image of the flight as the known, mundane life. Joanna (whom it is tempting to read as an analogue for Russ herself) also refers to birds, observing: "There are more whooping cranes in the United States of America than there are women in Congress" (Russ 1975b, 61). The whooping cranes were an endangered species, down to a few dozen breeding pairs, and felt worth preserving by various campaigns; in contrast, it seems that no one is much bothered about inequalities in Congress.

The other face of Cixous's *voler* image is the robber. Elaine is to some extent a thief figure: she steals equipment from her fellow survivors in order to prolong her own decline. More significant is the eponymous protagonist of the Alyx stories, described as working as a "pick-lock, a profession that gratified her sense of subtlety" (*Alyx* 9). While it is clear that Alyx can support herself by stealing things, the occasions on which we tend to observe it are when she is employed to do so, rather than straightforwardly engaging in robberies, and it is not necessarily for immediate personal financial gain. In "Blue Stocking"/"The Adventuress," Alyx is employed as a guardian by the seventeen-year-old Edarra who had arranged for her necklace to be stolen in order to gain money deceitfully. Alyx is able to arrange better terms by selling it, and then helps Edarra leave Ourdh in a stolen boat, another act of theft (Russ 1976a, 12–15).[12] Later in the collection, in "The Barbarian," she breaks into the governor's villa in the company of a sorcerer who wishes to kill a baby girl (perhaps a parallel to Elaine's boyfriend's suggestion of what to do to the baby sparrows. The act of burglary gives Alex pleasure: "breaking and entering always gave her the keenest pleasure; and doing so 'for nothing' (as he said) tickled her fancy immensely. The power in gold and silver that attracts thieves was banal, in this thief's opinion, but to stand in the shadows of a sleeping house, absolutely silent, with no object at all in view and with the knowledge that if you are found you will probably have your throat cut—!" (Russ 1976a, 52). Such thieving crosses various boundaries and thresholds, from the literal threshold of the entrance or exit of a house, to the metaphorical division of legal and criminal. These thresholds are also sexualized, metaphors for a "woman's body, with its thousand and one thresholds of ardor" (Cixous 1981, 256) The image of having your throat cut is telling, as "To decapitate = to castrate" (Freud 1955b, 273)—to be silenced, to not speak, is also to be castrated in metaphorical terms.

It is with the crossing and crossing-out, blurring and refuting of thresholds that the Medusan woman is most concerned. Having been identified by Cixous, the figure was taken up by film critic B. Ruby Rich (1998) in her article "The Crisis in Naming in Feminist Film Criticism." She argues that humor is a "weapon of great power. Comedy requires further cultivation for its revolutionary potential as a deflator of the patriarchal order and an extraordinary leveler and reinventor of dramatic structure" (77). In the Medusan film, females mock patriarchal structures through laughter. Natalie M. Rosinsky (1982) used this figure to offer an analysis of The Female Man, noting in particular its use of satire and parody to make feminist points about patriarchy, and equally "the ways in which humor has been used as a weapon against women" (32). This is a trope that can be examined throughout the rest of Russ's output.

An alternate to the Medusan woman is the unruly woman, a figure identified by Natalie Zemon Davis (1975, 124–151) in relation to early modern French culture. The unruly woman has an excessive body and produces excessive speech, and either dominates or tries to dominate men. Sometimes the figure is hermaphrodite or androgynous, sometimes an old crone—in other words, outside the social system of reproduction. She is sexually liberated, and is not afraid to break taboos and borders. She is associated with dirt, and with the crossing of thresholds, from one state to another. Most significant for this study, Kathleen Rowe's (1995) examination of rather more recent examples—such as Roseanne and Miss Piggy—notes: "Like Medusa, the unruly woman laughs" (10).

Cixous, in collaboration with Catherine Clément, describes the crossing over of boundaries and contagion caused by the unruly woman figure of the witch: "She laughs, and it's frightening—like Medusa's laugh—petrifying and shattering constraint. There she is, facing us. Women-witches often laugh, like Kundry in Parsifal" (Cixous and Clément 1986, 32). The laughter described by Cixous and Clément is tremendously powerful and even destructive, and seems always to be aimed at men, and aimed to wound: "All laughter is allied with the monstrous. . . . Laughter breaks up, breaks out, splashes over. Penthesileia could have laughed; instead, she killed and ate Achilles. It is the moment at which the woman crosses a dangerous line, the cultural demarcation beyond which she will find herself excluded" (33). The laughter takes the victim back to a time before he entered the Symbolic Order, back to the time of the Imaginary, the point at which the child is trying to come to terms with its image of itself, identifying itself with an idealized image of itself in the mirror: "To break up [with laughter], to touch the masculine integrity of the body image, is to return to a stage that is scarcely constituted in human development; it is to return to the disordered Imaginary of before the mirror stage, of before the rigid and defensive constitution of subjective armor" (33). In Kristeva's terms this is also the moment of the abject[13]—the inability to distinguish between states, inside or outside, alive or dead, and often featuring anxieties around bodily parts and fluids: "Spittle, blood, milk, urine, faeces or tears . . . bodily parings, skin, nail, hair clippings and sweat" (Douglas 1970, 145). It is a retreat to the stage of the chora, when the child was almost indistinguishable from the mother, was assailed by both life and death instincts, and was closest to the Lacanian Real.[14] It seems that these borders are defined by language as a series of repeatable, structured acts, rites, rituals, and taboos; in a patriarchal society these are a form of male-centered writing or *écriture masculine* even if they are not literally inscribed characters on a page. The Real is supposed to be outside of language, but must surely still be structured—albeit negatively—in relation to language.

In *Purity and Danger*, the social anthropologist Mary Douglas (1970) examined the rituals and taboos associated with the crossings of such boundaries and thresholds, the anxieties surrounding the blurring of such boundaries, and in particular the "desire to keep the body (physical and social) intact. [R]ules are phrased to control entrances and exits" (166). The rituals reinforce and reinscribe the boundaries even as they are transgressed, bringing harmony and order to the shift.

The joke, in contrast, may act as an anti-rite, pointing up chaos and disharmony, perhaps almost an irruption of the Real, although that would not be a term that Douglas herself uses. The joke "offers alternative patterns, one apparent, one hidden: the latter, by being brought to the surface impugns the validity of the first" (Douglas 1975, 149–150). Here Douglas is one in a long line of thinkers such as Sigmund Freud, Henri Bergson, and Mikhail Bakhtin who have situated comedy in the collision of double meaning.[15] Laughter has largely been located in three overlapping areas: a reaction to incongruity, relief from pent-up emotion, and the assertion of superiority. Each of these areas can be related in turn to the Medusan woman and feminist laughter.

First, the disruption of linguistic systems typical of incongruity, or more

specifically of verbal reversals, can be located in the various feminist transla-
tions of male language that Russ offers in *The Female Man* (1975b) or "Dear Colleague: I am Not an Honorary Male" (1980a) "It was only a joke," said by a man
after a woman has taken offense might translate as "I love the sex war because
I always win," or "I find jokes about you funny. Why don't *you* find jokes about
you funny?" (1980a, 180). "I'm all for women's liberation, but" might translate
as "I'm scared" (1980a, 179), and so on. Here Russ seems to be analyzing an
*écriture masculine* typical of the masculinist Symbolic Order.

The second suggested function of laughter is as a kind of safety valve to
relieve tension and the buildup of stress—in this case, from the pressures
of the contradictions and oppressions of patriarchal societies. This relief is
politically dangerous, however, as it may prevent society reaching the crisis
point that might provoke some form of revolution or overthrow of the existing structure. One example of this release of tension occurs in "The Second
Inquisition"—the apparently anomalous Alyx story at the end of the collection[16]—in the relationship between the visitor and Bogalusa Joe. Having told
him that she despises him, he offers to marry her, and she responds by laughing: "She began to laugh. I had never heard her laugh like that before. Then
she began to choke" (1976a, 184). After her laughter they go outside and engage in a sexual act—the anger and hatred defused.

The final suggested function of laughter is the assertion of one party
as being superior to the other. Sexist jokes, as already has been seen in the
Manhattan cocktail party, attempt to establish the male as superior over the
female. The woman who does not laugh at the joke—who does not find jokes
about herself funny, as it were—is further undermined, but if she does laugh
then she potentially affirms her own subjugation.

In contrast, women's humor can be used as a means of cutting men down
to size—a kind of castrating laughter. It might not be quite that simple, as
Regina Barreca (1992) suggests: "It's not even that men are afraid that women
will laugh at them during sex or guffaw at the size of their sexual apparatus.
Rather, it's that a man can't *really* laugh and maintain an erection at the same
time. A woman who can make a man laugh when he doesn't want to is as
dangerous as a Medusa" (19). Potentially this talent could offer an escape for
woman from unwanted sexual attention from males.

In the 1970s a number of feminists wrote about the risk that men's physical bodies, especially their erections, posed to women, and how, for example:
"Man's structural capacity to rape and women's corresponding structural vulnerability are as basic to the physiology of both our sexes as the primal act of
sex itself" (Brownmiller 1975, 13–14). In the discourse about (and against)
male supremacy and intercourse, the physical act was a metaphor for the
wider inequalities in society, intercourse within marriage being viewed by

some feminists as state-sanctioned rape as the female's option to consent was legally and financially undermined. In anatomical terms, the male was seen to penetrate and the female was seen to be penetrated, her lack filled.

Russ was able to envisage this action in an alternate way and to reverse the terms: "I myself can't see 'inviting penetration' as in any way degrading or humiliating *per se*—except of course that we still live in a culture that believes coitus to be symbolic of male dominance and that talks about male penetration rather than 'the capture of the penis'" (Russ 1985a, 12–13).[17] While the political need for cutting men down to size is understandable, simple reversals of the power structure are not sustainable. For Cixous the Medusan laughter can disrupt and thus destroy the entire system. Yet in time it may bring harmony and equality between the sexes. Rosinsky (1982) suggests: "[Whileaway's] humor is neither deceptive nor divisive. It is not used to subjugate" (34), offering a sense of utopian laughter.

Indeed, in the story "When It Changed" (Russ 1972c), we have a useful parable of the power and scope of laughter for communication and miscommunication. As the title suggests, the narrative covers a transition: the return of men to the all-female planet of Whileaway, where the original males had been wiped out in a plague thirty generations before. Janet (the narrator), her wife Katy, and Janet's daughter Yuriko are among the first people to see the men and try to communicate with them. From the first the encounter is awkward and the male ritual of shaking hands seems odd: "He seemed to mean well, but I found myself shuddering back almost the length of the kitchen—and then I laughed apologetically—and then to set a good example (*interstellar amity*, I thought) did 'shake hands' finally. A hard, hard hand" (235). The laughter here is a bit of social glue, partly to put the man at his ease, partly to ease the tension in general. As Douglas (1975) suggests, "all jokes are expressive of the social conditions in which they occur" (152), even if, as on this occasion, there is no joke as such vocalized.

On the next few occasions it is a man who laughs, when confronted with the fact that Whileaway surnames are based on the mother's name: "He laughed, involuntarily."[18] The laughter is repeated as the conversation continues: "I translated Yuki's words into *the man's* dog-Russian, once our lingua franca, and *the man* laughed again" (Russ 1972c, 235) The laughter here seems an attempt to mask the cultural differences between the two parties—and this masking is underlined by the mistake Janet makes when describing them: "'Like you?' I said. 'Like a bride?' For men were wearing silver from head to foot. I had never seen anything so gaudy. He made as if to answer and then apparently thought better of it; he laughed at me again" (235). From the male perspective, they have been unmanned by this (in their eyes) feminization of their appearance, and so they have to laugh to disavow the anxiety. From the

perspective of Whileaway, there is no insult, for in an all-female world everyone can be a wife if they choose.

In time—specifically, in retrospect—Janet can laugh at the men's social
awkwardness in dealing with the first encounter. It is perhaps meaningless
to describe the Whileawayans as lesbian in the context of a single-sex environment, but the men from a two-sex background are still grappling with a
dual notion of sexuality and gender as active and passive partners, rather than
something more neutral. Janet observes: "Sometimes I laugh at the question
those four men hedged about all evening and never quite dared to ask, looking at the lot of us, hicks in overalls, farmers in canvas pants and plain shirts:
*Which of you plays the role of the man?*" (239). What she fears is that the reintro-
duction of men will lead to the bad kind of laughter that belittles women:

> I do not like to think of myself mocked, of Katy deferred to as if she were
> weak, of Yuki made to feel unimportant or silly, of my other children
> cheated of their full humanity or turned into strangers. And I'm afraid
> that my own achievements will dwindle from what they were—or what
> I thought they were—to the not-very-interesting curiosa of the human
> race, the oddities you read about in the back of the book, things to
> laugh at sometimes because they are so exotic, quaint but not impres-
> sive, charming but not useful. I find this more painful that I can say.
> (239)

Here it is clear that laughter becomes a means to various kinds of power:
it can be used to belittle men when used aggressively by women, it can be used
to belittle women when used aggressively by men, and it can ideally be used to
establish a comradeship and equality between people if the joke is shared.

Ideally this laughter becomes a gender-free, unmarked language that will
allow space for both men and women. The hierarchy propped up by the mas-
culinization of the Symbolic Order is one that excludes and thereby alienates
women, but in the fixing of experience and expression it also alienates men
(albeit in a position of consolation through relative power).[19] The solution is
not to invert the hierarchy, as I have already noted, as that would trap women
in another alienated position (albeit with some consolation and with some
kind of payback for the inequities of several millennia of patriarchy). Instead,
a society should be built upon difference which is not sexed or gendered.

As the male visitors to Whileaway prove, such a space is difficult to imagine. It is difficult enough for them to imagine a female realm. The attempt
to imagine and write women's experience is rhetorically and politically vital,
to show the possibility of being otherwise. If the alternative *écriture* is designated as feminine, that should perhaps only be a temporary move to distinguish it from the masculinist tradition of writing. The whole range of possible

sentences should be available to both sexes. For now the notion of feminine *écriture* can allow us to recognize and decode the possibilities. As Sally Robinson (1988) argues: "When approached as *description* of (not *prescription* for) a feminine practice of writing, French feminist theory proves to be a valuable lens through which to read innovative women's fiction. In shattering the concept of unity—of meaning and of the speaking subject—Cixous, Irigaray, and Kristeva are working toward deconstructing traditionally masculine systems of thought, with the goal of constructing new modes of signification which do not exclude female specificity" (122).

It is up to writers to play with this new language and science fiction is a potential space for this play, although few, alas, have taken up the challenge. As Russ notes:

> One of the best things (for me) about science fiction is that—at least theoretically—it is a place where the ancient dualities disappear. Day and night, up and down, "masculine" and "feminine" are purely specific, limited phenomena which have been mythologized by people. They are man-made (not woman-made). Excepting up and down, night and day (maybe). Out in space there is no up or down, no day or night, and in the point of view space can give us, I think there is no "opposite" sex—what a word! Opposite what? The Eternal Feminine and the Eternal Masculine become the poetic fancies of a weakly dimorphic species trying to imitate every other species in a vain search for what is "natural." (Russ 1993, 43)

Certainly Russ, in most of the texts here, attempts to find new means of narrativizing that disrupt the traditional "masculine" form. The narrative of Elaine in *We Who are About To . . .* is fragmentary, depending upon what she has recorded for an unknown posterity, and, in at least one place, unreliable as to its faithfulness to actual events. The notion of a female protagonist in the Alyx stories is a revolutionary act, playing as it does against the sword-and-sorcery stories of, among others, Fritz Leiber. Russ later wrote: "People would say I wanted to be a man. Reviewers would howl in derision. By writing an adventure story with a female hero I was clearly breaking some basic taboo" (Russ "Creating" 5; quoted in Moylan 1986, 58) The Alyx stories slot together in numerous ways, potentially contradicting each other, certainly not respecting genre purity, and openly being narrated.

Most challenging to the traditional reader is the structure of *The Female Man*, containing as it does the four interleaved narratives and perceptions of Janet Evason (who may or may not be the Janet of "When It Changed") Jeannine Dadier, Joanna (a version of the author, or at least of the implied author), and Alice-Jael Reasoner (an agent who potentially seems a verbal echo of Alyx).

As Sarah Lefanu (1988) rightly notes: "*The Female Man* breaks all formal rules of narrative fiction. It has no beginning-middle-end, no clear relationship between author and characters and, indeed, no clear relationship between text and meaning . . . [it] challenges the simple notion of an author speaking and her readers hearing" (186–187). This is a long way indeed from the traditional male text.

Male language needs to be challenged by ambivalent monsters, to shake it to the foundations so that it can be rebuilt from scratch. The Medusa is one such beast: tagged as a monster (by men), a castrator (by men), yet actually "[s]he's beautiful and she's laughing" (Cixous 1981, 255). Laughter is one means for women (and ideally men too) to cut men who engage in oppressive practices down to size. Sometimes such laughter might reflect men's own anxieties back against themselves (or perhaps I should type "against ourselves," as I cannot maintain critical distance in this instance). This type, however, is laughter as excluding, which may just draw a new set of boundaries through enacting new rites (and rights).

Better still is the figure of the chiasmus, which undercuts boundaries and thresholds, and which might be reached by the nonaggressive humor. This is laughter as anti-rite, which offers access to other realities (perhaps even to the Real). This is laughter as a social lubricant, and is to be embraced. As Barreca (1992) suggests, "Humor is a show of both strength and vulnerability—you are willing to make the first move but you are trusting in the response of your listener. . . . A day during which we laughed is a day that has not been wasted—to laugh is affirm ourselves and our lives in a fundamental sense." (201). In shared laughter we can perhaps all meet, if only in the heart of the chiasmus.[20]

~

# 11 Violent Women, Womanly Violence
## Joanna Russ's Femmes Fatales

JASON P. VEST

In 1974, Philip K. Dick published an anti-abortion story titled "The Pre-Persons" that, Dick (1992) later recalled, "incurred the absolute hate of Joanna Russ," who, after reading it, "wrote me the nastiest letter I've ever received; at one point she said she usually offered to beat up people (she didn't use the word 'people') who expressed opinions such as [mine]" (393). Russ never physically "beat up" Dick, of course, although she had nothing gracious to say about his fictional representations of women. More intriguing, however, is that Russ informed Dick of her disagreement with his abortion politics in terms so strident that "The Pre-Persons" has never escaped its richly deserved reputation for misogyny. This exchange also illustrates a significant, but underappreciated, point about Russ's early fiction: the women in her short stories and novels of the 1960s and 1970s not only embrace implied or actual violence as effective means of expression, but also employ violent gestures as necessary components of achieving equality with the men who control their lives.

This judgment may be antithetical to traditional American assumptions about appropriate female behavior, but Russ's writing shares few of these assumptions. The stories in The Adventures of Alyx, an anthology of short stories and novellas originally published between 1967 and 1970, offer particularly significant examples of texts whose explicitly violent discourse suggests that women may only achieve full personhood by adopting the aggressive tendencies that American culture (especially canonical American literature) conventionally attributes to men. I am not arguing that Russ masculinizes her female characters by having them indulge in violent acts that prove a woman's worthiness to the men in her life (although this possibility certainly exists in The Adventures of Alyx, but rather that physical aggression, for Russ, is not an exclusively male trait foreign to female psychology. In this belief, she is out of step with her feminist contemporaries.

Russ, in The Adventures of Alyx, manipulates the conventions of the literary femme fatale to allow Alyx to fulfill her humanity through what I have chosen to call "womanly violence": the physical expression of aggression and anger that is entirely natural to a woman's character. This womanly violence is not mimetic—Alyx does not mimic the violent behavior of men—but is inherent to her status as a mature human being. The Adventures of Alyx deconstructs the assumption that women are incapable of extraordinary violence by linking its protagonist's intellectual and emotional passion to the physical harm that she sometimes gleefully inflicts upon other people. Alyx is an early literary analogue of the "ass-kicking women" that have become popular in late twentieth-century and early twenty-first-century American mass media (the eponymous lead characters in *Buffy the Vampire Slayer* and *Xena: Warrior Princess*, as well as Sydney Bristow, the secret-agent protagonist of *Alias*, are three obvious examples), as well as a fully realized woman whose personhood depends upon implied and actual violence.

By examining Russ's changes to the traditional femme fatale, I seek to dismantle the same dichotomies that Jeanne Cortiel (2000) questions in her fine essay, "Determinate Politics of Indeterminacy: Reading Joanna Russ's Recent Work in Light of Her Early Short Fiction." Cortiel believes that the "scholarship on sexuality in Russ's work has tended to reinforce the privilege of normative heterosexuality that the texts clearly undermine" (220); further, it endorses an essentialist division between men and women that apportions specific traits to each gender (in terms of my argument, aggression is assigned to men and peacemaking to women). "Russ's work, even in its explicitly feminist phase, never solely relies on such simple binary oppositions" (221), Cortiel (2000) writes in reference to Russ's 1975 novel *The Female Man*, although this judgment applies equally well to *The Adventures of Alyx*. Russ's fiction, in other words, cannot be reduced to mere feminist hostility toward an inevitably patriarchal symbolic order. "Russ's texts," Cortiel concludes, "do not wage all-out war against the heterosexist, patriarchal linguistic system because they are grounded in an awareness that they themselves are part of the same symbolic order. Russ's fiction is much too subtle and sophisticated in its political thinking to include such comparatively crude categories" (221).

The irony of Cortiel's incisive assessment of Russ's political project is that, although Russ may not declare all-out war against patriarchy in the Alyx stories, she nonetheless depicts a woman whose aggressive tendencies find expression in explicitly violent acts. *The Adventures of Alyx* provides several relevant examples of this phenomenon, particularly in the book's first two short stories, "Bluestocking" and "I Thought She Was Afeard Till She Stroked My Beard." "Bluestocking" finds Alyx in the City of Ourdh, making "a modest living as pick-lock, a profession that gratified her sense of subtlety. It provided her with a living, a craft and a society" (1983a, 9). Russ's prose is, as always, suggestively ironic. While it is appropriate that working as a pick-lock (an illicit enterprise that depends upon stealth and secrecy) satisfies Alyx's sense of subtlety, the fact that this profession provides her with a society indicates that community is important, if not crucial, to Alyx's highly individualistic character. Alyx's occupation is not overtly violent, but Russ's language suggests that the implicit violence it does to the social order—theft being the object of much bourgeois fear and loathing—does not mitigate Alyx's need for connection with other people (even if these people are fellow, professional pick-locks). The story, therefore, begins by intimating the violence that readers might expect from a crime plot, but the expected punishment that Alyx risks—namely, incarceration—never arrives. Russ adapts the linguistic and narrative conventions of both science fiction and crime fiction to tell a quirkier, more complicated story about a woman who employs, as well as endures, violence to achieve her own ends.

The ironies of Russ's well-crafted prose proliferate: Alyx's criminal career begins after she leaves a religious delegation that has come to Ourdh "to convert the dissolute citizens to the ways of virtue and the one true God, a Bang tree of awful majesty" (1983a, 9). Alyx, however, decides that "the religion of Yp (as the hill god was called) was a disastrous piece of nonsense, and that deceiving a young woman in matters of such importance was a piece of thoughtlessness for which it would take some weeks of hard, concentrated thought to think up a proper reprisal" (9). Alyx's rejection of religion leads to immediate thoughts of revenge, demonstrating that, from the story's opening lines, Alyx's passions include both the life of the mind and an aggressive emotional response to her intellectual manipulation by religious authority. Russ's prose is again notable, not for its violence, but for its understated humor. Parodying the biblical symbol of the burning bush by identifying the god of Alyx's religion as a tree before proclaiming that religion to be a deceit worthy of violent reprisal accentuates the protagonist's status as an antiheroine while elliptically foreshadowing her transformation into a femme fatale.

Violence is not far behind. A young noblewoman named Lady Edarra recruits Alyx to act as her personal bodyguard and guide. Edarra wishes to leave Ourdh to avoid marrying a wealthy landlord "who had buried three previous wives and would now have the privilege of burying the Lady Edarra" (12–13). The possibility of violence against women, or at least against Edarra, prompts Alyx to purchase two short swords and a dagger after making a telling comment: " 'Kill one, kill all, kill devil!' said Alyx gleefully" (14). She then commandeers an empty tramp boat to effect Edarra's escape from Ourdh and to prevent a marriage that will consign Edarra to the status of property. Alyx's excitement, the reader now understands, is an integral and innate part of her character. When, after slaughtering a sea monster that terrifies Edarra, Alyx sees three men in a sloop approaching the tramp boat, Russ's narration of

this scene complicates the reader's response to the forthcoming battle between Alyx and the sloop's male interlopers: "Now in Ourdh there is a common saying that if you have not strength, there are three things which will
serve as well: deceit, surprise and speed. These are women's natural weapons" (19). Russ may at first seem to indulge the essentialist notion that women
are less capable of inflicting bodily harm because they are physically weaker
than men. Alyx's violent behavior, however, quickly reduces this statement
to a common Ourdhian adage that is as patriarchal as the city whose social
economy allows Edarra to be sold to a landlord who wishes to enjoy conjugal
pleasure with a much younger woman. As the men climb aboard the tramp
boat, "Alyx saw with joy that two of the three were fat and all were dirty; *too
vain, she thought, to keep in trim or take precautions*" (19; emphasis in original).
The zest with which Alyx dispatches one of the men is significant:

> Then in a burst of speed she took him under his guard at a pitch of
> the ship and slashed his sword wrist, disarming him. But her thrust
> carried her too far and she fell; grasping his wounded wrist with his
> other hand, he launched himself at her, and Alyx—planting both knees
> against his chest—helped him into the sea. He took a piece of the rail
> with him. By the sound of it, he could not swim. She stood over the rail,
> gripping her blade until he vanished for the last time. It was over that
> quickly. (19–20)

Alyx's nonchalance at perpetrating violence against this man (and si-
lently watching him drown without giving a single thought to helping him)
illustrates how natural aggression is to her. Alyx then notices "Edarra standing over the third man, sword in hand, an incredulous, pleased expression
on her face. Blood holds no terrors for a child of Ourdh, unfortunately" (20).
Alyx's slight qualm about Edarra's youthful enthusiasm for violence does
not alter the basic narrative reality that Russ sketches with precision: these
women take control of their lives by harnessing violence in their own defense.
Alyx and, to a lesser degree, Edarra need no male protection because they
provide it for themselves. Women are not subservient to men in this regard,
even if they can be bought and sold on a patriarchal marriage market. They
are femmes fatales (literally, fatal women) when challenged by men who wish
to take physical and emotional advantage of them.

Russ's implicit invocation of the femme fatale, as Alyx and Edarra illus-
trate, alters received notions about how this character type functions within
American literature. Science fiction and detective fiction have, despite a broad
array of variations, cemented the femme fatale as a stock patriarchal character: a seductive cipher who employs mystification, sexual allure, and devious-
ness to lead men to moral, spiritual, and physical ruin. Russ's early fiction,

however, transforms this trope into a far more specific character that, by transgressing the role's conventionally sexist boundaries, proposes a different view of women. Russ's femmes fatales are women who not only claim direct control over their lives, but who commit violent acts to achieve or to preserve their independence from men. Such independence does not preclude mature sexual relationships with men, but it liberates Russ's femmes fatales from lives as sexual objects that merely bring pleasure and/or damage to the men they encounter.

The joy that Alyx feels when she sees that the sloop men will be no match for her enacts Russ's new vision of the femme fatale even as it encapsulates the mythological supremacy with which Russ begins "Bluestocking." "It is common knowledge," the narrator reveals in the story's first paragraph, "that Woman was created fully a quarter of an hour before Man, and has kept that advantage to this very day" (9). The cadences of this line parallel the rhythms of the opening sentence of Jane Austen's *Pride and Prejudice*—"It is a truth universally acknowledged, that a single man in possession of a good fortune, must be in want of a wife" (5)—to suggest that the narrator of "Bluestocking" is a woman. Even so, Russ's narrator does not reverse women's traditional oppression to demonstrate that women are, finally, innately superior to men. Rather, she underscores the irony of both Alyx's and Edarra's constrained position within Ourdh's sexist society. Edarra must still flee Ourdh to avoid an unwanted marriage (arranged, notably, by Edarra's mother), while Alyx is far more than a stereotypical man-hater. After defeating the sloops' male sailors, for instance, Alyx recalls a man with whom she enjoyed a brief, but lively, affair:

> "Ah! what a man. A big Northman with hair like yours and a gold-red beard—God, what a beard!—Fafnir—no, Fafh—well, something ridiculous. But he was far from ridiculous. He was amazing."
> Edarra said nothing, rapt.
> "He was strong," said Alyx, laughing, "and hairy, beautifully hairy. And willful! I said to him, 'Man, if you must follow your eyes into every whorehouse—' And we fought! At a place called the Silver Fish. Overturned tables. What a fuss! And a week later," (she shrugged ruefully) "gone. There it is. And I can't even remember his name."
> "Is that sad?" said Edarra.
> "I don't think so," said Alyx. "After all, I remember his beard," and she smiled wickedly. (26)

Alyx's sensual interest in this man celebrates her independence from his control while emphasizing her sexuality. Alyx unapologetically protects her physical and psychological integrity by enjoying men (and fighting them) before moving onto new experiences and passions. Her impish sense of humor, in which she dismisses a casual affair that brings her pleasure (but no emotional commitment), is not violently destructive, but it challenges traditional American formulations of women as conservative, passive, and silent receivers of male sexual attention.

This theme receives sustained development in *The Adventures of Alyx*'s second story, "I Thought She Was Afeard Till She Stroked My Beard." This tale, a prequel to the events of "Bluestocking," begins with a line significant for its revision of traditional patriarchal assumptions: "Many years ago, long before the world got into the state it is in today, young women were supposed to obey their husbands; but nobody knows if they did or not" (31). This final comment casts doubt on the sexist assumption that it simultaneously asserts, positioning young women as subservient to their husbands, yet questioning both the validity of this claim's historical accuracy and the notion of female subservience. This ambiguity, typical of the *Alyx* stories (and Russ's fiction in general), continues as the tale develops. "I Thought She Was Afeard" goes on to depict Alyx's origin as a femme fatale who discovers violence to be a meaningful method of self-assertion.

Alyx, who remains unnamed almost until the story's final line, begins as the wife of an abusive husband. When Alyx announces that she will leave him, her husband attempts to whip her and provokes an unexpected reaction that becomes the first expression of her womanly violence: "He swung [the whip] high in the air and down in a snapping arc to where she—not where she was; where she had been—this extraordinary young woman had leapt half the distance between them and wrested the stock of the whip from him a foot from his hand. He was off balance and fell; with a vicious grimace she brought the stock down short and hard on the top of his head. She had all her wits about her as she stood over him" (33).

Alyx's aggression is not purely defensive. She discovers a previously unsuspected talent for violence that, significantly, remains rational even as it liberates Alyx physically, socially, and sexually from her husband's control. Alyx uses violence to escape her husband rather than subjugating him to her will, and her vicious grimace unleashes a type of pleasure that, before her transformation into a femme fatale, was unimaginable: "Slowly she straightened up, with a swagger, with a certain awe. . . . She slapped [her husband], called his name impatiently, but when the fallen man moved a little—or she fancied he did—a thrill ran up her spine to the top of her head, a kind of soundless chill, and snatching the vegetable knife from the floor where she dropped it, she sprang like an arrow from the bow into the night that waited, all around the house, to devour" (33).

Russ demonstrates how integral aggression is to Alyx's character. This womanly violence, in fact, marks Alyx as a destructive nocturnal figure whose desire to devour, like the night's, has no specific object. She leaves behind her husband (and her former life) by rushing into the sea. Just as significant is the telling detail that battering her husband into submission arouses Alyx. The story, in this passage, rejects essentialist notions of women as gentle souls who may be driven to violence, only to later regret it. Alyx is not the traditional battered wife whose violent outburst drains her of spirit; instead, it energizes her in a singularly aggressive way. Alyx is freed to do as she pleases, without restriction or constraint.

This freedom resonates in, and in certain instances predicts, the women's liberation movement of the 1960s and 1970s. In 1972, Russ wrote "The New Misandry," an essay that opens with lines so sarcastic, so cutting, and so honest that they seem like direct descendants of the Alyx stories:

> Gee, isn't it awful for women to hate men?
>
> Of course lots of men despise women, but that's different; woman-hating isn't serious—at worst it's eccentric, at best sort of cute. Woman-haters (many of whom are women) can express themselves all over the place, as the latest cartoon about women drivers reminds me, but man-haters have fewer opportunities. Man-hating takes self-control. Besides, man-haters are in the minority; for every Valerie Solanas, how many rapists, how many male murderers are there? What male reviewer found Hitchcock's "Frenzy" one-20th as revolting as Solanas's "Scum Manifesto?" Of course Solanas went out and did it, but then so do many, many men—in the small town I live in there were several incidents of rape last year, and a common response to them was laughter. (1972d, 167)

When Russ reproaches what she terms "a fine case of double-think" (167), her tone conveys the silliness and mendacity of denying misandry's powerful presence in women's lives, or at least in the lives of women who no longer accept patriarchal control. "Perhaps the most important cause of the fear of misandry," Russ writes in one of the essay's most penetrating observations, "is the awfulness of facing the extent to which misandry and misogyny are an inescapable part of the texture of our lives" (1972d, 168). Russ neither accepts nor countenances the common view of man-hating as a malformed and distinctly *unfeminine* act; rather, she acknowledges the pervasive sexism that refuses women even the territory of their own, honest response to social, political, and domestic repression.

Violence is, in Russ's view, a natural reaction to this state of affairs: "I think we ought to decide that man-hating is not only respectable but honorable" (1972d, 169). Russ goes on to ask and answer a fundamental question: "Why is man-hating so dreadful? Because it is easier for everybody, male and female, to demand saintly purity of the oppressed than to tee off on the oppressor" (170). "Teeing off" indicates a variety of behaviors, especially the withering social analysis that Russ conducts in "The New Misandry," but violence is certainly one of this term's unstated connotations. Alyx, in *The Adventures of Alyx*, literalizes Russ's sarcasm by refusing to accept the oppressive instincts of her male counterparts and the repressive controls of her patriarchal society, even as she develops her violent impulses into admirable fighting skills.

Russ's ire in "The New Misandry," however, never rises to the level of Valerie Solanas (2000), who, in the "SCUM Manifesto," famously declares, "The male is a biological accident. . . . To be male is to be deficient, emotionally limited; maleness is a deficiency disease and males are emotional cripples" (201). While no single author can represent the whole of radical feminism, as Barbara A. Crow (2000) notes in her excellent introduction to *Radical Feminism: A Documentary Reader*, Solanas, more than any other participant in this diverse and complicated social movement, has come to personify the excesses of womanly violence that other feminists have found it necessary to condemn. Russ's fiction and nonfiction, however, by refusing to denounce violence, posit it instead as an essential tool of women's liberation and independence. Alyx does not believe, as Solanus asserts, that men are "walking abortions" (201), but Alyx enthusiastically rejects the patriarchal assumption that women are physically and psychological deficient.

In "I Thought She Was Afeard," Alyx steals aboard a pirate ship. Demanding to see its captain, Alyx meets Blackbeard, who trains her as a swordswoman and, eventually, becomes her lover. Their relationship is one of contest and conflict, with Alyx refusing to live simply as "the captain's woman." She takes great pleasure from their sexual union, but does not feel that this physical relationship relegates her to secondhand status. When Blackbeard announces that Alyx cannot accompany him into a port town in which he has business, Alyx protests:

> She said again, "Why not?" and her whole face lifted and became sharper as one's face does when one stares against the sun.
> "Because you can't," he said. . . . "I won't be able to take care of you."
> "You won't have to," said she. He shook his head. "You won't come."
> "Of course I'll come," she said.
> "You won't," said he.
> "The devil I won't!" said she. (39)

Alyx rebukes Blackbeard's belief that he must care for her. Her willfulness is notable in its aggressive stance toward a man whose huge physical size dwarfs Alyx. She is not afraid of Blackbeard, defying him, in Russ's intriguing comparison, as would a person who looks into the sun. Alyx's metaphorical recklessness remains ambiguous by implying that she risks blindness in her determination to remain independent, yet it is also another sign of her inner confidence. Alyx, in the story's next passage, follows Blackbeard to a small tavern to observe his conversation with an unknown man. Interrupting their meeting angers both Blackbeard and his interlocutor, but Alyx does not care.

In her exchanges with Blackbeard, Alyx becomes the healthy "angry woman" that Susi Kaplow (1973) discusses in "Getting Angry." Observing that the traditional woman "is a living, walking apology for her own existence— what could be more foreign than self-assertion?" (38), Kaplow (1973) outlines a position that neatly describes Alyx: "Healthy anger says 'I'm a person. I have certain human rights which you can't deny. I have a right to be treated with fairness and compassion, I have a right to live my life as I see fit, I have a right to get what I can for myself without hurting you. And if you deprive me of my rights, I'm not going to thank you, I'm going to say 'fuck off' and fight you if I have to' " (37). No matter how healthy or angry Alyx is, however, she cannot escape patriarchy, as subsequent events in "I Thought She Was Afeard" demonstrate. Blackbeard, the story soon reveals, does not have the best business mind. When he incorrectly concludes his transaction, Alyx cannot restrain herself: " 'No, dammit,' she cried, 'you're ten percent off!' He slapped her. The other gentlemen cleared his throat." (1983a, 41) The situation deteriorates when a third man, who has been eyeing Alyx from across the room, approaches her after Blackbeard concludes his business:

> "Well, baby," said the intruder.
> Blackbeard turned his back on the girl.
> The intruder took hold of her by the nape of the neck but she did not move; he talked to her in a low voice; finally she blurted out, "Oh yes! Go on!" (fixing her eyes on the progress of Blackbeard's monolithic back towards the door) and stumbled aside as the latter all but vaulted over a table to retrieve his lost property. She followed him, her head bent, violently flushed. Two streets off he stopped, saying, "Look, my dear, can I please not take you ashore again?" but she would not answer, no, not a word. (1983a, 41; emphasis in original)

In these passages Alyx is not only diminished to a nagging girlfriend who must be slapped back into line, but also reduced to a woman who must rely upon Blackbeard to rescue her from the intruder's sexual predations. Perhaps most objectionable for feminist readers, Blackbeard still considers Alyx to be his property, returning her to the role in which she began the story (namely, the subservient woman of a physically abusive man). Alyx's refusal to forgive

Blackbeard's behavior is a half-hearted affirmation of willfulness that merely emphasizes her impotence. Alyx cannot change Blackbeard's attitudes or the patriarchal system that encourages men to objectify her, and is left to sulk about her salvation at Blackbeard's hands.

This dispiriting development paradoxically signals the political maturity that Jeanne Cortiel (2000) notes in Russ's early fiction. Russ realizes that no matter how vibrant and independent her femmes fatales may be, they must still negotiate the limitations that patriarchy imposes upon them simply because they are women. Rather than proposing a utopian society that allows Alyx absolute freedom from sexist constraints, Russ gives Ourdh a sexual economy familiar to its American readership to demonstrate just how reductive patriarchy is, even for women who violently resist its many oppressions. In a 1994 interview with Aruna Sitesh, Russ acknowledged the complications of writing feminist fiction:

> I found science fiction a very congenial way of talking about feminism, although it's a mistake to think that I used science fiction to present my ideas. This sounds as if the ideas came first and the story second. I never write like that. The story always comes first as a story and I discover my ideas as I write the story. Often I don't know what the ideas are until quite a while after I've finished a book or a story. I do think the freedom of science fiction means that women or feminists can have more chance in it to depict the kinds of things they do envision as new for women than they could in other kinds of fiction. (Sitesh 1994, 198)

This freedom, which includes Russ's freedom to depict womanly violence, does not depart so completely from the realities of American patriarchal society that The Adventures of Alyx becomes total fantasy. "Certainly science fiction is about today's reality," Russ tells Sitesh (Sitesh 1994, 198). Alyx's womanly violence must be situated for effect within traditional attitudes that circumscribe a woman's life and that Russ's feminist contemporaries, whether or not they identified themselves as radical, actively contested during the time of the Alyx stories' composition.

"I Thought She Was Afeard Till She Stroked My Beard" embodies this dichotomy. It is a story whose very title suppresses Alyx's ability to speak on her own behalf. In the end, Alyx's only choice is to leave Blackbeard. After one final battle in which she enthusiastically kills the pirate ship's attackers, Blackbeard comforts Alyx by noting that she will not have to participate in more violence:

> "Well," she said, "perhaps I will all the same," and in pure good humor she put her arms about his neck. There were tears in her eyes—

perhaps they were tears of laughter—and in the light of the rising sun the deck showed ever more ruddy and grotesque. *What a mess*, she thought. She said, "It's all right; don't you worry," which was, all in all and in the light of things, a fairly kind goodbye. (1983a, 45; emphasis in original)

Alyx, a woman of intricate emotion, is as capable of anger, aggression, and violence as she is of joy, tenderness, and love. She demonstrates that a female character need not inevitably become a man (or even become like a man) when she claims traditionally masculine traits as her own. Alyx, indeed, personifies the definition of "bitch" that Joreen Freeman (2000) proposes in her 1970 essay "The Bitch Manifesto": "What is disturbing about a Bitch is that she is androgynous. She incorporates within herself qualities traditionally defined as 'masculine' as well as 'feminine.' A bitch is blunt, direct, arrogant, at times egoistic. . . . She disdains the vicarious life deemed natural to women because she wants to have a life of her own" (227).

A better characterization of Alyx, particularly in "Bluestocking" and "I Thought She Was Afeard," is difficult to imagine. Alyx neither accepts conventional limitations on her power nor restricts herself to traditional ideas of how a woman should behave. She refuses to live vicariously through men, instead claiming a life of courageous exploits for herself.

After saying goodbye to Blackbeard, Alyx arrives at Ourdh six weeks later, alone and ready for more adventure. She is, by this time, a fully realized character who—despite her attraction to, affection for, and even love of Blackbeard—reclaims an authentic and independent identity that may not fully transcend patriarchy, but that also refuses to submit to it. Alyx's power is compromised, complicated, and mediated by the sexist strictures of the society that has formed her, but she is also a memorable, passionate, and original femme fatale whom Russ imbues with great vitality.

Womanly violence and feminist power, therefore, do not enshrine Alyx as either a simpleminded or a simplistically drawn heroine. Russ does not celebrate the final triumph of women over sexism in *The Adventures of Alyx*; instead, she offers a more complex vision of female identity that demonstrates how significant violence is, for women no less than for men, in developing an authentic sense of self. Genuine personhood does not arise when Alyx mimics male aggression, but rather when she employs violence to satisfy her own longings, desires, and goals. This new spin on the literary femme fatale marks Joanna Russ's early writing as distinctive within the tradition of mid-twentieth-century science fiction. It also preserves Russ's reputation as one of America's most innovative, thoughtful, and fascinating feminist authors.

~

## 12 Art and Amity

*The "Opposed Aesthetic" in Mina Loy and Joanna Russ*

PAUL MARCH-RUSSELL

In her study of postmodernism and feminist science fiction, Jenny Wolmark (1994) briefly refers to Joanna Russ's novel, *The Female Man* (1975), as exploring "the pleasures of dissonance and incongruity that occur when gender and genre are in conflict." Wolmark continues by arguing that the novel's fragmented narrative disrupts "the familiar discursive practices of science fiction in a playful and witty way," so as to generate a series of female identities that are both multiple and decentered (21). This optimistic view of Russ's feminism, which emphasizes the pleasure to be found in her writing, also surfaces in Donna Haraway's (1991) passing reference to the "exuberant eroticism" of *The Female Man* as part of her landmark "Cyborg Manifesto" (178). Richard Law, in associating Russ with the metafictional experiments of writers such as John Barth, also stresses wit and playfulness as the defining characteristics of Russ's innovative fiction (146–156). While it is possible to see this type of reading as an appropriation of Russ's science fiction by postmodern thought, in its emphases upon irony, self-reflexivity, and decentered subjectivities (Luckhurst 2005, 159–160), a similar response to Russ's work can also be found in highly politicized accounts, such as that of Tom Moylan (1986) who equates Russ's utopianism with both personal liberation and collective resistance (55–90). As Alan Sinfield (1992), writing in another context, has suggested, to claim a text is subversive is "to imply achievement—that something *was subverted*," only for that subversion to be subsequently contained (49). To overemphasize the pleasure and delight of Russ's writing not only glosses the stylistic brutality that other critics have noted (Luckhurst 2005, 193), but also presents an overoptimistic reading of her politics that effectively forecloses the continuing dissidence of her fiction. Russ's work can still unsettle contemporary critics such as Adam Roberts (2000, 96–97). Yet even one of her most astute advocates, Sarah Lefanu (1988), concludes her account of *The Female Man* with a passage that makes her laugh—as if laughter was Russ' chief legacy (192).

In this essay, I shall explore the jarring and discontinuous elements of

Russ's prose, principally in The Female Man, but also the novel, We Who Are About To . . . (1977), and the short story, "Everyday Depressions" (in Russ 1984c). Their conflicting form describes a struggle amid generic conventions and gender stereotyping to express a notion of amity that would transcend pre-existing conceptions of love and friendship. This notional amity can be compared to Jacques Derrida's (1997) concept of aimance, and which David Ayers (1999) has summarized as "a form of loving which goes beyond the socially determined forms of love and friendship, and beyond the existing cultures and traditions of love" (220).

In order to throw this struggle into relief, I shall read Russ's fiction through the poetry and unorthodox feminism of an avant-garde precursor, Mina Loy, in particular, her sequence "Songs to Joannes" (1917), her "Feminist Manifesto" (1914) and her health and beauty proposal, "Auto-Facial-Construction" (1919). Loy's agonistic writing, especially on questions of female identity, not only suggests similarities with Russ; more important, it establishes a critical and historical framework through which Russ's own experiments with form can be assessed. While it is not my intention to propose Loy as an influence upon Russ, Loy is very much the kind of female author that Russ might be interested in. A poet and artist from London, by way of Florence where she worked under the influence of the Italian Futurists, Loy became a minor celebrity during her time in New York between 1916 and 1917.[1] She was profiled as an example of modern womanhood; Russ too has acknowledged her own interest in the "New Woman" of this period in such stories as "Scenes from Domestic Life" (in Russ 1984c). Loy was celebrated and condemned in equal measure for her transgression of conventional feminine roles: the same controversy that befell Loy's friends and contemporaries in Paris and New York, such as Djuna Barnes, H.D., Marianne Moore, and Gertrude Stein, and those whom Russ (1983b) discusses in How to Suppress Women's Writing. Of more particular importance, though, Loy prefigures Russ by retaining the utopian ideal of love as an order that would transform preexisting social relations. In this order, however, for both authors, conventional heterosexual romance has been abandoned (Loy participated in a bohemian lifestyle; Russ declared herself as lesbian). Loy's writing offers a perspective with which to view Russ's articulation of an "Opposed Aesthetic" in conflict with the hegemonic discourse of misogyny and homophobia. (All citations from Loy's work will be drawn from the 1985 Conover edition.)

## Mina Loy: "There Is No Love Alone"

Like Russ, who has drawn upon avant-garde influences while declining to identify her work with the avant-garde, Loy pursued an equally ambiguous pathway through the development of modernism. On the one hand, she associated with more avant-garde movements than any other Anglo-American modernist. In Italy, Loy was the lover of both Giovanni Papini and Filippo Marinetti, the leading figures within Futurism; in New York, she was part of the local Dada scene alongside such other émigrés as Marcel Duchamp; and in Paris, she mixed with the surrealist grouping built around André Breton. On the other hand, Loy was never a member of these avant-garde circles for long. In later years, she came to identify with other artists who worked outside of recognizable schools, such as the conceptual artist, Joseph Cornell. Part of the reason for Loy's lack of affiliation to any one movement, besides her own restless temperament, is the chauvinism that existed within these camps. Despite the avant-garde's claim to sever all preexisting social relations in order to discover new forms of self-expression (a major appeal for Loy, born into a respectable working-class family in London), this declaration failed to produce a radical agenda as far as women were concerned. In his "Futurist Manifesto" of 1909, Marinetti (1998) glorifies "war—the world's only hygiene—militarism, patriotism, the destructive gesture of freedom-bringers, beautiful ideas worth dying for, *and scorn for woman*" before concluding that "art, in fact, can be nothing but violence, cruelty, and injustice" (251, 253). As Mark Dery (1996) has also observed, the work of New York Dadaists such as Duchamp and Francis Picabia is both sexually explicit and strongly phallocentric (Dery 188–191).

In short, while the avant-garde of the early twentieth century represents a rejection of traditional romantic values and sexual norms, there prevails a bohemianism based upon male chauvinism and misogyny, a theme frequently satirized in Loy's poetry. "The Effectual Marriage" (1917), for example, is based upon Loy's affair with the painter and intellectual, Papini. Through the character of Gina, Loy questions the objectification of woman as muse, the fate of so many women (Nancy Cunard and Lee Miller among them) associated with the avant-garde:

> But she was more than that
> Being an incipience    a correlative
> an instigation of the reaction of man
>
> From the palpable to the transcendent
> Mollescent irritant of his fantasy
> Gina had her use (26)

By contrast, her lover, the artist Miovanni, thinks "alone in the dark," remains "Monumentally the same," while it is Gina who composes "a poem on the milk" bill as she shops and cooks for Miovanni (38–39). In poems such as

"Giovanni Franchi" (1916), Loy sharpens her attack by suggesting a homosexual attraction between the philosopher, Bapini, and his acolyte, Franchi—an appalling thought to the macho rhetoric of the Futurists—while, in "Lions' Jaws" (1920), Loy ridicules Marinetti's dream of agamogenesis, or male reproduction:

> burst in a manifesto
> notifying women's wombs
> of Man's immediate agamogenesis
>
> . . . . . . . . . . . . . . . . . . . . . . . . . . .
>                              Insurance
> of his spiritual integrity
> against the carnivorous courtesan (47)

As Loy suggests (and as Russ implies in The Female Man), fantasies of male reproduction are motivated not only by narcissism, bordering upon same-sex attraction as in the Freudian model of self-love, but also by a frightened demonization of the woman as sexual predator.

It is in this climate, then, that Loy attempts to formulate a poetic language that will not only address itself to the needs of women, in particular the female artist, but also articulate a notion of love that has been disavowed by the stridency of the male avant-garde. Though Loy's use of free verse, spacing within lines, and irregular syntax appear compatible with Futurist tactics to shock and disorientate the reader, Loy seeks to disrupt what she regards as a man-made language: a gendered take upon Dada's abolition of sense-meaning. As Tristan Tzara writes in his "Dada Manifesto" (1918), "I am against systems; the most acceptable system is that of having none on principle" (Tzara 1998, 278). Consequently, having affiliated herself to the avant-garde at the expense of mainstream feminism, Loy does not offer the consolation of an alternative female identity. In this respect, Loy's position is not unlike that of the former suffragette and editor of The Egoist, Dora Marsden, who in 1915 declared: "Our war is with words and in their every aspect: grammar, accidence, syntax: body, blood, and bone" (1998, 332). Loy's negative ethos, though, can be traced back to her "Feminist Manifesto" (1914).

The manifesto rejects contemporary concerns of the women's movement: political and economic rights, education, employment, and sexual morality. For Loy, these are all reformist measures whereas "the only method is Absolute Demolition" (153). Loy asserts that, under present social conditions, women's only choice is "between Parasitism, & Prostitution—or Negation" (154). She dismisses the feminist demand for social equality as, according to Loy, it defines female identity in relation to masculinity and masculine notions of womanhood. In particular, Loy rejects the idea of feminine virtue, which valorizes sexual innocence over experience, maternal destiny over personal desire. Loy goes so far as to demand "the *unconditional* surgical *destruction of virginity*" (154–155). By severing femaleness from sexual purity, Loy proceeds to dismantle the basis for marriage, to insist that women must first find themselves, and to emphasize that women must solely be responsible for child-rearing. Implicit in these demands is an egotistical call for self-fulfillment, in which women would no longer be objects in a masculine discourse but self-determining subjects. The sexual relation, where "there is *nothing impure*" (156), acts as a microcosm for Loy's idealized transformation of all political and social relations.

The manifesto is striking in a number of ways. First, in questioning the social category of Woman, Loy prefigures the thinking of third-wave feminists, such as Judith Butler and Julia Kristeva, with whom Russ has been compared.[2] Second, Loy presents language as an instrument of patriarchy in which women are objectified, a point that Russ, like other feminists of her generation, pursues in her fiction and criticism. Third, Loy privileges the sexual expression of women as a potentially subversive force that can be aided by technology. Loy not only applies Dada's use of technology "to ridicule and dismantle bourgeois high culture and ideology" (Huyssen 1988, 11) to sexual politics, but also prefigures feminist thinkers such as Haraway and Shulamith Firestone, the latter an important influence on Russ. In her bizarrely imaginative health and beauty proposal, "Auto-Facial-Construction" (1919), Loy presents the body as plastic, a commodity rather than a metaphysical essence that can be reconditioned through the power of thought:

> I will instruct men or women who are intelligent and for the briefest period, patient, to become masters of their facial destiny. I understand the skull with its muscular sheath, as a sphere whose superficies can be voluntarily energised. And the foundations of beauty as embedded in the three interconnected zones of energy encircling this sphere. . . . Control, through the identity of your conscious will, with these centres and zones, can be perfectly attained through my system, which does not include any form of cutaneous hygiene. . . . Through Auto-Facial-Construction the attachments of the muscles to the bones are revitalised, as also the gums, and the original facial contours are permanently observed as a structure which can be relied upon without anxiety as to the ravages of time. (165–166)

Loy demystifies the human body as a spiritual vessel while, at the same time, presenting it as a physical object that can be reinvented through the exertion of will. Just as historically produced women are dissociated from metaphysical notions of womanhood, so Loy extracts the material body from a cultural ideology that emphasizes its intrinsic autonomy. In advance of cyberfeminists such as Haraway and Sadie Plant, who tend to celebrate the utopian space of the interchangeable and spiritually divested body, Loy casts physical identity as porous and malleable. Yet, in effectively appropriating a decadent aesthetic whereby the female form was enjoyed for its superficiality (Beerbohm 1894, 65–82), Loy's vision emerges not from a celebration of physicality but from a masculine rhetoric in which the female body was viewed as a passive object. Consequently, the maneuverings within Loy's thought offer a clearer insight into the uncertain mix of pain and pleasure that underwrites feminist fictions of bodily modification, such as Russ's The Female Man and Angela Carter's The Passion of New Eve (1977). As Tim Armstrong (1998) has noted, the paradox of Loy's beauty regime is that it "is both natural and artificial; a cosmetics and an expression of the truth of the self" (122). Loy authenticates her method only by revealing the inauthenticity of the human subject. Appropriately enough, it is performers such as "the society woman, the actor, the actress, the man of public career" (166), whom Loy feels will benefit most from her scheme. Yet, performance is a role that Loy herself assumes in poems such as "Lions' Jaws" where she casts herself as:

> Nima Lyo, alias Anim Yol, alias
> Imna Oly
> (secret service buffoon to the Woman's Cause) (49)

The reproduction of identities is itself seen as a mechanical process in poems such as "Human Cylinders" (1917), though in a late poem, "Brain" (1945), Loy describes human consciousness as a mindless recording device that replays and sabotages memory, exposing the discrepancies between inner and outer expression (Last Lunar Baedeker 257).

The interpenetration of bodies and technology allows Loy to cast human identity as a spectacle in which fiction and reality are held in tension with one another. Russ, too, uses various forms of simulation, pretense, and disguise in novels, such as The Female Man, and stories such as "The Mystery of the Young Gentleman" (in Russ 1984c).

Yet, the tone of Loy's poetry is satirical rather than joyful. What is revealed by the comparison between technology and the human body are the shortcomings within bohemian love, suspended as a mirror to normal (patriarchal) sexual relations. As Loy emphasizes in her manifesto, the transition from subjection to self-knowledge will involve "a devastating psychological upheaval" (153) for both men and women. Consequently, Loy's utopianism is not founded upon the carnivalesque play of sexual freedom (glorified by the male avant-garde), but upon the difficult forging of a new relation between the individual ego and its external reality.[3] As the record of this transition,

Loy's poetry sets pain alongside pleasure. In "Songs to Joannes" (1917), the conflicting range of emotion is registered at the level of syntax and wordplay, as the poem moves between the respective poles of the "inviolate ego" and "the terrific Nirvana" (58) of heterosexual relations.

Having renounced both mainstream feminism and women's definition in marriage, Loy describes the vicariousness of sexual attraction where the promise of commitment is absent. She contrasts mindless physical pleasure, the "rosy snout" of the "Pig Cupid" "Rooting erotic garbage" (53), with a lament for what could have been: "We might have coupled / In the bed-ridden monopoly of a moment. . . . We might have given birth to a butterfly" (54). Yet, the use of the conditional "might" suggests also the uncertainty of the relationship, as if Loy's narrator is attempting to recall what exactly did happen. The indeterminacy of the narration is itself symptomatic of Loy trusting to an egoism that she celebrates, for example, in her "Apology of Genius" (1922). Yet, in the absence of traditional social certainties governing the conduct of heterosexual romance, Loy's egoism gives way to doubt and anxiety: "Is it true / That I have set you apart. . . . Or are you / Only the other half / Of an ego's necessity" (57). While trusting to her own ego, Loy's narrator is equally aware of her lover as a separate subject with no surety that her love will be returned, even if desirable:

> For far further
> Differentiation
> Rather than watch
> Own-self distortion
> Wince in the alien ego (66)

Yet, despite the precariousness of their relationship, there remains "Something taking shape / Something that has a new name" (57). This inexpressible presence embodies a new relation between self and other that would transform existing social relations, a utopian order that Loy can only signal as "Love—the preeminent litterateur" (68). Consequently, while "Songs to Joannes" witnesses the fragility of sexual relations that have abandoned the conventions of heterosexual romance, the frustration of desire implicitly describes the striving after some ideal that would radically alter this situation.[4] In an unpublished poem, "There Is No Love Alone" (possibly written in or around 1940), Loy ventures to suggest that this ideal is founded not on the metaphysical essence of the autonomous body but on the reciprocation of multiple bodies and identities that blend to become a new compound (233).

Loy questions, then, the objectification of the female form within the chauvinistic discourse of the avant-garde. She proceeds to demystify the autonomy of the body, in particular, through the role of technology. Last, in sequences such as "Songs to Joannes," Loy gestures toward a notion of love mediated through the openness and plurality of the body. This nonessential ethos surrounding the possibility of friendship at the expense of heterosexual romance can also be read as an emerging discourse in Russ's fiction.

## Joanna Russ: "Why Life Doesn't Match the Stories"

Russ severed her connection with heterosexual romantic conduct when, at about the same time as starting *The Female Man* in 1969, she came out as a lesbian. She had already begun to identify herself as a feminist soon after her return to Cornell University as a tutor in 1968. Yet, just as Loy attempted to articulate a discourse around sexuality that contravened the mainstream feminism of her day,[5] so Russ has criticized the more puritanical aspects of the American women's movement, especially in campaigns against pornography and the prohibition of sexual images. Much of Russ's fiction has been concerned with the expression of women, especially their capacity for violence or to take the initiative in sex, even where this conduct not only contradicts patriarchal norms of feminine behavior but also mainstream feminist notions of womanhood. Consequently, while Russ has aligned herself more closely with feminism than has Loy, she has also sought to test its ideological limits.

This testing can be compared with the experimental strategies that came to characterize the "New Wave" in science fiction, and with which Russ was affiliated.[6] Yet this quest had come in the context of Russ having abandoned the consolation of heterosexual norms. Like the avant-garde circles in which Loy moved, architects of the New Wave, such as Michael Moorcock, sought to break with the past by creating a mythology in which authors of the 1940s and 1950s, (for example, John W. Campbell and Robert Heinlein) were exclusively portrayed as reactionary and, even, crypto-fascist.[7] By the same token, journals such as Moorcock's *New Worlds* or Harlan Ellison's anthology, *Dangerous Visions* (1967), presented themselves as progressive and liberating, both in their writing and their politics. Yet, like the countercultural scene of the 1960s with which it came to associate itself, the New Wave reproduced traditional attitudes toward women and sexual behavior. For instance, while Moorcock has professed support for women's revolutionary activities, there is a concealed criticism of "the feminist typesetters" who "refused . . . on moral and political grounds" to print Norman Spinrad's sexually explicit tale, "Extracts from a Typewriter" (1979) (Moorcock 1983, 505). With the notable exception of Samuel R. Delany, much of New Wave fiction was dominated by the overt maleness and editorial policies of such writers as Ellison and Moorcock.[8] Despite the presence of female writers such as Hilary Bailey, Ursula K. Le Guin, and Pamela Zoline, they were outnumbered by their male contemporaries within the New Wave. Yet Russ was doubly discriminated against by what the poet, Adrienne Rich, has referred to as "heterosexism": the assumption that the experience of heterosexual women stands for the experience of *all* women (Rich 1994). Not only does Russ's lesbianism represent, in Bonnie Zimmerman's (1992) words, "a hole in the fabric of gender dualism," (4) it is also an enigma for the universalizing tendencies of both first- and second-wave feminism. Consequently, Russ's fiction works away at patriarchal representations of womanhood (including the assumptions of the 1960s counterculture) *and* at heterosexual discourse itself, through which the women's movement still largely participated. Like Loy, Russ is attempting to articulate something that has been suppressed: a new social relation that breaks not only with patriarchy but also with the male chauvinism of the avant-garde and the false optimism of orthodox feminism.[9] Yet, at the same time, Loy's example offers a perspective by which to view Russ' attempts.

The *Female Man* (Russ 1975b) effectively dramatizes the questions raised by Loy. Again, the certainties of heterosexual romance have been shaken, but this time by an engagement with feminism, lesbianism, and countercultural politics. Yet, just as the discontinuous sections of "Songs to Joannes" vary in terms of tone and style, so Russ's novel lacks a coherent narrative and consistent point of view. Having disavowed the traditional outcomes of heterosexual desire (marriage and childbirth), Russ's narrative lacks either linear development or plot resolution. Instead, just as Loy works through the inherent contradictions within bohemian love, so The *Female Man* works through fractures within the dominant sexual ideology to reveal the limitations within normal (heterosexual) discourse. As Patricia Waugh (1989) has argued, the novel's utopianism "is constructed through the fluid process of reading the whole text, forming a relationship which resists the fixed and the static" (212). Russ's utopianism, then, emerges as a cultural practice that involves both writer and reader. Herein, though, lies the fundamental problem for reading Russ's text.

For example, at one point, Joanna dismisses party politics as "X 'winning' and Y 'losing'" before insisting: "Concealing your anxiety over the phone when He calls" is the genuine political reality for women (203); in other words, the moment at which women are summoned to take a subject position in a discourse from which they are irreducibly estranged. Yet this moment recurs throughout the course of The *Female Man*. Political oppression is experienced at the level of discourse—a language that the characters, most notably Jeannine and Joanna, have internalized and from which they are alienated: "I decided that the key word in all this vomit was *self-less*" (205). Expression, though, is permissible only through this same language, so that the act of enunciation is fundamentally political. Like Loy, Russ views this language as man-made and sets about dismantling it through a variety of techniques, some of which

I discuss below. In doing so, Russ co-opts the reader as part of the process. Sometimes this appropriation is direct by the reader being addressed, sometimes self-mockingly ("This is the lecture. If you don't like it, you can skip to the next chapter," 29), rhetorically ("*I know who I am, but what's my brand name?*" 19), confidentially ("I'll tell you how I turned into a man," 133), and/or antagonistically ("If you don't, by God and all the Saints, *I'll break your neck*," 140). More often, though, the reader is co-opted indirectly by being encouraged to piece together the many fragments that constitute the text, such as "There are more whooping cranes in the United States of America than there are women in Congress" (61). This puzzling use of a fragmentary or epigrammatical style is overlaid by Russ's use of voice that draws attention to the artificiality of the language: "A dozen beautiful 'girls' each 'brushing' and 'combing' her long, silky 'hair,' each 'longing' to 'catch a man'" (75). The reader, then, becomes part of the text's drive toward doubt and anxiety. It passes its questions to the reader, whose own subjectivity is displaced on to the position of Russ' protagonists. Like Russ's characters, Russ's readers inhabit a series of conflicting discourses that they must decipher, but from which they are alienated.[10] To describe this activity of reading as pleasurable, even as a form of *jouissance*, glosses the effect of Russ's writing. Instead, like Loy's poetry, Russ's prose is painful to experience as what she is describing is the loss of social and sexual certainties—that were in themselves oppressive—while at the same time "seized by a hopeless, helpless longing for love and reconciliation" (202).

This agony is played out in the novel's fragmented structure that parallels the fractured subjectivities of the four protagonists—potential aspects of the same woman, but to which they do not add up. In one sense, Russ is seeking to recapture the multiple identities that have been suppressed by the objectification of women: the mechanical list of men's achievements that ends "Women get married" (126). But, in another sense, Russ shows the impossibility of this attempt. In recovering one fragmented series of identities, the text effectively covers over another set, an infinity of traces that complements the view of time travel described in book 1: "And with each decision you make (back there in the Past) that new probable universe itself branches, creating simultaneously a new Past and a new Present, or to put it plainly, a new universe" (7). Consequently, the moment of self-realization is endlessly deferred throughout the course of the text, a point invoked in the novel's series of farewells:

> We got up and paid our quintuple bill; then we went out into the street. I said goodbye and went off with Laura, I, Janet; I also watched them go, I, Joanna; moreover I went off to show Jael the city, I Jeannine, I Jael, I myself.
> Goodbye, goodbye, goodbye. (212)

The supplementary fifth character, the anonymous writer who effectively edits the text, evokes the other ghostly presences, the trace elements of all the other potential Js who shadow the four versions described in the text. This sense of haunting is developed in the novel by the use of animism: the infiltration of one character's narrative by the spirits of the other protagonists. For example, while Janet seduces Laura, the spirit of Jael hangs "by one claw from the window curtain" (71), not only observing but also experiencing and commenting upon the seduction. These episodes not only obscure the authenticity of perception (through whose eyes is this event being narrated?); they also tally with the experience of time travel where each of the four protagonists can slide into each other's universe once breached by Jael. In a sense, these four aspects of the same person haunt one another in a simultaneous movement of attraction and estrangement. Like satellites, they orbit one another but cannot be reconciled. They are one another's ghostly counterpart or, as Jael suggests, "Doppelgänger" (162), while at the same time haunted by their potential and unknown selves. While the novel is drawn to retrieving these shards of fragmented identity, it is neither a liberating nor a playful exercise; it indicates that wholeness is impossible and possibly undesirable even where it is most necessary (for example, in the pursuit of friendship). At one point, Joanna catches herself:

> Some of my best friends are—I was about to say that some of my best friends are—my friends—
> My friends are dead. (136)

Instead of an activity in play, the novel's textual strategies have an altogether more mournful function. While individual sections, such as "The Great Happiness Contest" (116–119), are amusing, the overall tone (as in Loy's poetry) is satirical and its effect negative. An example is the sketch dramatizing the "dominance game called I Must Impress This Woman," which concludes:

> He: You really are sweet and responsive after all. You've kept your femininity. You're not one of those hysterical feminist bitches who want to be a man and have a penis. You're a woman.
> She: Yes. (She kills herself.) (94)

The discourse in which heterosexual relations are conducted is criticized throughout the novel: at best, manipulative and doctrinaire, at worst, aggressive and violent. But Russ, through the persona of Joanna, is quick to deny the romantic compensation of a feminine discourse: "I am not saying 'Damn' any more, or 'Blast'; I am putting in lots of qualifiers like 'rather,' I am writing in these breathless little feminine tags, she threw herself down on the bed, I have no structure (she thought), my thoughts seep out shapelessly like menstrual fluid, it is all very female and deep and full of essences, it is very primitive and full of 'and's,' it is called 'run-on sentences' " (137).[11] Instead, the novel's collage structure—its abrupt and often inexplicable juxtapositions of inserts, sketches, interior monologue, anecdote, fairy tale, diatribe, essay, and metafiction—not only disturbs the logicality associated with phallocentric thought but also reveals the extent to which another discourse, unbounded by patriarchy, has been rendered impossible. Yet it is from this hypothetical nowhere, from this nonplace or utopian impulse that underwrites the novel, that Russ can mount a politically committed critique. As Derrida (1997) has commented on the abyss that underlies friendship: "The truth of friendship, if there is one, is found there, in darkness, and with it the truth of the political" (16).

This politically questing darkness emerges in the tensions and disagreements between the four protagonists. Jeannine, for example, defines herself through patriarchal codes of femininity. Yet her perceived failure in not marrying produces in her anxiety, irritability, and self-loathing: "Sometimes I want to die" (150). Of the other characters, Jeannine most admires Jael, who embodies the strength and self-assertiveness that Jeannine lacks, and dislikes Janet because of her self-satisfaction. Yet Jeannine's admiration of Jael is potentially misplaced while her envy of Janet's surety is potentially self-destructive. Joanna, though, who resents being "stuck with Jeannine" (83), is scarcely in a better position. Having renounced marriage in favor of a professional career, Joanna has also declined the promise of heterosexual romance for the vagaries of a male-dominated workplace. While Joanna is witty and insightful into women's lack of emancipation, her solution of becoming "the female man" (140) is politically inadequate. As she later declares, "You see before you a woman in a trap" (152). The predicaments that Jeannine and Joanna encounter tally with the stark choices of Loy's "Feminist Manifesto." Jeannine's desperate decision to marry Cal amounts to legalized prostitution while Joanna's pursuit of professional employment is a kind of parasitism; it replicates the values of patriarchy without subverting them. The only course left is negation. Yet, Russ offers two contrasting models, Janet and Jael, through whom the demand for change can be articulated.

Both Janet and the all-female society of Whileaway represent a tear within gender dualism *and* within the text itself. Information on Whileaway punctuates the narrative and serves to contrast the parallel societies with their utopian alternative, while also resisting the depiction of Whileaway as a monolithic entity. Unlike other separatist communities, such as Charlotte Perkins Gilman's *Herland* (1915) and Sally Miller Gearhart's *The Wanderground* (1978), which tend to be static and uniform, Whileaway is ambiguous and dynamic. Crimes are committed, lovers quarrel, and advanced technology jostles with a rural economy. Power is decentralized throughout the community; as Janet comments, "there is no one place from which to control the entire activity of Whileaway" (91). Social life is organized through clans in which, again, there is no center: "the web is world-wide" (81). Whileawayans tend to be polygamous and families are large and extended. Due to this libertarian ethos, the work ethic is more than balanced by a sense of carnival and play. Whileawayans celebrate equally at "Anything at all" and "Nothing at all" (103). Whileaway is configured, then, as an excess of libidinal desire in which the society is self-regulating but not self-limiting. When Janet is asked if this way of life "is considered enough, in Whileaway?" her immediate response is "My God, no" (15). For Russ, continuing dissatisfaction in the context of general contentment is a sign of the Whileawayans' humanity. Freed from any relation to the social signifier of Man, except as a distant memory, the Whileawayans are in turn released from the social category of Woman, another parallel with Loy's manifesto.

In contrast with Whileaway are Manland and Womanland and the terrorist figure, Jael, who moves between them. Whereas gender dualism has faded on Whileaway, here it has hardened into a form of cold war. Jael's cyborg body not only incarnates the profusion of bodies and technology within Dadaist collage, but also extends Loy's depiction (in "Auto-Facial-Construction") of the body as malleable and porous. As in Loy's representation, Jael's body is wholly spectacular: the intermeshing of flesh and mechanical parts not only demystifies the body but also disguises what is, in effect, an instrument defined by its (military) function. Jael not only discredits the essentialism associated with the physical body but also (partially) disturbs the gender dualism of her society. Her modified body not only allows Jael to enjoy masculine attributes of strength and mastery—the murder of Boss, the sexual domination of Davy—it also parades a hyperrealistic simulation of feminine sexuality: Jael's teeth, claws and catlike movement.[12] Jael's gender ambiguity mirrors that of Manland where two-sevenths of the population are either surgically refashioned to serve as prostitutes or "grow slim, grow languid, grow emotional and feminine" (167), and become caricatures of gay men.

Yet, in the context of overt sexual aggression, this ambiguity is also a disavowal of the feminine that plays such a role for both Loy and Russ. Jael distinguishes herself as "a man-woman" from the "woman-women" (188), who occupy the "sentimental Arcadian communes" of Womanland. She disparages them for wanting "to win the men over by Love": "There's a game called Pussycat that's great fun for the player; it goes like this: Meeow, I'm dead (lying on your back, all four paws engagingly held in the air, playing helpless)" (186).

Yet, while Jael caricatures Womanland as a litter of coquettish felines, her technologized body is itself a grotesque parody of the woman as catlike predator. Like the "half-changed," who are "artists, illusionists, impressionists of femininity" (167), Jael (to use the terminology of Jean Baudrillard) is a simulacrum in which the feminine is foregrounded as a sign but drained of its meaning. Though quintessentially postmodern, Jael's cyborg body effectively reinforces the sexual apartheid of Manland and Womanland where love is defined in terms of mechanics, desire in terms of lust and violence, and the feminine in terms of a debased and abused other.[13] The dystopianism of Jael's world turns upon this exclusion of the feminine: there is simply no place for love as amity, Loy's "preeminent litterateur," as opposed to phallocentric want. Consequently, there is the need for Janet, "whom we don't believe in and whom we deride but who is in secret our savior from utter despair" (212–213). Without the utopian vision of Whileaway, the alternative is Jael, "twisted . . . on the rack of her own hard logic" (212), Joanna's "female man" descended into the "blond Hallowe'en ghoul on top of the S.S. uniform" (19).

At the same time, Jael's "hard logic" is unsettled by the fragmented structure of the text itself. Russ's self-reflexivity not only demystifies the book as a finished product but also reconstitutes art as a living process that reconnects writer and reader. This avant-garde strategy is made clear at the novel's conclusion where the exhaustion of literary meaning is interconnected with the escape from oppression:

> Do not get glum when you are no longer understood, little book. Do not curse your fate. Do not reach up from readers' laps and punch the readers' noses.
>
> Rejoice, little book!
>
> For on that day, we will be free. (214)

The question raised in *The Female Man* of "why life doesn't match the stories" (108) recurs elsewhere in Russ's fiction, for example, in the short story "Everyday Depressions" (in Russ 1984c). The story takes the form of a series of letters from a middle-aged academic to her anonymous friend, in which she plots a gothic romance between two eighteenth-century women. The plot is a wild pastiche of gothic conventions that are turned inside out by the introduction of homoerotic desire. Yet the novel is left unwritten; what exists, instead, is the narrative in provisional form, scattered across the letters. More important than the finished work is the turning over of ideas between the writer and her correspondent. Even though the addressee is silent, the letters resemble a dialogue as the recipient is written into the correspondence, her name affectionately changing. The writer punctuates her plot description with questions: facts to be checked, revisions to be made. Each letter ends on a moment of suspense as the writer pauses to consider the next intrigue, the next revelation. The letters become, in themselves, a romantic adventure as we, in the position of the implied reader, pursue the writer's thoughts; her excitement in uncovering the next detail that will both enrich the overall design and delay the moment of its closure. As in *The Female Man*, desire—in this instance, an enthusiasm for imagination—courses through the correspondence but refuses to resolve itself in any more totalizing form than the individual letter. Even this fragment is transgressed by the writer's playful use of postscripts, typography, and pastiche, for example, where one letter turns into a convention of diary-keeping: "To bed, and dream up the next plot wrinkle" (153).

In the final letter, though, the writer decides to abandon her novel. The ending, she admits, is a cliché: "A walk into the sunset, hand in hand, and the obligatory prophecy that Some Day Society Will Accept a Love Like Ours" (158). Despite its content, the narrative remains constrained by generic conventions, principally closure, so that even taboo desire is ultimately reconciled to the consolations of romance. As the writer notes, these conventions mean that the narrative is also blind to historical realities of social, economic, and racial oppression. Despite the theme of same-sex attraction, the Gothic pastiche reproduces the hegemonic interests in class, wealth, and power to the exclusion of political dissent. Yet, this observation is made by an academic, who has been trained in cultural theory, a training that is in itself a bar to the pleasures of the imagination: "You are right; the book should be full of real politics, but Oh Susannah, what wishest thou? Marxism-Leninism? Too doctrinaire. Women's Studies? Too respectable. Lesbian separatism? Too unrealistic" (158–159).

She counters this list with "Other lists I enjoy: croissants, pain au chocolat, brioches (with or without raisins)." The mood turns reflective: "You have been a grand help," and concerned with private consolations, such as the narrator's "beautifully expensive" raincoat that consoles "one in Seattle as the days draw in." The underlying theme is mortality:

> When I was twenty I thought that life came to a point in some openly dramatic way (like in the movies) and somehow you got into adulthood at some point and then you were set, on a plateau that went on forever and ever . . .
>
> Now I look in the mirror and see my mother. (159)

Like the movies of her youth, the narrator's Gothic pastiche is a distraction from life and its inevitable passing. 'Does Life exist?' the narrator asks:

> Well, yes. It does. Life is, well life is . . . like this & like that & like that & like this & like nothing & like everything.
>
> That's what life is.

In place of the reification of Art, the narrator ascribes to an ontological experience of life without foundations or certainties. In their absence, though, friendship endures and, with it, a sense of the ethical: "Live, if you have the time" (160).

In contrast, *We Who Are About To* . . . (1977) the tale of survivors on a deserted alien planet, seems to cancel both art and life. Yet, from the outset, the narrator inscribes an addressee within her narration: "Imagine a flat world," "how would you get from one spot to the other?" "Don't ask me how" (7). As the narrator's mental and physical condition becomes more desperate, so the relationship with her imaginary confidant becomes more antagonistic: 'What do you know? Do you know anything? . . . *Who are you?*" (1977, 76). Even though the narrator admits, "I'm left talking to myself. Which is nothing and nobody," she continues to treat her listener as an actual person(s): "I'd better tell you about my politics because you're such nice people you might think I did something wrong" (115). Though she plays with her hypothetical audience, the narrator remains responsible to it by refusing to die until "it's time" (170). Through this responsibility to the other, the narrator reveals herself, a self that would have otherwise been objectified by the colonists' decision to use the women as childbearers.

Instead of self-negation, the narrator vocalizes her experience, converting her life story into a fractured form of self-expression that is dependent upon the ghostly presence of others: the fellow passengers she murders; Kennedy, the spirit-child; the audience with whom she converses. The narrator even regards her monologue as in some sense spectral: an external presence that "will live on years and years after I die, thus proving that the rest of me was . . . just an organic backup for conversation" (128). While demystifying her own authority, the narrator confers a material presence upon her recorded text, imagining it as a printed page with "punctuation" and parentheses; in effect, the text that we read. Nonetheless, this cannot be the text as it is recorded, complete with untranslatable "gutturals, spits, squeaks, pops" (9). Instead, the narrator speaks from "outside the outside of the outside" (119), a liminal space in stark contrast with authoritarian figures, such as John Ude, or the leftist groups with whom the narrator associated and "wanted to be inside History" (124).[14] Instead, while convening with various kinds of specters, the narrator is herself a ghost that haunts the text, and it is her radical alterity that forces the reader into an ethical relationship with the narrative. As in Loy's "Feminist Manifesto," the narrator accepts that women have no objective existence within patriarchal discourse. Instead, her narration emanates from a periphery in which all agreed positions are negated: "So it all cancels out" (164).

Arguably, then, both Loy and Russ are attempting to articulate a notion of amity that transcends both conventional heterosexual discourse and the limitations of countercultural rhetoric. Yet, this relation can only emerge through the cancellation of preexisting social relations. Consequently, the ending to *We Who Are About To . . .* and the narrative movement of "Everyday Depressions" can be usefully compared to the temporal abridgments that occur in *The Female Man* with the result that Laura can simultaneously, yet at different times, be seduced by both Janet and Joanna. This episode of narrative indeterminacy, in which "reality itself" is torn "wide open," creates an aperture through which the experience of *aimance* may be glimpsed:

> She kept on reading and I trod at a snail's pace over her ear and cheek down to the corner of her mouth. Laura getting hotter and redder all the time as if she had steam inside her. It's like falling off a cliff, standing astonished in mid-air as the horizon rushes away from you. If this is possible, anything is possible. Later we got stoned and made awkward, self-conscious love, but nothing that happened afterward was as important to me (in an inhuman way) as that first, awful wrench of the mind. (208)

Russ's fiction develops Loy's faith in love as "the preeminent litterateur" and in the political stance that accords with that commitment.

~

# 13 Joanna Russ and D. W. Griffith

SAMUEL R. DELANY

## I

My claims for Joanna Russ are large. She is one of the finest—and most necessary—writers of American fiction to publish between 1959, when her first professional short story, "Nor Custom Stale," appeared in the *Magazine of Fantasy and Science Fiction*, and 1998, when St. Martin's Press published her overview of feminism *What Are We Fighting For? Sex, Race, Class, and the Future of Feminism*. Between these dates fall six novels—seven, if we count her children's book *Kittatinny: A Tale of Magic* (1978). All but one are either science fiction or one or another mode of fantasy. The exception, *On Strike against God* (1980), is a moving and meticulously crafted story of a young lesbian academic's coming out in the early days of the women's movement, a book that has been all but ignored in a body of work that, despite a book-length study, *Demand My Writing: Joanna Russ / Feminism / Science Fiction*, by Jeanne Cortiel (1999), deserves far more attention.

Aside from her second novel, *And Chaos Died* (1970), all the books grow directly from feminist concerns, with which Russ was deeply involved from the second half of the 1960s on. In that second novel, a gay man, Jai Vhed, encounters a telepathic woman on a far world, who "cures" him of his sexual deviation. (It was written when homosexuality was still classified as a pathological condition). She also teaches him her telepathic skills, thus rendering him unfit for human society. On his return to Earth, the world that to us would appear normal appears to him a dystopian nightmare, because of his new knowledge. At the end, he can only leave Earth once more and rejoin his mentor. Here the feminist concerns are indirect, and in the extraordinarily rich text a range of interesting ideological problems ring in resonance with Russ's fiction written before and after it.

The problems of feminism no more limit the meaning of Russ's fiction, however, than the problems of slavery limit the meaning of, say, *Huckleberry Finn*. Rather, feminism provides a structure for her arguments, which range over everything from music to mysticism, from the direct perception of matter at a distance to the problems of running a late medieval convent besieged by Vikings. This is not to imply that Russ is other than perfectly serious about her feminism—or that, somehow, her work "goes beyond" it or engages it only accidentally. Feminism plays a role in Russ similar to the one that Marxism plays in the theatrical works of Bertolt Brecht. Indeed, another reason Russ's work may have escaped its due recognition is that her feminism has a decidedly Marxist leaning.

Alongside her novels, Russ has written a book-length study, *How to Suppress Women's Writing* (1983); two collections of essays; the aforementioned overview of feminism (*What Are We Fighting For?*); and three books of short stories, the second of which, *Extra(Ordinary) People* (1984), includes "Souls." Besides winning the Hugo Award in 1983, this novella easily stands on the same shelf with James Joyce's "The Dead," Willa Cather's "My Mortal Enemy," Glenway Westcott's "The Pilgrim Hawk," and Guy Davenport's "The Dawn in Erewhon." Russ belongs to a collection of modern stylists who excel at descriptive vividness: a collection one has to work at to extend it to include a dozen: William Gass, Guy Davenport, Virginia Woolf, David Foster Wallace, Richard Hughes, William Golding, G. K. Chesterton, and Vladimir Nabokov. At Cornell University Russ studied under Nabokov, who, along with S. J. Perelman, is a dedicatee of *And Chaos Died*. From time to time Lawrence Durrell, Angela Carter, John Updike, Eugene Garber, Jeanette Winterson, or James Dickey may flicker at the group's edges. Russ should be placed at its center.

*And Chaos Died* (1970a) contains such sentences as this delicious description of a starliner: "The Big One was obviously one of those epoxy-and-metal eggs produced by itself—the Platonic Idea of a pebble turned inside out, born of a computer and aspiring towards the condition of Mechanical Opera" (93). With its intertextual sweep, the sentence takes in everything from H. P. Lovecraft's pulp ponderosities ("the Old One") and the instructions on a cardboard backing from the hardware store ("This epoxy can be used with aluminum") to the Nicene Creed ("born of the Virgin Mary") and Walter Pater's obiter dictum from his 1877 essay "The School of Giorgione" ("*All art constantly aspires towards the condition of music*"). But these hypogrammatic resonances can make us forget how pleasurable such a sentence is simply as a mouthful of sound. Any extended consideration of Russ's works without a section devoted to style alone would be as radically incomplete as such a consideration of the works of Pater, Nabokov, or Joyce. In Russ, as in Nabokov, again and again the most precise observation breaks through the sumptuous euphony, the most vivid description, the coruscating wit, to produce an electric version of the ordinary that is anything but.

Little or none of the pyrotechnically accomplished rhetorical surface of Russ's prose is explored in Cortiel's (1999) study—or, indeed, even mentioned.

Cortiel does note that several of Russ's heroines kill men; she even devotes a chapter to the topic ( "Acts of Violence: Representations of Androcide"). What Cortiel avoids, if not suppresses, in her study is any mention of heroines in Russ who kill other women. Nonetheless, paradoxical as it may appear, these deaths are central to Russ's feminist vision. Whether the four anonymous duels fought by Janet on Whileaway in *The Female Man* ("I've killed four times") or her hunting down of the renegade philosopher Belin above the forty-eighth parallel—presumably the fourth time Janet has killed another woman, as only three of her duels resulted in death (55): "Whileawayans are not as peaceful as they sound" (49)—these deaths occur in situations in which women have achieved enough power that their removal is worth it or even necessary.

In what for me is Russ's most perfectly crafted novel, *We Who Are About To . . .* 1977), the narrator (whose name might be Elaine) murders Valeria Graham. Among those castaways out of touch with Earth, the Graham family—handsome and urbane Victor, bright, spoiled twelve-year-old daughter Lori (whom the narrator will also murder), and Valeria Graham herself—initially appears as the quintessential upper-middle-class social unit. As the story unfolds, however, we learn that the money—and there is considerably more of it than we might have supposed—is all Valeria's. Presumably she has made it herself. "How much money have I got? . . . You don't even know. . . . I'll tell you. Six mill a month. Eurodollar. That puts me in the top one-tenth of the top percentile, I believe . . . with a credit level-one you can have anything you want in this world, anything at all" (91). In the course of getting to where she is, Valeria has purchased for herself both a consort, Victor, and a daughter, Lori. "And maybe you think it's foolish and strange and rich to buy a man and strange and foolish and rich to buy a child. But one gets sick of renting people and even sicker of renting pets—it's dull—and I don't enjoy politics and there's one thing about bought people if you're wise: they stay bought" (92). The polysyndeton climaxed by the simple and singular clause "they stay bought" is a figure for Valeria's entire worldview, an interconnected and undifferentiated totality in which her dictum alone is the controlling factor, shaping all around it, like Wallace Stevens's jar in Tennessee.

Victor, who has taken Valeria's name, instead of her taking his, not only is happy with the arrangement but actively strove for it before he met his fabulously wealthy wife. "I worked on myself," he tells the narrator. "Made myself good looking, you know: clothes, accent, the works. Spent a lot on surgery; no whore could have done better. . . . I can satisfy anyone." No polysyndetons for Victor. His statements come out in the telegraphic rapid-fire of both the dying man and the sexual self-fashioner with an all-but-industrial commitment to the enterprise:

"Did you practice?" asks our narrator.
Answers Victor, "Of course."

"*What a way to spend a life,*" thinks the narrator, who goes on to comment, "*Here is the kernel of Victor Graham. I can satisfy anyone. Myself, I eat potatoes*" (67). We learn that Mrs. Graham purchased Lori to give Victor something to do, presumably while Valeria was making her multimillions. Lori was selected from a crèche specifically because she was sickly and not expected to live. Keeping her alive was a challenge to Victor's time and Valeria's wealth. "She needed money like mine," Valeria tells the narrator. "Do you know how many operations that child's had? She was hooked to a kidney machine when I first saw her and she needed a heart implant. And dozens of other things." (The *ands* let us know we are again listening to Valeria.) Through PD—psychic displacement—Lori has lived much of her life in the rented (or possibly purchased) bodies of other children, so that she did not have to undergo the trauma of so much medical intervention, which would have killed her had she experienced it all herself. "That child," Valeria tells the narrator proudly, "cost as much money as a small New England state" (92–93). The narrator sneaks back to the camp with the intention of murdering Valeria and her daughter, but the murder actually occurs during a struggle for the gun in the midst of an argument between the two women about which of them knows "how to live" (91), the spinsterish, drug-dependent, but coruscatingly observant narrator or the megalomaniacal Valeria.

Russ's point here is that the main oppressor and exploiter of women is not—another insight I sorely miss in Cortiel—defined by biological sex but rather ("by St. Marx and St. Engels," as Russ swears in at least one of her essays) constituted by socioeconomics as a power structure at work on what Foucault would call a biopolitical field. That is the significance of the hostility between the narrator and Valeria, fatal unto murder.

While Russ is contemptuous of Victor for what he has had to excise from his personality to fulfill his role, she is as understanding of the socioeconomic conditions that force him to do it as she is sympathetic with Cassie: her portrait of an ordinary working-class young woman trapped in the same deadly matrix as the other survivors of the spaceship crash on the lost world out of touch with Earth.

Victor Graham is the only person in the group of eight whom the narrator does not directly or indirectly kill. He dies because the heart medicine that would keep him alive is presumably no longer available. Though the narrator offers him a suicide pill from her extensive pharmacopoeia so he can avoid a protracted death, he declines it. Russ's refusal to avoid the realities of death, both as a social and personal fact and as a rich discursive field for metaphysical elaboration, is one of her major writerly strengths. Again and again, it takes her ironies beyond the place where we can easily resolve them into comedy or preachment.

In her essay-memoir *Feminist Accused of Sexual Harassment*, Jane Gallop (1997) gives a portrait of Russ in 1971, when Gallop was a student and most of Russ's novels were yet to be published:

> Earlier that evening [at the first all-women's dance at Cornell University, which male students tried to crash; the women physically kept them out and, elated at their victory, took off their shirts and danced], two women had made a spectacular entrance. One of them taught my first women studies course, which I was taking that semester. One of the campus's best known feminists, an early leader in the national movement for women's studies, a published writer over six feet tall, this teacher was a woman whom I looked up to in every way. She walked into the dance accompanied by a beautiful girl I had seen around and knew to be a senior. The teacher was wearing a dress, the student a man's suit; their carefully staged entrance publicly declared their affair.
>
> I thought the two of them were the hottest thing I had ever seen. I profoundly admired the professor; I found the senior girl beautiful and sophisticated. I wanted both of them. Although I would have loved to have an affair like theirs, I didn't feel left out and envious. I felt privileged to be let in on their secret. I felt it as our secret, the secret of our women's party.
>
> The couple could no more safely appear around the campus together like that than we could walk around with our shirts off. But the relation could be revealed within our women-only space . . . because we as a community could recognize them as our sexuality, could affirm them as part of the new possibility opened to us as women by feminism. The couple was performing for us; we were not only their special, exclusive audience, but they presented us with the spectacle of our daring communal possibilities. (13–14)

The charismatic six-foot-plus professor was Joanna Russ. Russ has noted that she is actually only five ten; the extra three inches Gallop allots her may be taken as an index of how impressed the young Gallop was, as well as of Russ's general aura of presence.

## II

When David Wark Griffith turned from the controversy following hard on his filmic masterpiece *Birth of a Nation* (1915) to his epic historical exploration

*Intolerance* (1916), I do not believe that in any way, shape, or form he set out to make a feminist film. No suffragist is visible anywhere in the epic's complex four-layered historical interweave. For this paper I watched two versions of the film: the 118-minute Blackhawk laserdisc and the 178-minute Image DVD (1997), which restores various passages omitted in the earlier and general release version. A number of passages that occur in the climactic battle between the Persian leader Cyrus and Prince Belshazzar of Babylon, occur as well in the subsequent Babylonian victory celebration, which distracts the Babylonians from Cyrus's surprise attack the next morning. Many were too licentious even for a pre–Hays Code audience.

We know of four versions Griffith himself released in 1916 or shortly thereafter. Some longer, some radically truncated, they played around the country over the next few years. But only the most inattentive viewer of either version I saw could fail to notice that women are the agents of most of the film's significant actions. In the person of the actress Josephine Crowell, Catherine de Médicis engineers the Saint Bartholomew's Day massacre of the Huguenots—and seems to go all but mad because of it. The lovely Margery Wilson loads her musket and, in her nightgown, fires on the French soldiers, only to be killed by one of Catherine's mercenaries, as others of them kill Wilson's true love, Prosper Latour, when he emerges in the doorway with her body in his arms.

Five centuries before the time of Christ, after having been found "incorrigible" by the Babylonian court for rejecting the tasteless advances, however sincere, of the rhapsode of Inanna, the Hill Girl (played by Constance Talmedge), dragged before the Babylonian marriage market's auctioneer by her brother, eats raw onions to render herself unmarriageable and threatens to scratch out the eyes of one of the bidders, who is in the market for a wife and makes the mistake of handling her skirt.

When the Prince, on whom the Hill Girl has previously fixated, comes by, Talmedge pleads from her knees on the very block where she has rejected her bidders, No one will marry me—what am I to do? In 1916, four years before the Nineteenth Amendment, at least while she is in Griffith's hands, our Hill Girl is incapable of explaining, Yes, I'd like a husband, but I also want my say in the matter; I don't want to be sold to the highest bidder from an auction block. Certainly the post–World War I audience took her inability to offer such a synthesis as comic.

The Prince is something of a mind reader, however, and because of the services that the Hill Girl has already rendered him, he grants her a special clay seal that gives her (alone among women . . . ?) the right to marry or not to marry as she wishes, despite her brother or—doubtless more important—the Babylonian court.

After returning to her house and putting a loaf of bread on a wooden paddle into her Babylonian oven, the Hill Girl decides, "Enough of this!" She dons armor, loops a sheaf of arrows over her shoulder, and takes up a bow in order to spend the rest of her brief life fighting for the Prince's honor. In her subsequent adventures, she *almost* manages to prevent the fall of Babylon to the Persian king, Cyrus. She fails only because the Prince is too busy with the Princess Beloved to listen to a report about Cyrus's renewed pre-dawn attack that Talmedge has risked life and limb to deliver.

Thus Babylon falls, and they all Die in the End.

Once the revels of Babylon have provided the film with its most spectacular sequence, a modern take proffers the film's melodramatic resolution. Looking like a younger sister of Margaret Hamilton from *The Wizard of Oz* (twenty-five years before the fact), the aging Miss Mary Jenkins (played by Vera Lewis) realizes she is too old for the world of youthful upper-class delights. Instead of giving balls at which no one asks her to dance any more, she decides to spend her millions on the Women's Reform League, a quartet of demonic dowagers who, with her backing, will now be powerful enough to seize Mae Marsh's infant, since they have decided Marsh is an unfit mother.

Marsh—the Dear One—and the Boy (played by Robert Harron) have been driven to the city in the aftermath of a workers' strike, in which the Boy's father was killed. For the film's first viewers, the strike's powerful presentation, however cleaned up and sanitized, must have recalled the Ludlow massacre of recent memory, where the National Guard, called out to defend the property of John D. Rockefeller in Ludlow, Colorado, fired into a crowd of men, women, and children.

In the strike's wake, the town's poverty also drives the Friendless One—played darkly on the edge of psychosis by Miriam Casper—into the city, where she becomes the mistress of the crime boss.

The Boy falls in with a gang and eventually spends a stint in jail because the crime boss wishes to punish him for pulling out of the life of crime to be a good father and husband (the Boy is now married to Marsh); the boss frames the Boy by planting a stolen wallet on him during a tussle with the boss's toughs in the street. While the boy is in jail, the Women's Reform League comes by and finds the child alone just as Marsh returns with some whiskey that she is taking purely for medicinal purposes. The whiskey is enough, however, for the busybody dowagers to run off with her child.

The crime boss takes a shine to Marsh and lures her with promises of getting her child back—just as the Boy is released from jail. A struggle involving all three takes palace. Goaded by the fires of jealousy, the Friendless One (recall, she is the crime boss's mistress) creeps along a second-floor ledge, fires through the window and kills her lover (who is manhandling the fainting Marsh). The Friendless One throws the gun inside, and the Boy un-wittingly picks it up just as the police arrive. Meanwhile Friendless Miriam Casper makes a spectacular leap down into the alley and staggers away, hav-ing somehow avoided breaking a leg.

Mae Marsh has fainted. The crime boss is dead.

The Boy is of course convicted of the murder and is sentenced to hang. The climax grows from Marsh's (one almost wants to write "manful") strug-gle to obtain her husband's freedom.

The entire film's rather diffuse point would seem to be that, while Baby-lon, with all its brightness and bravery in the person of the Hill Girl (Talmedge also plays Marguerite de Valois in the French sequence), falls before the forces of intolerance in the form of Cyrus's army and the city's own glamorous deca-dence and while the Huguenots are slaughtered by the intolerance of Cath-erine and her son Charles IX, two people triumph over adversities: Christ—in the skimpiest of the four interwoven tales, which restricts itself pretty much to the miracle of the water turned into wine during the Wedding at Cana, the Woman Taken in Adultery, and the Crucifixion—and Marsh, who shows unflagging, even hysterical, energy as she speeds in trains and motorcars to catch the governor to get a stay of execution. Brilliantly edited in briefer and briefer intercuts with the execution's preparation, Marsh's race against time produces an all-but-unbearable sense of velocity and hanging-by-the-finger-tips suspense. Finally she drags the conveniently repentant Miriam Casper to the scaffold's very foot, where, with not a second to spare, her husband's hanging is averted.

One cannot help noting that in the production, Christ, who rises now to preside over the finale, rather resembles Marsh: Mae with only slightly more manageable hair and a neat beard.

III

What suggests a relation between Griffith's confused if spectacular undertak-ing (a commercial flop, it broke Griffith and his studio, and he was never able to create another epic) and a number of Russ's works, specifically her first and third novels, ranges from content to context to specific textual moments. My description of Intolerance above is to establish the field that might have in-terested the young Russ, perhaps during her years at the Yale Drama School after her graduation from Cornell—a field that shows a shared concern with women even as it leaves ample room for Russ to criticize what remains of Griffith's post–World War I vision. That, I am convinced, is the structure nec-essary for the process that criticism so frequently speaks of as influence to take place.

Any reader of Russ who views the adventures of Talmedge as the Hill Girl, a woman who chooses to become a soldier rather than a wife, must think of Russ's adventuress from her early story series that includes her first novel, *Picnic on Paradise*, and that was collected as *The Adventures of Alyx* (1983a): Alyx the Barbarian. In the second of the Alyx ("I Thought She Was Afeared Till She Stroked My Beard"), the seventeen-year-old Alyx is married to a gruff husband who believes in using the whip on his rebellious wife. Shortly before she dispatches him, while he is trying to prevent her from leaving, he thinks, "That is what comes of marrying a wild hill girl without a proper education" (31). The use of the words "hill girl" is the first textual moment that recalls Griffith's "Hill Girl," as the name is indicated on more than a dozen of the film's intertitles. Alyx's adventures (she is soon enlisted by the far-future Trans Temporal Agency) take her through the far past, then into the far future, till finally one of her descendants, who might even be her incarnation, arrives in Greene County, USA, in 1925, in what, along with "Souls" (1983), is one of Russ's two great novellas, "The Second Inquisition" (1970).

Another textual connection appears with the first and third intertitles after the main title in Griffith's film:

Our play is made up of four separate stories, laid in different periods of history, each with its own set of characters.

Therefore, you will find our play turning from one of the four stories to another, as the common theme unfolds in each.

These statements describe exactly the structure of Russ's third novel, *The Female Man* (1975b), which deals with four women from four parallel universes, the story cutting back and forth between them. For those who wish to up the intertextual ante, at about a quarter of the way through act 1 of *Intolerance* (a film that consists, its titles tell us, of a prologue and two acts), the Hill Girl, after getting her seal of liberty from Prince Belshazzar and deciding to fight for him, runs into the rhapsode of Inanna, whose unwanted attentions initially helped to get her declared incorrigible by the Babylonian court. She tells the young man, who is apparently still taken with her, in a clearly worded intertitle, "Put away thy perfumes, thy garments of Assinnu, the female man. I shall love none but a soldier." Not only is the fundamental four-part structure of Russ's most overtly feminist novel all but identical with that of Griffith's film, but the rather unusual title of Russ's novel appears as a textual fragment in one of Griffith's intertitles.

Some differences suggest that the similarity of the Russ title and the Griffith intertitle might be happenstance or at least an inadvertent borrowing. The Assinnu, holy officers in the service of the goddess Inanna (whom the rhapsode serves), traditionally dressed in women's clothing as they attended the goddess. The historical assumption has been that the Assinnu were transvestites, possibly even eunuchs. They are figures of gender ambiguity, and Talmedge's remark, in keeping with the time of the movie's making, is clearly meant as a more or less lighthearted insult.

The title of Cortiel's (1999) study *Demand My Writing*, she tells us, comes from her mishearing of a line in a lecture by Rachel Blau DuPlessis (subsequently published as "The Pink Guitar," a riff on Wallace Stevens's "The Man with the Blue Guitar") (2). Wrote DuPlessis, "All the signs that emerge on the page (I put them there) (some were already there, in the weave of the paper, no tabula rasa) / demand my reading." But, attending the lecture, Cortiel heard "demand my writing" and took that misprision as the name of her book-length study of some of the plots in Russ.

Possibly Russ read Talmedge's homophobic jab in Griffith's intertitle as something else. The rhapsode (played by the handsome Elmer Clifton) takes Talmedge's exhortation to heart and a few scenes later presents himself to Talmedge in armor—like her. But he has come under the influence of the priest of Bel, who (for no clear reason other than that he is just "evil") hopes to betray Babylon and its prince to the invading Cyrus. Now willing to be more feminine and seductive, Talmedge learns about the plot along with the password to get through the gates of Imgur Bell, which close Babylon's walls against invaders.

Here the temptation for me to place a call or write a letter to Russ, who lives in retirement in Tucson, becomes almost overwhelming. Why not simply ask, Did any of these ideas in your fiction—the interweaving of the four worlds of Janet, Jeannine, Jael, and Joanna in *The Female Man*; the character of Alyx—have a source in Griffith's film? The first four women, each of whom inhabits a different historical reality, are all genotypically identical. What distinguishes them—and what defines Valeria Graham as the ultimate member of the oppressor class—is the intricate socioeconomic conditions of power that constitute their different worlds. Even this notion of a genetic body shared among them is figured in *Intolerance*, in the visual-verbal leitmotif that initiates the movie and provides more than a dozen transitions during the film's prologue and two acts as we move from epoch to epoch: the image of Lillian Gish seated at the head of a cradle while Walt Whitman's words appear on the accompanying title card, "Out of the cradle endlessly rocking" (from the first of his "Sea Drift" poems in *Leaves of Grass*), and three hooded women in the background spin, measure out, and cut their yarn.

I have *not* yet put this question to Russ because I think it's necessary first to discuss the status of such intertextual relations, especially in the field of

science fiction studies, with its highly uneasy connection to the greater enterprise of literature. A hundred and fifty years ago, critics such as Edgar Allan
Poe and James Russell Lowell regularly tagged far more tenuous correspondences between texts than these as clear signs of influence. Today the most
salvageable lessons from Freud tell us that the unconscious part of the mind
works by maneuvering the signifier rather than the signified (and discourse
controls what might be considered the signified excess). Certainly this seems
true of dreams, the revisions of memory through *Nachträglichkeit*, and imagination in general. (What can be imagined is what can be said or written.)
The critical interest of such correspondences does not require a finding of
intentional borrowing.

In the precincts of science fiction, Alfred Bester was generous in his citations of Alexandre Dumas's *The Count of Monte Cristo* as a source for *The Stars
My Destination* (1956) and Joris-Karl Huysmans's *A rebours* as a source for "Hell
Is Forever" (1942). I don't believe that anyone has ever discussed the overwhelming differences between parent text and textual offspring or how each
argues with the other. Such a critical relation is what, finally, any aesthetic
influence worth the name must be, so that the differences are as much a part
of the influence as the similarities.

In my discussion of Russ and of *Intolerance* as the possible source of several aspects of her early work, just such critical tension is figured in the distinction between the nameless Hill Girl, who dies futilely, and Russ's "hill
girl"—the clearly named Alyx, who enjoys a series of witty triumphs, each
presented with linguistic panache—and in a dramatic analysis of Russ's several milieus vis-à-vis Griffith's that makes both landscapes meaningful.

In his Babylonian sequence, Griffith shows a battalion of Nubian soldiers, played by African American actors; in the modern sequence, when the
Boy is set upon in the street and the stolen wallet is slipped into his pocket,
among the six street people who crowd around him is an African American
man—onscreen for no more than ten seconds—and all six are in physical
contact as they crowd around to see. What throws this moment into relief is
Griffith's previous film, *Birth of a Nation*, where there are many African American characters but any black character who must have physical contact with a
white one is played by a white actor in blackface.

One turns again to Russ's tale of Greene County, "The Second Inquisition," to examine the discomfort that "the visitor's" (Alyx's) racial ambiguity
sheds around her in her American family in the same year (1925) that *Birth
of a Nation* was revived at the Capitol Theatre in New York City and provoked
picket lines and protests among African Americans (many of whom were ar-
rested, among them W. E. B. DuBois and the sociologist E. Franklin Frazier).

Such racial ambiguity would have been present in *Intolerance* had the Hill Girl been played not by Constance Talmedge but by, say, a visibly Middle Eastern woman.

The highlighting and significations that constantly emerge through such comparative gestures do not hinge on intention. This is why, though I would certainly be interested in Russ's answer to my question, I am suspicious of the too quick establishment of an intention (or nonintention) to explain away Russ's work (or, indeed, Griffith's). Such explanation only distracts from the critical construction of new meanings that must fall out of the comparison of individual rhetorical moments from any two or more wonderfully rich and significant texts. The construction of further meanings, I hope, is the proper use of such a critical enterprise.

## IV

After I concluded this paper, I wrote Russ, who generously responded that, although she definitely saw both of Griffith's films, *Intolerance* and *Birth of a Nation*, while she was at the Yale Drama School as a graduate student and before writing any of her novels, she retains no conscious memory of modeling her plots or her language on anything in either. Thus, the vanity of general influences and thematic origins.

~

## 14 Extraordinary People
### Joanna Russ's Short Fiction

G R A H A M   S L E I G H T

> These folks are advancing backwards with all possible speed and calling themselves
> feminists as they do so. I ache for ——— because she's young but where is her anger?
> I think from now on I will not trust anyone who isn't angry. Hopelessness is not a first
> step. It may be the prelude to finding out where one is, but that's all. Nothing really
> good is ever easy—but it's worth it. The other sort of thing is merely the old feminine
> (not feminist) game of Ain't It Awful.
>
> —Joanna Russ, "Letter to Susan Koppelman" (1995b)

> In my story I have used assumptions that seem to me obviously true. One of them is
> the idea that almost all the characterological sex differences we take for granted are
> in fact learned and not innate. I do not see how anyone can walk around with both
> eyes open and both halves of his/her brain functioning and not realize this.
>
> —Joanna Russ, afterword to "When It Changed" (1972c)

Joanna Russ's "When It Changed" is one of the most well known—and
certainly one of the most quoted—stories in science fiction. It originally appeared in Harlan Ellison's anthology *Again, Dangerous Visions* in 1972, and was
subsequently collected in *The Zanzibar Cat* (1983). It begins urgently: "Katy
drives like a maniac; we must have been doing over 120 kilometers an hour on
those turns. She's good, though, extremely good, and I've seen her take the
whole car apart and put it together again in a day" (1972c, 3). In the car with
the narrator and Katy is the narrator's eldest daughter, Yuriko, and we are
told various details: their ages, their habits, that Katy is the narrator's wife,
that they live somewhere called Whileaway. But not until the end of the first
section are we told, by implication, the narrator's gender: " 'Men!' Yuki had
screamed, leaping over the car door. 'They've come back. Real Earth men!' "
(4). As the narrator says, "We've been intellectually prepared for this ever
since the colony was founded, ever since it was abandoned, but this is different. This is awful" (4).

So, with talk of colonies and abandonment, the reader can begin to guess that Whileaway might be the name of a planet, with a women-only society, and that we are in a science fiction frame. The first encounter with the men, therefore, plays off two levels of reference. It is, obviously, "about" gender, about the experience of gender difference being made manifest. But it also plays off the First Contact stories that the SF genre had been telling for many years, putting down the shock of alienness in prose. Except, in this case, "we" are female humans, and "they" are male humans:

> They are bigger than we are. They are bigger and broader. Two were taller than me, and I am extremely tall, one meter, eighty centimeters in my bare feet. They are obviously of our species but *off*, indescribably off, and as my eyes could not and still cannot quite comprehend the lines of those alien bodies, I could not, then, bring myself to touch them, though the one who spoke Russian—what voices they have!—wanted to "shake hands," a custom from the past, I imagine. I can only say that they were apes with human faces. He seemed to mean well. (1972c, 5)

After such a litany of incomprehension, that last phrase is beautifully placed, almost a comic note, but also the complaint of radicals through the ages about moderates: that they "mean well," but their meaning well is not sufficient. And indeed, the men are sympathetic as it's explained to them that Whileaway lost its entire male population in a plague, and that it's now entirely inhabited by women. One now sees how *placed* the information is in the story's first paragraph, that Katy can do traditionally masculine tasks like disassembling a car. It's not an assertion that on Whileaway women "take on male roles," but that they take on human roles. Whileaway is sketched within the compass of an astonishingly brief (nine-page) story not as a "utopia," in which human problems are solved by societal fiat, but as an enclave, a polis shaped by its history to the needs of its inhabitants. And the men's incomprehension of Whileaway is beautifully conveyed, as when discussing the tragedy of the plague:

> "Yes," he said, catching his breath again with that queer smile, that adult-to-child smile that tells you something is being hidden and will presently be produced with cries of encouragement and joy, "a great tragedy. But it's over." And again he looked around all of us with the strangest deference. As if we were invalids. (7)

The smile is another perfectly placed touch, the smile of power through the ages as it does what it wants and *assumes you will find it wonderful.* In this case, the wonderful news is that the men have come to redress the imbalance that, from their point of view, Whileaway represents. By the end of the story, it's utterly clear that the enclave will die. The men's motives may be recognizable—they're part of "the grand movement to recolonize and rediscover all that Earth had lost" (10)—making the story's ironies hit closer to home. The story is all the more powerful for understating the narrator's anger at what's happening: it's her wife Katy who thinks "we should have burned [the men] where they stood" (10). The narrator ends the story by reflecting on the original name of the planet, For-a-While, and the realization that her society, like all social constructs, is vulnerable to change. Hence the title: any story, by definition, will be a description of a cusp moment, of something changing. A defining characteristic of science fiction is that it depicts moments when societies change as well as individuals—often in ways only grounded in the author's speculations.

Justine Larbalestier (2002) places "When it Changed" within a tradition of gender-conflict SF stories. But, she argues, it also marks a turning point in that tradition. It is the first time, for instance, that a heterosexual way of life has to be argued for, has to make a case for itself against the Whileawayan norm: "[Yuriko's] first view of the manly form leaves behind the heterosexual equation of man plus woman equals person. Woman as love interest, woman who is not yet a woman until she is completed and molded into being by heterosexual penetration, is absent" (89). What makes the story tragic is Russ's awareness that this world can be unmade far more easily than it was made. Here, as in much else of her work, there is a constant awareness that worthwhile things are valuable, fragile, and above all have to be worked for.

I emphasise the reality of the story, the sense that it does not depict a frictionless utopia, because Russ did also. In a later story, "The Clichés from Outer Space" (1984b), she comes close to describing a not-very-good version of "When it Changed." The story opens with Russ visiting a fellow writer named Ermintrude, who is editing an anthology of feminist SF, and wading through piles of poor submissions. Russ's attempts to help Ermintrude cause her typewriter to become possessed by bad feminist SF, such as "The Noble Separatist Story." This begins: " 'Tell me Mommy,' said Jeanie Joan, snuggling up to her beautiful, strong, powerful, gentle, wise, loveing, eight-foot-tall Mommy who was President of the United States, "why aren't there Daddies any more?" (107). It gets worse, and funnier, from there; Russ notes that such stories are "to be avoided—at all costs."

The point is this: Russ has, as this chapter will demonstrate, an astonishingly varied body of speculative work to her name. But she also has a trait far less common in SF: a distrust of easiness, of solutions that magic away the human fallibilities. It is the tension between these drives and many others—a love of literature and historical periods, a delight in stylistic experimentation, and not least the anger alluded to in the words I quoted at the head of this chapter—that give her body of short fiction its unique stature.

≈ ≈ ≈

In a sense, the renown of "When it Changed" is understandable. It marks, as Larbalestier argues, something of a watershed in SF's treatment of gender. It appeared in an extremely high-profile anthology, and won a Nebula Award. It sparked, as contributors elsewhere in this volume record, a great deal of debate about science fiction's treatment of gender. And a somewhat different Whileaway also features in Russ's most famous novel, *The Female Man* (1975b). Indeed, any number of descendent stories can be traced, probably the most famous example being James Tiptree, Jr.'s "Houston, Houston, Do you Read" (1976), which movingly depicts the male point of view in a very similar all-female society. One of the men asks:

> "What do you call yourselves? Women's World? Liberation? Amazonia?
> "Why, we call ourselves human beings." Her eyes twinkle absently at him. . . . "Humanity, mankind. The human race." (222)

But there's also a paradox here. Tiptree's short fiction is readily available: first, through the Arkham House volume *Her Smoke Rose Up Forever* (1990), and then through subsequent reprints and new volumes such as *Meet Me at Infinity* (2002). Russ's short fiction, which arguably occupies a comparable place in the field, is currently little known among the SF community in general. At the time of writing (early 2007), all of Russ's short fiction collections are out of print in the United States and United Kingdom, and her stories are rarely re-printed. This neglect can, in part, be attributed to Russ's withdrawal from the field in the mid-1980s. Partly, also, many new writers with feminist concerns have come on the scene since then, as Larbalestier (1999) chronicles in her closing chapter on the Tiptree Award. But if you believe, as I do, that Russ has produced one of the three or four finest bodies of work in speculative short fiction, then her neglect is extraordinary.

Before I proceed, a word about inclusivity: in this chapter, I provide an overview of Russ's short fiction. I include the collections *The Zanzibar Cat* and *The Hidden Side of the Moon*, and also the volume *(Extra)Ordinary People*. This last is a borderline case, as the five stories within it are loosely connected, and have only a brief linking narrative. But Clute and Nicholls's *The Encyclopedia of Science Fiction* (1993) refers to it as a "collection," and most of its stories were published individually first. On the other hand, I do not treat in any detail the stories comprising *The Adventures of Alyx* (1983). These were also published separately, but their collection in volume form presents them as a novel and they are dealt with elsewhere in this volume. It's worth saying, also, that Russ's collections are all arranged with extreme cunning and reward being read in order.

To go back to the quotation at the top of this chapter, anger is indeed one of the most prominent affects in Russ's fiction: anger at the callous power that patriarchal society exercises, as the men do in "When it Changed," almost without noticing; anger at the lies we tell ourselves; anger at the shortcuts of the genre she works in. But it is far from the only tone. Her short fiction is varied, playful, and delights in experiments of tone and form. And anger cannot exist in a void. Anger is always in dialogue with the world in Russ's work. In "When it Changed," one only needs the women's side of the story because it's all too easy to imagine what the men's side would be like. It would be one of those early first-contact stories where a group of (male) astronauts touch down on some empty rock (or Pacific island), encounter natives with curious habits, and bring them round to the American Way by figuring out (in the hard-SF sense) *what's wrong with them*. Part of the brilliance of "When It Changed" is that it makes the reader supply that familiar other side of the story. But Russ is just as happy to supply both, when the story merits.

Take, for example, "Invasion" (1996), as it stands, Russ's most recent story, and currently uncollected. This hilarious tale depicts a human-run spaceship being invaded by tiny aliens from the planet Ulp. It alternates sections of human and Ulpian point of view, with most of the important plot development relayed in the Ulp sections. The human sections are formal, but with an undercurrent of hysteria at the disruption the creatures cause: "The Navigator walked into her study area and found two of [the creatures] sitting on top of her antique wooden bookcase. Normally a peaceful woman, even a bit shy, she threw herself at the intruders, shouting 'No!' only to receive a painful barrage of books in the face, most of which rolled under the bed as she grabbed for them, acquiring disc-destroying grit in the process" (176). And the Ulpian sections sound like this: "Now I will tell of the time the yoomin beans catched us, it was sad but o so fine. . . . It was big ship, big shape looming and glooming in the starlite when—no, not Glydd, I *me*—saw and took all in" (178–179). So there's an immediate contrast between the formal language of the humans and what is evidently intended to be the oral storytelling of the Ulpians. The Ulpians certainly don't see what they're doing as an invasion; they just lounge around on the ship playing poker, and are ultimately revealed to be shapeshifters whose natural form resembles a small pyramid of green Jell-O. Their shapeshifting problem resolved, the Ulpians depart for the moment.

"Invasion" looks like a piece of fun, a jape about space opera conventions, the sort of work that Robert Sheckley might write. But, by counterpointing two very different narrative voices, Russ is doing something very interesting.

Whenever we are reading one strand, we're conscious that the other side would perceive things very differently. Neither side, it's clear, really understands the other except in the most limited sense. The humans figure out the peculiar lipid protein that stops the Ulpians constantly being small pyramids of green Jell-O; but this, it's emphasised, is very different from knowing them.

"Invasion" is, as with almost all Russ stories, a short work. There's a sense that the fierceness she brings to bear on her material can tend to exhaust its potential, burn it to the ground, much more quickly than most other authors—even when, as in "Invasion," she's being fiercely funny. There's no more radical example of this intensity than "The Zanzibar Cat," which closes the collection of the same name. Russ states at the outset that it takes its starting point from Hope Mirrlees's great fantasy novel Lud-in-the-Mist: "Ms Mirrlees's novel does not depict Fairyland—so I did, half in affectionate parody, the other half very seriously indeed" (1983c, 234). The title is a reference to Thoreau's injunction not to count the cats in Zanzibar.

The story begins, in a fine imitation of Lud-in-the-Mist's tone, by recounting the reappearance of Duke Humphrey, who had died six hundred years ago, to terrorize the people of Appletap-on-Flat. He had, it was said, a demon cat from Zanzibar on his humped back telling him what to do. Eventually, the Appletappians come to confront him, led by a local Miller's daughter (sometimes referred to as the "Milleress," which is not quite "Mirrlees," but is not too distant either.) The Duke dismisses their challenge disdainfully, in tones that evoke God's voice from the whirlwind at the end of the Book of Job: "Do you know against whom it is you come to wage war? I have counted the cats in Zanzibar, I have numbered the waterspouts over the Red Sea. I am all-life-and-all-death" (240). But the Appletappians, and the Milleress in particular, stand their ground. It seems that the Milleress, not the Duke, is in control: she shifts the scene to a small front parlor that somehow contains the huge militia that stands behind her. She tells the Duke that he exists because she made him up, and kisses him; he disappears. The Appletappians are, naturally, shocked, and she speaks some final words to them:

> "Do not," said the Miller's daughter, "go around looking for the kingdom of Heaven as if it were a lost sheep, saying wow, here! and wow, there! because the kingdom of Heaven is inside you."
>
> "Who are you," said the people of Appletap-on-Flat, all kneeling down instanter, "who speak not as the scribes but with authority?"
>
> She said:
>
> "I'm the Author. (244)

And the story ends, and the book, without even closing the quotation mark. This is an extreme example, perhaps the most extreme example imaginable, of a story that exhausts itself precisely as it finishes, which is impossible to sequel. Beyond being a mere metaphysical game, "The Zanzibar Cat" does a number of things. It reminds the audience of who is really pulling the strings in any story. But also, by giving the voice of power the voice of God, it suggests quite how much chutzpah is needed to oppose that voice. And it replicates perfectly the sense in Mirrlees of the danger of Faerie, that it makes reality shimmer like a heat-haze.

"The Zanzibar Cat" is far from the only story Russ wrote as a tribute to another author. "The Extraordinary Voyages of Amélie Bertrand" (1979a) is headed "Hommage à Jules Verne," and is set in provincial France in the 1920s. The narrator, a business traveler, meets a woman at the train station of Beaulieu-sur-le-Pont. He walks with her through a tunnel in the station and finds himself, after a brief disorienting moment, facing an elephant in the middle of the jungle. Mme. Bertrand explains to him that she had found this portal some years ago while her husband was away, and has used it repeatedly ever since to visit exotic corners of the globe—or even Venus and Mars. The man is shocked that anyone—that a woman in particular—might be able to have such adventures; but he eventually finds himself following her and vanishes from the mundane world.

So one can see here how Russ's project is designed. If, as she argues in *How To Suppress Women's Writing* (1983b), patriarchy operates by the creation of narratives that diminish or efface the work of women ("She wrote an interesting book, but she wasn't really an artist," say) then one of the tasks of a feminist fiction would be to set out counternarratives. The counternarratives would create worlds that did not agree with patriarchy's story but that, nonetheless commanded assent. Moreover—and this, I think, is Russ's unique strength—they would show *how* such narratives are created. Russ's stories are about *process*, not ending: the scaffolding of argument is built up very publicly as you read. So they are not just arguments: they show you how to argue. (One remembers that the last words of the epilogue of *How To Suppress Women's Writing* are, "I've been trying to finish this monster for thirteen ms. pages and it won't. Clearly it's not finished. You finish it" [132].) A story like "When it Changed" makes the case that Whileaway is possible, is worth preserving, because it shows you how that conclusion is reached and that it is not, as it were, rigged.

Russ's directness in argument extends to arguing with herself on occasion, as in "The Little Dirty Girl" (1982), the first story in *The Hidden Side of the Moon* (1987a). Here, a narrator who resembles Russ in the outward circumstances of her life—living in Seattle, teaching at the university—befriends the little dirty girl of the title. The narrator is suspicious of the girl, but begins to allow her into her home, offering candy and other treats to entice her.

The girl is astonishingly sure of herself, clearly intelligent, but refuses to say where she comes from: she seemingly has no family. Eventually, after being tucked up in bed one night, the girl vanishes; but the narrator meets soon afterward with her estranged mother.

If one had to assign a tag to "The Little Dirty Girl," it would be a self-critique, and a scathingly honest one too. ("The Precious Object," reprinted in the Baen paperback of *The Zanzibar Cat*, is another example of Russ's seemingly mining her own life as material.) It shows how a life, how a sense of self, can be constructed. The things that we think are fixed are often only our own creations. The broader point made by much of Russ's work is that exactly the same argument can be made about gender roles; indeed, she says so explicitly in her afterword to "When it Changed" in *Again, Dangerous Visions* (1972c).

So Russ's short works depict the arguing out, with extraordinary fierceness, of a series of tensions. Perhaps the overarching one is the tension between the world we have inherited and live in, and the world we can imagine (and, therefore, could construct.) In a sense, it's not surprising that many of the stories are so brief: the miracle is that they hold themselves together at all under the stresses of Russ's arguments.

～ ～ ～

I'm not going to argue that these tensions are "resolved" or "answered" at any point in Russ's work; but she does provide some speculations about what other ways of dealing with them might look like. In particular, her collection *Extra (Ordinary) People* (1984c) can be seen as a sustained attempt to show another picture of gender relations.

The first of the book's five stories, "Souls" (1982), won a Hugo Award in 1983. It is, perhaps, unusual for Russ in a number of ways. For a start, it's more than sixty pages long, and reads like one single uninterrupted breath of story. It tells the story of a medieval monastery and its Abbess Radegunde, and what happens when Vikings come to pillage the monastery's treasures. The story is narrated, many years later, by a man who was a child at the time of the invasion, and who had been brought up around the abbey. The narrator is nicknamed "Boy News" for his habit of bringing Radegunde all the abbey's gossip. The abbey, he says, "had many, many books, more than any other nunnery or monastery I have ever heard of: a full forty then, as I remember" (2). As soon as the news arrives of the Norsemen's approach, Radegunde announces "briskly" that "God protects our souls, not our bodies," and goes to face down the Vikings.

So, in one sense, this opening lays the groundwork for a story of a kind we've seen before. Russ is describing a confident, capable woman in a context one might have thought such a person could not exist. As the Norsemen approach, one wonders how the story is going to proceed. Is Radegunde going to be able to turn them back by the power of her arguments? Certainly, her first dialogue with their leader, Thorvald Einarsson (7–8), is civil but firm.

But it swiftly becomes clear that words are *not* more effective than force in this world: again, Russ distrusts the easy outcome. The abbey is pillaged, and horrors are visited upon its inhabitants—both the nuns and the villagers sheltering there. The moment when the Vikings attack is passed over (18–19), as being too much for Boy News to take in. But once it has happened, the story moves into another realm, an almost meditative depiction of aftermath that allows much more insight into the characters.

Radegunde, who has survived with Boy News, begins consoling some of the other nuns who have suffered in the attack and, in this context, begins reflecting on her own time in Rome many years ago (28–29). She dwells particularly on certain statues she saw there including "one Apollo, all naked, which I knew I should not look on but which I always made some excuse to my companions to pass by" (29). So the first implication of this is that Radegunde regards sexuality as an inherent part of human nature, not one that her vow of chastity makes her regard as sinful. But the second message these passages convey is, somehow, that of Radegunde's otherness: that she perceives more intensely than others. These hints will be expanded on as the story progresses.

Through a series of dialogues between Radegunde and the Vikings, a kind of compromise is brokered, and some of the Abbey's treasures are preserved. At one point—astonishingly, given what has gone before—Radegunde offers to sail away with Thorvald, the Viking's leader, seemingly offering him what he wants: "You are a clever man, Thorvald, perhaps the cleverest man I have ever met. . . . But your cleverness has had no food. It is a cleverness of the world and not of books" (36). By offering Thorvald a chance at what he clearly wants—for his cleverness to be fed, in return for Radegunde's passage to a city like Constantinopol—Radegunde has terrified him, and he accuses her of being a witch.

So the story can be read, in a sense, as a discourse on value: on what matters, what price to put on it, and how to protect it. Again, as always with Russ, the *process* of argument is central. But then, in the closing pages, a further change takes place. Throughout the story there have been hints to genre readers that Radegunde's extraordinary empathy has been born of something more than merely human ability. But toward the end of the tale, Boy News perceives a transformation in her, seeing her become calmer and more terrible than she had been before (49); he thinks she is some kind of demon. Just before, she seemed to receive some kind of message from her "people" (47), that they were coming in a few days to meet her.

And so it proves, for the Abbess leads Boy News, Thorvald and the others out into the trees beyond the village a few days later. There they see a light among the trees and "folk inside the brightness, both men and women, all dressed in white, and they held out their arms to us and the demon [the Abbess] ran to them, crying out loudly and weeping" (53). From the way the story is couched and framed, we are clearly meant to read this as a science-fictional rather than a fantasy resolution. But before the Abbess departs into the light, she looks into Thorvald's eyes and confirms what we already know: "I hate thee and would be revenged upon thee" (54). She pronounces a kind of curse: "Henceforth be not Thorvald Farmer nor yet Thorvald Seafarer but Thorvald Peacemaker, Thorvald War-hater, put into anguish by bloodshed and agonized at cruelty" (54). Boy News, in the closing words of the story, says that he does not understand:

> "Abbess, you said you would be revenged on Thorvald, but all you did was change him into a good man. That is no revenge!"
> What this saying did to her astonished me, for all the color went out of her face and left it gray. She looked suddenly old, like a death's head, even standing there among her own true folk with love and joy coming from them so strongly that I myself might feel it. She said, "I did not change him. I lent him my eyes; that is all." Then she looked beyond me, as if at our village, at the Norsemen loading their boats with weeping slaves, at all the villages of Germany and England and France where the poor folk sweat from dawn to dark so the great lords may do battle with one another, at castles under siege with the starving folk within eating mice and rats and sometimes each other, at the women carried off or raped or beaten, at the mothers waiting for their little ones, and beyond this at the great wide world itself with all its battles which I had used to think so grand, and the misery and greediness and fear and jealousy and hatred of folk one for the other, save—perhaps—for a few bands of savages, but they were so far from us that one could scarcely see them. She said: No revenge? Thinkest thou so, boy? And then she said as one who believes absolutely, as one who has seen all the folk at their living and dying, not for one year but for many, not in one place but in all places, as one who knows it all over the whole wide earth:
> Think again . . . (58–59)

Out of context, this passage may seem over-the-top, even preachy. (One must remember that its speaker is, after all, an abbess.) But in context, at the end of a story of some sixty pages, it reads like the culmination of an argument, a stately yet furious peroration on what can be borne, on what it is like to be a feeling human in a world like this, or ours. There is no anger in Russ except that which is earned.

"Souls" is preceded and followed, as are all the stories in the book, by brief snippets of dialogue between a child and a robot history tutor. (This is one of the ways in which we're cued to read the Abbess's departure as science-fictional.) The section after "Souls" begins, "'So that's how the world was saved,' said the schoolkid. 'By those aliens with their telepathic powers'" (61). The hint is taken: the Abbess, and those who rescued her, might be part of a secret clan of not-quite-humans; and the tutor's words suggest that we should look out for more in the next story, "The Mystery of the Young Gentleman" (1984c).

This story is couched as a diary, written by someone crossing the Atlantic on the S.S. *President Hayes* in 1885 with a young companion named Maria-Dolores. The narrator is, we surmise, older than Maria-Dolores, who appears to be only fifteen. Their ultimate destination is somewhere in the mountains of Colorado. During the crossing, the narrator, who calls himself "Joseph Smith," befriends a doctor. It becomes apparent that for the narrator and Maria-Dolores, categories of gender are somewhat mutable; on more than one occasion, Maria-Dolores exclaims, "Next time I travel as your son!" The central argument of the story takes place between the doctor, Smith, and Maria-Dolores. The doctor is simply unable to parse how gender works for these two, "and believes, because he is a doctor, that his confusions have the status of absolute truth" (73). The painful confusions that result are, in the end, not indictments against the doctor but against—as Russ would argue it—the arbitrarily constructed ideas of gender he has inherited. It's beside the point exactly how, in science-fictional terms, Joseph Smith and Maria-Dolores are created or have evolved. The point is that they are going to an enclave of like-minded people in Colorado; although we never see this enclave, we can imagine it being a place worth fighting for and preserving.

The remaining three stories in the collection, "Bodies," "What Did You Do During the Revolution Grandma," and "Everyday Depressions" press these ideas further. "Everyday Depressions" is another of Russ's semi-autobiographical stories, couched (like "The Little Dirty Girl") as a letter to a friend. (One could make an argument that all of Russ's work is epistolary, a personal message awaiting the reader's reply.) "Bodies" (1984) seems to me the most remarkable of these three, perhaps the most moving in Russ's body of short fiction. It is also couched as a letter—in this case, a love letter. It is set, the robot tutor tells us, in Utopia.

The letter writer, whose name we are not told, lives in a desert town near

Pueblo. The letter is addressed to someone called James. Like the narrator, James (and, we suppose, many others in this future society) is a resurrected persona from the past. In the narrator's case, the past life was as a woman, a real-estate speculator in the Pacific Northwest from the late twentieth century. James was from London in the 1930s. Both died young, though at the time of the story the narrator—having been resurrected before James—is considerably older. The narrator recalls James's resurrection: "You stood in the tank like a museum specimen in a showcase. . . . You shook. The tank was draining; the water poured off you. You looked like Adam in terror. You looked suddenly rather lovely" (98). The narrator spends some time talking to James about this new world: he is like "a nineteen-year-old schoolboy hearing about Heaven" (101).

The story then moves on to a party held that night. As the narrator says, "If six foot four of sunburnt blond cowboy in range clothes came to carry me off, I'd go too. . . . I thought: *Shall I tell James that this vision's name is Harriet? No*" (102). James goes off with Harriet—whom the narrator refers to throughout as "he"—seemingly happy to have sex with another man. But soon the message comes back that James is upset, and the narrator goes to talk to him. Eventually, they get to the bottom of James's unhappiness: "He's not a man. It was horrible!" (105). The narrator's answer, "Well, you see, there aren't any men and women, James, not any more. No-one thinks that way any more" (105) may well be true, but it hardly helps him.

James then goes off traveling for some time and, as the narrator recounts, there is some interest in his adventures: evidently he is becoming more sexually comfortable in this new world. When he finally returns, the two of them—the narrator around age fifty and James, twenty—go off on holiday to the mountains of Taos. A painful argument ensues, again centred around sex, and the narrator sends James away. At least as it's put in the story, it seems that James's crassness may not have entirely deserted him. The letter is a request to James to come back. It acknowledges his faults (and the writer's), as well as their age difference; it says, in so many words, that "this is not a love affair," but the writer's feelings for James clearly have the strength of love. It leaves open the question of what James's response is.

The miracle about "Bodies" is that it manages to be extraordinarily moving about sex and gender in a situation designed, I think, so that we (like James) cannot easily parse how gender works. In her short fiction—only a fraction of which I have been able to examine here—Russ never lets her arguments or her agendas obscure the humans of both genders who are tied to them. For sheer inventiveness, formal range, and emotional force, I can think of only a few bodies of short SF to rival it: perhaps those of Theodore Sturgeon, James Tiptree, Jr., and Gene Wolfe. But Russ exceeds those, even

Tiptree, in the fierceness with which she addresses her material, the sense that she exhausts the material at the same time as the story. The challenge for readers now—when some feminist arguments have been, if not won, then at least normalized into Western culture—is to see that her fierceness is *necessary*; that these battles have not been won and that, as always with letters, the onus is on the reader: *what do you do now?*

~

## 15 Castaway
### Carnival and Sociobiological Satire in We Who Are About To . . .

Tess Williams

*We Who Are About To* . . . is an SF story of a doomed group of castaways, a "lifeboat population" stranded on a tagged but uncharted planet. It is also a dark tale about physical vulnerability and the failure of social identity and power. Eight characters, from very different backgrounds, suddenly lose context and/or authority. The millionaire family does not know what to do without money to protect them and the academic finds his particularized and theoretical knowledge useless in a survival situation. They all die, together with a football player, a wannabe government agent, and a hooker. The only character that retains power (but not life) in this hopeless situation is the narrator, a member of a despised religious sect and a witch figure. Russ's novel is driven by a feminist politic but it is clear from this story that the author is also interested in the genre because of its "seams," its potential to represent the irregular, aberrant, subversive, and grotesque. This is a carnival text with carnival characters acting to destabilize much of late twentieth-century mainstream Western culture. Drawing on Mikhail Bakhtin's carnival theory, and Mary Russo's feminist extension of it, I address here the various subversions of literary forms this work offers, the textual challenges of exploring carnivalized bodies and social identities, and Russ's lampooning of neo-Darwinist stories of science and survival.

The theory of carnival, as first developed by Mikhail Bakhtin in his work on Rabelais, is grounded in medieval spectacle but has considerable relevance to contemporary culture as a critical and philosophical tool. Carnival maps transgression and subversion in discourse and materiality, particularly in relation to bodies. It also speaks to society, the environment, and time in a very different way to both modernism and postmodernism. A broad-based and plastic theory, carnival embraces category crisis and provides a "guerrilla epistemology" (Hitchcock 1998) that undermines the dominant politics of the day, whatever they may be, and transforms currencies of meaning and significance into satire, farce, and vulgar humor. Despite criticisms of utopianism, naïveté and essentialism, based primarily on Bakhtin's uniting of the individual body with the social body and ultimately with the regenerative and fecund body of the planet, the theory of carnival remains relevant. As a tool, many critics who employ carnival express a degree of frustration with it; but they also acknowledge carnival as an antidote to repression, and concede that its transgressiveness and inclusivity is useful. It is particularly important, however, to recognize the ambivalence of carnival theory with regard to gender.[1]

Rabelais's women are unvoiced and generally portrayed as archetypal figures such as the birthing woman and "the bride" in popular festive forms (Bakhtin 1965). Bakhtin takes his critical cues from Rabelais's work and fails to further follow issues with women and carnival expression. However, Mary Russo extends carnival to address women through carnival and the grotesque. She argues that the male body represents the classic closed and transcendent body, with its connections to rationalism and individualism, while the female is the protruding, secreting, multiple, changing, and connected body. The female body, therefore, is "other" and is more identified with carnival space and time, a space and time needed for cultural rejuvenation and the possibility of real change: "The figure of the female transgressor as public spectacle is still powerfully resonant, and the possibilities of redeploying this representation as a demystifying or utopian model have not been exhausted" (Russo 1994).

Russo rehabilitates the feminine through dramatic flight, which she sees as "a freedom from oppressive bodily containment." When the hysteric decides to jump or fly, thus escaping a phallocentric world, she reconstitutes herself as central and forces male spectatorship. While this action may mean the literal death of the female subject, it is also, according to Russo, the point where the masculine becomes the liminal, the female subject becomes realized, and the arbitrary, imposed boundaries constructed between "individual and society, between genders, between species, and between classes" become blurred and brought into crisis (79). Russ's novel is consistent with Russo's feminist interpretation of carnival as she uses the philobatic moment of her particular narrator's escape to achieve a feminist critique of text and body, and her other archetypal/universalized characters demonstrate a carnival collapse of social mores and demystification of many cultural values.

## Genre

In the mid-1960s, there were two popular television shows about castaways that still have mild cult status. *Gilligan's Island* is a farcical story of a charter boat shipwrecked on an uncharted island. There are seven people aboard the S.S. *Minnow*, stereotypes all: the captain and his first mate (a sort of Laurel and Hardy team of buffoons); a millionaire couple; a somewhat abstracted professor; a breathy, glamorous starlet; and a "girl-next-door." The other program, *Lost in Space*, is a family/child-centered science fantasy show of weekly encounters with monsters, robots, and alien environments. Again, the castaways number seven: the five members of the Robinson family; a "first mate" who reinforces Professor Robinson's patriarchal authority within the group; and a stowaway, a comic scientist driven by greed and cowardice.[2] The premise of the two shows is similar. They share a certain comic stability as the cultural values of the castaways are transported whole and uninterrogated into the microcosms of the stranded groups. To maintain this stability, any history more detailed than a sketchy story of how the castaways appear in the present location is nonexistent, danger is only ever a convention and not truly confronting, and any kind of sexual activity is taboo between members of the group. *We Who Are About To . . .* takes a similar premise of a castaway group, but then undermines the familiar stories of innocence, timelessness, and naturalized social behaviors that are staples of the television shows.

The first lines of the narrator in *We Who Are About To . . .* are, "About to die. And so on. We're all going to die" (7). From this introduction it is clear that the danger to these castaways is immediate, yet it is not what might traditionally be expected from an alien environment, particularly an alien environment in an SF novel. Conflict occurs when one of the women does not want to have babies and join the other castaways in re-creating civilization. She resists and everyone dies. Some die by misadventure and some by her hand, but not before there is an unmasking of certain individual delusions and cultural deceptions. The castaway story is thus rewritten with resonances of *The Lord of the Flies*, except that the chaos and murder in this text do not come from unconscious psychology, but from a darkly celebratory, almost pagan, collusion with inevitable death. The conclusion of the two television series are never contemplated as anything but a possible rescue followed by happy-ever-after, whereas the conclusion of *We Who Are About To . . .* is violent and disturbing. Death is the hors d'oeuvre, just as it will be the main course and the dessert. This is the deliberate carnivalization of a genre from an author skilled in textual criticism and readings: "I had gotten to the point early on where I could watch the first two minutes of any TV show and know everything that would follow. The patterns became so predictable and so false that after a while you want to *play* with them, be sacrilegious . . . you have to be aware of these structures in order to resist them and allow your texts to create a dialogue or dialectic with them" (McCaffery 1990, 200).

The undermining of the popular castaway tale is only one of a number of genre challenges issued by this carnival story. Russ also confronts the genre boundaries of the novel itself, the genre of SF, and utopian writing within feminist SF. What is deeply ironic about this process is that she is not only a contributor to these traditions, she also defines them as a critic. Russ uses her knowledge of literary forms and narrative expectation to destabilize the genres she participates in when she writes imaginatively.

According to Bakhtinian dialogic criticism, complex book-length stories always contain evidence of multiple discourses; they defy stability or unity as a form by remaining open. The novel is part of a continuous chain of utterance, inevitably answering previous utterances and generating future utterances (Bakhtin 1981). Put differently, more in accord with carnival theory, the "novel" body is moving away from formalist unities of time, space, and hero-centeredness, toward carnivalized, seamed bodies and decentered, ironic subjects.

Russ writes carnival, fully aware of the history of the novel and capitalizing on both conventions of textual form and disruptions to textual forms, as she floats new possibilities for her reader. In this instance she offers an unidentifiable, antiheroic, archetypal narrator; a written text masquerading as an audio text, both broken and continuous, reliable and unreliable; and a text with an audience assuming a text with no possible audience. Thus, with regard to the novel form itself, Russ enlarges the territory of metafiction with this book, just as she did with *The Female Man*, published in the same year. Both *The Female Man* and *We Who Are About To . . .* are precocious treatises on their own existence, commentators on their own reception, and parodies of countless prior stories. In the case of *We Who Are About To . . .*, the satire constellates around Western phallocentric traditions of heroism, ingenuity, survival, and biological and cultural imperialism.

If Russ complicates Western writing by parodying the novel genre, she further carnivalizes it by working in the SF subgenre from a feminist standpoint. SF is, in both form and subject, eminently carnivalistic. Michael Holquist (1994), critical commentator on Bakhtin, nominates Mary Shelley's *Frankenstein* as the poster text for carnival, because it is an important case study of the grotesque body and intertextuality (94–106).[3] Shelley's novel is also nominated by Brian Aldiss (1973) as the primary science fictional text in the Western tradition (29–65). It is impressive that carnival and speculative fiction join together in the same historic text, but it is not really a surprise. Holquist says carnival writing and *Frankenstein* are about the "novel body," and the inevitably historically patched stories we tell, while Aldiss says speculative fiction and *Frankenstein* are about "our confused state of knowledge." The emphasis of both is on the seams of the body/text, rather than on an unseamed body/text. Both carnival writing and most SF texts foreground the heteroglossic rather than trying to conceal it: discourses such as politics, history, and science become focuses of storytelling, and bodies are seen as inscribed and unruly.

≈ ≈ ≈

In the common, and often frustrating, process of laying down rules in a rule-breaking field, we come to see SF as often allied to other forms of writing. We see this alliance most particularly when trying to distinguish speculative fiction from realist fiction or trying to identify its roots. Samuel Delany (1977), for example, compares SF to nineteenth-century symbolism and identifies good SF as generative of mystical insight,[4] while Darko Suvin (1979) sees a relationship between SF and the pastoral and says that, like the pastoral, SF is "metaempirical and non-naturalistic . . . an estranged, literary genre which is not at the same time metaphysical" (20). When Aldiss identifies *Frankenstein* as the primary SF text, he allies the genre with the gothic, but Russ identifies the genre through function rather than effect. She picks up on another comment by Suvin and elaborates on the "quasi-medieval," didactic nature of SF that holds the "idea as hero" (Russ 1995g, 112–118). Ironically, where Russ might argue that SF is the relative of medieval didacticism, her particular brand of writing is actually more closely connected to the medieval *subversive* form of carnival. Both medieval mainstream culture and medieval carnival were blunt instruments of ideology: one broadly serving the dominant culture and more formal morality of the church; the other, broadly representing the repressed nature-based culture and less regulated moralities of common folk. Carnival depended upon satire, parody, vulgarity, and farce as it mocked religious, civil, and academic authorities, often showing them as hypocritical, foolish, self-interested, and vulnerable.

Part of Russ's complexity lies with her multiple subversions of Western storytelling traditions. As a writer and critic, she understands the rich histories and heteroglossic constructions of drama and the novel, but she also understands the social potential of popular fiction and media. *We Who Are About To . . .* is a novel and a science fiction story, but it disrupts both these genres in terms of form and content. This disruption is often attributed to the feminist content of Russ's text, yet the disruptive qualities and powers of the story cannot be isolated to this specific political dimension of the book. Rather, they come out of Russ's refusal to be pious about literary and social institutions of any kind, and her determination to expose cultural vanities, patriarchal and otherwise. If her writing could be explained only as feminist polemic, it could be more readily understood within the critical framework of the very specific tradition of feminist science fiction, a tradition manifesting a field of utopian writings in the same decade that the anti-utopian *We Who Are About To . . .* was published.

Russ, as critic, describes this field of imagined worlds where masculinist hierarchies and models of authority are undone. They are "classless, without government, ecologically minded, with a strong feeling for the natural world, quasi-tribal in feeling and quasi-familial in structure, [and] the societies of these stories are *sexually permissive*." They also exhibit the "joys of female bonding" and often stage the rescue of a female child. Furthermore, they are reactive and "very limited in violence" (Russ 1981; 1995g, 144). These texts question existing social structures on the basis of a growing awareness of gender inequity, and propose alternatives that vary from nature-focused separatism to complete power reversals.

Russ effectively disrupts this form because she knows it so intimately. The castaway group in *We Who Are About To . . .* is far from classless. In fact, their differences in social status are severe and stark, and from the first they snipe at each other. Not just the narrator, who annoys everyone by articulating the hopelessness of the situation, but also Cassie and John Udon, Nathalie and everyone else, and the Grahams as a couple. The situation is far from utopian. Authority is a pivotal issue and cannot be resolved, partly because the assumption of authority in such a small group is public and therefore tricky, and partly because the covert nature of power is not easy to map and understand in such an unexpected and uncontained situation. Transactions within the group are inevitably unsettled, and sexual permissiveness is subordinated to the futile and embarrassing colonial priority of impregnation, initially enacted between Nathalie and the ailing Victor Graham in an attempt to preserve his sperm, and unaddressed in the taboo construction of nubile, preadolescent Lori.

Lori is a particular site of anti-utopian satire, representing as she does, the undermined convention of "rescued female child." Her rescue is (in the way of carnival) not simply oppositional and is not anti-utopian just because it is a failure to save. Lori, Valeria tells the narrator proudly, was originally destined to die but Valeria paid for extensive medical work, and Lori ended up costing "as much money as a small new England state" (93). Lori's life is a testament to Valeria's power, money, and cynicism. The girl is a project, an extended investment. She is a toy, bought to keep an already bought husband amused and happy, and her "café-au-lait" skin brings a resonance of slavery to this costing out of her life. Ironically, therefore, Lori wears many masks in the carnival and some of them are contradictory. She is both a purchase and a saving; she was saved from death before she could not—in this instance—be saved from death; and then she is saved as a genetic treasure (despite her medically suspect beginnings) so she (in turn) could save her own species when it became isolated on this planet. In the end she is victim, as opposed to being saved, but even then she may be saved from suffering. Russ's inspired irony carnivalizes the story of rescuing/saving the female child in all its Western, white, imperialist arrogance, but also reduces Lori's extreme (good *and* bad) luck to arbitrary events outside a political context.

Another specific "anti-utopian" feature of *We Who Are About To . . .* is found in Russ's portrayal of violence. Russ identifies speculative utopias as reactive and very limited in violence. However, interpersonal violence between women and men resulting in the death of the man is often a focus of her own work. Feminist utopias generally shift violence out of the sphere of women's desire and power, but Russ embraces it and explores its narrative complexities. Critic Jeanne Cortiel (1999) points out three strands of narrative values connected with violence in Russ's fiction. First, the female hero of the Alyx stories is an exceptional woman whose violence is instinctive and personal; second, failing to kill men illustrates a lack of agency for women in texts such as "When it Changed" and "My Dear Emily"; and third, murder is a way of regaining female agency in *The Female Man* and *The Two of Them*. Even so, there is also a carnival dimension to Russ's textual violence that Cortiel misses.

As well as having comic value, Rabelaisian abuse, thrashings, and beatings often represent a significant metamorphosis of power: the decrowning of kings. Such is what occurs to the castaways as they experience their falls. They lose dignity, become physically vulnerable, and are even pathetic. Alan-Bobby, the young footballer, rushes into a dark cave and knocks himself out on a ledge. On a sports field his impetuosity could bring him rewards; in an unknown environment, it is stupid behavior that results in his death. He is the admired athlete turned buffoon. Nathalie, the would-be government agent, and John Udon, the academic, fall off a ledge and die. Potential and ability snuffed out by more miscalculation, and a literal fall is symbolic for these two who appeared to have elevated social status. Valeria, like an overconfident villain in a TV script, commits the clichéd mistake of not shooting the narrator when she has the upper hand. Instead she delivers a standard just-before-I-kill-you speech that allows the narrator to use her ingenuity to turn the tables. All of this violence has comic content, but the fall of each of these individuals represents more than simply the demise of that individual. It also represents the bringing low of whatever social value they held as the sole representative of that group on the uncharted planet.

Little more than a novella, *We Who Are About To . . .* flies in the face of many narrative expectations. It is uncooperative and does not give pleasure to readers in traditional ways; it unsettles them and undoes expectations on all generic levels as novel, as science fiction, and as utopian feminism. Often carnival is identified on the basis of content, looking at grotesque bodies or the language of the marketplace, but the subversion of literary form itself has precedent in Rabelais, who parodies written forms from sacred liturgy to "les belles lettres" and scholarly treatises. This is a process that works to undo both historical and cultural authorities and demands a complex and tiered receptivity in the audience that relies on their recognition of form and recognition of deviation from that form.

## Body, Social Identity, and Carnival

The way that Russ maps the physical bodies of her characters, the social body they have left behind, the social body they try to construct, and the planetary body they are so precariously perched upon, also reveal carnival. Representations of body and social identity are unpredictable as the text reconfigures power and relationship. Bakhtin reads carnival as subversions of social authority. Mary Russo (1994) reads it as subversions of certain *naturalized* authorities of gender, with attention paid to physical and social reconfigurations. Russo's political reading of carnival, picking up on physical and social transgressions, subversions and distortions, and reading them from a feminist perspective, is apposite for the genre of science fiction and Joanna Russ's text in particular. For example, the Grahams present as a conventional heterosexual couple but closer examination undoes this illusion.

Samuel R. Delany reads Valeria as coded masculine. Because she is rich and exercised patriarchal powers prior to being shipwrecked, she is not "defined by biological sex but rather . . . constituted by socioeconomics as a power structure . . . what Foucault would call a biopolitical field" (see chapter 13, this book). Further, when the narrator and Valeria physically struggle and Valeria is killed when the gun goes off, Delany sees the struggle as the importance of both the fight and the murder, because the narrator is opposed to what Valeria represents. If this is true, the logical extension of this reading is that Victor is coded feminine. He groomed himself for a rich wife, subjecting himself to enhancing cosmetic surgeries and training himself to please to the point where he calls himself a "whore," both a feminizing and debasing term. And if Valeria's death is about power (struggles), his is about vulnerability due to a problem with his heart, the organ usually associated with love, romance, and femininity. Valeria and Victor are cross-dressed characters, practicing a social and cultural form of transvestism, who find this situation forces them back into more predictable roles. The reversal is reversed: Valeria, the financial mogul, is uncrowned while Victor, the fool and whore, is raised up.

*We Who Are About To . . .* hinges on a number of comic reversals, part of what Mikhail Bakhtin describes as the "gay relativity of prevailing truths and authorities . . . the peculiar logic of the "inside out," of the "turnabout," of a continual shifting from top to bottom, from front to rear, of numerous parodies and travesties, humiliations, profanations, comic crownings and uncrownings" (Bakhtin 1965, 11). Russ's text also offers carnival readings of cultural sites commonly representing safety and protection. Government training, formal education, money, family, and even organized sport become liabilities or useless to the group of castaways.

The Cartesian body is divorced from the mind, closed, complete, and problematically linked to the world, while carnival is preoccupied with the open, protruding, and secreting body that participates in the cycles of nature. The carnival body is often seen in terms of its parts, particularly those parts that relate to the "lower stratum," the bowels and the genitals, and it is fecund and excessive. The bodies in We Who Are About To . . . are affected by the romantic tradition, which divorces them from that fecund, excessive, regenerative power of the world, and they become "dismembered." On the untagged planet, however, there is an obsession with reproductive processes that isolates the genitals. In the absence of technology, human reproductive organs will take the place of tools; they will be used to dominate and control the environment. Nathalie and Victor's awkward mating speaks to the way that Western modernism divides mind and body, and body and environment. The mind will control the body, and the body, in turn, will control the planet. This dissociation is part of the social and cultural values that are lampooned in carnival. And there is a serious distinction between male and female genitals and the stories they have attached to them. Victor is an older, dying man but his genitals represent expansion, colonization, and the hope for the future, a way of preserving life (human) through possible reproduction. Cassie, on the other hand, remarks that her chances of coming through childbirth at her age and with a family history of difficult births is not particularly good. While the narrator points out that biology is not destiny with regard to birth histories, Cassie's doubts forcibly remind the reader of the difficulties of birth in pretechnological culture. The female reproductive organs represent contraction, fear, limitation, and potential death.

We have seen that liminal values are foregrounded and can be understood much better in a carnival space. But carnival also allows illumination of dominant or official cultural values in unexpected ways. In this text, a tiny cross-section of American culture has been transported onto an uncharted planet and with it come its very own cultural restraints, harassments, and threats. While the threats and violence appear to be contained by the trappings of civilization, this containment is only an illusion. The threats and constraints are not a force that civilization as we know it is counteracting; they actually represent part of civilization. The assumption that the urge of an isolated group to retreat to barbarism will be irresistible is yet another cultural story that makes up the carnival experience of the text. In We Who Are About To . . . , unlike Golding's Lord of the Flies, the layers of Western culture are not being slowly stripped away to reveal elemental humans, minus their technology and comforts. Rather, they are being stripped away in such a fashion as to reveal what Westerners *believe* are the underlying imperatives of human biologies. In Russ's book, domination and sexual access are preoccupations, not necessarily of an essential psychophysiology, but of a cultural belief relating to psychophysiology. That is, when the colonizing story of the castaways was countered by a different, skeptical story, the responding anger and threats come from contemporary notions of nature and survival, not from some base biology that is surfacing in the characters because of their predicament.

As the response to provocation in the book is deeply political, so is the original catalyst. The narrator stands as an unraveler, a character who refuses to collude with the other castaways' attempt to present their predicament as manageable and coherent in terms of the society they have left behind. Physically, she is a woman of late childbearing age and that makes her compliance with the group a significant issue. But she does not/will not comply and mocks the group dreams of colonization. The narrator is an important carnival figure because she is more than a personal challenge to the castaways on this planet. She is a mythic and historical challenge to the world they came from as well: configured as a witch, she takes possession of the "broomstick," a small motorized flier, and she is equipped with a pharmacopoeia of drugs. Being mythic and historical endows her a different kind of carnival presence, a more loaded and controversial presence.

Mary Russo's feminist emphasis in carnival critique is embodied woman, woman situated in opposition to the closed, classical body, woman as the grotesque. In contrast, Joanna Russ's most significant carnival character identifies herself as "nobody" (no body). She is disembodied and is the only character who really makes an escape in any physical or psychological sense. Her "philobatic moment" sees her flying free, escaping the privileges, illusions, and power abuses that have come to the planet with the castaways. All have the opportunity to do the same as the narrator, but she is the only one that can imagine a space not governed by the social and cultural constraints they have always known. She is the only one who can truly understand the possibility and non-negotiability of a "new world."

A world, a planetary body, inspires respect and interest by virtue of its massiveness, its immeasurable bounty and appetites, its agency in the life and death of lesser entities, and its longevity. Bakhtin speaks to the medieval attempt to negotiate the hugeness of the planet in Rabelais's stories of Gargantua and his enormous son, Pantagruel. Everything is done in excess, particularly in times of birth, and everything is eaten and drunk in enormous quantities. Gargamelle, Gargantua's mother, goes into labor with him after consuming a vast amount of tripe, and a caravan of wagons loaded with food follows Panatagruel from his mother's womb, while the child himself eats a cow's leg as if it were a sausage (Bahktin 1965, 220, 331). These carnival stories also include death in the Rabelaisian tradition, but they inevitably become cyclical, stories of fecundity and renewal, connected to the European, seasonal understanding of the planet. Russ's text is carnivalesque in its refusal of high culture and comic in its awkward violence, but it holds a modernist view on death and its world is an ancient, sinister stranger. The castaways are surrounded by life, but there is no birth in this novel, there are only a thousand creative, terrifying, ironic ways in which to die:

> Think of Earth. Kind old home. Think of the Arctic. Of Labrador. Of Southern India in June. Think of smallpox and plague and earthquakes and ringworm and pit vipers. Think of a nice case of poison ivy all over, including your eyes. Status asthmaticus. Amoebic dysentery. The Minnesota pioneers who tied a rope from the house to the barn in winter because you could lose your way in a blizzard and die three feet from the house. Think (while you're at it) of tsunamis, liver fluke, the Asian brown bear. Kind old home. The sweetheart. The darling place. Think of Death Valley . . . in August. (20)
>
> . . . . . . . . . . . . . . . . . . . . . . . . . . . . . . . . .
>
> We died the minute we crashed. Plague, toxic food, deficiency diseases, broken bones, infection, gangrene, cold, heat, and just plain starvation (46).

Bodies and social identities are mapped in sometimes unexpected ways in *We Who Are About To. . . .* Nothing of the physical or social is safe or stable; in this carnival, death is a prominent character. This is a darkening of Rabelaisan carnival, one that Bakhtin sees as a move to the Romantic grotesque and a context of terror—but it is still carnival (Bahktin 1965, 38)

## Carnival and Science

Major cultural discourses challenge and change both the science fiction genre and the inclusive, critical form of carnival. Russ's text lampoons not only perceptions of nature, but also perceptions of power over nature. The unstable position science holds in carnival is similar to the central but unstable position of science in SF. Science and technology are valorized in some texts and demonized in others. One day they will save the world; the next, they will destroy it. In SF the emphasis is often on technology, but Russ understands that less materially manifest science stories can also drive fiction. In "Towards an Aesthetic of Science Fiction," she reads entropy, a "dreadful and agonising iron physical law," as central to H. G. Wells's *Time Machine*, and says Ursula K.

Le Guin's story, "The Masters," "has as its emotional center the rediscovery of the duodecimal system" (1995g, 112–113).

Neither Russ's critiques nor her creative writing are innocent. Just as she writes about feminist utopias as an academic and then subverts them in *We Who Are About To . . .* , so she understands and subverts the science story that is at the heart of this novel. Neo-Darwinism is a combination of Darwin's theory of natural selection and molecular biology. The broad idea is that the fittest survive, though both fitness and survival are complicated concepts, and neo-Darwinism is historically and politically troubled, particularly where it intersects with the newer discipline of sociobiology. While both paradigms have redeeming features, they are deeply marked with the politics of patriarchy, colonialism, environmental exploitation, and eugenics, often failing to take into account the role played by culture over genes in creating particular behaviors, and the role played by culture in scientific understandings and perception.

Many feminist scientists in particular see problems with the reductiveness and determinism of neo-Darwinism and sociobiology. They contest such scientific research for its selective approaches (particularly, its reading violence and male promiscuity as natural).[5] Joanna Russ, however, is a different sort of critic. She is a fiction writer utilizing knowledge imaginatively and critically constructing fictional scenarios that confront, resist, and provoke.

That material circumstances limit genetic success and human ingenuity is something made clear in the baby bird story. As the narrator is dying, she hallucinates about her past and recalls time spent with a lover. They are woken one morning by the intense, hungry screeching of a nest of baby sparrows in the air-conditioner. The narrator's lover wants to kill the birds, possibly by piping boiling water over them. The birds' extreme vulnerability and their tenancy in an unnatural environment, one they were never designed to occupy, turn this story into a parable: membership of an aggressively populating species does not ensure individual or small group success in a bad situation. The castaways' colonization program is a self-deception, springing from cultural indoctrination and fear, rather than a biological imperative. The conclusion of the book reinforces this reading. Rather than the ultimate survivor being a wonderful physical and psychological specimen of humanity, it is a middle-aged woman, with swollen ankles and a bad attitude.

The narrator, the final member of the group left alive, is an apparent enigma. Does she represent authority or does she represent a knowledgeable and competent subversion of authority? She is a musicologist, but her knowledge is broader based than the study of music would imply. She is a failed resistance fighter, but she still has a lot of fight in her. Because the text is carnival, these instabilities do not resolve. In fact, they are compounded with other instabilities as the narrator continues to combine power and subversion unexpectedly. In a major Janus-like incarnation she is scientist and antiscientist. This is not a contradiction; it is a reflection of the ambivalent history of science itself embodied by the narrator. Carolyn Merchant (2001), ecofeminist theorist, has discussed the roots of science in the early seventeenth century. Francis Bacon, a "father" of modern science worked with James I after his coronation to destroy witchcraft in England and to set up science as a cultural project using the "modern experimental method—constraint of nature in the laboratory, dissection by hand and mind, and the penetration of hidden secrets" (71). In that period, which was pivotal in overseeing the original power shift from the feminine "black magic" to the "white magic" of science, witches were understood as servants of nature whereas science was a recovery of man's rights over nature.

This historic complexity is key to Russ's narrator. She has access to the discourse of science, but she is ultimately a servant of nature. When describing their situation, she uses language taken from a scientific epistemology that no longer exists for the castaways, a language that she recognizes will inevitably fall away and become meaningless in time:

> We are (O listeners note) one quarter the height of the trees, we are hairless, give birth to our young alive, are bipedal with two manipulating limbs, have binocular vision, we regulate our internal temperatures by the slow oxidation of various compounds (food), and we live no more than a century at the very, very most (at least it feels that way, as the joke goes) and we are caught rather nastily, very badly, and sometimes even comically between different aspirations. That is the fault of the cerebral cortex. (20–21)

Her language reflects their recent understanding of the world, but she knows Western science is not on their side and cannot be. This division is presented in comical-satirical ways. For example, any benefits that might appear in the technology they have with them tends to be time-limited: unrechargeable batteries, sealed powerpack, cast desalination unit, the winding watch that stops. Extinction, not evolution, is their very real bogey now. *We Who Are About To . . .* speaks strongly to theories of natural selection, genetic reductionism, and deep time. It is a work about people, a cross-section of culture, trapped not only by biology, but also by notions of biology. As the castaways struggle to come to terms with their predicament, scientific ideas that have almost become religious beliefs get in the way of understanding their situation. Science takes its place as one of the prevailing authorities that can be mocked and even dismantled in carnival, along with other cultural and social powers. Russ is iconoclastic, able to imagine stepping outside of what is known, capable of proposing that "history may just end arbitrarily, without the consolation of meaning" (Cortiel 1999, 209).

≈ ≈ ≈

Carnival and SF go well together, particularly if the SF is subversive. They both allow many liberties of imagination and expression. *We Who Are About To . . .* is not roistering, Rabelaisan farce, but it is humorous. Much of the comedy is situational and dark: Lori's abysmal ignorance of her vulnerability, Alan-Bobby's recklessness, Valeria's need to grandstand, the forced intimacy of Victor and Nathalie, and so on. In this place where money and conventional knowledge are no longer currency, characters are so out of context it is as if they have been caught with their pants down. The narrator, on the other hand, is smart, wry, and crafty, outwitting her companions at every turn. Other humor in the text is dependant on challenges to dominant cultural forms, discourses, and authorities. Novels, utopian dreams, sociobiology, natural selection, time and space—all are touched upon and tested for their assumptions and possibilities. Boundaries, perspectives, and subjectivities slip and slide in an unsettling story that prevents the reader from selecting one viewpoint, one understanding, one thematic thread. In the end a single powerful carnival image remains for the reader.

A central, fecund, and morbid archetype seems to appear with the death of the narrator. The archetype is that of the "pregnant hag," the grotesque twinning of death and birth that is the very *raison d'être* of carnival. Utterly starved, "skinny legs, big knees, hanging belly," the narrator produces a child in her hallucinations. The little girl is not a child she particularly liked, but one that was named after an airport and might be "a gateway, a sign or a messenger" (166). Moreover, while she reminds the narrator of the cycle of life and renewal, the narrator complains that she still doesn't understand. This is not surprising. The truth is, the little girl is not even a remotely hopeful figure. Kennedy is already dead herself, her potential cut off at an early age. Her visit to the narrator is not a promise but an act of closure. The narrator and the reader are left with only one option for continuity: it is time for the narrator to become part of the planet, to let the "kind" hill bury her. In Bakhtin's words: "The unfinished and open body (dying, bringing forth and being born) is not separated from the world by clearly defined boundaries; it is blended with the world, with animals, with objects. It is cosmic, it represents the entire material bodily world in all its elements" (1965, 26–27).

This return to earth should be an appropriate, deeply symbolic, psycho-spiritual finish to a twentieth-century carnival text, but in this story it creates yet a new, final level of absurdity. This is not the earth, but an earth that provides the ultimate resting place for the eight castaways. If human activity, individual and social, is satirized as insignificant against the indifferent majesty of nature when the species is at home and in its rightful context, how much more pretentious does human activity appear when it is enacted on the surface of an alien(ated) world?

# 16 The Narrative Topology of Resistance in the Fiction of Joanna Russ

BRIAN CHARLES CLARK

Narrative is both a kind of engine and a kind of friction, creating a tension that both drives and prescribes story. The stories of our lives motivate us along certain narrative arcs, but to stray from those arcs is to move out of bounds. Narrative, in other words, is a way of mapping and transacting with the epistemologically dicey territory of life, culture, and world. Narrative is epistemologically dicey in that knowledge of life and culture is riven with the gaps of the unknown and the plains of negotiated reality. We know and become ourselves in terms of our stories and it is thus appropriate and useful to theorize narrative in explicitly topological terms. Narrative, then, is not only literary. It is, in reality, primarily cognitive, due to the social formation of human ontology (Ochs and Capp 1996). Narrative exerts constraints on human epistemology (Harré 2001) and emotion (Hsu et al. 2005) as well as on human cultural and political constructs (Bhabha 1990).

How do we know when we've strayed out of the bounds of a given narrative arc? We know because we are edge-detecting animals. When we stray out of bounds our social milieu applies friction by various means: by indicating that we have not been understood; by critical remarks ("*those* shoes with *those* pants?"); and by more extreme measures, such as prohibition, arrest, exile, and even death.

Russ challenges the boundaries of a hegemonic narrative topology. In this essay I explore the edges and bounds—the topology—and uses of Russ's narrative through an analysis of her novels *On Strike Against God, We Who Are About To . . ., And Chaos Died*, and other works. I celebrate Russ's arc-defying fiction by showing, with the help of the theoretical and philosophical writings of Gilles Deleuze and Félix Guattari, that she resists oppressive territorialization. Deleuze and Guattari are especially valuable for understanding Russ's deterritorializing challenges, her resistance to authoritarian and *a priori* narratives, in that the French philosophers specifically work within a topological mode. Russ's radically feminist science fiction creates a refrain—a territorial call—that deliberately lures the engaged reader *out*: not just "off" the map of patriarchal-capitalism, with its colonial insistence on "straight" narrative, but out of the map completely in order to (1) disorient us through critical challenges to our molecular assumptions about syntax (such as the use of certain pronouns and prepositions) and (2) to reorient us in new directions such that we do not passively "dwell in possibility" (Dickinson 1998, poem 466). Rather, we actively or even violently work through the ramifications of minoritarian potential (see also Walker 1975).

## Narrative Edge Detection and Visual-Spatial Orientation

Reader perception of a narrative proceeds and is motivated by edge detection: by contrasting motivations among characters (Shakespeare), or by grosser contrasts between light and dark, good and evil, opportunity and crisis, doubt and certainty—and, significantly for Russ's work, between oppression and liberation.

When we are walking and we see a gap, we avoid the gap, thanks to the brain's primordial ability to detect edges. When we are reading or writing and we see a gap we very likely will want to explore that gap

John Le Carré writes stories about stories full of interpersonal gaps and about the bridges that only ever partially span those gaps. In The Little Drummer Girl, someone (an underground Palestinian cell?) has just blown up a number of people in the German town of Bad Godesberg. In the ensuing crime-scene investigation, Israeli agent Schulmann's detecting mind notes a chunk of wire.

This chunk of wire is too much: it is more than is required in the reconstruction of the terrorists' bomb. The other agents on the scene placate Schulmann: "It has no meaning, Mr. Schulmann. It is left over," the investigators say. "The moment was past," says the narrator, "the gap was sealed" (Le Carré 1983, 22–23).

Schulmann, a nationalistic vigilante with both qualifications and doubts, seeks signs, symptoms, and gaps. From previous investigations, he recognizes the wire as a signature. From the signature he constructs an edge-blurring narrative, as the central character (an out-of-work leftist darkling English rose) takes on the identity of another (Palestinian terrorist). Le Carré crosses a line with The Little Drummer Girl. He disrupts smooth space with his insistent narrative neutrality, forcing the reader to transact both the Palestinian and Israel ideological landscape simultaneously.

Genre writers, especially (think of the thriller with its vertical walls of epistemological walls of revelation), use edge detection as entrée to the potential, the incline and fall, of narrative topology. Gaps in the topology of power are often greeted with malice, however (witness the reception of Le Carré and, especially, of Russ). For reasons of maintaining order and selling goods and services, then, it is desirable to create a "smooth space," to use Deleuze and Guattari's (1987, 492) term, a narrative that allows no communicative or ideological gaps, no edges, no violations of the story-as-smooth-space.

In *We Who Are About To . . .*, the unnamed narrator, a mole, a subterranean with no direction home, starts off mildly enough by backing-and-filling her story after she and a few other men and women have crash-landed on an uncharted and uninhabited planet This female narrator interrogates the epistemological boundaries of the narratives functioning around her among the other crashed interstellar travelers: "Travel enough and you can make friends with the crew, what's this, what's that, ask questions; they even let you fiddle about in sick bay if you're careful. You see things, then" (1977, 5). She's retrospecting because she's in an archetypal Russiesque situation: the survivor of a crash who has been utterly deterritorialized. The crash site in *We Who Are About To . . .* is off all maps; the narrator is beyond cartographical redemption. She finally, and ultimately, is with the ones she's with, never mind how harsh love is and Steven Stills be damned.

We find a similar scene in *And Chaos Died*, in which the character Jai Vedh crashes on a planet of beings who are richly endowed with telepathic and telekinetic powers. Likewise in *On Strike Against God*—generally considered autobiographical and thus often treated as out of the bounds of the Russ science-fictional canon—the narrator, Esther (star), crashes when her lesbian lover unaccountably abandons her. Russ embraces science fiction's change of landscape for her own purposes: her narrative purpose is to interrogate the status quo. Russ is a bomber; she blows across entire landscapes and ideologies without notice, landing in a place unrelated to either Kansas or a mainstream science fiction novel plot.

The crash site as scene-of-crisis enables Russ to deterritorialize her narratives. Russ uses deterritorialization to interrogate "gaps and discontinuities" (Wolfson 1986, 19; see also Delany and Russ 1984, 29) in patriarchal and capitalist narratives. Russ isn't so much "deconstructing" these narratives as attempting to rethink narrative from a new perspective. New, that is, as in *novel* or *nova*, and with Russ the perspective is explosively queer-feminist. There is a powerful edge of utopian romanticism in Russ's work, one that seeks apocalyptic scenarios within which to play out stories of deterritorialization, however ephemeral such liberations be.

The crash site of crisis empowers a reconsideration of the (typically colonialist) foundations of culture. In *And Chaos Died* and *Extra(ordinary) People*, for instance, there is again movement toward a utopian moment. But Russ repeatedly rejects this moment; she turns away from the utopian edge by undermining the very narrative she is constructing.

## Resisting Smooth Space in *We Who Are About To . . .*

Russ resists the smooth space of edgeless narrative in a variety of ways, most cogently through relentless self-examination and interrogation. The Socratic axiom—"the unexamined life is not worth living"—works to counteract the perpetuation of story-as-smooth-space, of edgeless, authoritarian narratives. In her interview with Larry McCaffery, Russ remarks upon the unexamined life: "People accept all sorts of attitudes—about racism, sexism, and class—simply because they don't have the time or energy to think these things through. It's easier to accept the status quo, especially if you're part of a privileged group and want to think well of yourself" (McCaffery 183).

The nameless, almost faceless, narrator of *We Who Are About To . . .* survives and ultimately defeats the seemingly utopian and colonial potential presented at the crash site through her own memories. Without memory, we are edgeless, blunt, smooth: Russ's narrator punctuates this equilibrium with a braid of memoir; a life passes before our eyes. As Russ (1983b) says: "When the memory of one's predecessors is buried, the assumption persists that there were none and each generation of women believes itself to be faced with the burden of doing everything for the first time. . . . Without models, it's hard to work; without a context, difficult to evaluate; without peers, nearly impossible to speak" (93).

Even with memory (as armor, weapon, and edge-detector), Russ's characters are often defeated by the hegemonic agency of cultural narratives, as in this grasping after Marx parodying Hegel: "one could ask to be remembered but history is fake and memories die when you do and only God (don't believe it) remembers. History [is] always rewritten" (1977, 78).

Speculative fiction, at its heart, is an interrogative mode of inquiry. Russ's inquisition of the bonds of the patriarchal narrative arc ruptures ideological control—but where do we emerge? She continually catapults us into the unknown of striated space, into "temporary autonomous zones" (Bey 2003) where, freed of the conformities of smooth space, we are forced to confront difference.

The narrator of *We Who Are About To . . .* "dreamed" of her friend L.B: "we were back together at my place, all this sensuality a topography I couldn't describe to you, a sort of lovely pocket universe" (1977, 108). Russ discovers "pocket universes," shimmering zones of autonomy where utopian lights flicker, but wherein we never take comfort. More pragmatic than romantic, Russ's zones of autonomy are always only temporary; the monolithic authority of patriarchal capitalism is never truly defeated. Instead, Russ attacks authority with critical inquiry—*why must this be the way it is?*—and interrogative intensity in hopes of exposing the gaps, cracks, and seams of the monolith.

As Russ says, "Science fiction is a natural . . . for any kind of radical thought" (Delany and Russ 1984, 29).

"WE WUZ PUSHED," Esther insists, her reterritorialization of her and her sisters' stories being the topic of *On Strike Against God* (1980c, 37). Pushed by those great (as in overwhelming, not noble) tropes of male homoerotic bonding: a conversation at a party moves "from a Western to a hockey game to a fight," and then in comes "Olga Korbut, the Russian gymnast" in her skintight suit of prepubescent glory (35). Pushed, Esther says in response to the white-male-flung accusation that feminists are "selfish," because "radicals are people who fight their own oppression. People who fight other people's oppression are liberals or worse" (35). This, of course, is easily demolished nonsense that nevertheless tsunamis a wave of folk wisdom about how to deal with political battles. Keep 'em at home. It's that simple, and no wonder we were pushed.

A radically interrogative stance is needed to create "lines of flight," as Deleuze and Guattari say throughout *A Thousand Plateaus* (1987) and *Kafka: Toward a Minor Literature* (1986), lines that let out and open up territories of egalitarian alterity. The radical cannot work with the materials given her: they must be dynamited and then left behind. Russ's rugged alterity outs herself and attempts to imagine a narrative that suits her desire to speak the tongue of imagination and experience.

## Linguistic Reterritorialization

In *The Lone Ranger and Tonto Fistfight in Heaven*, Sherman Alexie (1993) asks, "How can we imagine a new language when the language of the enemy keeps our dismembered tongues tied to his belt?" (152). Alexie suggests that the way to reterritorialize a new language, to discover new narrative territory, is through the agency of imagination itself: "Didn't you know? Imagination is the politics of dreams; imagination turns every word into a bottle rocket" (152). Alexie's "politics of dreams" is kin to Adrienne Rich's "dream of a common language" and both are elaborated in Deleuze and Guattari's (1987) concept of the minor literature. The member of a minoritarian culture is, in postcolonial theory, the subaltern; therefore, membership has nothing to do with statistical numbers. Rather, the minoritarian is "a way of being 'a foreigner . . . in one's own tongue,' of being 'bilingual, multilingual, but in one and the same language' " (Bogue 2003, 120, quoting Deleuze and Guattari 1987, 98). Russ works through this concept in *How To Suppress Women's Writing*. The "dominant sapients" of "Tau Ceti 8," the "Glotolog," speak the majoritarian dialect of "Glotologgi" and who, with their superior "super-nerd essence," look down upon and do not understand the wide variety of Glotologgi dialects spoken around them by other sapients of lesser "essence" (Russ 1983b, 3). Russ is writing in a code here that infuriates the "dominant sapients" because they can't understand what is being said. Bruce Sterling's remark that "SF in the late Seventies was confused, self-involved, and stale" (in Gibson 2003, xi) is the perfect example of a "super-nerd" deaf to the voices of minoritarian alterity.

Russ is clearly in this mode of a "minor literature" in her attempt to inscribe lines of flight out of patriarchal narrative and into a new space of female autonomy. Indeed, the minoritarian community outlined in Kafka's *Diaries* is seen in the feminist community, and especially among feminist SF writers. Schools of thought in conflict work out their various ideas in small-press magazines, while the history of literature is an important project among feminists and other minoritarian groups, including the recovery of "lost" (that is, erased by the authority of the smooth patriarchal narrative) texts and the discovery of new logics of symbols, metaphors, and modes of speech.

## "The Skies Flew Open": Discovering Lines of Flight

Joanna Russ described to interviewer Donna Perry how she discovered feminism in late 1968 or early 1969 at a Cornell University symposium. "It was the first time feminism had hit Ithaca," she told Perry (Perry 1993, 295). Russ saw several of her students at the symposium including "two [female] students . . . who stood up and said, 'We've been lovers for several years' " (296). Although Russ told Perry that she'd had an inkling that she was a lesbian when she was eleven years old, it was this experience that I understand as a key deterritorializing moment for Russ: as she said, "The skies flew open" (295). She came out and began writing *The Female Man*.

*The Female Man* forces us to read in a deterritorialized fashion. The novel accomplishes this by "*freeing the molecular*" (Deleuze and Guattari 1987, 346; emphasis in original); that is, by freeing the details harnessed by the major forces at work in a milieu in an assault, in Russ's case, on the hegemony of the masculine pronoun. As Peircian philosopher Kathleen Nott (1970) points out, the negotiation of reality depends on "a system of categories which implicitly classify our concepts and experiences and thus provide us with a meaningful, hence a useful language" (89). The question, of course, is, Useful to whom? Nott notes in passing what becomes for Russ a territorial dispute: "abuses of language" must "be properly stated in order to disappear" (89).

But clearly stating the erasure entailed in the exclusive use of the masculine pronoun doesn't make the problem "disappear." In her interrogative wrestling with this problem, Russ forces open "lines of flight" that striate the space created by the edgeless use of the masculine pronoun. Russ doesn't consider the mere "proper statement" as a cure because, as Nott (1970) suggests, "the quest for 'ordinary language' [in the discourse of philosophy] may be a piece of epistemological Salvationism. . . . It is attached to the old hankering after the absolutely verifiable—at which we shall never arrive" (91). The epistemological stakes are high, in other words, and the battle over linguistic territory has been bloody. In *On Strike Against God* Russ (1980c) outs her position baldly: "One moves incurably into the future but there is no future; it has to be created" (85). Beyond mere statement of a problem lies (1) the dismissal of the extant narrative in which the problem is so deeply embedded and (2) a discovery or invention of narrative territory that more closely adheres to the truth of experiential reality.

Numerous critics (for example, Barr, Freedman, Hicks) have noted Russ's resistance to patriarchal hegemony in the Whileaway stories ("When It Changed" and *The Female Man*). It is instructive to map out a few of the resonances of this toponym, Whileaway. "*While away,*" that is, "while on an *outing,* I learned something about myself and about my culture." The peripatetic wandering implied in the toponym suggests a shaking off of the Glotologgi's static and smooth weltanschauung. Additionally, to "while away" the time is, in the majoritarian use of the term, to *waste* time. "Whileaway" invokes philosophies of anarchic laziness and proto-Taoist "aimless wandering" as a deterritorializing act of resistance, as, for instance, in the works of Bob Black and Peter Lamborn Wilson. In a minoritarian sense, to "while away" is to *resist* the hegemonic project of patriarchal-capitalism in the form of wildcat strikes, nomadism, and absenteeism.

The majoritarian territory of racist, paternalistic capital is an "imbrication of the *semiotic* and the *material*" (Deleuze and Guattari 1987, 337); that is, an ordered layering (as of fish scales or roof tiles) of signs and technologies (in the sense of *teknē,* "made-things," especially in its vernacular sense of "boy-toys"). " 'Man,' " Russ writes, "is a *rhetorical convenience* [that is, a *teknē*] for 'human.' 'Man' includes 'woman.' Thus: 1. The Eternal Feminine leads us ever upward and on. (Guess who 'us' is)" (1975b, 93; emphasis mine see also Barr 1987, 13). As Marleen S. Barr points out, Russ interrogates the assumptions in the masculine pronoun by substituting the feminine: "That single personal pronoun [that is, 'she'] signals that readers have a false view of the story's ['When It Changed'] beginning, that they have fallen into Russ's prearranged linguistic trap. The glaringly inappropriate use of 'she' announces that on Whileaway women have wives" (Barr 1993, 61). But (1993) this use of "she," while a "trap" for sure, is not "inappropriate" so much as interrogative. Barr writes of "When it Changed": "men take pains to emphasize the reestablishment of sexual equality on earth, [while] they still insist on falsely viewing Janet and Katy according to patriarchal conceptions of proper power relationships: 'Which of you plays the role of man?' " (61). The self-doubt and insecurity heaped upon the minoritarian victims of colonialist patriarchal-capitalism is here held up to a mirror; in The Female Man it is Medusa who holds up the reflecting shield against the patriarchal brutality of the Perseian hero. Russ's use of the feminine pronoun exposes a gap in the patriarchal narrative; a trap for the patriarchal reader, but a point of intensity (identification and emotive power) and potential for the minority reader.

In On Strike Against God, Russ unleashes a molecular interrogation of prepositions: "When you fuck someone, you are fucking with their eyes, too, with their hair, with their temples, their minds, their fingers' ends" (59; emphasis mine). This is a distinctly collaborative (and distinctly queer-feminist) way of theorizing "fucking." We can see the collaborative reterritorialization at work in this sentence by considering the political implications of two typical ways of talking about sex, which I present here as mere sentence fragments in order to highlight the difference in preposition use: "to make love to" as contrasted with "to make love with." It is a far different thing to have something done to one's person than to have someone collaboratively do something with one's person. The subtle matrix of syntax is spring-loaded and hair-triggered with explosive political potential and its detonation is a blow against the "slithery little man with his techniques and his systems and his instructions about what 'wives' do for 'husbands' and what 'husbands' do to 'wives'" (Russ 1980c, 41; emphasis mine).

These examples are particular formal blows against the story-as-smooth-space, molecular refrains in the creation of a minor literature in which various modalities of violence are Russ's primary tools of deterritorialization. Narratively speaking, Russ's deployment of violence is tantamount to going "nova," as Esther describes her burgeoning lesbian awareness in On Strike Against God: characters and entire narratives "blast into an intensity surpassing that of [the] normal state" (24; quoting Gamow 2005, 155).

## Interrogation as a Way Out

Russ begins her award-winning novella, "Souls" (the first chapter or story in Extra(ordinary) People), with an epigram from Emily Dickinson (1998, poem 872, lines 1–2):

> Deprived of other Banquet
> I entertained Myself—

The verb entertain connotes a holding, as in to hold attention or to contemplate. Emily Dickinson's poems enact a profoundly multiperspectival epistemology and she "entertained" herself by holding forth with her own inquisition. Roland Hagenbüchle (1986) puts this succinctly when he writes, "Dickinson's oeuvre is . . . an ever-renewed 'research,' and each of her poems a heuristic act" (143). The shared turf of poets, philosophers, and their hybridizing cousins, science fiction writers, is the deterritorializing contemplation of the interrogative, the unknown, the *"what if?"* As an explorer of questions, Dickinson lived in the dangerous wilds; so too do many of Russ's characters. In *Extra(ordinary) People* (1984c), narrative reality is a banquet. The question that lurks behind this novel composed of a linked chain of stories is, Who is to be served?

The subject is deprivation: Russ, like Dickinson, is an entertainer of dark doubts; both force us to consider difficult questions. Russ is an interrogator of the deprivation of women's cultural positions. Russ's questions entertain the possibility that we are all cognitively colonized. We have entertained a planet-wrecking capitalism that enslaves even the masters, though the masters de-monstrably and monstrously benefit by controlling access to the banquet. *Extra(ordinary) People* is a history of "extra" people, the losers whose history remains unwritten because they are *enchained*: the links that bind them are narrative because the narrative is controlled by those who sit at the banquet. *Extra(ordinary) People* thus says *non serviam* and deterritorializes itself.

There is "always a problem when you write anything with real social or political consciousness," Russ told McCaffery: "what you're describing *hasn't ended*" (McCaffery 1990, 187; emphasis in original). One of Russ's primary means of deterritorialization is that of doing violence to narrative in order to resist authoritarian closure. The smooth ending of most fictions is, in Russ's work, rejected, exploded, Freytag's pyramid is assaulted with a wreck-ing ball. For Russ, the interrogative mode is a means of writing oneself *out*. *Extra(ordinary) People* thus progresses through various manifestations of epis-temological uncertainty. In "Souls," the narrator, a man who as a young boy witnessed an alien intervention in human affairs, is told by the alien presence to *"Think again,"* to reassess what he presumes to know (59; emphasis in origi-nal). "The Mystery of the Young Gentleman" is precisely that: an epistemo-logical enigma in which the narrator tells us that some people "can't stand two kinds of knowledge that don't mix" (1984c, 83). The oil-and-water battle of engendered epistemologies is explicitly topological, "like a switchback on a train ride" (1984c, 84). The story ends with a self-referential enfolding when a manuscript called *The Mystery of the Young Gentleman* is placed "on the table" near the narrator's bed: the mysterious young gentleman is "a not-so-young lady, we find out" (1984c, 92). By outing "straight" SF's patriarchal, racist, and capitalistic tropes, Russ discovers terrain that is both "ordinary" (obvious to those who have eyes to see) and "extraordinary."

*Extra(ordinary) People*, ostensibly a document of the evolution of telepathy in *Homo sapiens*, doesn't "end" (as the brief links between the stories would suggest): it is written out, off, and away, Russ told McCaffery, as "a comment on the whole utopian theme" (187) of patriarchal-romantic science fiction. The chain-linked stories over which the author climbs in order to out herself, to free herself from the false consciousness of the romantic-utopian dream of the perfectly smooth space of telepathic omniscience, ends with an interrogative blastoff into the unknown:

> What is Life?
> Is it anything?
> Who invented it and when?
> Is it patented? (If so, what#?)
> Why does it always turn green in the wash?
> When does the guarantee run out?
> Does Life exist? (1984c, 160; emphasis in original)

The terminology of technological capitalism (boy toys) is rampant here. Invention, patent, guarantee, the parody of a laundry-detergent commercial—these are not the stuff of "Life" in any evolutionary biological sense but the metaphysical technobabble of patriarchal capitalism. The narrator (who, in this final link of the book, is an epistle-writing epistemologist plotting a lesbian gothic romance) scales the fence, answering the question "Does Life exist?" with "Well, yes. It does. Life is, well life is . . . like this & like that & like that & like this & like nothing & like everything" (1984c, 160). And then comes the final deterritorialization, a clambering over the fence and down the other side in a series of six vertically descending "Etc." We hear the deterritorializing intention here when we translate this Latin tag out of its abbreviated form into plain English: "And so on, and so on, and so on . . .": onward on words. And so out to the final lines, which are signed "With Love":

> P.S. Nah, I won't write the silly book.
> P.P.S. and on (160)

Extra(ordinary) People is a chain that refuses to bind, that breaks its own shackles, and so there's a coda, a final, unclosed link that loops back to the beginning, where a "tutor" tells a "schoolkid" that "'today we . . . study history'" (iv):

> "Is that the way the world was saved?"
> . . . "What makes you think the world's ever been saved?"
> But that's too grim.
> &c. (161; emphasis in original)

Again, Russ closes with "&c"—and so on. Here, as elsewhere, Russ mobilizes the political clout of her prepositional forces. Despite the disclaimer of "but that's too grim" there is a despair here, an ad infinitum of human agency that echoes the epigram for the entire book: "you think a place is just wild and then there's people" (attributed to Alice Sheldon, aka James Tiptree, Jr.). We say that "power is knowledge" but human culture is power *and* knowledge; human agency follows the wildest animal trail—and tosses a beer can "out there."

Full of poetry and humor, *Extra(ordinary) People* is ultimately a rebel yell of epistemological indeterminacy: how can we, as represented by a brilliantly imaginative writer, ever *really* (in the post-Peircian sense of the word) inscribe an egalitarian narrative when the very definition of "reality" entails negotiation within a racist-patriarchal human collectivity and where power and knowledge are—even in a telepathic utopia (as the relationship between the "tutor" and the "schoolkid" implies)—unequally distributed? The answer is a Dickinsonian "unknown" and resounds throughout *Extra(ordinary) People*, most particularly in a passage in "What Did You Do During the Revolution, Grandma?" where we read: " 'How does this work?' . . . 'Nobody knows' " (1984c, 127). The "flat earth" (to paraphrase the title of a recent book by Thomas Friedman) of authoritarianly privileged epistemology is revealed by Russ to be a deeply fissured terrain. Examples of the futility of instrumental knowledge in the context of biological reality appear throughout Russ's work, as in this pithy remark in *We Who Are About To . . .* : "tools and toolkit, all of this superficially showing immense order but in fact about as rational as the ooze of algae from a pond" (1977, 11).

## Being and Somethingness: Getting Out for Good

*And Chaos Died* (Russ 1970a) compounds epistemological uncertainty with ontological deterritorialization in the person of Jai Vedh, "a homosexual" (11) who, in the words of Samuel R. Delany, is "a quietly despairing modern man with a nearly psychotic desire to merge with the universe" as a response to "the meaninglessness and homogeneity of every day life" (1979, 333). Not only is life on "Old Earth . . . a void" but "every place [is] like every other place" as well (1979, 3). The void and vacuum of life on Earth is nothing, though, compared to the hard vacuum of space into which Jai Vedh ventures on a business trip: "Then the ship exploded" (4).

We return to the scene of the crash site and the crisis there invoked. With *And Chaos Died*, though, premised as it is on an ancient Chinese story from Chuang Tzu, crisis is both danger and opportunity. Chuang Tzu's story is simple: two gods meet Chaos, "the god of the center." The two note that Chaos has no sense "apertures": no eyes, ears, nose, or mouth. So these two gods, Fuss and Fret, poke holes in Chaos. On the seventh day they poke the seventh hole and "Chaos died" (Chuang Tzu ["The Inner Chapters" of *Tao Te Ching*], trans.

A. Waley; epigraph in *And Chaos Died*). The planet upon which Jai Vedh crashes is inhabited by people with "some form of ESP," as Delany says, that open up "*ordinarily invisible* communicational pathways" (333; emphasis in original).

The psi-powers–endowed humans on the crash planet, known to us only as "*whatitsname*" (1970a, 140; emphasis in original), are members of "[a] lost colony" (27). *And Chaos Died* is the revenge of the colonized, as if the abandoned colonists of Roanoke, instead of vanishing, had sent a deadly virus back to England. By endowing Jai Vedh with the power to teleport himself, the lost colonists enable him to Earth with this virus. By endowing Jai Vedh with sensory powers beyond the ordinary, the inhabitants of "whatitsname" poke holes in his defensive shield against the "social vacuum" (Delany 1979, 334) of Earth society. It is through these metaphorical holes that the novel's deep pessimism works its imaginative magic.

Vedh is "disoriented, frightened, and confused" throughout the novel (according to Delany 1979, 334); once he gains superior powers he is transformed from a meek "homosexual" (repeatedly called a "coward" in the first few pages [7, 8]) into a violent man who has sex with females (but "I don't like women," he say early on [10]), repeatedly commits murder, and attempts to murder the boy he loves. His enormous psi powers don't result in transcendent realization of utopian potential (pace Delany, 335): "*What eyes*"? Vedh thinks to himself: "*Half the time I don't see and half the time I can't interpret what I see*" (1970a, 146). Jai Vedh is a product of the cultural topology of Earth. When representatives from "whatitsname" come to Earth to teach its inhabitants the utopian technique of telepathy, they are met with violence: "the Earth people, terrified, bomb them" (Delany 1979, 335). Only then is Jai Vedh deterritorialized; he is telekinetically whisked away, back to "whatitsname" where he learns the colonial origins of its inhabitants.

The inhabitants of the nameless lost colony are "Earth people" and like all Earthlings were created "long, long ago" (1970a, 182). The creators were metallic beings "with nerve impulses of light"—"big, big beast[s]" (182):

> "They are all dead now, of course."
> "Why?" said Jai, though of course he knew why.
> *We killed them. . . . What else?* (183; emphasis in original)

Are the telepaths of "whatitsname" truly utopians? No: when confronted with true alterity—metal beasts with nerves of light—they commit genocide. With Russ, utopia is always rejected in view of the incorrigible and Kafkaesque nature of human ontology. (Jai Vedh's alternate personality's name is "Joseph K.") In Russ's work, human ontology is not a metaphysical stain but rather a biological one, and there is only one true means of deterritorialization: suicide.

Russ's ultimate means of deterritorialization, then, is physical violence. The story-as-smooth-space isn't just patriarchal, it is also the vector enabling the smooth flow of capitalism, racism, and molecular oppressions as yet unnamed. More, it is the space of colonization. As Frantz Fanon (1963) has argued, violence is the only way to overthrow a colonialist regime: colonialism "is violence in its natural state, and it will only yield when confronted with greater violence" (61).

In *We Who Are About To . . .* we hear the territorial refrain of fledgling sparrows in the walls of the unnamed narrator's remembered apartment: "SQUEEEEEEEECH!" (1977, 108). "Filthy, lousy, bird-brained birds," says the narrator's friend, L.B. (109). L.B. wants to "[k]ill them," but the narrator is repulsed by the idea of killing helpless animals: "They're just babies," she says (108). Rather, "[t]he trick is to get them when they're first nesting and repeatedly scare the living daylights out of them—birds are very emotional—until they get the idea there's a large, very irritable, dangerous mammal who comes with the site and they do, finally, go somewhere else" (109). The tragedy of patriarchal-capitalism is that all milieus have been colonized—not just the political geographies of human cultures (as in Fanon); the biosphere itself is smoothed over. The site of the minoritarian is surrounded by nasty animals and there's nowhere left to go.

*We Who Are about To . . .* is Russ's most powerful anticolonial narrative. When the spaceship crashes, the survivors are immediately embroiled in a colonialist crisis. The males want to impregnate the females in order to ensure the survival of their species on the new planet. The narrator objects; at first she withdraws from the group's campsite but then, pressured to conform, she resorts to violence. She contemplates suicide by poison, but then murders the other survivors. The murder of one of the women, Cass, is described in explicitly topological terms: "she [threw] her arms out in a cross, as if quartering the circle she was part of" (101). Cass falls *out* of the circle—the ideal smooth space—after having quartered or striated it in her death throes. Russ's narrator resists the colonialist narrative by violently striating it. The threat of sexual violence and its correlative, fetal colonization, is met with greater violence; first the women, then the men are eliminated. "Oppression," Russ told McCaffery, "is always mystifying and confusing. . . . Anger is a necessity. It's part of all radicalism" (McCaffery 1990, 209). The radical must deploy "sheer fury" in order "to resist looking at the structure and saying, 'It's us, it's our fault'" (209). The anticolonial project is full of gaps, mysteries, unanswered (and unanswerable) questions; it is not the formulaic, smooth-space nationalism of Fanon's revolutionary program, which Russ eschews as "second-generation" Marxism (McCaffery 1990, 209).

At the end of *On Strike Against God*, Esther-as-nova writes, "*Let's be reasonable.*

*Let's demand the impossible*" (107; emphasis in original). Throughout the works under consideration Russ demands that we rationally entertain the possibility of an egalitarian and utopian alternative to the smooth space of patriarchal capitalism. And throughout these same works she finds that alternative impossible. The desire to discover a new territory is constantly thwarted by the inherently colonialistic ontology of human culture. In a universe dwelling in possibility and potential, we are left, in *We Who Are About To . . .* , with the nameless narrator's cri de coeur: "I'm Nobody, who are you? Are you Nobody, too?" (*We Who* 20; quoting Dickinson 1998, poem 260).

Call it pessimism, if you must, but Russ is also a molecular activist, setting loose subversive forces that can be met with and joined: as Dickinson's poem continues, "Then there's a pair of us!" The minoritarian audience of radical science fiction is empowered to seize the power of interrogative introspection. The light of possibility is very dim, but it dwells on, outside the territory of the known, the mapped, and the ontologically bankrupt. If power is knowledge then "Don't tell! they'd advertise—you know!" (Dickinson 1998, poem 260). Russ's resistance to authoritarian closure doesn't "advertise," doesn't try to sell us anything. Least of all does it offer a (false) ray of hope. Rather, it exposes us to the harsh elements of authoritarian reality and challenges us to contest the usurpation of any and all territory by oppressive forces. Russ's project first crashes us and then challenges us to resurrect our lives somewhere *out there*.

# Notes

### 1. Alyx among the Genres (pages 3–18)

1. Reprinted as "Alien Monsters" in Knight 1977, 132–143. Another version of the essay, under the title "The He-Man Ethos in Science Fiction," was included in Wilson 1972, 226–230.

2. Sarah Lefanu, for example, quotes Samuel R. Delany's comment that the Alyx tales represent the end of "early Russ," and goes on to add, "Certainly it seems as if a proto-feminist consciousness has become a feminist one" (1988, 183).

3. See, for example, the Barbara Garland essay in Cowart and Rhmyer 1981.

4. (1995g, 8). The essay originally appeared in *Science-Fiction Studies* in 1975.

### 2. Russ on Writing Science Fiction and Reviewing It (pages 19–30)

1. December 1966, 36–37; October 1967, 28–30; January 1968, 37–39; July 1968, 54–57; December 1968, 16–21; April 1969, 44–48; August 1969, 24–30; September 1969, 20–24; January 1970, 37–44; July 1970, 40–47; February 1971, 60–66; April 1971, 64–69; November 1971, 18–23; December 1972, 39–45; February 1973, 25–31; July 1973, 65–71; February 1974, 67–73; January 1975, 10–16; March 1975, 39–45; April 1975, 59–67; November 1976, 66–73; February 1979, 62–71; June 1979, 48–56; November 1979, 102–108; February 1980, 94–101.

2. A list of her reviews in the *Washington Post* and elsewhere can be found in Cortiel 1999, 244. It should be noted that Cortiel does not list all the reviews from *The Magazine of Fantasy and Science Fiction*, and therefore her bibliography may well not be complete as far as other publications are concerned.

3. The January 1970 issue records average sales each month during 1969 of 50,299 (89); the advertisement on 130 claims 60,000, with an average of three people reading each copy.

4. For some earlier comments on SF criticism, see James 2000, 35. The reviews of M. John Harrison have now been collected and published: see Bould and Reid 2005.

5. The reference to *ghoti* soup is presumably an allusion to George Bernard Shaw's observation on the eccentricites of English spelling, whereby if *gh* is pronounced as in "rough" and *o* as in "women" and *ti* as in "nation," then *ghoti* can be pronounced "fish." But she is also making fun of Biggle's "smeerp" tendency: she had just quoted Blish on unimaginative SF writers turning mundane fiction into SF by calling rabbits *smeerps*.

6. Clute and Nicholls 1993, 11.

### 3. A History of One's Own (pages 31–47)

1. Such debates typically revolve around one of two issues. The first issue is one of generic categorization: is feminist SF best understood as a tradition unto itself (albeit with close ties to the rest of SF), or can it be more productively understood as part of a larger postmodern literary tradition? The second issue is one of political categorization: should feminist SF scholars hew to conventional understandings of literary feminism as writing produced in periods of overt feminist activity, or would it be more productive to think more broadly about what constitutes progressive women's politics—and thus progressive women's writing—in different historical periods? For more discussion of the first debate, see Robin Roberts 1995. For further discussion of the second, see Merrick 2000.

2. See especially Fiedler's *Love and Death in the American Novel* (1960) and Marx's *The Machine in the Garden: Technology and the Pastoral Ideal in America* (1964).

3. Of course, other modes of SF scholarship have become increasingly popular since the 1970s. These include anthropological examinations of SF fandom (such as Camille Bacon-Smith's *Enterprising Women* and Henry Jenkins's *Textual Poachers*); critical race studies of speculative fiction from the African diaspora (including Sherree R. Thomas's *Dark Matter* anthologies and Nalo Hopkinson's *Whispers from the Cotton Tree*); and, of course, feminist SF studies itself.

4. McCaffrey (1974) responds to Lundwall's charges by depicting him as a brilliant but misguided scholar who fails to understand her writing strategies. Indeed, McCaffrey insists that she never really gave in to editorial demands that she reproduce conventional gendered relations in her work, but that she made strategic concessions by depicting women in "the traditional role of mother-mistress-healer" while nonetheless making them the real heroes of her stories (283).

5. The uneven treatment of feminism in Scholes and Rabkin (1977) is perhaps most clearly illustrated by the indexing of the word "feminism" itself at the end of the book. Although Scholes and Rabkin describe a number of contemporary SF authors as feminists at various points in their book, the only page reference for feminism leads readers to a discussion of the *antifeminist* impulses in C. S. Lewis's *Perelandra*.

6. Nearly all of the early male SF critics agree on the significance of Campbell's contributions to the genre, as do feminist and feminist-friendly writers including Judith Merril and Anne McCaffrey. For further discussion, see especially Aldiss 1973, Merril 1971, and McCaffrey 1974.

7. For example, Russ notes, Parley J. Cooper's *The Feminists* (1971) depicts a dystopic near-future America ruled by a militant gynocracy that abruptly collapses when the mayor of New York realizes that the leader of the masculinist underground is her long-lost son. Realizing that "*Before she was a Feminist, she was a Mother!*" the mayor saves her son from execution and cedes her rule to the army of men (Russ 1995i, 45). Meanwhile, Edmund Cooper's *Gender Genocide* (1972) depicts a future England torn apart by a literal battle of the sexes: technologically advanced women rule the south

while trying to exterminate the remnants of a primitive patriarchy in the north. When one woman decides to help the wounded leader of the men, he responds to her mercy by knocking her down, allowing her to be gang-raped, and then claiming her as his wife. At this point Cooper's heroine promptly falls in love with her captor and spends the rest of the novel at his side, fighting the "hellbitches" who used to be her comrades-in-arms (51).

8. The other recent feminist utopias Russ mentions are Samuel Delany's *Triton*; Marge Piercy's *Woman on the Edge of Time*; Suzy McKee Charnas's *Motherlines*; Marion Zimmer Bradley's *The Shattered Chain*; Catherine Madsen's "Commodore Bork and the Compost"; and Alice Sheldon's "Your Faces, O My Sisters! Your Faces Filled of Light!" (published under the pseudonym Raccoona Sheldon) and "Houston, Houston, Do You Read?" (published under the pseudonym James Tiptree, Jr.).

9. Susan Wood advances similar arguments in "Women and Science Fiction" (1978b), another classic example of early feminist SF scholarship—and one that, significantly enough, directly quotes both Joanna Russ and Pamela Sargent on the subject of midcentury women's science fiction. Although Wood largely shares Russ and Sargent's skepticism about the meaning and value of such fiction, she does acknowledge it as providing some of the first explorations of feminine archetypes in modern SF.

10. See Larbalestier 2002 (esp. chap. 5); Larbalestier and Merrick 2003; Merrick 2000; and Yaszek 2003, 2004, 2005, 2006, 2007.

11. As Justine Larbalestier, Helen Merrick, and I have all demonstrated, a good deal of women's speculative fiction about galactic suburbia was also decidedly satiric in tone. Although Russ herself never explicitly discusses it as such, this tone may have contributed to her lack of interest in it. After all, as Russ notes in one of her early discussions of SF aesthetics, satire is "unfortunately" one of the most popular kinds of SF to write because it is one of the easiest both to write and to read, requiring little from its readers by way of extrapolation (1995f, 18).

12. SF scholars and authors alike generally agree on Anthony Boucher's lasting contributions to SF scholarship. For an example of the former, see especially James 1994. For an example of the latter, see Merril 1971.

13. Russ's first gothic tales include "My Dear Emily" (July 1962); "There is Another Shore, You Know, Upon the Other Side (September 1963); and "Mr. Wilde's Second Chance" (September 1966). Her first SF stories include "Nor Custom Stale" (September 1959); "I Had Vacantly Crumpled It into My Pocket . . . But By God, Eliot, It Was a Photograph from Life!" (August 1964); and "Wilderness Year" ((December 1964). Her seventh story, "The New Men" (January 1966), combines elements of both SF and the gothic tale.

14. For more extensive discussion concerning the political potential inherent in postwar women's SF, see especially Yaszek 2004, 2005, and 2007.

## 4. The Female "Atlas" of Science Fiction? (pages 48–63)

1. Russ's contributions to feminist academic criticism and theorizing could be the subject of a whole separate essay; see Russ 1972a, 1983b, 1995i, and 1998c. She contributed to such mainstream and academic feminist publications as *Ms* and *Signs* (Russ 1976d) See also the description of her impression as women's studies professor on the young Jane Gallop (cited in Delany 2004, 503).

2. Geis was the author of a number of "sf-and-sex novels," with titles such as *The Endless Orgy* and *Raw Meat*, which were described by Richard Delap as a "messy bit of sex-drenched but puerile humor" (Delap 1974, 5).

3. Not surprisingly, such reviews and responses to Russ's work rehearsed the criticisms she predicted in an interjection in *The Female Man* (Russ 1975b, 140–141).

4. In a letter to the following issue, Coney (1974) separates Aab from Russ and McIntyre, and situates her as "young and nice and genuinely upset about my remark," whose reading of Russ' story was "naive," co-opting McIntyre's statement of her "anger and hostility" to support his own argument. His tone of paternalistic tolerance reaches its peak in the final response to Aab's letter: "I find my penis just great and hope you are enjoying your vagina."

5. One of the most famous proponents of this argument was Isaac Asimov: see chapter 4 of Larbalestier (2002) for a detailed discussion.

6. Even fan/critic Sam Lundwall had criticized Heinlein's "harem" and Asimov's Calvin previously (Lundwall 1971). Incidentally, it may well have been the use of earlier female writers as "evidence for the defense" by male critics and authors who refused to acknowledge the validity of feminist critiques that led to their rather tenuous position in later feminist criticism.

7. This comparison to the Black civil rights movement appears in a number of other instances as a comparative point for the women's movement, and is used to argue both for and against the "justice" of women's liberation.

8. Although not published until 1975, *The Female Man* was in circulation in the SF community for a number of years previously, according to Samuel Delany (Moylan 1986: 57).

9. MacGregor was commenting as a fan; he later went on to become an SF novelist himself.

10. The impact of MacGregor's reasonable assessment is somewhat marred by the fact that his title is illustrated by a 3-cup brassiere (presumably for some "alien" female) hanging from the word "chauvinist"—a fact bemoaned by Russ in the next issue (1975c).

11. APA (Amateur Publishing Associations) are a form of fanzines. Members of the APA each produce a fanzine which is sent to a "general editor" who compiles, copies, and distributes them to the group. AWA (A Women's APA) was still active as of 2005 in a print version, although many APAs are now distributed electronically.

12. The contributors were: Joanna Russ, Ursula Le Guin, Suzy McKee Charnas,

Kate Wilhelm, Vonda McIntyre, Chelsea Quinn Yarbro, Virginia Kidd, Raylyn Moore, Luise White, Samuel R. Delany and James Tiptree, Jr. As Gwyneth Jones commented in the 1993 printing, 'It rather takes you aback, to realize how much of what's passed into the SF record—on feminism, on women—comes from this single source' (Gomoll 1993, 131).

13. Interestingly, only a few years later, Susan Wood reports on Wilhelm's active participation in "women's programming" at conventions, including panels and discussions at the 1977 WesterCon where she declared, "I think any woman who is aware has to be a feminist' (cited in Wood 1978a, 7)

14. To be precise, these were the first fanzines to be consciously aligned to and inspired by the women's liberation movement; there had been earlier personal fanzines by women who were feminist, also women-only fanzines in the 1950s that could be considered protofeminist (see Merrick 1999). *Janus* was the longest running zine, beginning in 1975, and continuing as *Aurora* from 1981 through to 1987, with a delayed final issue in 1990. The sadly short-lived *WatCh* published its final double issue (5/6) in 1976.

15. For example, a letter from fan Kris Fawcett commented on the "steadily growing feminist element" in SF fandom in the early 1970s, (Fawcett 1974).

16. Later republished with an introduction explaining they were actually produced by a "Thing in the Typewriter" as "The Cliches from Outer Space" (Russ 1984b).

17. I use "travels" here to connect with Katie King's observations on personal reading histories in her *Theory in Its Feminist Travels* (King 1994).

## 5. Learning the "Prophet Business" (pages 64–80)

1. This runs through Merril's books columns in F&SF. See, for example, September 1965, 79; August 1966, 57–60; March 1967, 26–27; December 1967, 28–33; February 1968, 53–54; June 1968, 47–48; January 1969, 34–37.

2. See Delany 1985, 116.

3. Merril 1967c.

4. Of the three letters from Russ to Merril in the Merril Papers, two were written in the late summer of 1968 at Baycon. In August Russ sought to meet up with Merril at Baycon (in Berkeley, California), and in September expresses regret that she missed Merril at Baycon (at which, Russ writes, she witnessed a "mini-riot" by radicals and pot smoking, a radicalizing experience for her)—noting that Merril chose instead to go to the Democratic National Convention in Chicago (which we know solidified Merril's decision to leave the United States shortly thereafter). Joanna Russ to Judith Merril (Russ 1968a).

5. See Aldiss 1973, 264, 284n; and Knight 1967, 122.

6. Samuel R. Delany would later in effect agree with Merril that Russ's stories in *Orbit* 2 were sword-and-sorcery (1977, 213–214), but he saw it as her strength. He

argued Russ's overall variation in approach was nothing short of a sign of her leadership in the evolving field of science fiction: "That Russ's stories move from sword and sorcery to s-f and beyond puts them directly in the tradition of the s-f of its time that was so busily stepping over so many boundary lines" (229).

7. Merril 1968a. For SF12, Merril wants to remove the "year's best aspect entirely."

8. Merril 1968c.

9. Fritz Leiber to Merril, 15 April 1969.

10. Merril became the key founding figure in the Canadian SF scene. In Toronto she was involved with the free university movement and in founding the Canadian Writers' Union as well as the movement to aid US draft resisters and anticensorship campaigns.

## 6. Joanna Russ's The Two of Them in an Age of Third-wave Feminism (pages 83–98)

1. As Freedman (2000) is careful to point out in his argument, the novel presents Ka'abah as a constructed culture of recent origin and thus as something of a "symbolic" rather than literal other space, one whose function in the novel has more to do with Irene's own journey to greater self-understanding than with a critique of any culture upon which the Ka'abah might be seen to be modeled. In this way, "The Two of Them emphasises its habitation of an epistemological level sharply different from that inhabited by its heroine; the text therefore distances itself from the precritical Orientalism that she initially displays" (140).

2. Kathleen Spencer (1990) argues that the motif of rescue from "the restrictions of patriarchal culture on the possibilities of [a young girl's] life" (167) is a persistent theme across all of Russ's work. Spencer argues that this rescue motif works across five stages, the fourth of which is "the rescue of the self, as the older woman in some kind of time-loop goes back to help her younger self" (168). Spencer concludes that in Russ's later work "we see her growing recognition that the rescuer herself often needs the validation, or the companionship, which the girl can provide" (184). My argument is similar to Spencer's in that I see Zubeydeh providing rescue for Irene as much as Irene is for Zubeydeh. However, it is not companionship that Zubeydeh provides in my argument but rather perspective.

3. Roiphe's (1993) work is guilty of even more pernicious racial and class stereotyping than that which weakens Hoff Sommers and Wolf's work. When discussing the "alleged" increase in the reporting (if not the occurrence) of rapes on American campuses, a phenomenon Roiphe attributes to the feminist agenda of teaching women to redefine bad sex as rape, Roiphe suggests that the real problem is cultural miscommunication because universities are no longer the privileged place of a class and racially homogeneous elite. She argues, "With the radical shift in college environment, with the introduction of black kids, Asian kids, Jewish kids, kids from the wrong side of the tracks of nearly every railroad in the country, there was an accom-

panying anxiety about how people were to behave. When ivory tower meets melting pot, it causes some confusion, some tension, some need for readjustment" (77). She tries to present her view as sensitive to such cultural differences, which feminists overlook, suggesting that "concern with rape, with verbal coercion, is part class prejudice and race prejudice. The dangerous 'miscommunication' that recurs through the literature on date rape is a code word for difference in background" (79)

4. This is Ernst and Irene's private nickname for the Trans Temp agency for which they work. For Irene it seems to be connected to her sense that in his life—as compared to the earth she was rescued from—she really is just "one of the guys." The term "gang" was also used to describe her own tomboy youth before the forces of gender discrimination began to make themselves felt in her life. She claims she spent her youth "not as a mascot or a boy-crazy girl but as one of the gang" (30).

5. Cortiel (1999) makes a similar argument about seeing the struggle between Ernst and Irene in more archetypal than individual terms, but her argument moves toward an analysis of its symbolism in psychoanalytic terms with which I do not entirely agree. She argues, "The two individuals represent 'woman' and 'man' in general, the gender antagonism which according to materialist feminist analysis can only be resolved by violent action—revolution—on the part of the oppressed. Making the death struggle analogous to sexual intercourse, the text lets the act of liberation directly refer to the act that instituted the oppression and that seems to confirm it every time a man (in a patriarchal culture) sticks his erect penis, charged with cultural meaning and significance, into / a woman. Unlike Jael, Irene does not wait for the dying man's recognition. It is not anger that drives her to kill the man, but plain necessity, not hatred of man, but love of self." There are similarities in our arguments in terms of an emphasis on Irene's crime as one that is motivated by her desire to escape self-loathing. My concern with Cortiel's analysis is the connection to heterosexual sex, which seems to suggest that the revolution Irene wages is one about symbolic and semiotic gender differences. My slightly different point is that Irene needs to kill Ernst because the structures of gender discrimination will always give him power over her, a power she cannot resist other than by overthrowing this system.

## 7. "That Is Not Me. I Am Not That" (pages 99–113)

1. This idea is typically found in women's science fiction, notably in novels such as Katharine Burdekin's *Swastika Nights* (1937) and Sherri Tepper's *The Gate to Women's Country* (1988).

2. By incorporating other genres, such as the ghost story, Russ is able to bring to the forefront of her debate the unspoken words of women. It is essential for Russ that women speak their own stories; there are many instances in her texts where men are silenced so that women may speak. In *The Thousand and One Nights* Dunyazad is mostly silent, but encourages Shahrazad to tell the stories that keep her alive.

## 10. Medusa Laughs (pages 143–156)

1. I steal this notion from Emmanuel Levinas as a parallel to that rather muddied term *deconstruction*—a reading open to difference, contradiction and proximity. As Simon Critchley (1992) notes: "If in any chiasmic dialogue, the two lines of thought are bound to cross in what Levinas calls 'the heart of a chiasmus,' then this should not blind us to the multiplicity of points where those lines of thought diverge" (13). It should be noted that I do not see deconstruction as a reversal of a hierarchy—which simply reverses the power structure—but one that demands the dualism to be entirely recast and rethought. Any reading against the grain still requires the grain.

2. Among the many objections to Freud's theories is that they assume the necessity for at least the basics of a nuclear family: an actual father, an actual mother and a child, and that the necessary result of, say, a single-parent family or a same-sex partnership would be a failure of the child to properly navigate the "proper" route to healthy and well-adjusted heterosexuality. My own unscientific polling of students I have taught over the years suggests a rigid sexual divide: to a man, all my male students have admitted to being anxious at the thought of being castrated. No more than a tiny handful of the women have admitted to penis envy, although no doubt Freudians would put this down to repression. It does not help that Freud slides between a metaphor of power (the phallus) and actual dangly bits (the penis, the testicles), nor that as a male Freud was clearly invested in his own power/organ. Do all female children have the chance to compare themselves with their playfellows or their father in order to perceive "that she has 'come off badly' " and therefore "feels this as a wrong done to her and as a ground for inferiority." (Freud 1991a, 320)? Would they see themselves as envious of this "famous bit of skin" (Cixous 1981, 261), or fearful of the male as having an unfortunate growth?

3. There is, of course, a contradiction here that emphasizes the image's ideological work: if the Medusa is castrated and an image of power, then surely the castrated is not necessarily powerless.

4. Lacan places the penis as a signifier for the phallus—the symbol of (masculine) power—at the head of the Oedipal triangle, and assumes that the mother desires the phallus. The child craves the attention of the mother, and desires to be desired by her: "man's desire finds its meaning in the desire of the other, not so much because the other holds the key to the object desired, as because the first object of desire is to be recognized by the other" (Lacan 1977, 58). In order to reconcile these two desires, the child attempts to become a phallus for the mother, to become central to her attention. However this is forbidden by the power of the phallus, which operates in the Name/No-of-the-Father [*Nom/Non du père*]. Again we reach the point of differentiation between children's reactions split along sexed lines: this is when the child becomes gendered. The male child can choose to accede to phallic order, and console himself that the set back is merely temporary: "one day my son, all this will be yours . . ." In the meantime he can enter into the Symbolic Order, the logical,

rational language-as-system that structures all of society. The female, on the other hand, being already castrated, can nostalgically look back to the nonexistent time before she was castrated, or at the least to the time before she *knew* she was already castrated; ignorance being bliss, or at least *jouissance*.

5. Is there phallic symbolism in "cocktail"—a sign of a masculine space?

6. Russ is being ironic, of course.

7. Are all texts actually feminine then? Certainly even the simplest sentence will admit to multiple meanings according to context; an alternative term might be "polysemic"—which derives from the same root as *semen*, *sēmen*, seed.

8. Translation: "I find you strangely attractive. Shall we go to your place or mine?"

9. I still have not quite recovered from the cognitive dissonance engendered by an otherwise intelligent and smart student asking me whether I knew "that Gwyneth Jones bird." He meant no offense, but it was a strange clash of registers.

10. See discussions in, for example, Goodman (1996), and Gilbert and Gubar (1978).

11. The choice of the word "siren" in close conjunction with "banshee" raises the image of female specters.

12. For the recurring trope of the older woman helping the young to escape, see Spencer (1990).

13. For Kristeva on the abject see her *Powers of Horror: An Essay on Abjection* (1982).

14. It is curious that gender only enters at the point of entry into the Symbolic Order, and yet the prelinguistic is characterized as feminine. The Real—the third part of the Lacanian *hérésie*/heresy/RSI along with the Symbolic and Imaginary—is that which cannot be Symbolized or Imagined. This is another version of the (alleged) unrepresentability of woman—along with those familiar twins, sex and death.

15. See, for example, Freud 1976, Bergson 1921, and Bakhtin 1968, 1981.

16. The story does not appear to feature Alyx, but has been read as a depiction of the coming of age of the narrator of the rest of the book—and great-granddaughter of Alyx—bringing the narrative full circle. See Cortiel 1999, 135.

17. Curiously this is a viewpoint that can be found in Freud, in particular in the case study of the Wolf Man, who (believes he) has observed his parents engaged in sexual intercourse, albeit probably anal intercourse: "during copulation in the primal scene he had observed the penis disappear, . . . he had felt compassion for his father on that account, and had rejoiced at the reappearance of what he thought had been lost" (Freud 1991c, 327). Freud makes no comment on this space for an anal dentata (along with the more traditional vaginal variety), but the rejoicing appears to be a variation of the Fort-Da game discussed in *Beyond the Pleasure Principle* (Freud 1995a).

18. Russ 1972c.

19. Compare: "The male is expected to be the strong rock, the sexual performer,

expected to always cope, not to collapse, expected to be chivalrous, to mend fuses and flat tyres, to make the moves in courtship, expected not to be passive or weepy or frightened, expected to go to war and be killed, or be prepared to kill others" (Horrocks 1994, 143). I should, however, note my own discomfort at the oh-woe-is-me-I'm-so-guilty tone that creeps into so much men's studies.

20. Respect is owed Elizabeth Billinger for comments on an earlier draft of this piece and Maureen Kincaid Speller for raiding libraries on my behalf. Anything stolen is my own responsibility.

### 12. Art and Amity (pages 168–184)

1. For further biographical details, see Burke 1996.

2. See, for example, Boulter 1999 and Cortiel 1999.

3. Potter 2000, esp. 259–261.

4. Ayers's reading of "Songs to Joannes," 2004, 36–38.

5. For a detailed background analysis, see Bland 1995.

6. Luckhurst (2005) has recently questioned the usefulness of the "New Wave" in explaining developments in science fiction, especially with regards to American literature (see 160–166). Russ, though, like other American writers such as Thomas M. Disch, John Sladek, and Pamela Zoline, shares much of the avant-garde ethos associated with the British journal, *New Worlds*.

7. See, for example, Moorcock's essay, "Starship Stormtroopers" (1986, 279–295).

8. In this respect, see Russ 1995a. Whereas Russ limits her criticisms to the film version of Harlan Ellison's story, I personally find the misogyny of Ellison's original tale smug and repellent.

9. See Andermahr's comparison of *The Female Man* with the separatist ideal of Sally Miller Gearhart's *The Wanderground* (1978) in "The Politics of Separatism and Lesbian Utopian Fiction," in Munt 1992, 133–152.

10. Bartkowski (1989, 59–61) has suggested Russ' debt to Brecht's theories of theatrical alienation.

11. Kristeva's criticism of a commodified *écriture féminine* in 'Women's Time' (1981), in Belsey and Moore 1989, 204.

12. On Russ's use of cat analogies, see Cortiel 1999, 70–74.

13. See Soper's (1999) critique of Haraway, "Of OncoMice and FemaleMen: Donna Haraway on Cyber Ontology," esp. 170–171.

14. On the role of history and agency in *We Who Are About To. . . .*, see Cortiel 1999, 207–209

### 15. Castaway (pages 210–224)

1. See Mary Russo (1994), which is a text using carnival, the grotesque, and feminism, while Dale M. Bauer and S. Jaret McKinstry (1991) and Michael Mayerfield Bell

and Michael Gardiner (1998) are edited collections on Bakhtin that include articles on carnival and the cyborg, and carnival and modern parody. Other conference paper and journal writers include David Shepherd, Wayne C. Booth, and Evelyn Cobley. Their predominant theme is that Carnival is problematic because of its utopianism, essentialism, and its concessions to authority for the space it occupies. But there are redeeming qualities to carnival, particularly in the notion of subversion, the grotesque, and the different treatment of time. Bakhtin studied Rabelais's work very specifically, but his interpretation of carnival acts as a point of critical transfer and his model remains—in real Bakhtinian style—dialogic with, open to, and inclusive of other interpretations of subversion and transgression. A few critics resist this, for example, Peter Stallybras and Allon White (1986), who consider carnival's relevance to lie in the performance, not the theory. They are now becoming outnumbered by critics prepared to entertain and adapt Bakhtin's ideas to cultural studies and literary theory.

2. There was also a robot in *Lost in Space*, which was anthropomorphized to some degree and contributed to the farcical relationship between Dr. Smith and Will, the youngest Robinson child. The robot's speaking part was limited and much of the humor involving the machine relied on verbal repetitions, difficulties moving, or programming problems.

3. As well as saying the book is a site for the grotesque, Holquist points out it is a site of mirrored multiplicity and intertextuality; it incorporates classical stories, origin myths from different traditions, and literature and science contemporary with the book.

4. Samuel Delany (1977), "About Five Thousand Seven Hundred and Fifty Words" in *The Jewel-Hinged Jaw: Notes on the Language of SF*. This essay grew out of a talk presented to the MLA in New York and was originally published in Clareson (1971).

5. Patricia Adair Gowaty, Sarah Blaffer Hardy and Ruth Bleier are just some of the feminist scientists who have worked with sociobiological stories, and the issues of anthropomorphic and androcentric language and masculine biases in interpreting links between genes and behavior.

# Works Cited

**Works by Joanna Russ**

1959. "Nor Custom Stale." *Magazine of Fantasy and Science Fiction*, September, 75–86.

1962. "My Dear Emily." *Magazine of Fantasy and Science Fiction*, July, 91–116.

1966. "On Books." *Magazine of Fantasy and Science Fiction*, December, 36–37.

1967a. "Bluestocking" ["The Adventuress"]. In *Orbit* 2, edited by Damon Knight, 185–210. New York: Berkley.

1967b. "I Thought She Was Afeard Till She Stroked My Beard" ["I Gave Her Sack and Sherry"]. In *Orbit* 2, edited by Damon Knight, 164–184. New York: Berkley.

1967c. "On Books." *Magazine of Fantasy and Science Fiction*, October, 28–30.

1968a. Correspondence, Joanna Russ to Judith Merril, 2 August, 2 September, 1968. Box 14, file 49. Merril Papers, Ottawa, Library and Archives of Canada.

1968b. "On Books." *Magazine of Fantasy and Science Fiction*, January, 37–39.

1968c. "On Books." *Magazine of Fantasy and Science Fiction*, July, 54–57.

1968d. "On Books." *Magazine of Fantasy and Science Fiction*, December, 16–21.

1968e. *Picnic on Paradise*. New York: Ace.

1968f. Review of *Sf: The Best of the Best*, edited by Judith Merril. *Magazine of Fantasy and Science Fiction*, July, 54–55.

1969a. "On Books." *Magazine of Fantasy and Science Fiction*, April, 44–48.

1969b. "On Books." *Magazine of Fantasy and Science Fiction*, August, 24–30.

1969c. "On Books." *Magazine of Fantasy and Science Fiction*, September, 20–24.

1970a. *And Chaos Died*. New York: Ace.

1970b. "On Books." *Magazine of Fantasy and Science Fiction*, January, 37–44.

1970c. "On Books." *Magazine of Fantasy and Science Fiction*, July, 40–47.

1970d. "Review of *The Ship Who Sang*, by Anne McCaffrey. *Magazine of Fantasy and Science Fiction*, July, 40–42.

1970e. "The Second Inquisition." In *Orbit* 6, edited by Damon Knight, 1–39. New York: Putnam.

1971a. "On Books." *Magazine of Fantasy and Science Fiction*, February, 60–66.

1971b. "On Books." *Magazine of Fantasy and Science Fiction*, April, 64–69.

1971c. "On Books." *Magazine of Fantasy and Science Fiction*, November, 18–23.

1971d. "The Wearing out of Genre Materials." *College English* 33, no. 1: 46–54.

1971e. "The Zanzibar Cat." In *Quark* 3, edited by Samuel R. Delany and Marilyn Hacker, 234–44.

1972a. "The Image of Women in Science Fiction." In *Images of Women in Science Fiction: Feminist Perspectives,* edited by Susan Koppleman Cornillon, 79–94. Bowling Green, Ohio: Bowling Green University Popular Press.

1972b. "On Books." *Magazine of Fantasy and Science Fiction,* December, 39–45.

1972c. "When It Changed." In *Again, Dangerous Visions: 46 Original Stories,* edited by Harlan Ellison, 253–260. New York: Doubleday.

1973a. "On Books." *Magazine of Fantasy and Science Fiction,* February, 25–31.

1973b. "On Books." *Magazine of Fantasy and Science Fiction,* July, 65–71.

1974a. "The Image of Women in Science Fiction." *Vertex* 1, no. 6: 53–57.

1974b. Letter. *The Alien Critic* 3, no. 1: 36–37.

1974c. "On Books." *Magazine of Fantasy and Science Fiction,* February, 67–73.

1972d. "The New Misandry." *Village Voice,* 12 October.

1975a. "Alien Monsters." In *Turning Points: Essays on the Art of Science Fiction,* edited by Damon Knight, 132–43. New York: Harper.

1975b. *The Female Man.* New York: Bantam Books.

1975c. Letter. *Notes from the Chemistry Department* 10: 38–39.

1975d. Letter. *The Witch and the Chameleon* 3: 26–27.

1975e. Letter. *The Witch and the Chameleon* 4: 15–18.

1975f. "On Books." *Magazine of Fantasy and Science Fiction,* January, 10–16.

1975g. "On Books." *Magazine of Fantasy and Science Fiction,* March, 39–45.

1975h. "On Books." *Magazine of Fantasy and Science Fiction,* April, 59–67.

1975i. "Towards an Aesthetic of Science Fiction." *Science Fiction Studies* 6, no. 1: 112–118.

1976a. *Alyx.* New York: G. K. Hall.

1976b. "A Letter to Marion Zimmer Bradley." *The Witch and the Chameleon* 5 and 6: 9–13.

1976c. "On Books." *Magazine of Fantasy and Science Fiction,* November, 66–73.

1976d. "Outta Space: Women Write Science Fiction." *Ms,* January, 109–111.

1977. *We Who Are About To . . .* New York: Dell.

1978a. *Kittatinny: A Tale of Magic.* New York: Daughters.

1978b. *The Two of Them.* New York: Berkley.

1979a. "The Extraordinary Voyages of Amélie Bertrand." *Magazine of Fantasy and Science Fiction,* September, 146–157.

1979b. "On Books." *Magazine of Fantasy and Science Fiction,* February, 62–71.

1979c. "On Books." *Magazine of Fantasy and Science Fiction,* June, 48–56.

1979d. "On Books." *Magazine of Fantasy and Science Fiction,* November, 102–108.

1980a. "Dear Colleague: I Am Not an Honorary Male." In *Pulling Our Strings: Feminist Humor and Satire,* edited by Gloria Kaufman and Mary Kay Blakely, 179–83. Bloomington: Indiana University Press.

1980b. "On Books." *Magazine of Fantasy and Science Fiction,* February, 94–101.

1980c. *On Strike Against God.* Brooklyn, N.Y.: Out and Out Books.

1981. "Recent Feminist Utopias." In *Future Females: A Critical Anthology*, edited by Marleen S. Barr, 71–85. Bowling Green, Ohio: Bowling Green University Press.

1982a. "The Mystery of the Young Gentleman." In *Speculations*, edited by Isaac Asimov and Alice Laurence. Boston: Houghton Mifflin.

1982b. "Souls." *Magazine of Fantasy and Science Fiction*, January, 7–46.

1983a. *The Adventures of Alyx*. New York: Timescape-Pocket Books.

1983b. *How to Suppress Women's Writing*. London: Women's Press, 1983.

1983c. *The Zanzibar Cat*. Sauk City, Wis.: Arkham House.

1984a. "Bodies." In her *Extra(Ordinary) People*. New York: St Martin's.

1984b. "The Clichés from Outer Space." *Women's Studies International Forum* 7, no. 2: 249–253.

1984c. *Extra(Ordinary) People*. New York: St. Martin's.

1985a. [Ed.]. *Magic Mommas, Trembling Sisters, Puritans and Perverts: Feminist Essays*. Trumansburg, N.Y.: Crossing Press.

1985b. "Not for Years but for Decades." In her *Magic Mommas, Trembling Sisters, Puritans and Perverts: Feminist Essays*, 17–42.

1985c. "Powerlessness and the Women's Movement." In her *Magic Mommas, Trembling Sisters, Puritans and Perverts: Feminist Essays*, 43–54.

1987a. *The Hidden Side of the Moon: Stories*. New York: St. Martin's.

1987b. "The Little Dirty Girl." In *Elsewhere II*. New York: Ace.

1993. "Commentary: Perhaps We Should All Back up and Start Again." By Joanna Russ, Virginia Kidd, Jeffery Smith, Samuel R. Delany, Chelsea Quinn Yarbro, Vonda McIntyre, and Raylyn Moore. *Khatru* 3 and 4: 40–55. 2nd printing.

1995a. "A Boy and His Dog: The Final Solution." In her *To Write Like a Woman*, 66–76.

1995b. "Letter to Susan Koppelman." In her *To Write Like a Woman*, 171–176.

1995c. "On Mary Wollstonecraft Shelley." In her *To Write Like a Woman*, 120–132.

1995d. "On the Yellow Wallpaper." In her *To Write Like a Woman*, 159–166.

1995e. "Recent Feminist Utopias." In her *To Write Like a Woman*, 133–148.

1995f. "Speculations: The Subjectivity of Science Fiction." In her *To Write Like a Woman*, 15–24.

1995g. "Towards an Aesthetic of Science Fiction." In her *To Write Like a Woman*, 41–59.

1995h. "What Can a Heroine Do? Or, Why Women Can't Write." In her *To Write Like a Woman*, 79–93.

1995i. *To Write Like a Woman: Essays in Feminism and Science Fiction*. Bloomington: Indiana University Press.

1996. "Invasion." *Isaac Asimov's Science Fiction Magazine*, January, 44–52.

1998a. "For Women Only; or, What Is That Man Doing under My Seat?" In her *What Are We Fighting For?* 84–103.

1998b. "I Thee Wed, So Watch It: The Woman Job." In her *What Are We Fighting For?* 126–153.

1998c. *What Are We Fighting For? Sex, Race, and the Future of Feminism.* New York: St. Martin's.

2000. "The New Misandry." In *Radical Feminism: A Documentary Reader,* edited by Barbara A. Crow, 167–170. New York: New York University Press.

N.d. "Creating Positive Images of Women: A Writer's Perspective." Women Writers' Conference, Cornell University, Ithaca, New York.

## Secondary Sources

Aab, Marjorie. "Letter." *The Alien Critic* 2, no. 4: 47–48.

Aguair, Sarah Appleton. 2001. *The Bitch Is Back: Wicked Women in Literature.* Carbondale: Southern Illinois University Press.

Aldiss, Brian W. 1973. *Billion Year Spree: The History of Science Fiction.* London: Weidenfeld and Nicholson.

Alexie, Sherman. 1993. *The Lone Ranger and Tonto Fistfight in Heaven.* New York: Atlantic Monthly Press.

Amis, Kingsley. 1960. *New Maps of Hell: A Survey of Science Fiction.* New York: Ballantine.

Anderson, Poul. 1974. "Reply to a Lady." *Vertex* 2, no. 2: 8 and 99.

Anzaldúa, Gloria. 1987. *Borderlands/La Frontera.* San Francisco, Calif.: Spinsters–Aunt Lute.

Armstrong, Tim. 1998. *Technology and the Body: A Cultural Study.* Cambridge: Cambridge University Press.

Austen, Jane. 2003. [1813]. *Pride and Prejudice.* Edited by Vivien Jones. New York: Penguin.

Ayers, David. 1999. *English Literature of the 1920s.* Edinburgh: Edinburgh University Press.

———. 2004. *Modernism: A Short Introduction.* Malden, Mass.: Blackwell.

Bakhtin, M. M. 1968. *Rabelais and His World.* Translated by Hélène Iswolsky. Cambridge, Mass.: MIT Press.

———. 1981. *The Dialogic Imagination: Four Essays.* Edited by Michael Holquist. Translated by Caryl Emerson and Michael Holquist. Austin: University of Texas Press.

———. 1987. *Alien to Femininity: Speculative Fiction and Feminist Theory.* New York: Greenwood.

———. 1993. *Lost in Space: Probing Feminist Science Fiction and Beyond.* Chapel Hill: University of North Carolina Press.

Barr, Marleen S. 1987. *Alien to Femininity: Speculative Fiction and Feminist Theory.* New York: Greenwood.

———. 1993. *Lost in Space: Probing Science Fiction and Beyond.* Chapel Hill: University of North Carolina Press.

Barreca, Regina. 1992. *They Used to Call Me Snow White . . . But I Drifted: Women's Strategic Use of Humor.* New York: Penguin.

Bartkowski, Frances. 1989. *Feminist Utopias*. Lincoln: University of Nebraska Press.

Bateson, Gregory. 1972. *Steps to an Ecology of Mind: Collected Essays in Anthropology, Psychiatry, Evolution, and Epistemology*. San Francisco, Calif.: Chandler.

Bauer, Dale M., and Susan Jaret McKinstry, eds. 1991. *Feminism, Bakhtin, and the Dialogic*. Albany: State University of New York Press.

Bede, The Venerable. 1969. *History of the English Church and People*. Translated by Leo Sherley-Price. Revised by R. E. Latham. Harmondsworth, Middlesex, Eng.: Penguin.

Beerbohm, Max. 1894. "A Defence of Cosmetics." *The Yellow Book* 1: 65–82.

Beilke, Debra. 1994. " 'What's So Funny?' The Explosion of Laughter in Feminist Criticism." *Contemporary Women's Issues Database* 16: 8–12.

Bell, Michael Mayerfield, and Michael Gardiner, eds. 1998. *Bakhtin and the Human Sciences: No Last Words*. London: Sage.

Belsey, Catherine, and Jane Moore, eds. 1989. *The Feminist Reader: Essays in Gender and the Politics of Literary Criticism*. Basingstoke: Macmillan.

Bergson, Henri. 1921. *Laughter: An Essay on the Meaning of the Comic*. London: Macmillan.

Bester, Alfred. 1976. "Hell Is Forever." In *The Light Fantastic*. New York: Berkely: 154–254.

———. 1998. *The Stars My Destination*. New York: Vintage.

Bey, Hakim. 2003. *T.A.Z.: The Temporary Autonomous Zone, Ontological Anarchy, Poetic Terrorism*. New York: Autonomedia.

Bhabha, Homi K., ed. 1990. *Nation and Narration*. London: Routledge.

Bland, Lucy. 1995. *Banishing the Beast: English Feminism and Sexual Morality, 1885–1914*. London: Penguin.

Bob, Black. 1991. "The Abolition of Work". <http://www.primitivism.com/abolition .htm>.

Bogstad, Janice. 1977. "The Science Fiction Connection: Readers and Writers in the Sf Community." *Janus* 3, no. 4: 4–8.

Bogue, Ronald. 2003. "Minority, Territory Music." In *An Introduction to the Philosophy of Gilles Deleuze*, edited by Jean Khalfa, 114–132. London: Continuum.

Boucher, Anthony, ed. 1956. *The Best from Fantasy and Science Fiction*. 5th ser. New York: Doubleday.

Bould, Mark, and Michelle Reid, eds. 2005. *Parietal Games: Critical Writing by and on M. John Harrison*. Vol. 5, Foundation Studies in Science Fiction. London: The Science Fiction Foundation.

Boulter, Amanda. 1999. " 'Unnatural Acts': American Feminism and Joanna Russ' *The Female Man*." *Women: A Cultural Review* 10, no. 2: 151–166.

Bourdieu, Pierre. 1995. *Outline of a Theory of Practice*. Translated by Richard Nice. Cambridge: Cambridge University Press.

Bradley, Marion Zimmer. 1974. *Darkover Landfall*. London: Arrow.

———. 1975. Letter. *The Witch and the Chameleon* 4: 19–25.

———. 1976. *The Shattered Chain*. New York: DAW.

———. 1977–78. "My Trip through Science Fiction." *Algol* 15, no. 1: 10–20.

Brown, Fredric. 1970. "Arena." In *The Science Fiction Hall of Fame*, edited by Robert Silverberg, 1:225–249. New York: Doubleday.

Brown, Lyn Mikel. 2003. *Girlfighting: Betrayal and Rejection among Girls*. New York: New York University Press.

Brownmiller, Susan. 1975. *Against Our Will: Men, Women, and Rape*. Harmondsworth, Middlesex, Eng.: Penguin.

Bryant, Dorothy. 1976. *The Kin of Ata are Waiting for You*. Berkeley, Calif: Random House.

Bunyan, John. 1882 [1678]. *The Pilgrim's Progress*. New York: Scribner.

Burke, Carolyn. 1996. *Becoming Modern: The Life of Mina Loy*. New York: Farrar, Straus and Giroux.

Butler, Judith. 1990. *Gender Trouble: Feminism and the Subversion of Identity*. New York: Routledge.

Charnas, Suzy McKee. 1978. *Motherlines*. New York: Berkley.

———. 1981. "A Woman Appeared." In *Future Females: A Critical Anthology*, edited by Marleen S. Barr, 103–108. Bowling Green, Ohio: Bowling Green University Press.

Chernin, Kim. 1982. *The Obsession: Reflections on the Tyranny of Slenderness*. New York: Harper and Row.

Cixous, Hélène. 1981. "The Laugh of the Medusa." In *New French Feminisms: An Anthology*, edited by Elaine Marks and Isabelle de Courtivro, 245–260. Brighton, Eng.: Harvester Wheatsheaf.

———, and Catherine Clément, 1986. "The Guilty One." In *The Newly-Born Woman*, translated by Betsy Wing, 1–57. Minneapolis: University of Minnesota Press.

Clareson, Thomas D., ed. 1971. *SF: The Other Side of Realism: Essays on Modern Fantasy and Science Fiction*. Bowling Green, Ohio: Bowling Green University Popular Press.

Clute, John. 1999. "Russ, Joanna." In *The Encyclopedia of Science Fiction*, edited by John Clute and Peter Nicholls, 1035–1036. London: Orbit.

———, and Peter Nicholls, eds. 1993. *The Encyclopedia of Science Fiction*. London: Orbit.

Coney, Michael G. 1973. Letter. *The Alien Critic* 2, no. 3: 52–53.

———. 1974. Letter. *The Alien Critic* 3, no. 1: 38.

Cornillon, Susan Koppleman, ed. 1972. *Images of Women in Science Fiction: Feminist Perspectives*. Bowling Green, Ohio: Bowling Green University Popular Press.

Cortiel, Jeanne. 1999. *Demand My Writing: Joanna Russ/Feminism/Science Fiction*. Liverpool: Liverpool University Press.

———. 2000. "Determinate Politics of Indeterminacy: Reading Joanna Russ's Recent Work in Light of Her Early Short Fiction." In *Future Females, the Next Genera-*

tion: New Voices and Velocities in Feminist Science Fiction Criticism, edited by Marleen S. Barr, 219–236. Lanham, Md.: Rowman and Littlefield.

Cowart, David, and Thomas M. Rymer, eds. 1981. *Dictionary of Literary Biography*. Detroit: Gale Research.

Critchley, Simon. 1992. *The Ethics of Deconstruction: Derrida and Levinas*. Oxford: Blackwell.

———. 2002. *On Humor*. New York: Routledge.

Crow, Barbara A., ed. 2000. *Radical Feminism: A Documentary Reader*. New York: New York University Press.

Crowder, Dianne Griffin. 1993. "Separatism and Feminist Utopian Fiction." In *Sexual Practice/ Textual Theory: Lesbian Cultural Criticism*, edited by Julia Penelope and Susan J. Wolfe, 237–250. Cambridge, Mass.: Blackwell.

Davis, Natalie Zemon. 1975. *Society and Culture in Early Modern France: Eight Essays*. Stanford, Calif.: Stanford University Press.

Delany, Samuel R. 1968. "Picnic on Paradise, a Book Review." *Nozdrovia*: 20–25.

———. 1976. *Triton*. New York: Bantam Books.

———. 1977. *The Jewel-Hinged Jaw: Notes on the Language of SF*. New York: Dragon Press.

———. 1979. "The Order of Chaos." *Science Fiction Studies* 6, no. 3: 333–336.

———. 2004. "Joanna Russ and D. W. Griffith." *PMLA* 119, no. 3: 500–508. [Reprinted in this volume.]

———, and Joanna Russ. 1984. "A Dialogue: Samuel Delany and Joanna Russ on Science Fiction." *Callaloo* 22: 27–35.

Delap, Richard. 1974. "Tomorrow's Libido: Sex and Science Fiction." *The Alien Critic* 3, no. 1: 5–12.

Deleuze, Gilles, and Félix Guttari. 1986. *Kafka: Towards a Minor Literature*. Minneapolis: University of Minneapolis Press.

———. 1987. *A Thousand Plateaus: Capitalism and Schizophrenia*. Minneapolis: University of Minnesota Press.

———. 2004. *Desert Islands and Other Texts, 1953–1974*. Edited by David Lapoujale. Translated by Michael Taormina. New York: Semiotexte.

Derrida, Jacques. 1997. *Politics of Friendship*. Translated by George Collins. London: Verso.

Dery, Mark. 1996. *Escape Velocity: Cyberculture at the End of the Century*. London: Hodder and Stoughton.

Dick, Philip K. 1974. "An Open Letter from Philip K. Dick." *Vertex* 2, no. 4: 99.

———. 1992. *The Collected Stories of Philip K. Dick*. Vol. 5, *The Eye of the Sibyl*. New York: Citadel-Carol.

Dickinson, Emily. 1998. *The Poems of Emily Dickinson*. Reading ed. Edited by R. W. Franklin. Cambridge, Mass.: The Belknap Press of Harvard University Press.

Disch, Thomas M. 1998. *The Dreams Our Stuff Is Made Of: How Science Fiction Conquered the World*. New York: Touchstone Books.

Donawerth, Jane L. 1994. "Science Fiction by Women in the Early Pulps, 1926–1930."
    In *Worlds of Difference: Utopian and Science Fiction by Women*, edited by Jane L.
    Donawerth and Carola A. Kolmerton, 137–152. Syracuse, N.Y.: Syracuse Uni-
    versity Press.

——. 2002. "Russ, Joanna (b. 1937)." In *glbtq: An Encyclopedia of Gay, Lesbian, Bi-
    sexual, Transgender, and Queer Culture*. Chicago: glbtq. Accessed 30 January 2005,
    <http://www.glbtq.com/literature/russ_j.html>.

——, and Carola A. Kolmerton, eds. 1994. *Worlds of Difference: Utopian and Science
    Fiction by Women*. Syracuse, N.Y.: Syracuse University Press.

Douglas, Mary. 1970. *Purity and Danger: An Analysis of Concepts of Pollution and Taboo*.
    Harmondsworth, Middlesex, Eng.: Penguin.

——. 1975. *Implicit Meanings: Essays on Anthropology*. London: Routledge.

Dworkin, Andrea. 1993. "I Want a Twenty-Four hour Truce in which There Is No
    Rape." In *Transforming a Rape Culture*, edited by Emilie Buchwald, Pamela R.
    Fletcher, and Martha Roth, 11–22. Minneapolis: Milkweed Editions.

Eco, Umberto. 1984. "The Frames of Comic Freedom." In *Umberto Eco, V. V. Ivanov, Monica
    Rector, Carnival*, edited by Thomas A. Sebeook, 1–9. Berlin: Marton Publishers.

Edut, Ophira. 1998. *Adiós, Barbie: Young Women Write About Body Image and Identity*.
    Seattle: Seal Press.

Ellis, Kate, Sebern Fisher, Marian Meade, Vivian Neimann, Gloria Schuh, Mary
    Winslow, and Rosemary Gaffney. 1973. "Men and Violence." In *Radical Femi-
    nism*, edited by Anne Koedt, Ellen Levine, and Anita Rapone, 63–71. New York:
    Quadrangle Books.

Engel, Barbara. 1972. Letter. *Time*, March, 6.

English, James F. 1994. *Comic Transactions: Literature, Humor, and the Politics of Commu-
    nity in Twentieth-Century Britain*. Ithaca, N.Y.: Cornell University Press.

Estés, Clarissa Pinkola. 1992. *Women Who Run with the Wolves: Myths and Stories of the
    Wild Woman Archtype*. New York: Ballantine Books.

Faderman, Lillian. 1981. *Surpassing the Love of Men: Romantic Friendship and Love between
    Women from the Renaissance to the Present*. New York: Morrow.

Fanon, Frantz. 1963. *The Wretched of the Earth*. New York: Grove.

Fawcett, Kris. 1974. Letter. *The Witch and the Chameleon* 2, 4.

Ferree, Myra Marx, and Beth B. Hess. 1994. *Controversy and Coalition: The New Feminist
    Movement across Three Decades of Change*. New York: Twayne.

Firestone, Shulamith. 1970. *The Dialectic of Sex: The Case for Feminist Revolution*. New
    York: Morrow.

Fitting, Peter. 1987. "For Men Only: A Guide to Reading Single-Sex Worlds." *Women's
    Studies* 14: 101–117.

Franke, Jackie. 1975. Letter. *Notes from the Chemistry Department* 10: 37.

Franklin, H. Bruce. 1978. *Future Perfect: American Science Fiction of the Nineteenth Century*.
    New York: Oxford University Press.

Freedman, Carl. 2000. *Critical Theory and Science Fiction*. Middleton, Conn.: Wesleyan University Press.

Freeman, Joreen. 2000. "The Bitch Manifesto." In *Radical Feminism: A Documentary Reader*, edited by Barbara A. Crow, 226–232. New York: New York University Press.

Freud, Sigmund. 1995a. *Beyond the Pleasure Principle*. In *The Standard Edition of the Complete Psychological Works of Sigmund Freud*, edited by James Strachey, 18:7–64. London: Hogarth Press.

———. 1955b. "Medusa's Head." In *The Standard Edition of the Complete Psychological Works of Sigmund Freud*, edited by James Strachey, 18: 273–274. London: Hogarth Press.

———. 1976. *Jokes and Their Relation to the Unconscious*. Edited by Angela Richards. Translated by James Strachey. London: Pelican.

———. 1991a. "The Dissolution of the Oedipus Complex." In *On Sexuality*, edited by James Strachey, 313–322. Harmondsworth, Middlesex, Eng.: Penguin.

———. 1991b. "Female Sexuality." In *On Sexuality*, edited by James Strachey, 371–392. Harmondsworth, Middlesex, Eng.: Penguin

———. 1991c. "From the History of an Infantile Neurosis [the Wolf Man]." In *Case Histories II*, 233–366. London: Penguin.

Friedan, Betty. 1963. *The Feminine Mystique*. New York: Norton.

Frye, Northrop. 1966. "Varieties of Literary Utopias." In *Utopias and Utopian Thought*, edited by Frank E. Manuel, 25–49. Boston: Houghton Mifflin.

Gallop, Jane. 1989. "Heroic Images: Feminist Criticisms, 1972." *American Literary History* 1, no. 3:612–636.

———. 1997. *Feminist Accused of Sexual Harassment*. Durham, N.C.: Duke University Press.

Gamow, George. 2005. *The Birth and Death of the Sun: Stellar Evolution and Subatomic Energy*. Mineola, N.Y.: Dover Publications.

Gardiner, Judith. 1994. "Empathic Ways of Reading: Narcissism Cultural Politics and Russ's 'Female Man.'" *Feminist Studies* 20: 87–111.

Garland, Barbara. 1981. "Joanna Russ." In *Dictionary of Literary Biography*, Vol. 8, *Twentieth-Century American Science Fiction Writers*, edited by David Cowart and Thomas M. Rymer, 88–93. Detroit, Mich.: Gale Research.

Gearhart, Sally Miller. 1979. *The Wanderground: Stories of the Hill Women*. Boston: Alyson Publications.

Gee, H. 2000. *Deep Time: Cladistics, the Revolution in Evolution*. London: Fourth Estate.

Gerlach, Neil, and Sheryl N. Hamilton. 2003. "A History of Social Science Fiction." *Science Fiction Studies* 30, no. 2: 161–173.

Gevers, Nick. 2000. "The Joy of Knowledge, the Clash of Arms: An Interview with Mary Gentle." *Infinity Plus*. <http://www.infinityplus.co.uk/nonfiction/intmg.htm>.

Gibson, William. 2003. *Burning Chrome*. New York: Eos.

Giddings, Paula. 1984. *When and Where I Enter: The Impact of Black Woman on Race and Sex in America.* New York: Bantam.

Gilbert, Sandra M., and Susan Gubar. 1978. *The Madwoman in the Attic: The Woman Writer and the Nineteenth-Century Literary Imagination.* New Haven, Conn.: Yale University Press.

Gilligan, Carol. 1992. *In a Different Voice: Psychological Theory and Women's Development.* Cambridge, Mass.: Harvard University Press.

Gilman, Charlotte Perkins. 1979 [1915]. *Herland.* New York: Pantheon Books.

Gomoll, Jeane. 1986–87. "An Open Letter to Joanna Russ." *Aurora* 10, no. 1: 7–10.

———. 1991. "An Open Letter to Joanna Russ." *Fanthology 87.* <http://www.geocities.com/Athens/8720/letter.htm>.

———, ed. 1993. *Symposium: Women in Science Fiction, Khatru 3 and 4.* 2nd ed. Madison, Wis.: Corflu SF3.

Goodman, Lizbeth. 1996. *Literature and Gender.* New York: Routledge.

Goodwin, Michael. 1976. "On Reading: A Giant Step for Science Fiction." *Mother Jones* 1: 62–65.

Gordon, Linda. 1991. "Birth Control." In *The Reader's Companion to American History,* edited by Eric Foner and John A. Garraty, 99–103. Boston: Houghton Mifflin.

Hagenbüchle, Roland. 1986. "Emily Dickinson's Aesthetic of Process." In *Poetry and Epistemology: Turning Points in the History of Poetic Knowledge: Papers from the Poetry Symposium, Eichstätt, 1983,* edited by Roland Hagenbüchle and Laura Skandera, 135–47. Regensburg, Ger.: Verlag Friedrich Pustet.

Haraway, Donna J. 1991. *Simians, Cyborgs, and Women: The Reinvention of Nature.* London: Free Association Books.

Harré, Rom. 2001. "How to Change Reality: Story v. Structure—a Debate between Rom Harré and Roy Bhaskar." In *After Postmodernism: An Introduction to Critical Realism,* edited by José Lopez and Garry Potter, 22–39. London: Athlone Press.

Henden, Josephine G. 2004. *Heartbreakers: Women and Violence in Contemporary Culture and Literature.* New York: Palgrave-Macmillan.

Heywood, Leslie, and Jennifer Drake. 1997. *Third Wave Agenda: Being Feminist, Doing Feminism.* Minneapolis: University of Minnesota Press.

Hicks, Heather J. 1999. "Automating Feminism: The Case of Joanna Russ's *The Female Man.*" *Postmodern Culture* 9, no. 3 <http://www3.iath.virginia.edu/pmc/text-only/issue.599>.

Hilf, Heidi. 1972. Letter. *Time,* 20 March, 6.

Hillegas, Mark. 1980. "Science Fiction in the English Department." In *Teaching Science Fiction: Education for Tomorrow,* edited by Jack Williamson, 97–101. Philadelphia: Owlswick Press.

Hitchcock, P. 1998. "The Grotesque of the Body Electric." In *Bakhtin and the Human Sciences,* edited by M. G. Bell, 78–94. London: Sage.

Hoff Sommers, Christina. 1994. *Who Stole Feminism? How Women Have Betrayed Women.* New York: Simon and Schuster.

Holquist, M. 1994. *Dialogism: Bakhtin and His World.* New York: Routledge.

Holt, Marilyn J. 1981. "No Docile Daughters: A Study of Two Novels by Joanna Russ." *Room of One's Own* 6, nos. 1–2: 92–99.

Horrocks, Roger. 1994. *Masculinity in Crisis: Myths, Fantasies, and Realities.* New York: St. Martin's.

Howard, June. 1983. "Widening the Dialogue on Feminist Science Fiction." In *Feminist Re-Visions: What Has Been and Might Be,* edited by Vivien Patraka and Louise A. Tilly, 64–96. Ann Arbor, Mich.: Women Studies Program, University of Michigan.

Hsu M., M. Bhatt, et al. 2005. "Neural Systems Responding to Degrees of Uncertainty in Human Decision-Making." *Science* 310, no. 9: 1680–1683.

Huebl-Naranjo, Linda. 1988. "From Peek-a-Boo to Sarcasm: Women's Humor as a Means of Both Connection and Resistance." *Studies in Prolife Feminism* 15, nos. 1–3: 347–341.

Hull, Gloria, ed. 1981. *All the Women Are White, All the Blacks Are Men, but Some of Us Are Brave.* Oldbury, N.Y.: The Feminist Press.

Huyssen, Andreas. 1988. *After the Great Divide: Modernism, Mass Culture and Postmodernism.* Basingstoke: Macmillan.

James, Edward. 1994. *Science Fiction in the Twentieth Century.* Oxford: Oxford University Press.

———. 2000. "Before the *Novum*: The Prehistory of Science Fiction Criticism." In *Learning from Other Worlds: Estrangement, Cognition and the Politics of Science Fiction and Utopia,* edited by Patrick Parrinder, 19–35. Liverpool: Liverpool University Press.

Johnson, David M. 1990. *Word Weaving: A Creative Approach to Teaching and Writing Poetry.* Urbana, Ill.: National Council of Teachers of English.

Jones, Libby Falk. 1990. "Gilman, Bradley, and Piercy and the Evolving Rhetoric of Feminist Utopias." In *Feminism, Utopia, and Narrative,* edited by Libby Falk Jones and Sarah Webster Goodwin, 116–129. Knoxville: University of Tennessee Press.

Kamen, Paula. 1991. *Feminist Fatale: Voices from the Twentysomething Generation Explore the Future of the Women's Movement.* New York: Fine.

Kaplow, Susi. 1973. "Getting Angry." In *Radical Feminism,* edited by Anne Koedt, Ellen Levine, and Anita Rapone, 36–41. New York: Quadrangle Books.

Kava, Beth Millstein, and Jeanne Bodin. 1983. *We, the American Women: A Documentary History.* Chicago: Science Research Associates.

Kaye/Kantrowiz, Melanie. 1992. *The Issue Is Power: Essays on Women, Jews, Violence, and Resistance.* San Francisco, Calif.: Aunt Lute Books.

Keough, Carol. 1972. Letter. *Time,* 20 March: 6–7.

Kerber, Linda, and Jane Sherron De Hart, eds. 1995. *Women's America: Refocusing the Past.* 4th ed. New York: Oxford University Press.

Kessler, Carol Farley, ed. 1995. *Daring to Dream: Utopian Fiction by United States Women before 1950.* Syracuse, N.Y.: Syracuse University Press.

King, Katie. 1994. *Theory in Its Feminist Travels: Conversations in U.S. Women's Movements.* Bloomington: Indiana University Press.

Kingston, Maxine Hong. 1989. *The Woman Warrior: Memoirs of a Girlhood among Ghosts.* New York: Vintage International.

Knight, Damon. 1967. *In Search of Wonder.* 2nd edition. Chicago: Advent.

———, ed. 1977. *Turning Points: Essays on the Art of Science Fiction.* New York: Harper and Row.

Kress, Nancy. N.d. "Speech." <http://www.lysator.liu.se/lsff/mb-nr21/Speech_by_Nancy_Kress.html>.

Kristeva, Julia. 1982. *Powers of Horror: An Essay on Abjection.* New York: Columbia University Press.

Kumar, Krishan. 1987. *Utopia and Anti-Utopia in Modern Times.* New York: Basil Blackwell.

Kurlansky, Mark. 2004. *1968: The Year That Rocked the World.* New York: Ballantine Books.

Lacan, Jacques. 1977. *Ecrits: A Selection.* Edited by Jacques-Alain Miller. Translated by Alan Sheridan. London: Tavistock.

Lamborn, Wilson Peter. 1994. "Aimless Wandering: Chuang Tzu's Chaos Linguistics." <http://www.thing.de/projekte/7:9%23/chuang_tzu_linguistics.html>.

Larbalastier, Justine. 2002. *The Battle of the Sexes in Science Fiction.* Middleton, Conn.: Wesleyan University Press.

———, and Helen Merrick. 2003. "The Revolting Housewife: Women and Science Fiction in the 1950s." *Paradoxa* 18: 136–156.

Laskin, David. 2000. *Partisans: Marriage, Politics, and Betrayal among the New York Intellectuals.* New York: Simon and Schuster.

Law, Richard. 1984. "Joanna Russ and the "Literature of Exhaustion." *Extrapolation* 25: 146–156.

Le Carré, John. 1983. *The Little Drummer Girl.* New York: Knopf.

Le Guin, Ursula K. 1969. *The Left Hand of Darkness.* New York: Ace.

———. 1972. *The Farthest Shore.* Toronto: Bantam.

———. 1974. *The Dispossessed.* New York: Harper & Row.

———. 2004a. "Dogs, Cats and Dancers: Thoughts About Beauty." In her *The Wave in the Mind: Talks and Essays on the Writer, the Reader, and the Imagination.* Boston: Shambhala.

———. 2004b. *The Wave in the Mind: Talks and Essays on the Writer, the Reader, and the Imagination.* Boston: Shambhala.

———. 2004c. "The Wilderness Within: The Sleeping Beauty and the Poacher." In her *The Wave in the Mind: Talks and Essays on the Writer, the Reader, and the Imagination*. Boston: Shambhala.

Lefanu, Sarah. 1988. *In the Chinks of the World Machine: Feminism and Science Fiction*. London: The Women's Press.

————. 2004. " 'The King Is Pregnant.' Rereadings: The Left Hand of Darkness, by Ursula K. Le Guin." *The Guardian Review*, January 3.

Longino, Helen E., and Valerie Miner. 1987. "A Feminist Taboo?" In *Competition: A Feminist Taboo?* edited by Helen E. Longino and Valerie Miner, 1–7. New York: The Feminist Press.

Loy, Mina. 1985. "Anglo-Mongrels and the Rose." In *The Last Lunar Baedeker*, edited by Roger L. Conover, 142–143. Manchester: Carcanet.

Luckhurst, Roger. 2005. *Science Fiction*. Cambridge: Polity Press.

Lundwall, Sam. 1971. *Science Fiction: What's It All About?* New York: Ace.

MacGregor, Loren. 1974. "A Reply to a Chauvinist." *Notes from the Chemistry Department* 9: 2–5.

Madsen, Catherine. 1976. "Commodore Bork and the Compost." *The Witch and the Chameleon* 5/6, 331–332.

Mann, Susan Archer, and Douglas J. Huffman. 2005. "The Decentering of Second Wave Feminism and the Rise of the Third Wave." *Science and Society* 69, no. 1: 56–91.

Manuel, Frank E. and Fritzie P. Manuel. 1979. *Utopian Thought in the Western World*. New York: Basil Blackwell.

Marcus, Jane. 1988. *Art and Anger: Reading Like a Woman*. Columbus: Ohio State University Press.

Marinetti, Filippo Tommaso. 1998. "The Founding and Manifesto of Futurism." In *Modernism*, edited by Vassiliki Kolcotroni et al., 249–263. Edinburgh: Edinburgh University Press.

Marsden, Dora. 1998. "I Am." In *Modernism*, edited by Vassiliki Kolocotroni et al. Edinburgh: Edinburgh University Press.

McCaffery, Larry. 1990. *Across the Wounded Galaxies: Interviews with Contemporary American Science Fiction Writers*. Champaign: University of Illinois Press.

McCaffrey, Anne. 1974. "Hitch Your Dragon to a Star: Romance and Glamour in Science Fiction." In *Science Fiction, Today and Tomorrow*, edited by Reginald Brettnor, 278–294. New York: Harper and Row.

McGuire, Gail M., and Jo Reger. 2003. "Feminist Co-Mentoring: A Model for Academic Professional Development." *NWSA Journal* 15, no. 1: 54–72.

McIntyre, Vonda N. 1973. Letter. *The Alien Critic* 2, no. 4: 52.

————. 1974. Review of *Darkover Landfall*. *The Witch and the Chameleon* 2: 19–24.

Mendlesohn, Farah. 1994. " 'Subcommittee' by Zenna Henderson." *Extrapolation* 35, no. 2: 120–129.

Merchant, C. 2001. "Dominion over Nature." In *The Gender and Science Reader*, edited by Muriel Lederman and Ingrid Bartsch, 68–81. New York: Routledge.

Merrick, Helen. 1999. "From Female Man to Feminist Fan: Uncovering Herstory in the Annals of Sf Fandom." In *Women of Other Worlds: Excursions through Science Fiction and Feminism*, edited by Helen Merrick and Tess Williams, 115–139. Nedlands: University of Western Australia Press.

———. 2000. "Fantastic Dialogues: Critical Stories About Feminism and Science Fiction." In *Speaking Science Fiction: Dialogue and Interpretations*, edited by Andy Sawyer and David Sees, 52–68. Liverpool: Liverpool University Press.

Merril, Judith. 1953. "Daughters of Earth." In *The Petrified Planet: A Twayne Science Fiction Triplet*. New York: Twayne.

———. 1966a. "Merril, Judith, Memo to Dell Publishing." Box 5, File 16. Merril Papers, Library and Archives of Canada, Ottawa.

———. 1966b. Merril Papers, Library and Archives of Canada, Ottawa.

———. 1967a. Introduction to *Sf: The Best of the Best*, edited by Judith Merril, 1–7. New York: Dell.

———. 1967b. "Merril Papers, Library and Archives of Canada, Ottawa. 9 December 1967." Box 9, File 7, Merril Papers, Library and Archives of Canada, Ottawa.

———. 1967c. "Merril, Judith, to Kay Bernard." Box 9, File 7, Merril Papers, Library and Archives of Canada, Ottawa.

———. 1967d. "They Call It the New Thing." *Magazine of Fantasy and Science Fiction*, November, 24–29.

———. 1968a. *England Swings Sf: Stories of Speculative Science Fiction*, edited by Judith Merril. Garden City, N.Y.: Doubleday.

———. 1968b. Introduction to *Path into the Unknown: The Best of Soviet Science Fiction*, edited by Judith Merril, 4–7. New York: Delacourte.

———. 1968c. "Merril, Judith to Brian Aldiss." Box 1, File 5, Merril Papers, Library and Archives of Canada, Ottawa.

———. 1968d. "Review of Joanna Russ, *Picnic on Paradise*." *Magazine of Fantasy and Science Fiction*, September, 35–37.

———. 1970. "Review of Anne McCaffrey, The Ship Who Sang." *Magazine of Fantasy and Science Fiction*, July, 40–42.

———. 1971. What do you Mean: Science? Fiction? *Extrapolation* 7 and 8: 30–36 and 2–19.

———, and Emily Pohl-Weary. 2002. *Better to Have Loved: The Life of Judith Merril*. Toronto: Between the Lines.

Meyerowitz, Joanne. 1994. "Beyond the Feminine Mystique: A Reassessment of Postwar Mass Culture, 1946–1958." In *Not June Cleaver: Women and Gender in Postwar America, 1945–1960*, edited by Joanne Meyerowitz, 229–262. Philadelphia: Temple University Press.

Miller, Alice, 1997. *The Drama of the Gifted Child: The Search for the True Self*. Translated by Ruth Ward. Revised and updated, with a new afterword by the author. New York: Basic Books.

Miner, Valerie. 1987. "Rumors from the Cauldron: Competition among Feminist Writers." In *Competition: A Feminist Taboo?* edited by Helen E. Longino and Valerie Miner, 183–194. New York: The Feminist Press.

Moi, Toril. 1991. *Sexual/Textual Politics: Feminist Literary Theory.* New York: Routledge.

Moorcock, Michael. 1983. *New Worlds: An Anthology.* London: Flamingo.

———. 1986. *The Opium General and Other Stories.* London: Grafton.

Moraga, Cherríe, and Gloria Anzaldúa, eds. 1981. *This Bridge Called My Back: Writings by Radical Women of Color.* With a foreword by Toni Cade Bambara. Watertown, Mass.: Persephone.

Moskowitz, Sam. 1963. *Explorers of the Infinite: Shapers of Science Fiction.* New York: World Publishing.

Moylan, Tom. 1986. *Demand the Impossible: Science Fiction and the Utopian Imagination.* New York: Methuen.

Munt, Sally. 1992. *New Lesbian Criticism: Literary and Cultural Readings.* London: Harvester, Wheatsheaf.

Nehring, Neil. 1997. *Popular Music, Gender, and Postmodernism: Anger Is An Energy.* Thousand Oaks, Calif.: Sage.

"New Woman, 1972." 1972. *Time,* 20 March, 6.

Newell, Dianne, and Victoria Lamont. 2005a. "House Opera: Frontier Mythology and Subversion of Domestic Discourse in Mid-Twentieth Century Women's Space Opera." *Foundation: The International Review of Science Fiction* 95: 71–88.

———. 2005b. "Rugged Domesticity: Frontier Mythology in Post-Armageddon Science Fiction by Women." *Science Fiction Studies* 32, no. 3: 423–441.

Newell, Dianne, and Jenéa Tallentire. 2007. "For the Extended Family and the Universe': Judith Merril and Science Fiction Autobiography." *Biography: An Interdisciplinary Quarterly* 30, no. 1: 1–21.

Nicholls, Peter. 1993a. "Force Field." In *The Encyclopedia of Science Fiction,* edited by John Clute and Peter Nicholls, 438. London: Orbit.

———. 1993b. "Sword and Sorcery." In *The Encyclopedia of Science Fiction,* edited by John Clute and Peter Nicholls, 1194–1196. London: Orbit.

Nicholson, Linda. 1994. "Interpreting Gender." *Signs: Journal of Women and Culture in Society* 20, no. 1: 79–105.

Nott, Katherine. 1970. *Philosophy and Human Nature.* London: Hoddard and Stoughton.

Ochs, Elinor, and Lisa Capps. 1996. "Narrating the Self." *Annual Review of Anthropology* 25: 19–43.

Ortner, Sherry B. "Making Gender: Toward a Feminist, Minority, Postcolonial, subaltern, Etc., Theory of Practice." In *Making Gender: The Politics and Erotics of Culture,* edited by Sherry B. Ortner, 1–20. Boston: Beacon.

Ostriker, Alicia Suskin. 1986. *The Emergence of Women's Poetry in America.* Boston: Beacon.

Parrinder, Patrick. 1980. *Science Fiction: Its Criticism and Teaching.* New York: Methuen.

Peirce, Charles Sanders Chance. 1998. *Love and Logic: Philosophical Essays*. Lincoln: University of Nebraska Press.

Perry, Donna. 1993. *Backtalk: Women Writers Speak Out: Interviews*. New Brunswick, N.J.: Rutgers University Press.

Pfaelzer, Jean. 1984. *The Utopian Novel in America, 1886–1896*. Pittsburgh, Pa.: University of Pittsburgh Press.

Phillips, Julie. 2006. *James Tiptree, Jr.: The Double Life of Alice B. Sheldon*. New York: St. Martin's.

Piercy, Marge. 1976. *Women on the Edge of Time*. New York: Fawcett Crest Books.

Pipher, Mary. 1994. *Reviving Ophelia: Saving the Selves of Adolescent Girls*. New York; Ballantine.

Plimlimmon, Judy. 1974. Letter. *The Alien Critic* 3, no. 2: 18.

Potter, Rachel. 2000. "Waiting at the Entrance to the Law: Modernism, Gender, and Democracy." *Textual Practice* 14, no. 2: 259–261.

Quindlen, Anna. 1996. "And Now, Babe Feminism." In *"Bad Girls"/"Good Girls": Women, Sex, and Power in the Nineties*, edited by Nan Bauer Maglin and Donna Perry, 3–5. New Brunswick, N.J.: Rutgers University Press.

Reuther, Rosemary Radford. 1985. *Womanguides: Reading toward a Feminist Theology*. Boston: Beacon.

Rich, Adrienne. 1978. *The Dream of a Common Language: Poems, 1974–1977*. New York: Norton.

———. 1979. "When We Dead Awaken: Writing as Re-Vision." In *On Lies, Secrets, and Silence: Selected Prose, 1966–1978*, 33–49. New York: Norton.

———. 1994. "Compulsory Heterosexuality and Lesbian Existence." In *Blood, Bread, and Poetry: Selected Prose*, 23–75. New York: Norton.

Rich, B. Ruby. 1998. "In the Name of Feminist Film Criticism." In *Chick Flicks: Theories and Memories of the Feminist Film Movement*, 62–84. Durham, N.C.: Duke University Press.

Roberts, Adam. 2000. *Science Fiction*. London: Routledge.

Roberts, Robin. 1995. "It's Still Science Fiction: Strategies of Feminist Science Fiction." *Extrapolation* 36, no. 3: 184–197.

Robinson, Sally. 1988. "The 'Anti-Logos Weapon': Multiplicity in Women's Texts." *Contemporary Literature* 29, no. 1: 105–124.

Roiphe, Katie. 1993. *The Morning After: Sex, Fear, and Feminism*. New York: Little, Brown.

Rosinsky, Natalie. 1982. "'A Female Man': The Medusan Humor of Joanna Russ." *Extrapolation* 23, no. 1: 31–36.

Rowe, Kathleen. 1995. *The Unruly Woman: Gender and the Genres of Laughter*. Austin: University of Texas Press.

Rubin, Gayle. 1975. "The Traffic in Women: Notes on the Political Economy of Sex." In *Toward an Anthropology of Women*, edited by Rayna R. Reiter, 157–210. New York: Monthly Review Press.

Russo, M. 1994. *The Female Grotesque: Risk, Excess, and Modernity*. New York: Routledge.

Sargent, Lyman Tower. 1979. *British and American Utopian Literature, 1516–1975: An Annotated Bibliography*. Boston: G.K. Hall.

Sargent, Pamela, ed. 1975. *Women of Wonder: Science Fiction Stories by Women About Women*. New York: Vintage.

Scholes, Robert, and Eric S. Rabkin. 1977. *Science Fiction: History, Science, Vision*. New York: Oxford University Press.

Schulz, Max F. 1973. *Black Humour Fictions of the Sixties: A Pluralistic Definition of Man and His World*. Athens: Ohio University Press.

Seigfried, Charlene Haddock. 1996. *Pragmatism and Feminism: Reweaving the Social Fabric*. Chicago: University of Chicago Press.

Sheldon, Raccona. 1976. "Your Faces, O My Sisters! Your Faces Filled with Light." In *Aurora: Beyond Equality*, edited by Vonda N. McIntyre and Susan Janice Anderson, 16–35. Seattle, Wash.: Fawcett Gold Medal.

Shinn, Thelma J. 1985. "Worlds of Words and Swords: Suzette Haden Elgin and Joanna Russ at Work." In *Women Worldwalkers: New Dimension of Science Fiction and Fantasy*, edited by Jane B. Weedman, 207–222. Lubbock: Texas Tech Press.

———. 1986. *Worlds within Women: The Traditional Myths Retold*. New York: Greenwood.

Showalter, Elaine. 2000. "Laughing Medusa: Feminist Intellectuals at the Millennium." *Women: A Cultural Review* 11, nos. 1–2: 131–38.

Silverberg, Robert. 1970. *Science Fiction Hall of Fame*. Garden City, N.Y.: Doubleday.

———. 1978. Introduction to *And Chaos Died*. By Joanna Russ. Pp. v–xi. Boston: Gregg.

Silverstein, Cathy. 1976. "Joanna Russ: Author and Professor." *Cthulhu Calls* 3, no. 3: 13–16.

Sinfield, Alan. 1992. *Cultural Materialism and the Politics of Dissident Reading*. Oxford: Clarendon Press.

Sitesh, Aruna. 1994. *Her Testimony: American Women Writers of the 90s in Conversation with Aruna Sitesh*. New Delhi: Affiliated East-West Press.

Smith, Jeffrey, ed. 1975. *Symposium: Women in Science Fiction, Khatru 3 & 4*. 1st ed. Baltimore, MD: Phantasmicon Press.

Solanas, Valerie. 2000. "Scum Manifesto." In *Radical Feminism: A Documentary Reader*, edited by Barbara A. Crow, 201–222. New York: New York University Press.

Soper, Kate. 1999. "Of OncoMice and FemaleMen: Donna Haraway on Cyber Ontology." In *Women: A Cultural Review* 10, no. 2: 167–172.

Sorisio, Carolyn. 1997. "A Tale of Two Feminisms: Power and Victimization in Contemporary Feminist Debate." In *Third Wave Agenda: Being Feminist, Doing Feminism*, edited by Leslie Heywood and Jennifer Drake, 134–154. Minneapolis: University of Minnesota Press.

Spencer, Kathleen L. 1990. "Rescuing the Female Child: The Fiction of Joanna Russ." *Science Fiction Studies* 17, no. 2: 167–87.

Stallybrass, Peter, and Allon White. 1986. *The Politics and Poetics of Transgression.* Ithaca, N.Y.: Cornell University Press.

Sturgis, Susanna J. 1990. "A Vindication of Heras and Heraism." In *The Women Who Walk through Fire: Women's Fantasy and Science Fiction.* Freedom, Calif.: Crossing Press.

Suvin, Darko. 1979. *Metamorphoses of Science Fiction: On the Poetics and History of a Literary Genre.* New Haven, Conn.: Yale University Press.

Tara, Walker Alison. 2005. "Destabilizing Order, Challenging History: Octavia Butler, Deleuze and Guattari, and Affective Beginnings." *Extrapolation* 46, no. 1: 103–119.

Tickner, Lisa. 2002. "Mediating Generation: The Mother-Daughter Plot." *Art History* 25, no. 1: 23–46.

Tiptree, James, Jr. 1976. "Houston, Houston, Do You Read?" In *Aurora: Beyond Equality,* edited by Susan Janice Anderson and Vonda N. McIntyre. Seattle, Wash.: Fawcett Gold Medal.

———. 2000. *Meet Me at Infinity.* New York: Tor.

Tuttle, Lisa. 1995. "Women Sf Writers." In *The Encyclopedia of Science Fiction,* edited by John Clute and Peter Nicholls, 1344–1345. New York: St. Martin's.

———. 1997. "Gender." In *The Encyclopedia of Fantasy,* edited by John Clute and Peter Nicholls, 393–396. New York: St. Martin's.

Tzara, Tristan. 1998. "Dada Manifesto, 1918." In *Modernism,* edited by Vassiliki Kolocotroni et al. Edinburgh: Edinburgh University Press.

Vayne, Victoria. 1975. Letter. *Notes from the Chemistry Department* 10: 37–38.

Walker, Barbara. 1983. *The Women's Encyclopedia of Myths and Secrets.* San Francisco, Calif.: Harper and Row.

Walker, Paul. 1975. "Sexual Stereotypes." *Notes from the Chemistry Department* 10: 9–11.

———, and Joanna Russ. 1975. "Interview." *Moebius Trip:* 4–9.

Watling, Clare. 1993. "Who's Read *Macho Sluts?*" In *Textuality and Sexuality: Reading Theories and Practices,* edited by Judith Still and Michael Worton, 193–206. Manchester: Manchester University Press.

Waugh, Patricia. 1989. *Feminine Fictions: Revisiting the Postmodern.* London: Routledge.

Weimar, Annegret. 1992. "Utopia and Science Fiction: A Contribution to Their Generic Description." *Canadian Review of Comparative Literature/Revue Canadienne de Littérature Comparée* 19: 171–200.

Westfahl, Gary. 1998. *The Mechanics of Wonder: The Creation of the Idea of Science Fiction.* Liverpool: Liverpool University Press.

Willis, Connie. 1992. "The Women SF Doesn't See." *Isaac Asimov's Science Fiction Magazine,* October, 48–49.

Wills, Deborah. 1995. "The Madwoman in the Matrix: Joanna Russ's *The Two of Them* and the Psychiatric Postmodern." In *Modes of the Fantastic: Selected Essays from* the Twelfth International Conference on the Fantastic in the Arts, edited by Robert A. Latham and Robert A. Collins, 93–99. Westport, Conn.: Greenwood.

Wilson, Robin Scott, ed. 1972. Clarion II. New York: New American Library.

Wittig, Monique. 1971. Les Guérillères. New York: Viking.

Wolf, Naomi. 1993. Fire with Fire: The New Female Power and How to Use It. New York: Vintage Books.

Wolfe, Susan J., and Julia Penelope, eds. 1993. Sexual Practice/Textual Theory: Lesbian Cultural Criticism. Cambridge, Mass.: Blackwell.

Wolfson, Susan J. 1986. The Questioning Presence: Wordsworth, Keats, and the Interrogative Mode in Romantic Poetry. Ithaca, N.Y.: Cornell University Press.

Wollhein, Donald A. 1971. The Universe Makers: Science Fiction Today. New York: Harper & Row.

Wolmark, Jenny. 1994. Aliens and Others: Science Fiction, Feminism, and Postmodernism. Iowa City: University of Iowa Press.

Wood, Susan. 1978a. "People's Programming." Janus 4, no. 1: 4–7 and 13.

———. 1978b. "Women and Science Fiction." Algol: A Magazine about Science Fiction 16, no. 1: 9–18.

Wu, Dingbo. 1993. "Understanding Utopian Literature." Extrapolation 34: 230–244.

Yaszek, Lisa. 2003. "Unhappy Housewife Heroines, Galactic Suburbia, and Nuclear War: A New History of Midcentury Women's Science Fiction." Extrapolation 44, no. 1: 97–111.

———. 2004. "The Women History Doesn't See: Recovering Midcentury Women's Sf as a Literature of Social Critique." Extrapolation 45, no. 1: 34–51.

———. 2005. "Domestic Satire as Social Commentary in Mid-Century Women's Media Landscape Sf." Foundation: The International Review of Science Fiction F95: 29–39.

———. 2006. "From Ladies' Home Journal to the Magazine of Fantasy and Science Fiction: 1950s Science Fiction, the Offbeat Romance Story, and the Case of Alice Eleanor Jones." In Daughters of Earth: Feminist Science Fiction in the Twentieth Century, edited by Justine Larbalastier, 76–96. Middleton, Conn.: Wesleyan University Press.

———. 2007. Galactic Suburbia: Gender, Technology, and the Creation of Women's Science Fiction. Columbus: Ohio State University Press.

Zeldes, Kiki. 2005. "Our Bodies, Our Selves." Boston Women's Health Book Collective. <http://www.ourbodiesourselves.org/about/history.asp>.

Zimmerman, Bonnie. 1992. "Lesbians Like This and That: Some Notes on Lesbian Criticism for the Nineties." In New Lesbian Criticism: Literary and Cultural Readings, edited by Sally Munt, 1–15. New York: Columbia Press.

# Contributors

**Andrew M. Butler** is the former features editor of *Vector* and has authored *The Pocket Essentials* on Philip K. Dick, Cyberpunk, Terry Pratchett, Postmodernism and Film Studies, as well as articles on Iain Banks, Jeff Noon, Jack Womack, and many others. He has been a recipient of the SFRA Pioneer Award.

**Brian Charles Clark** was the founding editor and publisher of Permeable Press (named by Larry McCaffrey as one of the most important independent presses of the 1990s). Clark is the author of a science fiction novel, *Splitting*, and three chapbooks of poetry, as well as numerous essays, stories, and reviews. His semi-autonomous digital avatar, DJ Funken Wagnalls, is the composer of, among many other pieces, an epic history of science fiction rapped in rhyme by MC Cottonmouth that ends in a video game (see briancharlesclark.com). Clark has lived in the Mojave Desert, the Ozark Plateau, and among the wheat fields of the Palouse in eastern Washington, where he continues to write sentences and music and to occasionally teach literature and film to college students.

**Samuel R. Delany** is a novelist and critic who lives in New York City and teaches at Temple University. His novels *Babel 17, Nova, Dhalgren*, and *The Fall of the Towers*, and a short story collection, *"Aye and Gomorrah" and Other Stories*, were recently reissued by Vintage Books. His essays are collected in three volumes, from Wesleyan University Press: *Silent Interviews, Longer Views*, and *Shorter Views*. A new novel, *Dark Reflections*, will appear this year from Carroll and Graf.

**Edward James** is currently professor of medieval history at University College, Dublin; he has also worked at the University of York and Reading University. From 1986 to 2001 he was editor of *Foundation: The International Review of Science Fiction*. For his work on science fiction (which includes five authored, edited or coedited books) he has received the Eaton Award, the Pilgrim Award, and a Hugo.

**Keridwen Luis** is pursuing her Ph.D. in anthropology at Brandeis University; her dissertation is a project exploring community, culture, and gender in women's communities and lesbian lands. She also studies nonheteronormative sexualities cross-culturally; she created and taught a course on this subject at Brandeis in 2005. Her broad academic interests range from personhood, gender, and agency in *shoujo*

Japanese anime and manga, to feminist approaches to SF as a field, to anthropology of the body, and to the meaning of belief in modern ghost phenomena.

**Sandra Lindow**, recently retired from a quarter-century stint working as a reading specialist in a treatment center for emotionally disturbed children and adolescents, is looking forward to a relatively less stressful life of writing, teaching, and editing. She has published five books of poetry, and is in the process of completing a book of essays on Ursula K. Le Guin. Her essays have appeared in *Extrapolation*, *Foundation*, the *New York Review of Science Fiction*, and *Women in Science Fiction and Fantasy: An Encyclopedia*.

**Paul March-Russell** teaches English and comparative literature at the University of Kent, Canterbury. His publications include articles on Joseph Conrad, E. M. Forster, William Gibson, and Douglas Oliver. He recently edited May Sinclair's *Uncanny Stories* (Wordsworth Editions, 2006) and is coeditor, with Carmen Casaliggi, of *Ruskin in Perspective* (Cambridge Scholars Press, forthcoming). His introduction to the short story is forthcoming from Edinburgh University Press, while his current research project is the British neoromantic movement, 1925–55.

**Farah Mendlesohn** was the editor of *Foundation* from 2001 to 2007. In 2005 she and Edward James won the Hugo for *The Cambridge Companion to Science Fiction*. Her most recent book is *Rhetorics of Fantasy*, also published by Wesleyan University Press. She is reader in science fiction and fantasy at the University of Middlesex.

**Helen Merrick** lectures in the faculty of Media, Society & Culture at the Curtin University of Technology, Western Australia. She has published various articles on the cultural history of feminist science fiction, including contributions to the *Cambridge Companion to Science Fiction* (2003); *Speaking Science Fiction* (Liverpool University Press, 2000); *Trash Aesthetics: Popular Culture and its Audience* (Pluto, 1997) and the forthcoming *Queer Universe: Sexualities in Science Fiction* (Liverpool University Press) and *The Joy of SF* (Open Court, 2007). With Tess Williams she coedited the collection *Women of Other Worlds: Excursions through Science Fiction and Feminism* (University of Western Australia Press, 1999). Her current research focuses on the intersections of feminist science fiction and science studies.

**Dianne Newell** is professor in the Department of History and director of the Peter Wall Institute for Advanced Studies at the University of British Columbia. She has published on women's postwar science fiction (with Victoria Lamont) in *Foundation: The International Review of Science Fiction*, and *Science Fiction Studies*, and on Judith Merril's nonfiction writings in the *European Journal of American Culture*; *Journal of International Women's Studies*, and (with Jenéa Tallentire), *Biography: An Interdisciplinary Quarterly* (forthcoming). She is preparing a book-length study of Judith Merril's intellectual circles in postwar Anglo-American, Canadian, and Japanese science/speculative fiction.

**Graham Sleight** (Web site http://www.gsleight.demon.co.uk) was born in 1972, lives in London, started writing about science fiction and fantasy in 2000, and became editor of *Foundation* in 2007. He writes regularly for the *New York Review of Science Fiction*, *Locus*, *Interzone*, *Strange Horizons*, and *Science Fiction Studies*. In 2006, he started writing regular columns for *Locus* and *Vector* (the latter are available online at www.vector -magazine.co.uk). His essays appear in *Polder: A Festschrift* for John Clute and Judith Clute (ed. Farah Mendlesohn), *Christopher Priest: The Interaction* (ed. Andrew M. Butler), *Parietal Games: Non-Fiction by and about M. John Harrison* (ed. Mark Bould and Michelle Reid), *Snake's-Hands: The Fiction of John Crowley* (ed. Alice K. Turner and Michael Andre-Driussi), and *Supernatural Fiction Writers* (ed. Richard Bleiler). He is grateful to John Clute and Geneva Melzack for the loan of books for work on this chapter.

**Jenéa Tallentire** completed her doctorate in history at the University of British Columbia in 2006. Her dissertation centers on defining marital status as a category of analysis for women's history, concentrating on the auto/biographical writings of ever-single women in British Columbia, 1880–1939. She is coauthor (with Dianne Newell) of " 'For the Extended Family and the Universe': Judith Merril and Science Fiction Autobiography," *Biography: An Interdisciplinary Quarterly* (forthcoming, 2006). She is cofounder, coeditor, and webspinner for *Thirdspace*, the e-journal for emerging feminist scholars (www.thirdspace.ca), and the founder of the Scholars of Single Women network (http://medusanet.ca/singlewomen/).

**Jason P. Vest** is an assistant professor of literature in the University of Guam's Division of English and Applied Lingustics. His research interests include twentieth-century American literature, modernism and postmodernism, American literature and culture of the 1950s and 1960s, science fiction, crime fiction, and media studies. He is currently writing a book titled *Future Imperfect* that examines the eight films adapted from the fiction of Philip K. Dick.

**Sherryl Vint** teaches American literature and cultural studies at Saint Francis Xavier University. She has published *Bodies of Tomorrow: Technology, Subjectivity, Science Fiction* (University of Toronto Press, 2006) and other essays on science fiction. She is currently working on a book-length project about the human/animal boundary in science fiction.

**Pat Wheeler** is principal lecturer in English Literature at the University of Hertfordshire. She has published articles on contemporary British fiction, feminist science fiction, and chapters on British women's working-class fiction. Her books include: *Sebastian Faulks's Birdsong* (New York: Continuum, 2002); *Contemporary British and Irish Novelists: Introduction through Interview* (with S. Monteith and J. Newman; London: Arnold, 2004); *Introduction to Science Fiction* (forthcoming, Continuum, 2006) and *Dark Cities and Brave New Worlds: Representations of Dystopia in Literature and Film* (forthcoming, Jefferson, N.C.: McFarland, 2007).

**Tess Williams** is currently completing her doctorate at the University of Western Australia. She has taught in universities for more than twenty years and her areas of interest are feminism, evolutionary sciences, women's literature, creative writing, and science and art. Her major publications include two novels, *Map of Power* (Random House, 1996), *Sea as Mirror* (HarperCollins 2000), and a collection edited with Helen Merrick, *Women of Other Worlds: Excursions through Science Fiction and Feminism* (University of Western Australia Press, 1999). She has published articles in journals and books, as well as a number of short stories in anthologies, and is currently working on a memoir that will include her personal experiences with dialysis and renal transplantation.

**Gary K. Wolfe**, professor of Humanities and English at Roosevelt University in Chicago and contributing editor for *Locus* magazine, is the author of the critical studies *The Known and the Unknown: The Iconography of Science Fiction* (Kent State, Ohio: Kent State University Press, 1979), *David Lindsay* (San Bernardino, Calif.: Borgo Press, 1982), *Critical Terms for Science Fiction and Fantasy: A Glossary and Guide to Scholarship* (New York: Greenwood, 1986), and *Harlan Ellison: The Edge of Forever* (with Ellen R. Weil; Columbus: Ohio State University Press, 2002). His most recent book, *Soundings: Reviews, 1992–1996* (Boston; Beacon, 2005), received the British Science Fiction Association Award for best nonfiction, and was nominated by the World Science Fiction Convention for a Hugo Award for Best Related Book. Wolfe has received the Eaton Award, the Pilgrim Award from the Science Fiction Research Association, and the Distinguished Scholarship Award from the International Association for the Fantastic in the Arts.

**Lisa Yaszek** is associate professor in the School of Literature, Communication, and Culture at the Georgia Institute of Technology, where she also curates the Bud Foote Science Fiction Collection. Yaszek's essays on the relations of gender, science, and science fiction appear in scholarly journals including *Foundation: The International Review of Science Fiction, Signs: Journal of Women in Culture and Society,* and the *electronic book review.* Her most recent book, *Galactic Suburbia: Gender, Technology, and the Creation of Women's Science Fiction,* is forthcoming from Ohio State University Press.

# Index

Note: Titles of works by Joanna Russ are indicated by **bold type**.